I0761772

THEA HAWTHORNE

Proofreading by Phoenix Rising Literary

Cover & illustrations by Thea Hawthorne

www.theahawthorne.com

www.instagram.com/thea.hawthorne

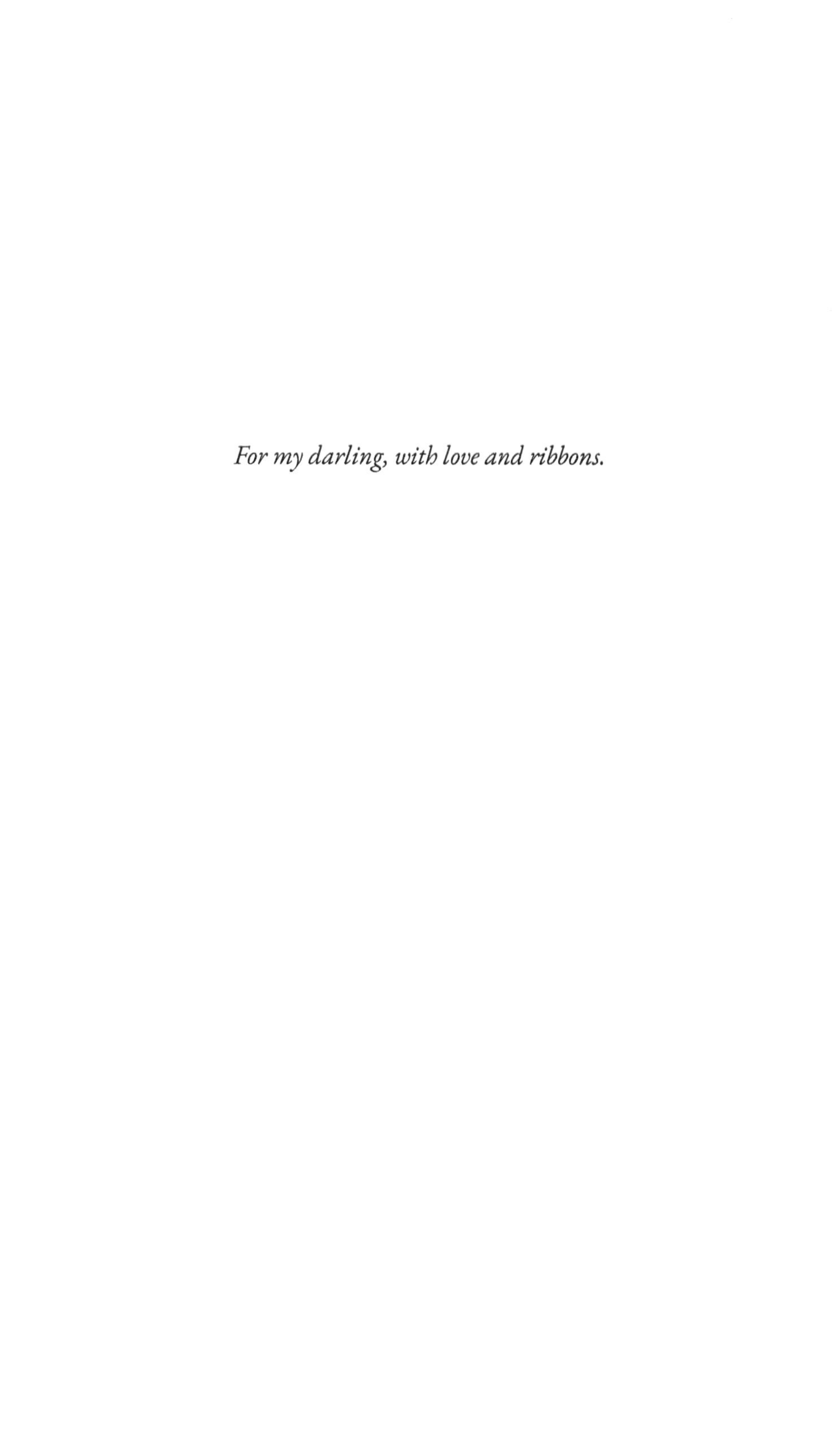

For my darling, with love and ribbons.

A note from the author

All Woven With Ivy is a fantasy romance set in a queernormative world. It is a warm-hearted story, with family (both found and otherwise), strong friendships, and a gentle, devoted romance with a HEA. While many aspects of this book are cosy, it does have medium stakes, a haunting mystery, and some stressful moments. If you are unsure, please read the rest of this note to best judge if this book is the right one for you.

Content Warnings: open door/fade-to-grey scenes between consenting adults, drinking, swearing, ritual death, poison, mild consensual non-monogamy, mentions of parental death, fantasy religion, mild violence, emesis, and drowning.

THE HOUSE OF
THE CROWN
secret
archive door
Casca Manor
THE GARDENS
Garden Hall
Emlyn's
studio

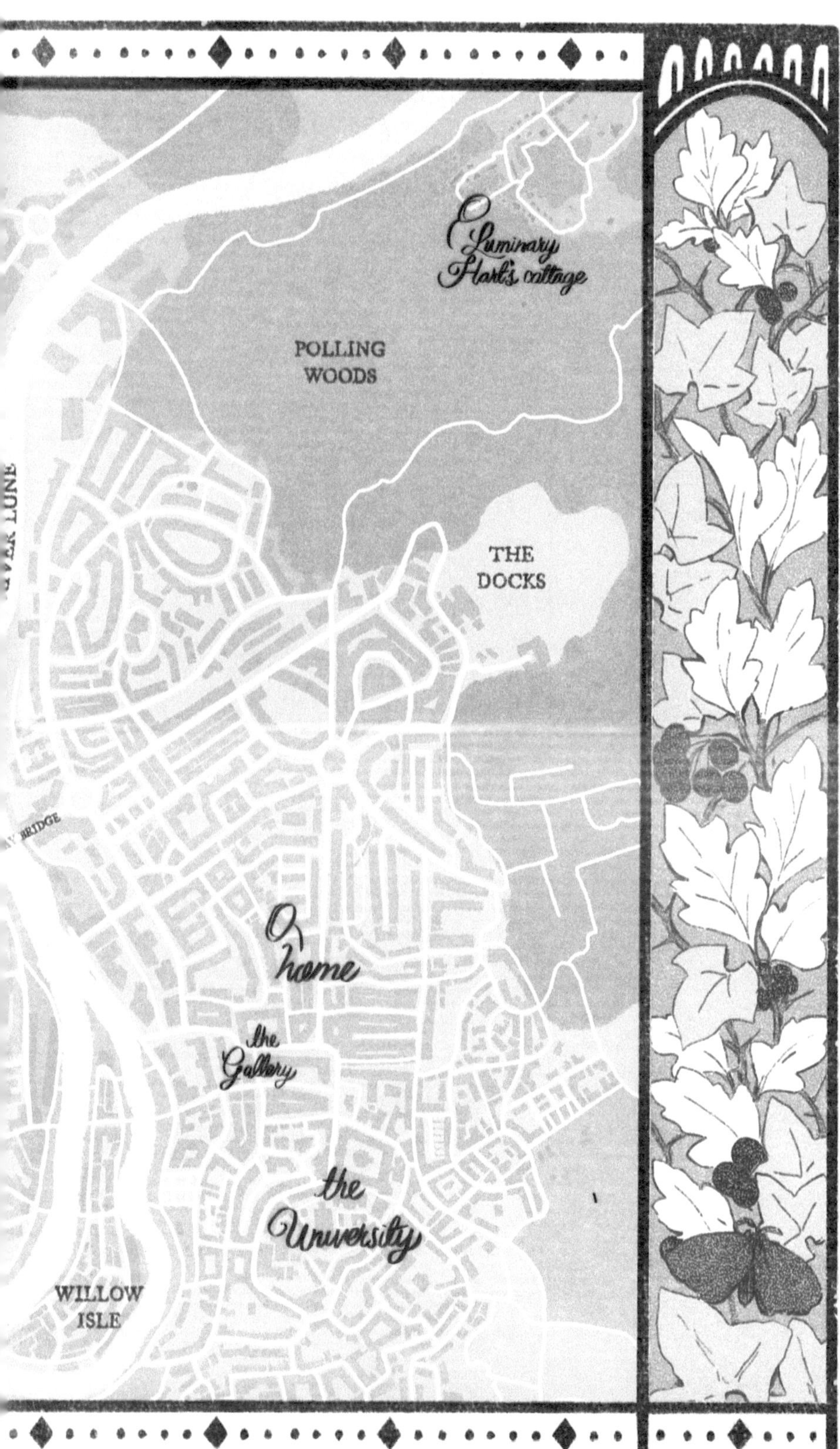
Luminary Hart's cottage
POLLING WOODS
THE DOCKS
home
the Gallery
the University
WILLOW ISLE

PART I
ALL THE
IVY
CROWNED
spring
-
summer

Chapter One

Somewhere in Esk, there is a funeral. The mourning bell ripples through the university archives, and Zanthi holds her aether lantern higher, as if the fall of golden light can keep the sound at bay. She's never liked the weeping toll of the funerary bell, but she can't deny it's fitting. She is deep in the cold earth below the city, amongst all the buried things, with a tunnel as dark as the underworld before her.

The bell rings on, and Zanthi does not move. She has a decision to make.

She's at the turning of the path, the furthest she's ever been in the archives, and further than the other archivists ever go. Beyond the carefully marked boundaries of aether lanterns on the archive walls, there is a vast warren of tunnels, unmapped and unlit. The archive holds many forgotten records and a good few curses in its darkness, and that's reason enough for most to avoid it. Rumours, too, of a strange, fey beast buried in the depths of the passages, but she's a practical sort. Superstitions don't scare her, and she has long since figured she's already cursed enough for no new curses to stick.

What scares her is the thought of what lies upstairs, the news and gossip that flows faster than aetherlight. They'll already be retelling the disaster of her morning's presentation. If she goes back up to the vault, people will *look*. She doesn't want to be seen by the archivists, or by the other students. Or by Theron.

The hook of failure is still in her chest. It had nestled in as she'd been standing in front of the Luminary board, her careful, practised words on her lips, and all those solemn, bored faces staring at her. Silent. Scornful. She doesn't know how to be rid of it.

And so, she'd fled underground, because she knows she'll see no pitying faces here.

There is nothing around her but damp and river mud, the passages still reeking from the spring floods. The River Lune lies above the passage, still rushing with storm-swell and snowmelt. But the floods have receded. This passage should be traversable. There might be a flooded way or two, though. There might be a collapsed wall. Or it might all collapse while she's in there, crossing beneath the river.

But she's spent four long years familiarising herself with the dark, with the old hollows and tumbled in chambers that lie within the boundaries of the known archives. She's spent whole days here, longer than the mandated two-hour limits, and never once has she felt the creeping disorientation that addles the senses. If anyone is ever able to delve deep enough to cross beneath the river, then it will be Zanthi.

And now, having failed to entice even a single mentor to be interested in sponsoring her studies, Zanthi has no reason not to do so. What can the university do now? Throw her out? Without a mentor, she'll be out by the end of the month.

Unless, of course, she goes and gets work as a research clerk for the Crown. Zanthi might have suffered many indignities in her time at the university, might have been called a wraith and a witch and a night-sprite, but she won't sink so low as to be an *unrobed researcher*.

Better to be expelled, honestly.

Here, Zanthi is beyond those worries. She is beyond any mortal dominion. The passages are old, older than the university. Older than Esk, maybe. Older than the Crown. That sort of thinking is why her study proposal was rejected by the Luminary board. High claims with no proof, they said. Anti-Crown sentiment. Heresy.

Cowards. It's all so clearly ancient. The stones here are worn down in sloping grooves made not by water, but by many, many years of people passing through. Anyone with eyes can see it. Anyone with a working mind would wonder *who* and *why* and *when*. The Luminary board, clearly, has no working minds at all between them, because they had taken one look at her proposal and denied her further study.

For the last two years, Zanthi has been working on a theory. It is a loose-woven thing, more gaps and holes than it is anything substantial, but the mystery has devoured her. She had thought... *Well*, she had thought others might see the value of uncovering unknown history, but clearly not.

Since Zanthi had first read a collection of founding myths from all the crest cities in the archipelago and found Esk missing from the pages, she has been searching for a hint of that history. Esk, as far as recorded history is concerned, sprang up, wealthy and prosperous under the hands of the first Crown. Before the Crown conquered the natural upwelling of magical aether-energy they called the Well, Esk did not exist.

Esk's Well is not the only aether well in the archipelago, but it is the strongest by far. It is the most potent. And it is the only one not connected to a god-myth or guardian spirit. Zanthi has barely started in her academic career, but she sees the gap in the pattern as well as any historian might. A skipped thread in the weaving of stories.

A secret is buried deep in the beginnings of Esk, and everyone is content to have forgotten it. Zanthi is determined to know what it is. And if she is to be cast out from her academic robes, then this will be her last chance to confirm her suspicions about the deep archives.

That is why she is standing here, at the river tunnel.

She just can't bring herself to go down it.

The broken shard of white chalk sticks to her fingers. She always carries it when she's in the archives, but she's never needed to rely on it like she'll need it now. Beyond the river tunnel, the paths could lead anywhere. She marks the wall at the mouth of the passage, a small, sharp dash of white that disappears into the dark as soon as she moves beyond it and takes her light with her.

The river tunnel is low, a curtain of water dripping from the ceiling. She pulls up the hood of her cloak. It's her favourite cloak, the woollen fabric woven with a rosemary-leaf pattern. It had been a gift from her brothers when she'd first started her studies in the archives, and it's always kept her warm.

The chill seeps through now, though. Each breath slicks her mouth with water, leaving it tasting of mud, and the river echoes haunt her footsteps. The stone roof sinks down and the echoes shatter all around. She grips her lantern, barely breathing, until the ground slopes up again. Up, leaving the sound of the river behind her.

And then, as if she had traversed further than a single passage, everything is different.

The plain, worn stonework of the archives is gone. The stone here is all ruined grandeur, better suited to the House of the Crown than the deep earth. It ripples under dust and soil, the faintest smudge of what it once must have been. Time and damp have worn it down to almost nothing.

She leaves a dash of a chalk mark and, gathering her courage, strides on.

Her lantern holds steady, a golden shield of light against the shadows. She marks the wall at the forking of the path, and then again when her passage melds with another. The ruined ornamentation continues, and she follows it. She should have brought a drawing kit, something to record it with.

Her feet fall into the ancient grooves of the tilted flagstones, walking where others had once walked. Surely, the university *knew* this lay just beyond their domain. And still, they make her out to be a fool and a fancy-seeker for wanting to explore it. Despite the dark, despite the chill, a hard pit of fury burns in her.

She turns into a passage braced by arched columns, stopping for a moment to admire it, and wonder at the ghost of what it must have been. The cold sinks through her, heavier than she's ever felt it. How deep is she? She must be under the artisan's quarter of Esk, or perhaps the Old Town. There is no way to know.

Ahead, the stonework ripples as if something is hiding. Curious, she presses a palm to the wall, and the grime gives way with a burst of stone-and-water scent. Underneath is pale stone, grooved against her fingers.

Carvings. Friezes. An endless scroll of figures carved into the stone walls, stretching out into the dark ahead of her.

She wipes at the stone. A stylised face in profile stares out at her, half-crumbled with age, with one shadowed eye. It looks at her like she's somewhere she shouldn't be. And beside it, the remains of another. And another.

When she stands back, her sleeve damp with grime and wet, and holds her lantern high, she sees it for what it is. A procession of dancers, maybe. The damage of age is too severe for her to pick out any details other than in part. A foot, a basket of tangled foliage.

She hardly notices her feet carrying her forward. The broken figures move in the aetherlight, flickering like ghosts, and she follows them like someone wisp-spelled. The carvings disappear into ruined stone and then, a mere four steps further down, leap back into form, beckoning her on. Disappear. Reappear. The path splits and splits again.

Ahead, a carved hand, still clinging to the wall. A sprig of a strange plant bearing fruit. A pattern like fish scales, carved into the wall, over and over and over. A ribboned foot, outstretched in a leap, though the rest of the dancer is gone.

And then, nothing. Only plain walls.

She stumbles back, swinging the lantern in a seeking arc. Nothing. Plain walls all around. She runs her tongue against her lips, and tastes damp. Has she gone back towards the river? But *no*. She's been forging upwards this whole time.

Back down the passage, she reaches the last turning. There is no chalk mark. A chill claws up her back. Surely, she'd remembered to mark the way? She looks at her hand, her fingers white with chalk dust. She is not holding her chalk.

When had she dropped it?

The lantern light catches the broken remnants of fingers carved in the wet stone, and the relief is like a roaring flood. She can follow the frieze back the way she came. She only needs to chase the dancers down in reverse.

She does so for a while, searching for chalk marks and finding only damp walls. Sometimes, she finds gouged marks at passage corners, as if some lost explorer marked their way through the labyrinth long ago. She finds less and less of the frieze remnants until she must admit to herself that she's lost them altogether. And then she takes a wrong turn, and the path ends in a crumbled cave-in of old earth and stone. She backtracks, turns the other way, and finds another, and another.

The unease latches in deep when she finds the stairs, and she knows she is not following her old trail at all. She is lost. Now, there is a drumming beat inside her, as loud as festival drums. It's her own heart, louder and louder, as she pushes into the darkness as if it is chasing her. All she wants is a way out.

Down, her thoughts tug. *Down, and you'll reach the river.*

But her path refuses to turn down. It pulls her further in, further up, until the passage tumbles back into the arched procession way, and the friezes are there once more, flickering in the golden light.

"Oh, thank the gods," she breathes, and then she looks up, and her words fade to dust on her lips.

Above her is the most finely preserved frieze yet. For the first time, she sees a face. A woman, with hair tangled like creeping vines, a strong, lovely nose, and a beautiful face. All of her is there, graceful body arched in a weightless pose, right down to her ankles.

There is nothing to clothe her but a wreath of ivy woven through her hair.

It seems, with all the shadows leaping up the walls, that the woman is casting a gaze down on her. Imperious, but not unkind. Her arm is outstretched. She is pointing.

Zanthi forgets she is lost. She turns to see that the passage splits. One path goes on, into the darkness, the other ends in a shadow-soaked tumble of rubble. Which is the frieze pointing at? Is the end of the procession in the shadows, or collapsed under rock?

She could never sleep again if she turned her back now.

The lantern light sways drunkenly as she strides ahead. In the flash of gold, she sees a gap halfway up the heap of stone that blocks the caved-in passage. When she sets her face to it, a breeze kisses her cheek. Living air, warm and inviting.

This, then, is a way out.

She squeezes through the gap, tumbling into shadows, and reaches back for her lantern. In the moment before she grasps it, she hears the funeral bell again. It is faint and faded, an echo trapped in the rolling passages of the archives, and it sets all her nerves on edge.

She slides down the rubble heap in a shower of dust. It makes the aetherlight milky and dull until she shakes the glass clear, and she hurries on. The darkness shifts even darker, and the hollowed groove of a path breaks into uneven stairs. As Zanthi lifts her lantern higher, trying to see ahead, the light gutters and dies.

She curses, loud.

The minutes stretch, the blackness thickens. The stairs go on and on, endless, and she has a horrid, quavering thought that perhaps she's climbed all the way to the heights of Esk, that maybe she'll emerge into the House of the Crown.

Forget heresy, if that's the case. They might skip straight to treason.

Her boots collide with solid wood. A door. It squeaks open, but it's a quiet sort of squeak, as if it's doing its very best to whisper. The velvet gleam of twilight greets her and the fear-splinters melt from her chest.

Air. Light. *Safe.*

She clips her useless lantern to her satchel, then eases the door shut behind her. She's in a hedge. It's a lovely, fragrant sort of place, with sweet-scented flowers vining through the glossy, dark leaves of a hawthorn tree. There's enough of a gap she can squeeze through, and then she's stumbling into a forest. No, a garden.

No, *the* Gardens, she realises. The Old Gardens.

No wonder her aether lantern had died.

The House would have been a worse place to intrude upon, but only barely. Only Esk's best and finest are graced with an invitation inside the hallowed grounds of the Gardens. She is firmly neither. If she's caught trespassing in such a place, Theron will never recover from the shame of it.

But she is, for the moment, unnoticed. She can't be in the main pleasure grounds, the place that hosts society parties, musical performances, and social bathing. It's too quiet, even for a spring night. There are no performers, none of the garlanded 'nightingales' that staff the grounds. No bathers. Only drifting steam and silence.

She must be in the older, sacred grounds. Objectively, that is worse. Practically, it means she has a chance of escaping her predicament unseen. She only needs to find an outer wall, and a gate through it, and she'll be safely back in the streets of Esk.

Why had the frieze pointed her here? Because she has little doubt that this is where that carven procession led. The sacred springs of Esk, as much Esk's lifeblood as the Well.

And, she realises, perhaps she finally has proof of something *older* than the Well and the Crown. She takes a heady breath of sweet-scented air and calms her thoughts. An old frieze and a pointing figure are no proof of anything, not on their own.

But it's a start. She must get home so she can write down everything she remembers, before the memory is dulled.

Each step stirs up the earthy scent of the mossy ground. It smells the same as the water in the remedial baths by the river—all wet stone and soil and a gentle, sweet scent that reminds her of steeping tea leaves or river rushes in the summer. It is a scent that any Esk-born person associates with rest and healing. The Casca family presides over the sacred healing springs, second only to the Crown and the Heirs in the vast social hierarchy of power and play that Zanthi does her very best to avoid. They would be dangerous enemies to have if they found her where she oughtn't be.

She's barely had that thought when she stumbles through a mossy thicket and right into trouble.

In the thicket is a pool, and in the pool is a man. An oil lantern sits on the moss nearby, flickering gold. It gives a wholly inconvenient light.

His dark hair is curling in the damp, clinging to his brow and neck. His eyes are closed, head tipped back. He's got a lovely, strong nose, and she sees his ears are pinched with gold, and then she notices his mouth, slack and soft.

And then she looks away, because he is very much naked. She is quite sure that bathers in the pools should wear bathing shifts, but she supposes this man thought he was alone. She tries to leave him alone, but the soil crunches beneath her boots and the man looks up.

He blinks at her.

"You are not supposed to be here," he says. His voice is low, lilting. It's really very pretty, in an entirely awful way. She supposes he's a nightingale. She *hopes* he's a nightingale, because the alternative is too awful to bear thinking about.

"I took a wrong turn," she says, because she's always found just forging on to be a formidable option when she's in the wrong. "I don't suppose you know the way out?"

His eyes are as green as the deep moss that clings around the pool. She notices because she is trying her very best to not look away from his face.

The water is rather clear, is all.

He leans back again, lifting a hand to point through the trees. The water runs down his arm, pattering to the moss with the sound of rain.

“Straight ahead, if you are set on leaving,” he says. Then, silken. “Might I tempt you to stay?”

Zanthi stares. He smiles.

“No, thank you,” she says, almost on instinct. It comes out sharp. She hurries on, refusing to look his way again. Even through the drape of her rosemary-patterned cloak, his gaze feels heavy on her until the dark falls thick between them.

Chapter Two

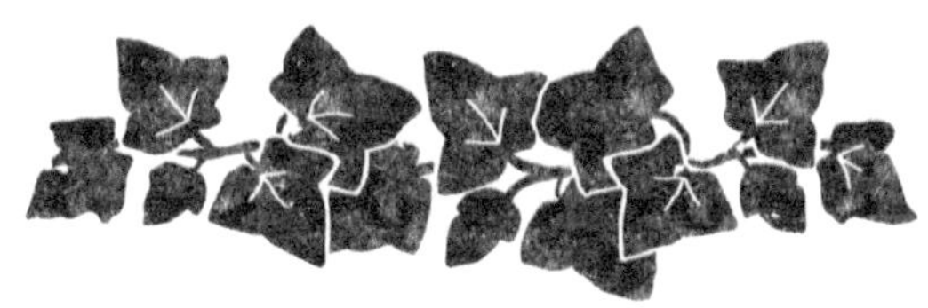

It's her turn to make breakfast, and so the toast is burnt.

Her brother Theron has his nose in the *Society Papers*, chasing gossip and wouldn't notice if she served him coal from the fireplace instead. She's grateful for it. Her tangled shame and mortification over her failed presentation still sits glass-cold in her stomach, refusing to shatter, and beneath that is a new shame and secret. She had trespassed in the Gardens, and she had been seen. She can only hope the dark hid her face, and that the bather she had disturbed does not care enough to find her. The more she thinks on it, the more she is sure that he was not a mere nightingale. She may have disturbed the Casca heir himself.

Theron looks over his paper, as if catching her thoughts. "Where were you yesterday afternoon?"

She breaks off a corner of her toast. "I went for a walk. Sorry if you waited for me."

He makes a dismissive noise, but she doesn't know if it is for her apology or for the audacity of thinking he'd wait for her. "About the presentation—"

"I'd rather not talk about it," she says, and takes a vicious bite of the crust. Especially not with him. He'd been there, after all, watching her fail. It's enough to make her want to crawl back into bed.

"We must talk about it. What are your plans?"

"Archivist Acanthus will give me my notice, no doubt."

"That is to be expected."

Expected. Did he expect her to be such a failure, then? He might have told her so, and spared her four years of trials. Four years of focusing on this one chance. The burnt-toast bitterness coats her tongue. She is adrift. She has very few friends and no allies at the university. No interests that aren't dark and old and covered in dust. No skills that aren't cross-referencing old records and sorting forgotten objects.

She is uniquely useless for anything but the thing she enjoys doing.

"There's no need for such dour faces." Theron's husband Fletcher pulls out a chair and drops into it. He's less put together in the morning than Theron is, but Zanthi likes the way he slowly gathers himself in stages. It's so consistent one could set a watch by it. Breakfast Fletcher has uncombed hair and an unfastened collar, but he has managed his braces and jacket. He'll manage the rest of it by eight o'clock, and have found where he left his pen by half past. "You might consider other areas of study, if you wish to continue on."

She takes another bite of toast. "They won't have me back in the folklore set." The less said about how her brief foray into that social circle had gone, the better. She might have known that the folklorists would be more superstitious about her eyes than most. "Nowhere else would have me either."

"You could consider something other than research," Fletcher tries. "There's an entire world outside the university, Zan. You have some rather unique abilities. Chester—"

Theron makes a noise deep in his throat. A warning.

Zanthi knows what Fletcher had been about to say. Chester, her eldest brother, is high-ranked in the airguard and would find work for her with the Admiralty if she needed it. Theron has always been vehemently against it. Her abilities, her witch-eyes that allow her to see glimpses of aether-patterns and other intangible things, are nothing they like flaunting.

People are unnerved enough at her dark, almost black, irises. They'd be throwing protection charms at her if they knew she could see the unseen. No, she is far better suited to shadows and library dust. If only they'd let her remain there.

"I said I didn't wish to talk about it."

Fletcher purses his mouth. "You have some time, at least. Your term has a few weeks left. Think on it."

"Two," says Theron, already with his nose back in his papers. "At most. Best figure something out."

She stares into her teacup. Her options are very few. She could, as Fletcher says, choose a new area of study and start over. Or she could take a second glance at the letter sitting on her dressing table upstairs.

It had been delivered some weeks ago, but she had ignored it because she had been so sure she'd find a mentorship. The letter is an offer of research work from the Crown clerks under the Guild of Records, signed by Secretary Fairthorne himself.

It's a generous offer, but she wants more from her career than becoming a clerk at the Guild of Records. But she doesn't want to go into aether studies or languages either. There *must* be a better option.

Theron makes a noise deep in his throat, pure disgust, and throws the paper down. The page is open to an article about a new wing opening at the remedial baths, full of adulations. She can see *Casca* in bold type from across the table.

"Gods, spare me from hearing about Casca for one day."

Zanthi tries to look unaffected. "Are they troubling you?"

"One can't say no to Sabine Casca, not since she has her claws in the chancellor. Her irritating spawn is constantly trying to get something or another from one of us, and we must run to his call." He stabs a piece of fig.

"I've always thought him rather charming," Fletcher says. "What has he done to offend you?"

"Everything. His smile. You know. You've met him."

"Of course. Smiling at you. What a crime that is, my dear."

Zanthi, who rather suspects she has met him too, takes a sip of tea and tries to look like she hasn't been trespassing into secret, hallowed Gardens. Especially not ones with handsome, naked men inside.

She can't know if it had been Casca for sure, because she's never seen an aethergraph of him. Aether doesn't work in the Gardens, not with all the steam and spring water, and so there are rarely aethergraphs of him for the papers. It doesn't stop the papers talking, but mostly it's salacious gossip about his many varied lovers and his formidable personality. It would be her cursed luck if it turns out it *was* the Casca heir she'd disturbed.

"Zanthi," Theron says, as if he's repeating himself.

"Yes?"

"Archivist Acanthus wants to see you this morning. It wouldn't do to keep her waiting, not with your precarious position."

Her precarious position which *he* has done nothing to help with. She tosses her last uneaten crust under the table. Fletcher's sleek hound, Susan, snaps it up. "I've errands to run today," she says. She needs no other sign from the world to avoid the university as long as possible. Luminary Acanthus had been on the board that witnessed her catastrophic failure, too. And she had enjoyed every minute. Zanthi had seen her smirk. "I'll try to go by later."

"I don't think—"

"No," she says, getting up. "You don't."

"Let her go, love," Fletcher says, over Theron's huff.

She glances back and regrets it. Fletcher is leaning over to kiss Theron. It's a chaste, dignified sort of kiss. They always pretend like that, but she's walked in on them unawares in the parlour once or a hundred times, and it's nothing at all like the way they kiss when they think they won't be seen.

She can't fathom what it would be like to have someone like

that. Someone to love with wild abandon, someone who *loves* with wild abandon. To never be thought too much, or too strange, or unwanted.

She unhooks her cloak in the hallway, and beside it, Theron's Luminary robes hang stately and golden in the drifting morning light. Three bands of twisting, gold-thread embroidery mark his achievements, the stitching bright in the quiet of the hall. She pulls her rosemary cloak over her student robes and lets the door shut firmly behind her.

Zanthi goes to hide. She scurries over the Lune—above it this time—across the spindly, lace-like bridges that tether Willow Isle to the banks. The wind whips off its churning surface, sharp with spring mountain chill, and she hunches up and hurries past red-cheeked artisans and students. The streets are always busier on the townside.

She loves Esk. The honeyed stone, the clock-like turn of seasons and festivals that keep it loud and lively. The secrets and history etched deep into the bedrock. The hollow grooves that run in the oldest streets, and the abandoned shrine-hollows in the oldest walls. She loves it, but lately she's feeling like it doesn't love her.

Acanthus will want to tell her to pack her desk and get out of the vault. She will block Zanthi from the archives, and Zanthi will never see those beautiful friezes again. Not that she's eager, exactly, to go back into the dark. If she ever does, she'll do it better prepared, with chalk and string. Perhaps she can persuade Chester to steal her some of the small, glowing aethermarkers they use on the airships next time he's home for shore leave.

In any case, the longer she can avoid Acanthus, the longer she can pretend she doesn't know she has to leave.

A tram ambles past, golden aether swirling in its wake. It creaks to a stop and a flood of townsfolk stream out like doves from a dovecote. Even now, when the airships are mostly all gone and all the ephemeral Wintering Season residents have fled back to their country towns and port cities, Esk is strung with colourful flags and the streets are full. Bright town carriages trundle down narrow streets, toted about by sedate ponies. Shops spill out their crafts and wares. Tearooms waft the warm scent of hot tea and freshly baked biscuits to entice idlers inside.

She can see the walls of the Gardens in the distance up the street, sitting in velvet silence. Dark trees rise above the walls and ancient ivy hedges, the steam of the sacred springs making it so everything within remains a mystery.

She gives it one last glance before she turns down the lane to her destination, a narrow sandstone building of artist studios. She feels as out-of-place as a hatpin in an archivist's pencil box whenever she comes here, but it's the one place she's ever reasonably sure of finding Emlyn Fairthorne. He only exists in badly written letters and forgotten tea dates, otherwise.

Despite that, she adores him. Neither of them had meant their friendship to happen, and neither of them can properly say *how* it happened, only that it had. They'd met three summers ago, when she'd been lying on the riverbank waiting for Chester to finish at an Admiralty lunch, and Emlyn had been idling about waiting for his father to do the same. He'd sketched her without permission, and she'd scolded him over it. He had been blunt, and she'd been rude, and they'd gotten along marvellously. They've been getting along much the same ever since.

He's quite happy to ignore that her brother is the infamous Captain Chester Locksley, and in return, she does her best not to think about his high-ranking fathers, either. Instead, they swap gossip, and books, and on one occasion, a very lovely painting that Zanthi had fallen for in an instant, and Emlyn had handed over without question or cost.

The studio is on the second floor, and the door is open. The scent of linseed and wax is already over her before she's three steps inside. He's at a canvas, a fistful of ragged brushes in one hand and his palette precariously balanced on a stack of books on the table beside him.

She doesn't interrupt, and he makes no acknowledgement of her. That's very usual, and she settles in the window seat while she waits. It isn't long before Emlyn's brushes clatter back into their pot.

"What brings you here?" He wipes his hands on a rag that looks dirtier than him by far. There's a smudge on his cheek, too. He has his father's looks. Not Secretary Fairthorne, but Admiral Fairthorne. There's a trustworthy set to his face that Zanthi supposes suits the admiral, but is entirely a lie on Emlyn. He can be a twisty sort of weasel, but she likes that about him.

She makes a frustrated gesture, finally letting her mood hiss out of her. "It's a mess. It's all a horrid bind."

"Sounds dire. I'd make you tea to fret over, but one should never ingest any substance in an artist's studio." He's all virtue as he says it.

"Is that half-bottle of wine there a prop, then?"

He picks it up, as if surprised to see it. "No idea. Tell me about this bind." He takes a sip and wrinkles his nose.

"I've had a nightmare of a week," she admits, as he tips the rest of the bottle down the sink. "I didn't get a single mentor offer, so that's it for me."

"Just like that?"

"More or less."

He makes a low noise of disgust. "That's rubbish. What now?"

"Gods, I don't know. It only happened yesterday!"

"I thought you academic types had plans for everything."

"Not for failure."

He *tsks* at her. "There's your problem. Always make peace with failure."

She levels him with her best Theron-esque look. It only makes him laugh.

"But why are you really here?" He's shrewd when he cares to be. His father was made admiral of the airguard for good reason, and Emlyn, for all he pretends, is not so different from his famous parents. "You look on the cusp of agony."

"I had an offer from the Crown clerks," she admits. "I ignored it, but since I haven't got a mentorship... Well, it's return to being a student or join the Guild of Records."

"An offer from Pa?"

Zanthi nods. Secretary Fairthorne is a well-known figure in academia, if only for the research he often commissions on behalf of the Crown, Esk's highest authority. But to be an independent researcher solely under his purview? That means working apart from the other scholars, outside of the factions and sets, away from the debates and seminars and presentations.

It means not being a part of the university anymore, and she's *always* been a part of the university. At her mother's side, and then at Theron's, following them up the hill to the old stone gate that marked the university grounds.

She lets her head fall against the window. It's cracked open and the breeze tugs at her. "I thought you might have put him up to it, if I'm honest."

"Not me. I don't interfere with his work. Barely know what he does, other than running around after the Heirs."

"I'm thinking about accepting," she says, voice small. "I'm barely a step away from an outcast already. How different can it be?"

Emlyn sits next to her. The breeze stirs his rush-gold hair, except where it's stuck with paint. His sleeves are pushed up his arms in some small attempt at keeping his shirt neat, but it's a lost cause. He is not a neat painter in the least. "Pa won't make you an outcast. Those pigeons on the Luminary board don't know what they had with you. And Pa has an eye for quality. See it as a compliment."

She tucks her knees up to give him room. It doesn't really work. He just slouches to fill it like a cat basking in sunlight. "The scholars will sneer even more at me, knowing I wasn't good enough to make it the proper way."

"The proper way can go sink in the river. Do it your way. I can't say I ever know what Pa means to do about anything, but he's a good man. If you run into strife, he's all you'd ever need to have on your side."

It's more than the university has ever offered her. She scrubs her hands down her face. She's never wanted protection—she's never thought she needed it.

"You want to stay for a while?"

"Do you mind?"

He smiles. He's got a good smile when he can be bothered to use it. He remembers to turn it on when he's trying to charm a collector or a potential subject, but otherwise he rather forgets it's in his arsenal. Now though, she supposes he's just in a good mood. "I never mind."

"That's a lie."

"*Once* I minded," he says.

She makes a sound of disagreement.

"Fine, sometimes I mind. But not today. You're very welcome today."

She narrows her eyes. He pats her foot, leaving a smudge on her boot that she's going to have to remove before it stains. "What are you painting?"

"I honestly had no plan," he says breezily. He pats her boot again. "But now my model has arrived."

He shuffles her on the window seat, then goes to shift his easel so he's facing her. She turns to gaze out the window instead of staring at him.

"Hey, no. Look towards me."

She hesitates. Emlyn has painted her before, but rarely so directly. Never her face, staring right out of the canvas. It's hard for others to look her in the eyes for any length of time, though Emlyn has gotten better at it. He's stubborn like that.

She settles for staring at the vase of flowers just behind Emlyn's head instead. It'll make things easier for him, and they're pretty things. Lacy yarrow in peach and cream and butter yellow, all spilling from a brass urn.

Emlyn must know exactly where she's looking, because he smiles as he flicks his brush into his fingers again. "They're from mother's garden. I'll get an earful tonight, no doubt." He is unashamed, and his smile is sweeter when he talks about his mother. "She says I hack at the best ones."

"I hope you at least painted her a portrait of them."

He makes a lazy gesture that flicks paint across the floor. "She has too many of my paintings already. You should come around and see the garden, though. You like gardens, don't you?"

It tugs a laugh from her. Here, in the window's warmth, in Emlyn's bright-lit studio, the cold dark of the archive tunnels feels a world away. "I suppose I do. I trespassed into the Gardens yesterday, you know. The properly old part."

His brush stops and he peers around his canvas. "*Why*?"

"It's a long story. I didn't mean to."

"Zanthi," he says, all reproach. "You might have led with that, before all that faff about your mentorship."

"It's not so interesting. I won't be doing it again."

"Not so interesting, she says," he mutters. "Gods fear what she *does* find interesting. Were you caught?"

"Obviously not, because Theron hasn't had to rescue me from the cityguard."

He makes a few vigorous marks on the canvas. "Only you would find it an inconvenience to peek behind the veil of one of Esk's most enthralling mysteries."

She thinks of water running down lantern-kissed skin. Enthralling is one word for it, certainly. Then she tries to think of something else, before Emlyn catches anything in her face. "Well," she says. "It wasn't entirely an inconvenience."

"That's the spirit," he says, cheered. "We'll make a romantic of you yet."

Visiting Emlyn never fails to calm her. Perhaps it's the way he just doesn't *care* about anything outside his tightly-curated world of paints and fits of passion. For a little while, while she's with him, she can feel like she doesn't care about a whit of it, either.

He makes her feel like it wouldn't be the worst to work for the Guild of Records. It might even be admirable. She carries that feeling right through the rest of the day, skirting through the vault, and avoiding Acanthus as she slips into the storage alcove she's claimed as a workspace. She's almost decided to accept the research position, which means she needs to tie up her loose ends in the vault.

Her current unfinished work is the sorting of tiny fragments of ancient pottery from an uncatalogued box. It's tedious, but she's never minded this style of work. She likes the mystery of ancient things. Likes the story she can pick from shattered clay and ancient brushstrokes. Most of the decorations in this collection have star-marks or faded, flowing markings of foliage. There are a lot of apple leaves and laurel. *Love and victory*. A wedding scene, perhaps.

She's sifting through the fragments, setting them down with soft, earthen clinks, when a voice disturbs her work. It's one of the senior archivists.

"I can't help you with that, sir. I'm only responsible for the new collections."

There is a quiet response. She listens, because there is something about the voice that tugs at her. It certainly isn't another scholar.

The archivist again. "We don't have those records in the vault. They might be down lower, but there's no record of what's there." Then he laughs. "You could try the wraith. She knows more than most, and she'll go wherever you ask. Best be quick, though. I hear she won't be around long."

If only the dead gods of the archipelago were still around to hear her prayers, she'd pray for them to keep her hidden. Instead, she makes it through only a few more fragments before the door to her alcove swings in.

"Excuse me?" It's a low, lovely sort of voice. She's never heard an academic speak like that.

"Yes," she says, after too long a pause. She hasn't quite got the standing to issue something like Theron's famous *go away*, even if she'd like to. "Come in."

He does. It is the man from the Gardens.

Casca.

Chapter Three

He's wearing clothes, which she is thankful for, but his outfit sends alarm right through her. It's all as fine as evening wear, steeped in rich brown and blackberry tones, and his hair is tousled and plaited at his temples like he's off to a society dinner. He smiles at her, and it's polite, and sweetly charming, and has none of the promise of the look he'd given her in the springs. "I was told you might help me?"

"Possibly." She turns back to her work, ducking her face. "If I must."

He hesitates on the threshold before stepping in. He doesn't shut the door behind him, just angles it towards closed. "I'm Madoc Casca. I'm conducting some research for the Gardens."

She pauses, glaring at the shard in her fingers. So modest, like he needs the introduction. Like she hasn't seen his name a hundred times in the papers, like every other townsperson of Esk. The fragment in her hands is decorated with oak leaves. *Protection and blessings*. She sets it aside in its own pile. "And?"

He clears his throat. "I'm looking for historical records."

"You're not a scholar."

"I have permission from the chancellor to seek whatever I need."

That has her glancing up. Her interest turns keen as a paper knife. He's holding a small, gilt-edged paper, and she takes only a moment to recognise it as a chancellor's writ. She's only ever seen one *once*, and that was airguard business. Theron had not been lying when he'd said the Casca family had their claws in the university. Not even Acanthus could bar someone from the archives if they had that writ.

He knows he has her attention. His mouth turns in a very sly, sharp line as he leans on the edge of her desk, watching the work she's doing. He picks up one of the pieces she's been unable to identify.

"What history are you seeking?"

He turns the fragment over in his hands, frowning. It's a very artful frown. "I'm looking for any records that might have come from the Gardens prior to the eighth storm cycle. Anything written by a Casca."

The short glance he gives her has no recognition in it. No real interest either. It's a relief.

"You've found nothing in the library?"

"Not anything useful. I think it must be buried deeper than a library shelf." He places the pottery piece down, but not in the unsorted pile. He places it with the ones that have star-marks and measurements.

"Why there?" she says, because he's done it too deliberately for it to be thoughtless.

He hesitates, then picks it up again. "Here," he says. His thumb rests against a tiny scratch in the clay, right by the break line. His hands are a warm shade lighter than the earthen clay, his nails neat and polished. Then she remembers to look at what he is marking, and not his hands. "That's the sort of sky-mark you'd see on an ancient celestial chart. We still use them today."

She takes it and places it back in the pile he chose. She doesn't know much about celestial charts, but she can always check it later. His eyes must be sharp as an airship gunner's, because she'd missed that mark entirely.

"Very well," she says. "I'll look for you. You'll have to leave the writ, though. They won't let me do anything without it."

It's a mistake, looking up. His gaze meets hers. There's a moment, his brows twitching down, where she thinks she's been recognised. But all he says is, "Why do they call you that?"

"Call me what?"

"Wraith."

"I go places only the dead would easily go, or so they say." She nods to the pottery fragments. "There are a lot of forgotten things in the archives, and most of the scholars think it's bad luck to spend any amount of time down there. But I've never minded it."

"Even though everyone thinks it's cursed?"

"Someone has to go," she says. "It would be sad, don't you think, for all the things in there to rot away unknown just because those that should care for them were too scared to try?"

The polished edge is gone from his expression. Now, he's watching her like he's trying to see through her. No one ever looks at her for as long as this.

"You remind me of a friend," he says at last, and the words are so gentle that she realises just how glass-like his voice had been, until then.

She turns to her work again. "I shouldn't think that's flattering for your friend, unless they also like dark and forgotten places."

"Metaphorically, maybe." He places the writ on her desk. "Thank you for being willing to help me. You can contact me at the Gardens any time. Just ask for me at any door." He hesitates. "May I have a name? I'll put you down for entry."

It's a bribe, but it's not necessary. He's already given her the only thing she could possibly want. She has no need for the Gardens, or for society, or for handsome men with green eyes.

"I can hand a letter over without such a thing."

There is silence. Has she offended him? But no. The smile is undaunted.

"Very well," he says. "I'll tell the nightingales to look out for a surly archive-dweller with a letter in hand."

He is teasing her. He doesn't know her well enough to be allowed to tease her. She opens her mouth to tell him so, but he has turned to leave, and is caught staring at the back of the door. Her rosemary cloak hangs there, plain to see.

She puts the fragment down carefully.

"Or perhaps," he says, "you needn't help to enter my Gardens, after all. Do tell me your name. It seems unfair for you to know so much of me when I know so little of you."

Her mouth tastes of pottery and archive dust. Almost unbidden, she replies, "Ilyston."

His eyes widen, just a fraction. "I'd quite forgotten Theron had a sister."

"Feel free to continue forgetting it," she suggests. Her blood is drumming in her, bright with alarm. She doesn't want to come to his attention. She doesn't want him knowing her.

He throws her one last look before he goes, and Theron was right. His smile *is* entirely offensive.

The Casca heir, if the *Society Papers* can be believed, has the sort of personality that Esk society turns around. From his seat in the Gardens, the entirety of Esk's social Season is his to open or close to whom he pleases. He is a lord of the glittering masses. Zanthi should never have crossed paths with him. Not once. Not *twice*.

And certainly not without even trying.

One isn't truly part of the Season unless they get on the Casca invite list. People spend the entirety of autumn vying for the notice of the Gardens, and when they get it, they dress in their finest silks, drink the Gardens' finest spirits, and tumble into each other's beds. If someone is fortunate, they might catch the eye of a nightingale and win their notice. Every now and then, someone might get *extremely* fortunate and catch the eye of Madoc Casca himself.

The *Society Papers* love catching the scent of scenes like that. It's always cause for gossip when someone makes too much of a show in public, but having even the dusting of a Casca scandal is a blessing for the socially ambitious. It can make any person desirable, and if they are smart, they make the most of that. A little gossip in return for a world of newly-opened doors is an easy trade for most to make. And according to the papers, Casca likes best those who are beautiful, talented, and charming.

All to say, Zanthi spends the rest of the day caught between disbelief that she has encountered Madoc Casca and survived, and foreboding that the next time she might not be so fortunate. Scholars gossip like breathing, and there are few things in this world that Zanthi wants less than to be mentioned in the papers.

She is not a society person. It's not that she doesn't like the idea of dressing finely and dancing under aetherlight—or at least, she hadn't once. But her eyes make it impossible.

Witch-eyes, some call it. Zanthi has always called it her side-sight. Her talent only works when she isn't properly looking, and only at the edges of her vision, but sometimes she can see things that no one else can see. Mostly, she sees aether—stronger and more clearly than anyone else she knows.

Esk lives on aether, thrives on it. There is the pale gold aether of the Well, near invisible even to her side-sight. The strong gold of harvested aether, used by aetherworkers and artisans, hewn from the bone, blood, and scale of stormbeasts. And then there's the deadly wild aether, silver and striking, that dances through the skies when the aetherstorms hit.

In truth, the last is something anyone can see, if they're close enough and the storm is strong enough. But in Esk, where the storms rarely reach, people only see aether as the warm golden glow that blooms when harvested aether is set into glass or metal. They know it as the magic that lights rooms, or powers trams, or flies airships. Invisible, until it lights up.

It's pretty when it's glowing. Beautiful when it's worked up to be decorative. Invisible when it's latent, when it's pooling in the streets and clinging to people like burdock seeds stick to socks.

But Zanthi sees all of it.

She sees the patterns the aether makes, sees the ripples and tidemarks left on the stones of Esk. She sees the radiant ship-aether cut through airguards, tearing them apart bit by bit. And she sees the way all the harvested aether still moves in the echoes of the living beasts it once was. It writhes and coils, as if desperate to tear itself away from the gold and glass and gemstones it is captured in.

Wearing aether is like adorning oneself in ghosts, as far as Zanthi is concerned. She'd tried to venture to an evening party years ago, and the sheer overload of aetherghosts flickering in the edges of her vision had sent her running home before dessert, suffering from a splitting headache.

The Gardens, aether-void and lit by candle-flame, are perhaps the only place in all of Esk that Zanthi might ever have a chance to enjoy a Season. But her passing interest in society fled years ago, and she hasn't the time for that life anymore. She has her studies, and her mysteries, and all she wants is to be left to pursue them.

So, no. Zanthi will not entertain thoughts of Madoc Casca, even if he sorts pottery fragments as well as any student of antiquities.

She runs her finger down the fold of the chancellor's writ, the gilt edges as sharp as the gold of a Luminary robe. She *will* research Casca's request, of course. But she'll research her own interests first.

The chancellor's writ causes a fuss, as she knew it would. Theron stares it down, then stares her down with equal reproach.

"Casca."

"He wants something no one else can find. The archivists directed him to me."

"It won't buy you more than a month, at most." He's at his desk in the study at home, and he goes back to marking his papers. "And what did Acanthus say?"

Zanthi tucks the writ in her pocket. "I didn't see her."

A muscle in his jaw twitches. "Didn't you?"

"Perhaps I'll see her tomorrow."

"You are burning bridges."

"I can't burn what wasn't there. Theron, be honest with me. What chance do I have of staying on without a mentor?"

He makes a harsh slash with his pen. Gods, he's probably marking some poor sod's paper, and she's making his mood mean. "None, as things are. You'd best prepare another proposal and submit it at the Vestmere panels."

That's his suggestion? Another year, maybe more, in her black, ungilded robes. She doesn't *want* to be a student anymore. She wants to be a sopharion—a mentored scholar under the tutelage of a Luminary, able to submit papers and take part in closed debates. "What sort of proposal?" she says, voice flat.

He's silent for a long while. "Something that doesn't challenge the foundations of the Crown, Zanthi. Gods, did you have to strike to the heart so hard? Why not move to aetheric studies? You are uniquely suited for it."

"I'm a historian."

"You risk being nothing," he says. "Not until you sort this out."

She takes a sharp breath. It sticks like sand in her throat. Theron was the youngest scholar in decades to win his Luminary robes. He had blazed his way to the top of the language faction. She's sure he's going to be the next faction head. He's going to be chancellor one day. She's watched his ascension for years, and he hasn't looked back for her, not once.

It's not that she wants him to make it easy for her. It's only that it might have been nice to have him speak in her favour, even just once. Just this once, when no one else had.

"I have another offer," she says. It falls from her mouth before she means it to. "The Crown clerks."

His pen stops. "Fairthorne? I expect you have better sense than to accept."

"It will allow me to continue my research in some manner. No other option gives me that."

"You will throw away the last four years of work." His voice is brittle. "It was good work, Zanthi. You can't let it take you nowhere."

"You just told me to throw it away."

"No, just to put it aside for now. One day you can come back to it. Think of Luminary Hart. He does as he pleases and none can speak against him. He's too entrenched. You only have to play along for a time."

"I'd rather spend my time going somewhere."

"Nowhere worth going," he says, flatly. "What is there for you, as an independent researcher? Jumping from wage book to wage book? You cannot debate, you cannot publish, you cannot teach, you cannot advance—"

"I don't want those things. I don't want any of that. I just want to study the things that interest me. I don't care about the rest." It's not true, of course. She cares about the looks the others give her. She cares about the bands of Luminary gold and how she'll never have them. But caring means little when the ways are shut to her. She can't care, because it will hurt too much.

Theron pinches the bridge of his nose, takes a calming breath. "Without the backing of a mentor, any scholar might take your research and publish it as their own. Independent work is not protected. You will not be able to claim any of it—"

"May they have better luck with it, if they dare," she says, patience finally splintering. "I intend to accept."

"You're making a mistake," he says, but he doesn't say a word more on it that night. He barely says a word to her at all.

The next day is a half-holiday, grey and overcast. Clouds slink low over the rooftops, and the sky curls up against the river and smothers the city between. Esk is a city of rain. There's not a season that spares it, but it's most unpleasant as summer nears.

Fletcher congratulates her with true enthusiasm when she tells him about the writ, and her intention to join the Crown clerks. "Is that what Theron was stewing about all night?" He twirls his pen idly in his fingers. His lunch is mostly untouched, and all his focus is on the thick stack of typed pages that have replaced his plate. He is very single-minded when he's in edits. "I think it's a good thing. Working for the Crown is a fine position to be in, and having the Casca family's favour can't hurt."

"You aren't going to warn me about the great lack of debating I will suffer?"

"I have seen your debating. I think Esk will survive its loss." Fletcher's soft-edged smile melts the worst of her edges away. It always has.

"I wish Theron wouldn't be such a blanket about it."

"He believes in you. He's frustrated your path is far thornier than his ever was."

"He hasn't been helping it. I don't *want* to be a researcher, but it's the closest thing to what I *do* want to do. If I can't be a scholar, it's the only other thing I can stand. Why can't Theron accept that?"

Fletcher sighs. He underlines a few words with an aggressive sweep. "I don't dare claim to know what goes on in that wonderful, complicated head of his." Another underline, this one even more aggressive. "Rivers weep, I fear I will never write a good book again."

That, at least, is a fear that Zanthi is entirely sure won't come to pass. She sneaks an olive off his untouched plate. "Nonsense. I think you're an excellent writer, and so does Esk."

"I'd take your opinion with more weight if your favourite writer wasn't Aster Starling," he says, and then holds up a hand against her outrage. "Don't get all puffed up. I only mean that you don't read fiction."

"Starling writes adventure novels."

He frowns. "They're travelogues. *Journals*."

She reaches for his apple next, but Fletcher beats her to the little cutting board. He pulls it between them and spins the apple around.

"Shall we?"

Zanthi hasn't played the fortune-telling game for years. She smiles, despite herself. "Go on," she says.

"Choose."

"Mountains," she says, as she always does.

"Valleys," he agrees, as he always does, and slices the apple right through the round middle.

She takes the top half with the stalk. The apple flesh is pale and snow-white, the core immature and barely defined against the rest of the apple.

"One seed, intact," she says, examining it. "A single path or choice lies ahead. No crown, so I am unseeing and unprepared. Well, that seems accurate."

Fletcher is looking at his half with resignation. He has three seeds, all clumped together. Muse-blessings, perhaps, but focused in intensity in one aspect of his life. "This had better be for my current book," he tells the apple in dire tones, "and not a new project coming from nowhere."

"Oh, and one damaged seed," adds Zanthi, frowning at her half. It's a small, dark nick of a seed, sliced by the knife. "A warning, then."

Fletcher turns his apple over, but he hasn't got the other half of it. "Perhaps for Theron's mood," he says, grinning.

"I needn't an apple to tell me that," she says, biting into her half. Theron's footsteps are rattling down the stairs, in any case. "I should be off. I have work to do."

"Zanthi," Fletcher says. He hesitates, turning the apple over in his hands. "I know the writ will make the next few weeks easier, but tread carefully, would you? Don't get tangled in anything with Casca."

"I'm not at risk of that. Of anything. I'm only going to find some old records for him."

"Send them to him, when you do. Don't go in person, not to the Gardens."

She frowns, nibbling at the apple. "Why ever not?"

He glances at her–right at her, at her eyes. "It's a strange place," he says finally. "I worry what they might think of you there."

She picks the half-cut seed from the apple heart and flicks it into the tray with the olive pits. "I'll keep my head down."

"Just step carefully," he says, and turns back to his work.

Chapter Four

For a few long weeks, all is unchanged. Spring tumbles on, until all the freshness is gone from the air and mugginess clings to everything. The reed beds in the river droop. Even her robes, though she is grateful to be wearing them a little longer, are too heavy and far too cloying against her skin.

Casca's writ keeps her safe from academic exile and Casca himself makes no further appearances. He is clearly content to leave her to her own business.

Truth be told, she thought the research he wanted would be easy. It is not.

She starts in the library, but it is as Casca had said—there is nothing on the history of the Gardens and very little on the springs. That strikes her as strange...and wrong. It's the same bell-strike feeling as she'd gotten when she'd realised that before the Crown, Esk did not exist in the history books. Whatever forgetting has devoured Esk's history has swallowed the Gardens, too.

She combs through the record chambers in the archives, after that. The record chambers are the dreariest spots, barely lit by the sconces, and full of breathless, dusty rows of ledgers and scrolls, all faded beyond colour and mostly beyond legibility.

She spends far more than her allocated time down there, but no one ever comes to collect her. She doesn't mind. The longer it takes, the more she is determined to find *something* for the Casca heir. It's personal pride at stake now.

She has always found what she seeks in the archives. It's the only reason she's been given the allowance she has from the archivists, so far. If they can't find what they need, there's never any doubt that Zanthi will.

The river tunnel sits in the dark, beyond the reach of her lantern. The awareness of it never fades, though. She wants to go back to the friezes and record them properly. Measure and sketch. Document. If she lay *that* in front of the Luminary board, they'd not be able to deny her a mentor.

But when she finally bolsters herself enough to return to the river tunnel, she freezes up, right through. She cannot reason with herself as to why her footsteps hesitate past the lower stairs or why the dark—which never bothered her before—now seems a living, stalking thing. Zanthi has only ever feared two things: deep water, and failure. Now, it seems she fears the dark cold of the earth, too.

Cursing herself, she hurries back up towards the lantern-lit archives. It's stark, the difference between that living, breathing dark and the defanged, slumbering softness that marks the university territory. The line between them is so sudden, so sharp, that she stumbles and almost misses the braided charm sitting at the top of the lower stairs.

It is a strange twist of braided river rush, about the size of her palm when she picks it up. The reeds must have been fresh when it was made, which can't have been too long ago. The faded colour is holding, and it hasn't yet turned brittle with dryness. She sniffs it. The scent of grassy sweetness is faint, but still clinging.

She tilts it again, and the pattern of reeds looks almost like fish scales. She *has* seen something like it, she realises. Recently. In the tunnels across the river, carved into the borders of the stone friezes. A scale pattern just like this one.

Stone scrapes ahead of her. The echoes ripple around her, and she turns to see a shape emerging from the shadows of the corridor. Black robes lined in the thin gold sopharion band of a mentored student. Then acorn-brown hair and a familiar face. Orrey.

"Oh, thank the waters. It's only you," Orrey says, pale and pinched. "I heard a noise. I thought I was the only one down here."

"I was heading to the records chamber again," Zanthi says, though she knows it's no explanation for being on the lower stairs. Orrey doesn't look like she's puzzling over it. Her gaze is fixed on the charm in Zanthi's hand.

"Oh. Another one." She smiles, though it is forced. "We keep finding them here. Acanthus says to throw them away. Someone's idea of a joke, I suppose. To be honest, I find it creepy."

"I've never seen anything like it." Zanthi pockets the charm to look at later. "What brings you down here?"

"Records chamber," she says, wry. "Geological maps of Calder. Are you still on the Casca hunt?"

"I am."

"Gods, they really waste our time, that lot. Well, I wouldn't mind so much if I got to meet him, but it's only ever say-so from Witten."

Luminary Witten is Orrey's mentor. He's as boring as old stone dust, but she still envies Orrey for it. "Shall we go together?"

Orrey's smile is bright and relieved. She chatters as they search —gossip about the archivists, about a professor who was caught stealing from another professor's office, and then about Casca.

Zanthi shuffles through the folders on her section of the shelf, barely listening.

"He caused a big fuss at the Gardens last week," Orrey is saying. "With one of the Alpins. Kissed them right on the steps of the Hall, in full view of the street." She tuts as if she isn't entirely delighted by this sordid level of gossip.

Kissing, as a rule, is not done outside of private settings. Casca, as a rule, kisses where he pleases. It's not like scandal ever sticks to someone like him. "Fancy that," she says, pushing a row of warped folders aside. "How nice for them."

"Maybe, maybe not. Casca was kissing someone else by the next day, or so the papers said."

"If only there were as many mentions of Casca down here as there were in the *Society Papers*."

"We'd be drowning in them, if so," Orrey says. "He really is good to the scandal writers. Makes sure they always earn their wages."

"Very benevolent of him."

Orrey laughs. It's a jarring sound in the swallowing dark, bright and then gone, without even an echo left behind. "Did you really meet him?"

"Briefly. He was very amiable."

Orrey peers through a gap in the shelves. The lantern chisels her face out in golden light. "Is it true that you're not continuing with us, Ilyston? Because it's a pity."

If she'd had to weather Orrey's platitudes weeks back, she might have been more bitter about it. Now though, she manages a resigned sort of shrug. "I'm working on some things."

She misses what Orrey says in response, because she opens a box and finds a ledger. It's bound in leather, the pages swollen and crisp from old water damage. The spine cracks when she opens it, and the ink is faded. She squints until she recognises readings of water levels and flow. It's almost certainly regarding the springs, given the list of various streams, all marked with arcane little symbols she's never seen before. The dates are old, old enough to be of interest to Casca.

Orrey sticks her head around the shelf, summoned by Zanthi's silence.

"Did you find something?"

Zanthi passes her the ledger and reaches for the case that was hidden behind it. The leather flakes under her hands, and when she pries it open, a stack of letters tumble out. They're old, old enough to be written on thick, crinkled paper made from river reeds. Beneath them, a small book sits. The cramped, flowing writing is in a language she doesn't recognise, crammed edge-to-edge on every page.

She recognises the name in the front leaf, though.

Casca.

❧

She could curse herself for finding exactly what Madoc had asked for, and for finding it in front of Orrey. Half the archivists will know by evening that she's completed the duties she was set by the writ, and the rest will know by morning. If she'd *thought* for a moment, she might have hidden the discovery and eked a few more weeks from the writ. She might have had time to gather enough courage to go back to the friezes.

She's not in the best mood when she enters her alcove and sees she has a visitor. He's a neatly-dressed man, with a cane in hand and an air of quiet irritation. He looks up. Beneath his dark brows, his eyes are ice-grey and just as cold.

"Ilyston?"

"Yes." She tilts her head just-so as she passes him, angling so she can see him better from the corner of her eye. Her side-sight reveals very little. Aether clings to him, pale and strong. He must spend time either at the House of the Crown, or at the airdocks, or both. She lets her eyes rest, and the faint pattern of aether disappears.

He looks her over. "You're not what I expected."

"Perhaps you are after my brother, then."

"No. I've been looking for you." He speaks with the smoothly rounded tones of the high classes of Esk. He's certainly not an academic.

"Have you? That's new. And you are?"

"Joren Fairthorne," he says, and a few things fall into place.

Joren Fairthorne. Secretary to the Crown. Emlyn's father.

"Oh," she says, struck wordless. She places the ledger and box down on her desk and sits.

"I have been waiting for a reply from you for some weeks. Is there somewhere we can talk privately?"

She gestures to the tiny room. If he wants anything fancier, he'll have to find it. This is as good as it gets for her. "I apologise for my lack of response. I had been considering my options."

"I wasn't aware you had any."

It's delivered with all the brutal grace of Theron in the debating hall. She clenches her jaw. "There is always a choice."

"Idealistic, but you are still young. Well, Ilyston. What answer do you have for me?"

She looks up, then, and looks him in the face. He lasts longer than most do, staring straight into her strange, dark eyes. His brow crooks as he tries to keep his gaze steady, but he fails.

"Why did you send me that offer?"

"I always need talented researchers. I know your brothers well and respect them greatly. I have no reason to believe you will be anything other than admirable yourself."

She stares at him, wondering. "And because you tried to recruit Theron and failed."

His smile turns sharp. "I never had a chance with him. He is destined for the stars of academia."

"And I'm not."

"I'm sure I don't know. I'm only offering you something the university can't. Work for me, Ilyston, and I will pay your researcher's fee and permits. I will put no strictures or limits on what you do with your time. All I ask is that you complete some small bouts of research here and there."

She freezes. It's almost too good to believe.

"I had the pleasure of seeing an early set of your notes, Miss Ilyston. Don't ask me how. But I find myself captivated by this absence of history you have uncovered. I am disappointed that the Luminary board did not see fit to grant you further support, but I would have approached you even if you had claimed your sopharion robes. It is research that must be undertaken, and the Crown agrees."

The Crown, as she is now called, had once been known as Heir Elanor and had been quite beloved in the town. She had ascended to the Well some years ago and was seen only rarely now. She spent her days in the House, by the Well, where she watched the aetherpatterns and predicted the stormfalls that ravaged the archipelago. It was a grim fate, in Zanthi's opinion.

"The university thinks my studies are heretical and full of anti-Crown sentiment."

Joren smiles, all amusement. "Ela is fond of antiquity," he promises. "She's always been interested in the passages under Esk."

"The deep archives, you mean?"

"Historically, there have been very few people able to delve into them. I was very curious to learn that you are both eager and capable, Miss Ilyston."

She swallows. "Scholars are superstitious, as a rule."

"Not superstition. Good sense. Ill things happen to those who go too far beneath the city, and very few ever possess the desire and will to do so. You, apparently, are an exception. That is very remarkable."

She's never been called remarkable in her life. "No amount of research fees will grant me access to the archives, not if I'm not a scholar."

"And are you intending to give up your scholarly aspirations?" He watches her, a pleased curl at the corner of his mouth. "No, I didn't think so. But you will need time, and working for me will give you that."

He's not wrong. It will allow her to pursue her studies without having to detour into another area of academia entirely. "The scholars aren't kind to those they deem beneath them, and independent researchers are the lowest of the low."

"And I imagine you are quite versed in surviving such treatment," he says, unconcerned. "Yours are not the first set of witch-eyes I have seen."

"Is that so?" She has never heard of anyone in Esk with eyes like hers. Either Joren is lying, or he's travelled the archipelago widely. "I'm not eager to join the Guild of Records."

"Then don't. I will employ you as a clerk directly under my oversight. No deadlines, no oversight, no strictures on what you delve into. It may not get you your sopharion robes, but it will buy you the time you need to find other ways to the Luminaries. At the very least, consider it."

"I do not need to consider, Secretary Fairthorne," she says, wishing she could sink her head into her palms and maybe cry a little. "You are right. I have no other options. I accept."

He places a card on her desk. "Excellent. Then continue as you are. I will sort your permissions. There will be a formal agreement sent along, but do not wait on it. It may take some time."

She nods. She can't trust herself to do anything else.

He takes up his cane. "Good day, then. It was an unexpected pleasure, Miss Ilyston."

She doesn't look up as he leaves. She's staring at the elegant calling card. No strictures, no deadlines, and no oversight is a potent offer. She can almost taste it, the absolute freedom of it. But the cost is a bitterness she isn't sure she can swallow.

When she wakes tomorrow, she'll have no reason to put on her black student robes. She can only hope she will manage to remain unnoticed and unremarkable through all the shame of her failure.

At least, with the Secretary of the Crown himself behind her, no one can tell her not to delve into the history of the town. Her research cannot be held to have anti-Crown sentiment if the Crown herself is paying for it. That little spark of victory is a sharp and shining thing.

Joren is right that she needs time, and under his protection, the university cannot run her out entirely. Close the archives to her, yes. Lock her out of the vault, maybe. But they cannot close the library to her, and they cannot stop her from requesting documents. It is, mostly, a success.

It's still nothing she is eager to announce to Theron, though. She reaches for the ledger and the letters instead.

It is time to visit the Gardens.

Chapter Five

The idea of seeing Casca's sweet-mouthed smile again is a daunting one, but the day has already turned so strange that the thought of the Gardens and the nightingales stirs nothing more than a hungry curiosity in her.

Her buried procession of friezes had pointed her right to the Gardens. Perhaps she'd be able to glean some sort of answer why, if she could peek inside. A ruined column or two. A pattern of fish scales in an old wall. *Something* to link it to the vaulted passage in the deep archives.

She bundles the books and the letter box into her satchel, tugging her rosemary cloak over it. The writ might allow her to be free and easy within the collections, but she is quite sure it doesn't extend to taking anything outside of university grounds.

She has no guilt over the smuggling, though. The items have the Casca name on them. Why shouldn't they be returned to the Gardens, rather than left in the dark to rot without even a catalogue card to mark them?

The Lune is softer today, gentling as summer approaches. The river reeds rattle in the breeze as she crosses through Willow Isle, and she hums an old river song under her breath as she strides up through the artisan's quarter.

The Garden Hall is a grand, lounging presence at the northern point of the old festival square. It is not as old as the walls or soil of the Gardens, but it's old enough to be nearly as stately as the House of the Crown. A solitary attendant guards the ornate doors at the crest of the sandstone stairs. He's a handsome nightingale, stone-still as he watches over the raucous bustle that floods the square.

Warm evenings like this bring out all the chattering students and apprentices to gather under the old oaks. They feast on baked apples and roasted fish, whiling away the last hours of daylight until the dance halls in the town open. A pair of nightingales sing at the foot of the stairs, entertaining the crowds, and Zanthi skirts them as she climbs to the attendant. He's keeping a watchful eye on the performers, and when she approaches, he doesn't give her more than a glance. He's wearing a draped linen tunic and tight trousers, and the effect is rather like an effortless princeling leaning against the threshold to some other kingdom.

"Yes?" he says. His eyes are lined in a smoky sort of way. "Have you a token? Only the Oak Pavilion is open for bathing today. You'll have to go to the riverside door."

"Not that," says Zanthi. She gathers herself. Just like talking to the professors, she thinks. No need to let him see she's unsure. "I've some items that Madoc Casca requested. May I pass them on to someone?"

He shifts. The linen of his tunic shimmers under the square's aetherlamps. "Name?"

"Ilyston, but I don't think—"

He straightens, and this time looks at her properly. "I have your name," he says, which feels rather ominous, even if he says it with a touch of a smile. "Come on, then."

The door frame is carved with a tangle of ivy leaves, and as he opens it, the scent of rosemary and candle wax spills out. He ushers her into a grand receiving hall, the music of the square disappearing into velvet softness. A mural of garlanded revellers in a forested landscape wraps around the walls, and she is struck still at the uncanny resemblance to the frieze in the archives.

A coincidence, she thinks. It is a recent mural. She remembers reading about it in the papers.

During the Season, this room will be full of people, but now it only holds a scattering of nightingales, all lounging about on sofas and wicker chairs. They rouse at the disturbance, flocking close to her. The candlelight dances around them, shimmering in the stones they wear in their ears and around their necks and on their fingers. They're each in draped linen bathing robes, like summer gods from some old folktale, with silken slippers on their feet and silken ribbons in their hair. They all have some variation of a smile, but none are friendly.

Her lips press down. She's been in debating halls that felt less dangerous than this.

"What's this?" says a woman. She reaches out to tweak the collar on Zanthi's university robe, where it is peeking above her cloak. "An academic?"

"An Ilyston," the doorman says. "For Casca. Be nice."

He steps back out, pulling the door shut behind him. The sound of the catch is loud in the hall. A murmur ripples around the group. When Zanthi steps back, startled, she collides with another nightingale coming up behind her.

There's an arm around her shoulder, a face close to hers. They all smell of perfume—heady scents of florals or spice. Her nose wrinkles before she can help it.

"Madoc, is it?" A man stands at the back of the crowd, leaning against a pillar. He has piercings along the shell of his ear, and he raises his fine brows as his gaze drifts down her body. "He's been hunting far afield."

"A poor hunt, if his quarry comes seeking him instead," says the voice by her ear. There's a sharp tug at her head, and then her hair tumbles free from its clasp.

"Pardon me," she says, grasping at her hair. "I don't know you nearly well enough for that."

The girl laughs, and her mouth is petal pink and bright. "But you could, sweetheart," she promises. "There's got to be something under all that dust to entice Casca, surely?"

"You're all mistaken—Do you mind?" She grabs at her satchel as deft hands try to pull it away. The thief grins, eyes bright in the candlelight, and then her cloak is stolen from her shoulders. She turns, but she meets a nightingale instead, who catches her fast. Her arms are soft as silk, twined around Zanthi's waist.

"Oh darling," she says. She has pretty eyes. "Not his usual songbird, are you?"

Zanthi takes a deep breath. She doesn't want to lose her temper, but she can feel it simmering at the back of her throat. They're just so *handsy*. One nightingale, draped in her stolen cloak, is strutting about while the others laugh. *Merciful gods.* Madoc Casca was less irritating than this. Even with that smile of his. Even naked.

"Would you stop for a cursed minute and listen to me?"

The nightingales stop. The girl with the pretty eyes smiles. "We're only playing."

"Perhaps," Zanthi says, with all the coldness she can muster, "you could play at having better manners."

The man leaning against the column laughs. He's been watching her with a sharp regard this entire time, and when she catches his gaze, she knows he's noticed her eyes. Most people do, given long enough to look. Dark eyes aren't so common in this part of the archipelago, and hers are darker than most.

"You'll need to learn our games if you want to stick around, songbird."

"I don't wish to stick around. If one of you would deliver Madoc's parcel to him, then I will gladly leave." She had hoped to look around more, but she had not expected to be mauled by bored nightingales.

None of them take any notice of her words. Zanthi pulls her hair over her shoulder. Her clasp is long gone. It had been a gift from Fletcher, and she *will* make sure it is returned. The girl with the stolen cloak is now perched on another's shoulders, declaiming something from some play or another. She has marvellous voice projection, which only makes Zanthi more irritated.

"Fine. I'll deliver them myself," she says.

They don't let her go easily. She's nudged forwards, then forwards again, nightingales crowding in on all sides, herding her. Lips brush against her ear, murmuring something sweet and promising. It's all beginning to be a bit much. She hasn't any idea how to respond to it. *This* is why she wants nothing to do with society.

A nightingale slips his hand down to her palm and spreads her fingers. "Actual ink stains," he says, amused. "I suppose you spend all your days with your nose in a book."

"Mostly. Better than wherever you stick your nose, I'm sure."

He grins. "Oh, I don't know. Would you like to compare?"

There's a titter of laughter all around, and then his head is pushed aside by a pale hand.

"Whatever is going on?" says a newcomer. "Thom? Why is there an academic here?" It is said in much the same way as someone might ask why there is a pony in their parlour.

"That," says the one against the pillar, "is an Ilyston."

The newcomer is fair-haired, with lilac ribbons twisted through her curls and a milk-pale dress. She blinks at Zanthi. "Is she?"

"Are you here to waste my time with games, too?" Zanthi extracts herself from the tangle of nightingales. Someone has tried to unbuckle her satchel, but they didn't get far. She snaps it closed again. "Or are you going to be helpful?"

The woman smiles. Her cheeks dimple. Unlike the other smiles, there's nothing sharp in it. "They aren't playing, lovely thing," she says. "They're trying to scare you off."

"Then they have failed. Perhaps you should find more impressive guard dogs."

"Come along," the woman says, taking pity on her. "I'll take you to Madoc. The puppies can amuse themselves."

The nightingales laugh, but there's a friendlier tone to it than before. A few hands pat against her shoulders.

"We'll see you," says one. "Ilyston."

Zanthi decides she likes the Gardens even less than she thought she would. Absurd to think that people consider a pleasant social evening is being tormented by these creatures.

Her saviour leads her out a side door, past the column-ringed society baths with its stunning mosaic, and into the first terrace of the Gardens. Great billows of steam drift past, hooked on the evening breeze. The springs tip merrily down from the terraces above and soak from the earth in great blooms of steaming water. It is as if the entire garden is dancing in the breeze, beds of fragrant thyme swaying and the thick drape of oak leaves rustling.

Under the trees, violet evening shadows sit like overfull inkwells, and amongst them are scattered figures on strewn blankets and low wooden benches. Nightingales, yes, but also townsfolk. Those fortunate enough to be allowed access, which means they are probably all remarkable people in their own right. All the air is spiced with damp, with the scent of herbs, with the waft of perfume.

Zanthi stares, and then, not wanting to be caught gaping, looks to her feet. Her boots aren't faring any better in the moss than last time.

"I'm Chicory," says the nightingale, and the dimples are back.

Zanthi glances up at her, and then swiftly away. Is it a rule, then, that all the nightingales must be so delightful? "Zanthi."

"You hardly seem impressed with the Gardens. I do hope we're able to change your impression in time." She says this, ducking in close, tucking a lock of Zanthi's loose hair behind her ear.

Zanthi isn't blushing, but it's a very near thing.

The terrace ends with a wooden gate and a wall, and Chicory pulls a key from around her neck. "Family and personal friends only, beyond this point," she explains. "The high terrace is off limits otherwise."

"Is it a large family?"

Chicory laughs. "Just Sabine Casca and her son," she says. "And the rest of us lifelong nightingales."

Zanthi hadn't realised there were lifelong nightingales, though she supposes it makes sense. Just like there are lifelong scholars, painters, and artisans. The dances and performances of the Gardens are an art form of their own, and that's without mentioning the arcane talents of the Gardens' unsurpassed healers.

Chicory leads her up a steep cut of stone steps, and once they are on the high terrace, the lower gardens are spread out beneath them in a beautiful, steam-clouded map. The bright hedges, the weightless spheres of oil lanterns, the thyme and the vervain, all growing lushly. The air on her tongue tingles with limestone and copper and sand.

Ahead, the path crosses a rivulet of spring water, and all around it the rock is stained in deep jewel tones of green. It leads to a wide, quartz-sand pool she can only glimpse through the trees. Another twist of the path, and they're crossing through an arbour of grapevines, with a small, verdant garden growing all around. And around the next bend is the manor. It is a grand old building covered in roses and ivy, its many-panelled windows all glowing from within.

Chicory invites her in. "Up to the second landing," she says, pointing to the staircase at the end of the hall. "You'll know the one. Knock on the door."

The manor is drenched in the same rich forest hues as the Gardens themselves. Even the wooden stairs are carpeted with an emerald runner patterned with twisted oak leaves. She runs her hand along the balustrade, the polished wood warm beneath her fingers.

Chicory is right. She knows when she's on the right landing.

A statue stands wreathed in the gold of the evening light, framed against a great, arched window. He is tall, clothed in nothing but stone ivy vines and an ivy crown, head tipped back and goblet in hand. She stares for a long moment. It's nothing modern, she can see that. It has the gravitas of antiquity. It's beautiful. It's wild abandon.

There is something in the sinuous, strong twist of the statue's body that is nothing other than indecent. It's an entirely shameless thing to put in a *home.*

Heat floods her cheeks, and she presses the back of her hands to her face, willing herself to calm. It's just a statue, after all.

When she finally tears her gaze away, she spots the door. She tiptoes past the statue and lifts the knocker. After three sharp raps, a muffled voice sounds on the other side.

Zanthi waits. And waits.

Just as she's lifting her hand to knock again, the door swings open.

Chapter Six

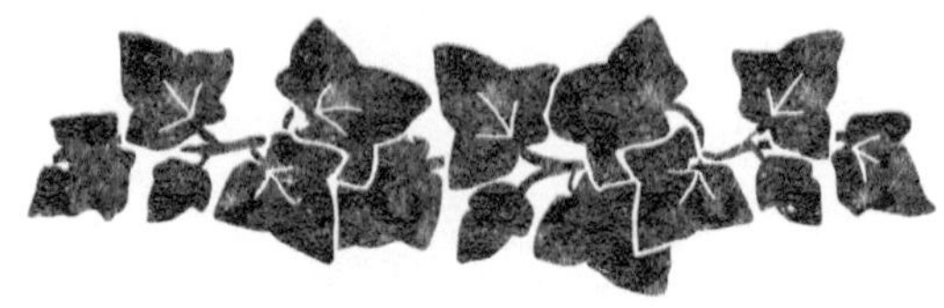

Madoc Casca is not dressed for company. His curls are tumbled up in a moth-shaped clasp, and his velvet wrap is barely tied, clinging to him idly. Beneath it, he wears an evening shirt with pearl buttons, as if she's caught him unfinished in his preparations for something grand.

"Ilyston," he says, gaze dropping to her toes and back up the length of her. "Whatever are you doing here?"

"Facing trials I was not prepared for," she says, sour. Whether her sourness is at his perfect disarray, or his polite surprise, she can't say. "I've some things for you."

"I'm sure you've been very brave." He steps back. "Will you come in?"

She glances at the statue on the landing. From the festival square to the manor, it has felt like delving through the rings of the underworld. What more is one further ring, really? "Do you have tea?"

"I very much do," he says, his smile tipping into something genuine. He gestures her in. "I was thinking I'd never hear from you, after all. What have you uncovered?"

"There wasn't much to find, I'm afraid. It's just a few things."

She grips the strap of her satchel as she steps into an artfully chaotic parlour. An ornate sofa bench basks beneath a panelled window, and a set of beautifully crafted armchairs lounge by a tiled hearth. Everything is beautifully crafted, so rich that she can barely rest her eyes anywhere without being enthralled by some loveliness or another. Dark, twisting brambles twine across the wallpaper, the secret gleam of berries half-hidden in the thicket. The panelled half-wall beneath is a deep, ancient brown. She turns in a slow circle. It's rather like sinking into a forgotten hollow of a forest.

And Madoc Casca *lives* here.

Being surrounded by so much beauty all the time would give her a splitting headache, she thinks. The window is no relief, as distracting as a painting. It frames a view of the garden terraces and the steaming pools, all sweeping down to the curve of the Hall. The manor is astonishingly like a palace. A palace over a tiny, ancient kingdom.

Madoc disappears through a narrow door off to one side, and she supposes that there is a kitchen space somewhere. She hears the noise of a kettle lid being opened and takes it as a sign that Madoc will be busy for a few moments.

She casts a curious glance over his bookshelf—a mix of novels, sheet music, naturalist journals, and astronomy books. Also, a few very dull books on things like mathematics, economics, trade, and guild politics. Theron always said one could assess a good deal about character from a person's bookshelf. She's not sure what to make of Madoc, then. A curious mind? Or a restless one?

On the other side of the bookshelf is a curtain. She tugs it back without thinking and immediately regrets her curiosity. She has found his bedroom. There is his bed with its dark green quilt, unmade and entirely covered in cast about clothes. She snatches the curtain closed and takes herself to the cushioned bench beneath the window. Her cheeks heat, and she knows she is flushed. She didn't mean to be quite so nosy. The place must be smaller than she thought.

By the time Madoc comes back, carrying a tray with a steaming teapot, two cups, and a small plate of sweets, Zanthi has extracted her finds from her satchel. She stacked them on the tea table and so must move them aside to make room for his tray.

"I must ask what happened to you," he says, sitting next to her. He has the same unconscious ignorance of personal space as his nightingales had. "You were much neater when I last saw you."

"Your tedious nightingales happened."

"You couldn't have picked a more cutting insult for that lot."

"I could find worse, if you gave me a moment," she promises. "Do they do this to all your supposed songbirds?"

"Ah," he says, thrown for a moment. "They shouldn't have called you such."

"They shouldn't have stolen my robes or my hair clasp either, and yet they did."

"I'll get them back for you," he says, and his mouth turns stern.

Somehow, though it startles her to think it, she prefers it soft. She clears her throat. "They're hardly as vicious as they think they are. They've clearly never been in an academic debate."

"I'll be sure to tell them you thought them both tedious and underwhelming. I promise you, nothing will give me greater pleasure than to do so."

She sips her tea to give her an excuse to look away from his face. He so easily makes one feel like they are the best thing to have happened in his day. It's probably unconscious, that artifice. It must come to him as naturally as breathing. It's entirely astonishing to her, though she supposes her only point of reference is Theron, who has the opposite talent of making everyone feel they are uniquely the worst thing to have happened to him all day.

"You came to the archives. It's only fair for me to venture outside my walls in turn. But I confess, I didn't expect the front door to be more harrowing than the secret one."

"Ah, yes," he says. "How *did* you get in here that time? I've been curious."

"I was exploring an archive tunnel. You've a doorway in your hawthorn thicket, if you didn't know."

"I did not." He glances out the window. "Though that certainly seems like something I should know about. Will you show me where it is?"

"I'd need to come from the other side. I'd never find it from this one."

"Another time, then," he decides. As if it is a done thing, them seeing each other again.

"Your finds," Zanthi says, desperate to wrestle the conversation back. She nudges the stack towards him. "The first is a ledger of water readings. I think it must refer to the springs, though I couldn't say for sure. It's certainly old enough." She touches the box on top. "And I found a small box belonging to a Casca that died during the seventh cycle and left a stack of letters and a journal. I found the bequest note—it's at the bottom."

He looks over the finds and gently opens the journal. He doesn't seem at all surprised at the strange language inside. "You do fine work. Better than anyone else that I asked."

"Scholars aren't helpful, as a general rule."

"You are."

"I'm not a scholar," she says. "Though not for lack of trying."

"Then they're missing out on good sense, a good mind, and a pretty face. More's the pity for them, and all the better for me." He takes a sweet biscuit and places it on her plate. It's an old-fashioned style of biscuit, the dough twisted like river reeds. "Try these. They're good."

"You needn't flatter me *after* you've got what you wanted."

"You are assuming I do, in fact, have everything I want."

She gives him a sharp look. It's the same warning she gives anyone who thinks they can charm anything from her. Usually, it has them backing down. But Madoc's cool smile is unflinching, and he studies her with the sort of intensity a scholar would be proud of.

"You really are Theron's sister," he says, after a moment. "You must have learned that look from him."

"Was it ever in question?"

"No, not really," he says, amused. "And the letters? What do they contain?"

"I didn't look. I've my own questions I'm trying to answer. I'm hardly going to do your research for you." She gathers her satchel up, preparing to leave. She has been here quite long enough, and far longer than she had ever intended to stay.

"Thank you, Ilyston. This is exactly what I had hoped for." He runs a gentle thumb along the edge of the journal. "What is your research, if I may ask?"

"The founding of Esk, mostly," she says, wary. Mostly, when someone asks, they're trying to trick her into looking boring or foolish, or both.

"In what manner? Is there some mystery to it?" he asks, and she is, for a heartbeat, at a loss.

No one ever asks for *more*.

"Well, yes. Tell me the founding story of Esk."

Madoc opens his mouth and looks, for the briefest of moments, hunted. Then he shrugs it off with a grin. "Well, the Crown—"

"That's the founding history of the *Crown*," she says, cutting him off. He looks fascinated. "In which the Crown makes a great sacrifice to rescue Esk and its people from destruction, but that implies Esk already existed. Already had people. Something was there before the Crown was, and whatever was there first must have been controlling the Well just as the Crown did in its place."

Madoc settles back against the lounge and bites into a biscuit.

"Did you know we're the only major settlement in the archipelago to have survived with such an active aether well? All the other documented wells are fairly dormant, the latent aether can barely recharge a single airship, let alone an entire fleet." She's hitting her stride now, satchel and her plan to leave forgotten. "We're also the only city without a founding god-myth. I started in folklore, you know, hence the interest in founding myths. We don't have a god-myth, or any remnant of one. Not even an accepted temple ruin! The day I ended up disturbing your bath, I had found a frieze that seemed to depict some sort of festival or sacred procession."

Madoc leans in, eyes bright, dark and green. "And this is why you spend so much time underground? Hunting out buried treasures?"

"The archives are so much older than anything else in Esk, and there's no clue *why* they were built or abandoned. We don't even know if the catacombs predate Esk, though I would propose they do. They might be our first temple."

He smiles. She's not used to that response, either.

"I believe I'm honour-bound to say the Gardens were the first. After all, the Gardens came from the old forest, and the forest was the first."

She sets her satchel back by her feet, forgotten. "The forest was the first? Wherever did you hear that?"

"It's an old Casca family saying." He considers her, amused. "Perhaps if you show me the hawthorn door, I can tell you more."

As far as unwise deals with unknown entities go, she's fairly sure of her safety. Madoc seems the type for a specific sort of trouble, and it's not the sort of trouble she's generally concerned about. "That seems fair," she allows.

"And if you tell me the rest of your name." He seems quite serious.

"Do you truly not know? It's Zanthi."

"Zanthi," he says, satisfied. "Now I will know you, when you next walk out of the darkness and startle me."

"I don't make a habit of it. That the passage led here really was a surprise."

"A pleasant one, it turns out," he says, sinking back against the cushions again as if he's finally at rest. It's a quiet look. She likes it more than his pretty smiles and laughter.

"Well," she says, turning back to her tea. "I don't know about that."

He gives her an amused glance. "You haven't eaten your sweets."

He's right, so she does. The biscuit is sweet and spiced and just as good as he promised. When she's finished picking the crumbs from her plate—a bad habit that Theron tirelessly scolds her for—she realises he is still watching her.

"Let me fix your hair," he says. "It's the least I can do."

It's an odd request, but a gracious one. Rather old-fashioned, too. An apology in an act of service is a custom so antiquated that she wouldn't have expected even the Heirs to follow it. She half-turns from him. "Go ahead, then. I've no desire to go home looking like I've tumbled through a bramble patch."

"I imagine there would be questions," he agrees. His fingers are warm against her temples as he plaits her hair back with deftness. When he's done, she turns to see his loose crown of curls has come down to skim his jaw.

"I'll return it," she says, as her fingers find the clasp he's taken from his own hair.

"When you can," he says, unconcerned. "More tea?"

There's no reason to say yes. Her work is done, the conversation is concluded, and her brothers will wonder when she's not home for supper. The last of the evening light is sinking beyond the roofline of the Hall, making dark shapes of the surrounding trees, and the lanterns glitter like little fires in the darkness. It's another world entirely.

It's not *her* world, not in the slightest. But she doesn't want to go. Not yet.

"If I may," she says, and holds out her cup.

Her letter arrives a week later. Joren's note is concise and brief, her papers of employ bundled in the same envelope. She reads through them in the quiet of her bedroom with Susan curled at her feet. Then she signs them, returns them to the envelope, and sets it aside to post in the morning. With that, she is officially working for the Crown. She is no longer a student.

The next day, she stands in the front hall and stares in the mirror. Her pale face glares back. The reflection shows a plainer creature than she remembers. Perhaps it is a lack of sun or confidence, or perhaps it's only that she has something more sparkling to compare herself to now.

Either way, the truth is that without her university robes, she feels unarmoured.

When she tilts her head, the moth clasp flashes in the morning light. It's made of polished copper and finely wrought, and far too flashy for the library or the vault. People will certainly notice, but she has no other option. Madoc has yet to return her clasp or her cloak, though she expects he'll do so when he remembers. She's thought about writing him a letter to remind him. Only every time she gets out a sheet of paper, she quails from the task.

"Ah, the Ilyston vanity is finally surfacing," says Fletcher, coming up beside her. He checks his buttons—he's clearly planning on going outside. "I was starting to think it might have skipped you."

She gives him a weary look, but he only smiles back. He's immune to glares at this point. One has to be to live in this house. "I was only checking my hair."

"That's a pretty thing," he says, nodding at the clasp. "Where in the isles did you get it?"

"I borrowed it from a friend," she says. She's stretching the definition, maybe, but Madoc had certainly been a polite and generous host. And despite all the rumours to the contrary, entirely well-behaved.

"Moths, though, are a very particular affectation in this town."

"Are they?"

"Madoc Casca is quite known for them, is all," he says. "And other things besides. Ignored my warnings about the Gardens, didn't you?"

Her fingers twitch, and she battles down the impulse to tear it from her hair. This is the sort of thing she doesn't know, not concerning herself with society. She forgets how much everyone is entangled in everyone else's business. "I misplaced the one you gave me. I'm still waiting for its return."

"Sweetheart," he says, delighted. "What have you been up to?"

"Nothing exciting."

"Jewellery is a particular sort of gift."

Another of those society customs she doesn't think much about. Giving jewellery to loved ones, but never buying it oneself. Never touching bare skin in public, not so much as handholding. Never visiting a house before mid-morning, unless you intend to start a courtship by arriving at breakfast.

Things are simpler at the university. You fall into beds or you don't, and no one cares either way, and not many bother with the whole courtship thing, either. Well, Fletcher had, but Fletcher is the most hopeless sort of romantic.

"It is not a gift. It is a loan." She steps aside, giving Fletcher the mirror, and reconsiders wearing the clasp entirely. If Fletcher knows, Theron will know. Others will know.

"It's a very eye-catching piece, but that's no reason not to wear it." Fletcher brushes an errant piece of hair from her face and tucks it behind her ear. "It's okay to want to be seen, you know."

"I know that. I'm not sure what I want, is all."

"And that's okay, too. Some things are easy to know, and some creep up while we aren't looking." His gaze shifts in the mirror. "Speaking of, whatever are you doing lurking there, dear?"

Theron is at the foot of the stairs. His Luminary cloak glints sharply in the morning light. A band of gold embroidery at the hem, for the work that first got him into the top ranks. Another three above it, each with a different design. She knows the motifs like she knows his face. She's spent so many hours staring at them—the twining elm leaves and willow branches, the arching irises. So many hours daydreaming of what her own might look like one day.

He's looking at her too, scraping a judging gaze over her blouse, tapestry waistcoat, and wool skirt. "I suppose it's acceptable," he says. "An Ilyston as an unrobed researcher. Gods, what a mess."

Despite all her reasoning with herself, shame still flares hot through her. Fletcher settles a tense hand on her shoulder.

"Theron, watch your tongue." He says it with dangerous calm. It should be a warning sign for anyone, but Theron looks uncowed.

Zanthi digs her hands into her pockets. "If you have such stakes in me keeping my robes, you might have made more of an effort to help."

He glances at his timepiece, her words brushing past him. "I'm off. Are you coming?" As she passes him to fetch her boots, he adds, "And don't think I haven't noticed that clasp."

Zanthi usually tries to act her age, but Theron brings out the worst in her. She tugs her boots from the hall cupboard. "What? Worried I've been unrobed in other ways?"

His face goes tight. "I'm sure that's none of my business—" he begins.

Fletcher chimes in with, "But be sure to drink the tea, sweetheart."

She's been drinking the stalling tea since her monthlies first started, if only for the benefit of not having to suffer through them, and Fletcher knows that. He's only riling Theron up, and it works. Theron stalks out the door, and Zanthi is left scrambling to catch up.

It's not an auspicious start to the week. When Zanthi arrives at the vault, Orrey beckons her over with a desperate air. It's early enough that there aren't many archivists around, but there is a pair by the far wall watching with a look she does not like.

She slides into the spare seat at the desk, and Orrey caps her pen.

"It's true? No more robes?" It's the way she says it. As final as the last line drawn under a word. Orrey has a gift for being concise.

Zanthi presses her lips together. "Yes."

Orrey gives one nod, then glances over at Acanthus behind her desk. "They've cleared your spot out. Said they needed the space."

She should have expected that. She could kick herself that she didn't. It is only a storage alcove—she didn't think they'd take it from her so swiftly. What have they done with her notebooks, her lists? Her organised stacks of folders and catalogue entries?

Gods, the scholars here are a writhing knot of weasels.

Under the table, a hard object hits Zanthi's foot. "I got everything from the desk. Sorry, I couldn't grab the rest of the library volumes. They've probably all been shelved now."

Zanthi stares at her in wonder. Orrey grins.

"I think they're all spit-sparrows," she says simply. "Your work is interesting, by the by. I hope you don't mind that I read some of your notes."

"No. Not at all. Thank you."

"There aren't enough folklorists in the faculty. Bad things seem to happen every time one starts coming up."

Zanthi gives her a hapless look, gesturing to her bare outfit.

"Well, if that's the worst, you got off lightly. You don't want to end up like Luminary Hart."

And, well, she has a point. Zanthi tries not to think too much about Luminary Hart, if she can help it. The hauntings of his accident still ripple around the history faction, distorted and full of wispy holes. There isn't much solid truth to any of the rumours she's heard, and Hart certainly isn't telling, because he's been a recluse for over a decade and rarely turns up to anything.

"And I *do* like your clasp," Orrey continues, with a careful lack of inflection. "You've interesting friends, Ilyston."

Zanthi draws herself back to the present. "We're not friends. It's a passing acquaintance."

Orrey's face tells Zanthi she's understood precisely the wrong thing from that statement. "I'll be keeping an eye out for you in the papers—" she starts, but is interrupted by a throat-clearing from their table neighbour. She rolls her eyes. "Far too many pigeons in the rafters, here. Shall we get tea sometime and talk more?"

Zanthi has known Orrey for four years. Orrey has never asked her out for tea. Zanthi, in fact, can count on one hand the number of times she has been asked for tea by anyone but her brothers. She gathers her box from under the desk, and in a soft flush of gratitude, agrees.

"I'll send you a note." Orrey uncaps her pen in a friendly dismissal. "And you can use my desk if you need space to work."

"I might, time to time, but I have other places."

"I thought you would. You don't seem the type to be cornered easily."

Zanthi hopes that is true. She doesn't know how many more knots she can twist in to keep going. She bids Orrey farewell and leaves the vault with all the Ilyston pride she can summon.

May all the priggish archivists be river-damned.

She lugs her box up to Theron's office, bracing for his displeasure. He takes one look at it and sighs.

"You shouldn't be here. University only," he warns, but he doesn't object when she sets up at the little table in the corner.

"Yes, I know. It's a mess, and I'm a mess, and all that," she says. "You've been useless so far, so maybe you might unbend a little and help me with this."

He pulls his scholar's cap over his hair, setting it at the correct angle with an absent-minded nudge. "I have a lecture to teach. Try not to get yourself in strife before I get back. And if anyone comes by, have some care for university rules and pretend you're not here."

Chapter Seven

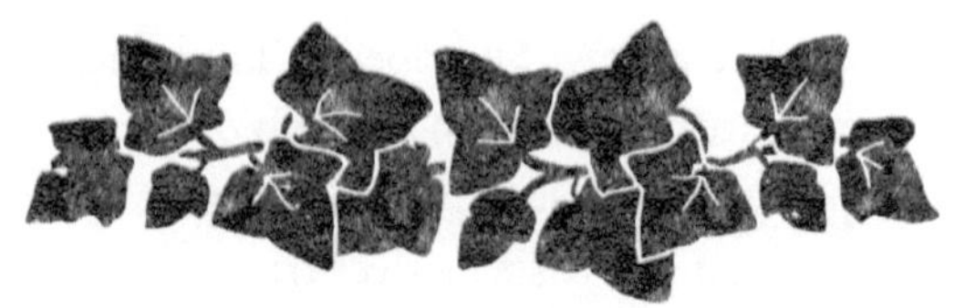

Summer stalks into Esk with warm breath and sticking rain. And midges. All along Conning Street, shops and townhouses hang decorative burners in their doorways, wafting scented drifts of thyme-scented smoke through the streets. It deters the midges, but it makes everyone smell of burnt herbs.

Theron's Luminary neighbours all know she's using his space, of course. She nods stiffly to them each day, and they pretend not to see her, and everyone gets along without fuss. Theron himself is stuck in a translation war with a scholar from East Cana, a university in the Eastern Isles, and Zanthi learns a fair few new curse words in a range of archipelagic languages from his under-his-breath commentary on his rival's letters.

She has been disallowed access to the archives, as she suspected. Instead, she has some success in entreating Orrey to dredge up records for her. There's no longer any chance of going under-river, not for now. She tries to sketch what she remembers of her path through the archives, but can't remember past the first glimpse of the friezes. After that, the passages had frayed and unspooled like unravelling carpet, on and on. The cave-ins are curious, too. She's working on a vague theory that it all happened around the same time, in some violent and all-encompassing event.

An earthquake, perhaps. They're rare, but Esk has suffered them in the past.

And Joren's work keeps her busy, too. He has her chasing ancient pottery styles, poetic forms, and even a few pointed questions on early aethercraft. It's all fascinating work, even the aethercraft, though none of it is very relevant to her own interests.

She's still working on the theory that the Isle of Elveresk had a god once. The Central Isles, of which Elveresk is the heart, are not religious lands. The north clings to their traditions, the west to their superstitions, and the east has their own worship of ocean and tide, but the Central Isles and the south have only memories of such things.

Oh, there were gods in the Central Isles once. The remnants of day-to-day worship still echo through society, even here, even in Esk. Artisans honouring their muses. The festival blessings. Offerings. The festivals themselves.

But there is no true belief. Superstition, perhaps. A sense of celestial fortune. But no gods.

There are fourteen crest cities, including Esk, so-named for their aetherwells. The faded wells in the other cities are each linked to founding gods, marked with fractured epithets or half-remembered names. She's made a list of them in her research. Some are well-known, others took more digging. But if recorded history is to be trusted, Esk's Well has never belonged to anyone but the Crown, and though the Crown might be a god-like figure in Esk's history, they have never been anything other than mortal. The current Crown, for all she has an aether resilience that eclipses even the most famous of the airship captains, will die young. The Crowns always do.

The other aetherwells slumber, soft and gentled, like kiss-marks left when a lover is gone. Esk's well is spilling over, tormented, and it has been for centuries. It is no kiss-mark. It is a gaping wound, a bite torn out and left bleeding. It would destroy Esk if the Crown did not stand at the Well's altar and stem the tide.

She is searching through the library's collection of submitted studies into aethercraft, trying to hunt down a reference for her commissioned research, when she finds a small, bound essay called *The Blooding of the Heirs.* It is written by *E. Hart*. Luminary Hart, the famous recluse.

She's always been fascinated by Luminary Hart. He'd had an accident in the archives, and had disappeared from academia for years, before returning with a work ethic that even Theron admires. He is well entrenched in the history faction, writing on festivals and traditions of Esk. She's been using several of his publications in her research, in fact, and so she takes the essay and reads it.

It leaves her restless with disquiet. It deals with the ceremony of the Blood, an old ritual in which the Heirs are chosen from bloodlines of the Crown.

The ceremony recorded must have been Heir Evelyn's, from the dates, and that's odd to think on, too. Heir Evelyn is a beloved, if not scandalous, figure in Esk. An airguard hero. Chester's friend. She doesn't know what to feel, knowing he's survived what is documented in Hart's paper.

In the essay, Hart refers to the act as one of sacrifice. A sacrificial offering, made to keep the Well from overflowing. The Crown and Heirs give their bodies and minds to the Well's currents, holding it back until they are worn entirely away.

She doesn't know how such a work is related to her delving into Esk's ancient history, only she has the feeling it isn't entirely unrelated either.

When she returns to Theron's study, the door is ajar. Inside, a man is sitting at her desk, reading her papers. Somehow, she isn't all that surprised.

"Casca," she says, because it *is* him. He's dressed down, and yet it's still entirely too much for the university. He is wearing a gathered silk shirt in deep hazelnut brown and he has little emeralds in his ears. "Are you reading my work?"

"Mm, it's fascinating," he says. He puts the papers back in order. "You have a wonderful writing style. I wouldn't have thought it, considering."

"Considering what?"

He smiles, leaning on the desk and resting his chin on the back of one hand. "I'd say you're a fair bit more to the point, in speech. I'm surprised you haven't published this. Or submitted it. It's very good."

"I did submit it. It was rejected."

"That seems unfair."

"A pity for me that you aren't on the Luminary board, then."

"Your brother is, isn't he?"

Zanthi feels pinned. She shoves her hands in her pockets. "He is. He abstained."

Madoc's lip curls. "Interesting choice."

"One vote wouldn't have made a difference."

"That's not the point, though, is it?"

He's very uncanny, with those eyes. People have accused her of seeing right through them with her dark gaze, but she's never felt it so keenly from another until this moment.

"It's done now," is all she says. "I can't submit it again."

"Will you publish it, anyway? I know a house or two you might approach."

She folds her arms, leans against the closed door. "Do you really?"

He smiles, a little unsure. "Yes? I wouldn't have said so, otherwise."

"I can't decide about you," she says. "Are you really so helpful, or are you just trying to get something?"

"Ah, academics," Madoc says, and he settles back into his unruffled cheer. "I do want something, though that's one thing, and the other is another. I want to go into the archives."

She puts her stack of books on the edge of her desk. It has her far too close to Madoc, and he smiles up at her. His eyes really are *so* green. It doesn't seem quite natural, and she knows that is a rich sentiment coming from her. "You can't."

"I suppose I could waste a day charming the chancellor into giving me permission. But I'd much rather spend my time charming you."

"I'm not meant to go to the archives, either."

He is undaunted. "I rather got the impression you went where you pleased. Or am I wrong?"

Her refusal is on her tongue, and then she stops. Lately, when she thinks of going down into the deep archives, there is a sharp alarm all through her body. But the thought of Madoc in the dark under the town doesn't feel sharp. It is soft and wistful, and if it were a creature, it'd be purring.

"Also, I have these for you, though I am sorry it took me so long to remember to return them to you." He pushes a bundle to the edge of her desk. Her rosemary cloak and hair clasp. "You should have written me a note if you were missing them."

"I didn't know if I could," she admits. She reaches back to her own hair, intending to switch the clasps over, and then Madoc is on his feet, stopping her.

She blinks up at him. He tugs her hand away from her hair, and his touch is startling in its warmth. "You're still wearing it?"

"I didn't think you'd mind." Gods, her pulse is making a racket in her ears, as if he's kicking it up just by being close. "Do you?"

"No," he murmurs. He fixes the moth clasp back up, tucking a stray piece of hair back into her bun. "Keep wearing it. It suits you. It was a gift, and I enjoy giving gifts to my friends."

"Are we friends?"

He steps back, and he's amused. "Are we not?"

She sighs. She hasn't many friends, but she does tend to pick up the oddest ones. "I suppose we can be friends."

"You needn't sound so tired about it."

"I suspect you will be entirely tiring. People usually are." She picks up her rosemary cloak. The familiar weight of it in her hands gives her a sliver of courage she had been lacking before. "Why do you want to go into the archives?"

"Curiosity," he says. "And also, this. I suspect it leads somewhere important, only I couldn't find the door in any of our hawthorn thickets, so I decided I'd have to go the long way around."

Zanthi snatches the paper he waves at her. It's a set of directions, written as a list of instructions. *Left turn, pass three, right turn, four steps up, left turn*...and so on, and so on. "From the journal?"

"Yes. Though it didn't say what it led to, only it sounds like it must be in the archives, mustn't it?"

She swallows. "Alright," she says, because her curiosity is burning like a hearth flame now. "You think it starts from the door?"

"Why wouldn't it?"

"The first line says, *'from the waymarker.'* There is a carved figure pointing towards the passage to the Garden's door. That might be the waymarker?"

"Can you take me there?"

"I can." She pauses. "We'll have to be discreet about it."

"Not my strongest skill, but I'll try."

"And I got lost for a bit last time."

Madoc takes the paper back. "Don't fret about that. I always know where my Gardens lie. Now, how do we sneak down there?"

In the end, she gives Madoc one of Theron's university robes, the plain black ones he wears when his Luminary robes are not needed. He always has a spare hanging in his office.

Madoc shrugs them over his too-much-like-evening-wear clothes, and it is entirely irritating that even dull black looks good on him. The university is probably lucky that he never took to studying there, because Madoc in Luminary robes would be a sight. She's a little disappointed that she'll never see it.

"Let's go," she says to cover her thoughts, and strides off, lantern in hand.

She sneaks them into the main archives without trouble, though she doesn't dare light her lantern. They make do with the flicker of the aether sconces that mark out the safe perimeter. It's thankfully quiet in the gloom. There is only the distant sound of footsteps, too far away to cause concern. She presses a finger to her lips and forges on, smuggling Madoc down the lower staircase. There, she lights her lantern but still doesn't risk speaking. Whispers carry far in here.

It's not until she's at the mouth of the river path, the water rustling furiously in the darkness, that she speaks. "We'll have to go under the river."

His mouth twitches. An amused grin, quickly tamped down upon. "I am uniquely suited for such a thing," he says, gravely.

He takes to the deep archives better than she'd expected. He doesn't flinch at shadows. He walks into them like he's walking into a room of lamplight and company—like there's something there waiting for him and he's eager to meet it. It has never occurred to her that someone might walk into the shadows and dark as easily as they walk into light and laughter.

The cold seems to be the only thing that gives him pause. He is glad for Theron's robes when the deep chill of the stone falls on them—it is clear from the way he clutches at it, drawing it tight around him.

"Stay behind me," she says, holding the lantern out and taking the lead. She doesn't want him falling over a loose stone and knocking himself out cold. The gods know she couldn't carry him out.

It is easier crossing under the river with him beside her. Even the air is different. The thick damp that had haunted the passage has turned crisp and cool, like the river has swept through and taken all the mildew and silt away.

"These are fascinating," he says, as they pass the friezes in the vaulted passage. Then he stops, head tilting. A sharp look comes over his face as he looks down the run of figures.

"It's a procession–though of what, I couldn't say. I haven't found a record of a matching festival yet."

He makes a noise in the back of his throat. When he turns to her, the sharp look has been packed away. "You'll have to tell me when you find out."

"Why would you need to know?"

"I'm a Casca," he says, like that explains it all. "It's my work to know all sorts of things."

"I thought your work was throwing parties."

He laughs. "What do you know of the Casca family?"

"Only what I read in the papers."

"The scandal and speculation, you mean?" He sounds amused, and she thinks if she looked back, he'd be smiling. "There's enough of that, to be fair. I do sing and dance, and steer conversation, and host parties, and cause spectacle." His voice turns light. "Like I said, all sorts of things."

"I get the picture," she says. "And the star charts?"

"Pardon?"

"You recognised the markings on the old fragments I was sorting. It was an old fresco, turns out. A star chart from a southern villa."

"Oh," he says. "I had an interest in astronomy for a while."

He says that like he's embarrassed by it. Madoc Casca, sheepish, and about astronomy of all things. She remembers his nature journals and astronomy books, tucked on a lower rung of his bookshelf and out of sight.

"I can't dance," she says, restoring balance on the scale of embarrassing things. "I never learned."

"Truly?" He catches up to her, and his footsteps are light and even. "How is that?"

"Well, there's nowhere to dance at home, and I never was interested in going elsewhere. I shouldn't have a clue about music or good conversation."

"Your conversation is perfectly charming," he says.

"You flatter people too easily."

"It's a habit, I'm afraid. Why have I never seen you in society before now?"

"I never wanted to be seen," she says. "And there was no one who was going to force me. I have a few friends, and I have my work. I have a good family. I don't need much more."

"Aren't you a little curious?"

"Not really," she says. "Don't you find it boring, after a time?"

"Thankfully, I enjoy it all well enough," he says. "Though I admit, a quiet evening in my rooms with a book is something I treasure."

She can almost see it; that warm, soft room with the bramble-patterned wallpaper and tiled hearth, all glowing on an autumn evening. The bench by the window would be perfect for curling up to read upon. Then she packs that thought away, because she is feeling rather envious.

"Ah," she says, as the light bounces back at them. She holds the lamp aloft. "We're here."

Madoc doesn't answer. He's staring at the pointing figure, eyes wide and unguarded. It's a raw expression, and she can't figure out whether it's only awe, or if there is grief in it, too. He blinks and it's gone, hidden away.

"It shouldn't be far from here," he says, holding the paper up to her lantern. He reads each line as they follow it, away from the pointing figure and into the darkness.

It leads, as most passages here seem to lead, to a dead end. She sighs, the disappointment choking her throat. And then Madoc makes a low noise, startled and curious.

"Where does that go?"

She freezes. Slowly, she holds out the lantern. Ahead, darkness seeps from the natural rock of the wall, like a spreading ink spill across parchment, bleeding onwards. Any other time, she'd have dismissed it as a shadow and walked past it.

But Madoc is right. It is an opening in the rock, hidden in the darkest, blackest shadow she's ever seen. They are silent for a long moment. In the spaces between their breaths, she can hear a distant shifting, like a colossal tide. And beyond it, a bell.

"I don't know," she says, cold fear sinking her heartbeat.

In the soft light of the aether lantern, Madoc's eyes are as black as the shadows. Before she can stop him, he wades into the darkness and disappears.

Cursing, she follows.

Chapter Eight

The darkness is complete. Her aether lantern flickers, and she grips it with whitened knuckles.

"Casca?"

This is no archive pathway. The rock seeps cold, and deep gouges pattern the walls. Tool marks, she tells herself. Definitely tool marks, and not at all claw marks. She hoists the lantern higher. There is only darkness ahead. Her lantern light does her little good, other than throwing the dark shadows dancing around her.

This is something else entirely. They shouldn't be here. Water drips down the walls and moss appears, thin at first and then thick. Moss, then dirt, then clay. The path forks, and she is left stranded, staring into the darkness like a lost soul in the River.

"Madoc?"

The shifting tide roars in the darkness now. An underground river, perhaps? A dark chasm ahead, waiting to swallow them? She's almost convinced she's lost the Casca heir to some unfortunate end in the dark, when she hears him.

"Here," he calls. He doesn't sound at all frightened. Cautious, yes, but not scared. He appears to the left of the fork, coming back towards her. He holds out his hand.

She hesitates. For all she scoffs at Esk's moral customs, taking his hand feels too much like intimacy, even in a place like this. He grabs her palm anyway, and his hand is warm, startlingly so. She hadn't realised the passage had grown so cold.

"There's something ahead. I want to know what it is," he says.

"I'm not sure this is safe."

"Oh, it definitely isn't," he agrees, low and focused. "Keep sharp."

From the corner of her gaze, she can see ghostly water seeping up from the earth. It shimmers in her side-sight like tide marks on a riverbank or flood marks on a city street, fading from her gaze when she looks directly at it. And as much as she tries to ignore it, she can't ignore that it is following them. Lapping at their footsteps.

It's not aether. It looks nothing like aether. It is the clearest, darkest water she's ever seen, and it disappears everywhere she looks at directly. She doesn't know what to make of it. Of any of it.

Madoc holds her hand tight, an anchoring point of warmth in all the cold, and she focuses on the strangeness of unknown fingers woven with hers, the weight of his palm against her own. Best to focus on that, and not how they keep delving down and down, deeper into the grave dirt of the dark earth.

The roof sweeps low, and the path twists on and on. The walls turn roughened, wild stone dripping with a damp as chill as winter. They're walking right into the bedrock of the mountains.

Madoc makes a sound, like surprise has been punched from him. He draws Zanthi up beside him, and ahead, the passage ends in a small chamber. She steps forward, lantern aloft.

"A spring," he says.

It's not a spring. At least, she wouldn't have thought so at first glance. The chamber is clearly carved by human hands, with marked stone walls and cracked flagstones. In the centre, a raised hollow sits, filled with silt and sand. She holds her lantern higher, and the light glances across the hollow. Quartz, sandstone, and a darker, blacker stone she has never seen before, all glinting back.

A crumbled stone edge runs around the hollow in a graceful curve, cupping it against the chamber wall, and in the centre is a wider stone, worn down in two shallow dips. Madoc moves towards it like he's drifting in a dream. He sinks to his knees, all grace, his knees cradle perfectly in those worn-away dips. When he ducks his head, she sees his lips move without sound, as if he's praying. At least, what she imagines praying to look like. It has been many, many centuries since anywhere in the archipelago has had a god to truly pray to.

"Might it be connected to your springs at the Gardens?" she asks, coming up behind him. There's enough room for her to crouch beside him, and so she does.

He looks at her sidelong, as if she's asked a foolish thing. "I am sure of it. Why else would it have been in the journal?"

The quartz pebbles glint in the lantern light, and she catches the shape of other things in the silt. Darkened discs that might be coins, fractures of rotted wood. A twist of metal poking up—a bracelet, perhaps? She reaches for it, and Madoc seizes her hand.

She stares at him. His grip is claw-tight.

Then he tugs her hand back and laughs, an easy smile falling onto his face. It's not a very convincing one. "Let's not disturb anything. You're the one who said things were cursed down here."

He tries to play it off, but she saw the alarm on his face and, for a moment, it had been fierce. Not frightened, no. Protective.

"Are they offerings, do you think? I've read about such things." She eases her hand back and lets the moment pass. "Perhaps it was a place of worship."

"What else would it be?"

She makes a thoughtful noise. "A water well, I suppose. A bath? That is what *your* springs are, are they not?"

He smiles again, and again it is the easy, socialite smile. It is, she suspects, how he lies. It is all the answer she needs. Her thoughts are skipping ahead like a stone across a river.

"The question is, worshipping *what*?"

"That is your particular interest, isn't it?" he says, and the smile turns more honest.

"I forgot you were nosing about my writing earlier."

"Mm. The search for Esk's unknown god-myth. What interests you about it?" He settles back on his heels as if he's ready for a story.

"Why wouldn't I be interested? Shouldn't that be something we know and remember? You can go to any settlement or town with a history, and they'll be able to tell you which god they worshipped in the time before the gods left. But in Esk, nothing. We are one of the oldest cities in the archipelago, and we have forgotten the name of our founding god."

"Perhaps we were meant to forget it," he says softly.

"We have forgotten we even *had* a god," she counters. "And I am called a heretic for daring to suggest the First Crown did not build Esk with her own two hands."

He brushes his fingers against the back of her hand, where she is gripping the edge of the stone lip. "Not a Crown loyalist, then?"

"Oh," she says, blinking. His touch, unexpected, has scattered her thoughts. "No, I suppose I am. I just don't understand why that means being unwilling to learn our history." She brushes her palm across the worn stone. "Centuries of devout people knelt here, enough to leave their shape in stone. That is no small thing. Even if no one ever kneels here again, even if there is no more devotion to give, don't we owe better to our old gods than pretending they were never here? We might, at the very least, remember their names."

"You said something similar the first time we spoke," he says. "You have appointed yourself a champion for lost and forgotten things, haven't you?"

She turns to him, and her side-sight leaps into life. Her words shrivel in her throat. In the corner of her sight, the spring brims with clear, dark ghost-water. It moves as if with a tide, back and forth, and then, in a flash, the roar of a river crashes through her. The echoes roll around the chamber like a bell tolling, echoes layering and layering again.

It's only the thinnest flash of a moment. A heartbeat of a nightmare.

But long enough to see, in the ghost-water of the dead springs, their reflections stare out with blackened eyes. Madoc's reflection is bloodless, his lips blue. And the both of them are crowned in woven river rushes.

She wrenches her gaze to the hollow, unable to stop herself, and there's nothing. Just silt, and dust, and age.

"Zanthi?"

Her name falls into her with a shock. She takes a shaky breath. "I thought I saw something," she says, and her voice comes out thin. "Something unpleasant."

He frowns. "The shadows must be getting to you. It is a little unnerving down here, isn't it?" He stands and helps her to her feet. "Let's find the surface once more."

His eyes are green, his lips are curved in a smile, and his hand is warm against hers. She buries that glimpse of a vision deep in her mind. She doesn't wish to think on it a moment longer, not on where it came from or what it might mean. It must be the archive playing tricks, as it does. Perhaps she's finally fallen to it.

They do not speak until they are back in the archive, retracing their steps to the vaulted passage that leads to the Gardens. Here, the darkness feels like a moonlit evening compared to the smothering dark they have come from. It is not until they are at the foot of the pointing figure once more that Zanthi feels she can finally breathe again.

"Well," Madoc says, running a hand through his hair. It makes a mess of his styling. "That was fascinating."

"You are entirely too eager," she says. He doesn't deny it. "Don't ever run off like that again."

"I will stick to your side like the most stubborn thistle-thatch."

"No need to go that far," she mutters, and he laughs.

She leads him to the caved-in passage past the pointing figure. "It's fallen in ahead, but I cleared a space last time. It might be a squeeze for you."

"I'm rather flexible," he says, unconcerned. And then, before she can even *begin* to figure out how to respond to that atrocity, he adds, "Shall I go first?"

Despite his claims of being flexible, it still takes some effort to squeeze through the gap into the passage beyond the cave-in. Zanthi waits for him to go over, then passes the lantern through and slides after him, once again kicking up a cloud of dust.

"So," Madoc says, as he leads the way onwards. She lets him—there's no way to run off or get lost from here. "You are a believer in gods, then."

She makes a wordless sound. Asking such a thing is like asking a person to disrobe in front of you. Like asking them what they think about at night, alone in bed. You just *didn't*.

"I've shocked you," he says, and laughs. "You talk so easily of gods. I didn't think you'd mind."

"Academically," she says, sourly.

"Then answer me academically."

She isn't the best at making a sound argument. Academically, everyone goes on like gods are stories, and superstition, and literary metaphor. Zanthi has never believed that. "I suppose I think they were real in some aspect or another. Aether is real, after all, and gods were likely creatures of aether. Just because we *called* them gods doesn't mean they were actually divine, though. In Esk, we are expected to regard the Crown and Heirs with the sort of awe and worship we once called devoutness, all because their bloodline can survive the Well and withstand aether that would quickly kill a normal person. That's not so different from worshipping a god."

"How unsettling," Madoc says, rich with amusement, and then startles when the aether lamp dies, plunging them into darkness.

Darkness, and Madoc's sudden laughter.

"I forgot about this part," she says. She reaches out and curls her fingers into the fabric of his sleeve. "We're beneath the Gardens now."

"I know," he says. "Can't you feel it?"

She can't. She tugs his sleeve. "There are steps ahead. Watch your feet."

They make their way up, carefully. It's daylight outside this time, and she's warned of the upcoming door by a thin spill of light from the crooked corner.

"This is it?" He shuffles up, puts a hand to the wood. It's warped, and perhaps she didn't shut it well enough last time because it almost jumps open under his hands. "Ah. How did you get out?"

The summer has thickened the hawthorn hedge into a dense mat of spiny branches. The breeze skips in, warm and sweet.

"It was a little less wild back then." She wriggles past, pressing between the door and his chest. The way out is there, though she must fight her way through it. She holds enough of the tree back that Madoc can follow.

He makes it out mostly unscathed. He's laughing, and there's a hawthorn twig caught in his curls. She lets the branches whip back behind him.

"So, this is where it lets out! No wonder you were lost."

Zanthi looks around and believes she is lost again. Summer has changed everything into a dense world of whispering green. How Madoc knows where he is at a glance, she can't say.

Then he looks at her, and all the summer warmth is in his face, too. "After all that, I believe we're owed a cup of tea. Might you come up to my rooms?"

She glances up at the sky. Through the pattern of oak and willow, the sun is still high. She could. She has no reason not to. Only, there is the memory of a shifting tide, and a ringing bell, and Madoc's face, blue-lipped and black-eyed in the ghost-waters of her side-sight. She's never in her life seen anything other than aether. Why now? Why *him*?

She wants to write it all down while it's still fresh.

"No," she says. "Sorry. I have other things to attend to."

He smiles, unbothered. "You're very good at that."

"At what?"

"Putting me in my place," he says. He brushes her face with his fingertips, and there's a sting. "You've a scratch. Here, I'll walk you to the gate. Do you need a carriage?"

"At this time of day? No." She takes her lantern back from him and falls into step. "I don't mean to be rude—" she starts, but he makes a sound, cutting her off.

"You weren't rude. You don't owe me a whit of your time, and you've given me quite a lot of it already. I really am grateful for your indulgence."

Madoc, she thinks, would be a very easy man to indulge. He'd make it feel like a privilege. The more she is around him, the more she understands the fascination the papers and society have with him. The more she is around him, the surer she is that he is more than a pretty-faced socialite hosting parties. He's got secrets as interesting and as deep as any archive path.

She only wonders what it would take to have him spill them.

He looks up, eyes widening. He curses.

She hears it a moment later. Footsteps, quick and sharp, on a nearby path. Madoc tugs her along, right through the thicket ahead. The trees are low and close here, but once they're through, things make more sense. If she'd come through in the day, that first time, she might not have been so lost, because there is the distinct line of the far wall in the distance.

They emerge onto a quartz-white path. There is a woman heading their way, her emerald dress skimming the stones.

"You've been causing trouble, Madoc," she says. She has dark hair plaited back in a graceful twist, and emeralds in her ears that match her eyes. Her look could cut glass. "You were to be overseeing the auditions at midday."

She can only be Sabine Casca. Her son looks very much like her.

Zanthi might only know about the Gardens from the papers, but even she knows of Sabine Casca. She's almost a mythological creature in Esk society—much whispered about, much sought after, and rarely ever seen. Only she's here in broad daylight, staring Madoc down like he's a wayward child skipping class. The whispers got one thing right, though. She is beautiful.

"Sorry, Mama," Madoc says, entirely unbothered. "I got caught up."

"Did you." Her tone is the sort of scathing that Theron could only aspire to. "How, exactly, did you manage that?"

He shrugs, and there's a smile in the corners of his mouth. "How do I ever manage anything?"

She sighs. "The gods only know." Her gaze cuts across Zanthi's face. Her lip curls at the corner in an expression Zanthi is sure an invited guest of the Gardens has never seen. She turns back to her son. "They're waiting for you in the theatre. They've been there two hours, and no one will decide until you show your face."

"Of course. I'll head there directly."

Zanthi smiles at him, warmer than she thought possible. It's not that she's faking it, but she knows she's mostly doing it because Lady Casca is right there, ignoring her. She thinks he knows it too, because there's an amused light in his eyes.

"I know my way out. Good day, Madoc. Lady Casca."

"Perhaps we can have that tea another day," he calls, as she leaves.

"Perhaps," she says over her shoulder, and then the path turns and the garden folds in, hiding them from view.

If she's honest, she doesn't expect to see him again.

Chapter Nine

The unsettling summer air fills her chest each morning, bringing damp and silt to her tongue. She sleeps with her window open and tracks the stars, sometimes waking to find Susan standing in her doorway, a dark shadow in the night, watching her with solemn eyes. She feels as if she's on a threshold to somewhere she didn't realise she was going, and if she tips over, she won't find her way back.

She's gotten herself all caught up on nothing, she knows. Seers and oracles have not existed for a long age, and even if they still did, Zanthi would not be one of them.

Even so, she cannot shake the dread that something bad is coming.

She reads the papers more diligently than usual, searching for glimpses of Casca amongst the stories of guild happenings, rail disasters, and storm news. Each time she finds his name in neatly printed ink, she feels a gentle burst of relief.

She has been spending long days in the library. In truth, she's sent more to Joren Fairthorne than he has asked for. She researches old religions and old trading accounts. She trawls through fables about seers and oracles, tracing back folksongs and folktales to the first seeds of possible truth. She'd have scoffed at it all months ago, before she'd seen that ghost-water pool and their dead-eyed apparitions. It hadn't escaped her notice that the river rush crowns had been braided like the charm from the archive steps.

When she exhausts herself on seers and portents, she visits Luminary Hart's office. He's not there. She didn't expect him to be —she's never seen him once in all her years at the university, even though they had been in the same faculty. Instead, she writes him a quick note and slips it under the door. She'd like to ask him about the braided rush charm from the archives. If anyone would know, it would be him. No other scholar alive has delved as deeply into Esk's festivals and customs.

"You've become very attached to the papers," Fletcher says one morning, as she's scanning the gossip columns once more.

She pretends not to see the look he and Theron swap. "I realised I don't pay enough attention to goings-on, that's all."

"Well, keep paying attention. You've been attracting notice," Theron says, sipping his tea.

"I can't see how."

"Your diligent research for the Crown. Apparently, some professors are wondering if they can hire your skills."

"They can lick river mud," Zanthi says tartly, and Theron grins, a flash of reed-sharp amusement. "I'm off. I have a tea date."

They look up in interest.

"With Archivist Orrey, from the natural history faction," she adds.

Theron gets a calculating look on his face, like he's trying to remember who exactly, Orrey is, and why Zanthi might be meeting with her.

In truth, Zanthi barely knows why. Only Orrey had followed through on her promise of sending an invitation, and so Zanthi is following through on her word, too.

When she walks into the teashop, Orrey is already there.

"Apologies. I made the mistake of catching a tram. I forget I can walk faster, half the time."

Orrey laughs. "Not in this spiteful weather. It's not even so hot, is it? I've spent enough time south, and that's properly warm. But there's something dreary about how everything here turns so soggy."

"It's soggy year-round."

"But it's so much more bearable when it's cold."

The tea shop is one she's often visited. A small stream runs right alongside the windows, and the windows are propped open to allow the water-music inside. She slumps into her seat, glad to be out of the muggy, overcast weather. "How are your studies coming?"

Orrey chatters on about geological aether deposits, year-on-year accumulations, and the effect on the patterns of storm spawning and strength. "The thing is," she says, as the server finally delivers their chosen teas, "if we can develop a system of prediction, there will be less need to rely on the Crown alone for knowing when and where a storm might eventuate."

"You could certainly identify risk areas, but the Crown will still be the only one able to tell when the aether is gathering."

"Sure, we'll always need the Crown. She's the *Crown*. This will make things easier for her, though. We could know, year to year, where the worst storms might be, weeks before the height of storm season hits. Have airships posted where they'll do the most good."

"Have you met a man called Joren Fairthorne?"

"Fairthorne? Like the admiral?" Orrey purses her lips in interest. "No."

Zanthi makes a note to mention her to Joren in her next letter. He might find her work useful, too.

"You know a lot of interesting people. I heard a rumour you know the admiral's son, too."

"I do," she admits. "I can't say I recommend it, though."

Orrey stirs her cup. "So, midsummer is coming. Do you attend the dance halls, Ilyston?"

"Never."

"Would you like to? I'd take you dancing, for midsummer, or for any other night." She smiles, easy and sweet.

Zanthi blinks, her cheeks heating. "Oh. Well, no. Dancing isn't really my thing."

"Isn't it? Ah, pity." Orrey grins and pinches a sesame cake from the plate between them. She is unruffled by Zanthi's rejection and settles into her cake with pleasure. "It's only I noticed you haven't been wearing the moth clasp lately. I thought it worth a try."

She hasn't. She's back to wearing her old oak-leaf clasp. The moth is sitting on her dressing table, and she looks at it every morning and wonders what she should do with it. It had been a gift, so she cannot return it. But after the strange happenings underground, and Lady Casca's scathing displeasure, and the silence since...it all feels tangled.

"That's nothing to do with anything," Zanthi says, a bit stiffly.

"If you say so." Orrey leans in, eyes bright. "You wouldn't have heard yet, would you? Acanthus has closed the archives."

"Pardon?" She grips her cup, light-headed. *Closed.*

"Locked and shut fast. She got sick of these appearing everywhere." She pulls a braided rush charm from her pocket and drops it by Zanthi's plate. "I brought this for you, by the way, because you seemed interested in them."

The sight of it makes that unsettled feeling rise in her again. She runs her finger across it, and a shiver echoes through her. "Is Acanthus letting anyone in?"

"A few people, here and there, but someone must stand at the archive doors the entire time they're open, and they're locked again right after."

The archives have never been locked. Not even in the worst of the spring floods.

Orrey taps her cup against her lips in thought. "There are rumours, of course."

"There are always rumours." Academics and socialites had one thing in common—they *thrived* on gossip.

"Aren't there just? A fair deal about you lately, too."

Zanthi makes a noise in the back of her throat. "I haven't been doing anything."

"Sure. First, you're walking around without robes. And then you're wearing a Casca favour. Then you're not. Is he really like the rumours say?"

"I wouldn't know. I haven't heard any."

Orrey waves her hand dismissively. "Oh, you know. His parade of lovers. That sometimes he takes more than one. That if you're in his bed, you can dive into the bathing pools whenever you please. Are they so very different from the remedial baths? I heard they leave you blissed-out and content for days."

Zanthi has an uncomfortable feeling that the gossip wheel has linked her independent researcher status to her association with Madoc Casca. She supposes waving his writ around hasn't helped—and *River wept*. She really should return it.

"I haven't bathed in the pools." Her dislike of deep water makes the thought unappealing. Even the remedial baths are unpleasant to her. She prefers to bathe at home, in the little bathroom off the kitchen, where the half-bath is shallow and safe. She only visits the remedial baths for her health, and even then, as little as possible. "I couldn't say."

Orrey grins. "Pity. I'd almost pick the pools over his bed, if the rumours were true."

That makes Zanthi laugh, because she greatly suspects that if the pools leave one content and blissed, Madoc's bed must do no less.

It's a pleasant tea date, and her good mood lasts until she is home again, and walks right into Theron looming on the landing. She takes one glance at his face and tries to flee. He does not let her.

"Sit down." He points her to his study, pink-cheeked with righteous fury. She has no idea what she might have done.

She sits. "What?" It's not the wisest opening to proceedings.

"What?" he says. "What, exactly, do you mean by *what*? Or has your language deserted you, along with your common sense?"

"*What*," she grits out, "is the problem, Theron?"

He matches her tone with a biting look. "Explain to me why my *own* robes were returned to me today with a thank you note. From *Madoc Casca*."

Gods, Casca. The man hadn't been lying when he said discretion wasn't his strength. She rolls a sigh around her mouth, but swallows it back. "I lent them to him."

"Clearly. I want to know why."

"I smuggled him down into the archives."

The silence crushes down. Theron draws in a needle-sharp breath. "You dressed Madoc Casca as a scholar."

"I needed to get him in unseen."

"If you had been caught—"

"We weren't."

"*Zanthi*. Do you have any idea? You are not under the university's charge any longer. You shouldn't have been in the archives unsupervised, and you certainly should not be bringing in passers-by from the street. They would have you removed from university grounds permanently."

She glances at the clock, wondering how long Theron has been stewing. He's certainly worked up a proper strop. "We were not caught. It's done. Don't get pinched over it now."

"You are being reckless. You have never been reckless, and now you are nothing but. What would it have looked like if Madoc Casca had been found trespassing in my robes?"

She stiffens. "Oh, so that's what this is about. Your reputation, again."

"My reputation keeps us fed and clothed. It helps pay our costs. It is necessary. What you are doing is chasing dead-end research that is helping no one, least of all you!"

She almost wishes she had something to hand to throw, because he deserves it. "I am employed. It is a job, and I will do it and be grateful for it, because no one else would give me half a chance. *You* wouldn't give me a chance. So, it is none of your business."

"*You* are my business. And you're making poor decisions." He's gearing himself up for one of his lectures. They must be shouting now because the creak of the parlour door means they've disturbed Fletcher. "You have become reckless, and selfish—"

"That's bold, coming from you," she mutters, and he whips around, furious.

"I do nothing but look out for you."

"You must do so with marvellous discretion then, because I've certainly been missing it entirely."

"I am trying to keep you safe."

"From what? Rumours? Someone besmirching our good name? That's still about you, not me."

"You know better, Zanthi. Mother didn't raise you to—"

"No," she says, her words sticking in her throat. "She didn't. You raised me, Theron. You're the one who taught me to chase my theories and never leave a stone unturned. So don't get sore at me now for daring to have half the passion you've enjoyed all your life." She snatches up her satchel and heads for the door. "I don't have to listen to this. I'm going out."

"You have nowhere to go," he calls after her.

She responds with a rude gesture and slams the door behind her.

The *gall* of him. Every action of hers reflects on him, every decision she makes must account for him. She stands a moment on the front steps of their townhouse, in amongst the tall yarrow and tangled cosmos of their tiny garden, and feels like she is twelve again. He always knows how to make her feel small.

She has places to go. Emlyn would let her sulk in his studio, even if he grumbled about it. She could sit and stew in a tea shop for a few hours. She could sit by the river and watch the ducks, like she used to do as a child.

She sets out for the river, still undecided, and she truly doesn't mean to end up at the Garden Hall. It's almost a surprise when she stumbles into the festival square, where the cart-sellers are setting up for the evening.

The late afternoon is cloying, the breeze sweetened with river thyme and hollyhocks. The ancient oaks in the square soak in the golden shadows, and she has barely stepped into the dappled light when a shrill whistle has her looking up.

The nightingale standing sentinel at the Hall's doors is waving to her, wide and eager. Zanthi looks around, but *no*, the nightingale is certainly trying to get her attention. She's halfway up the stairs before she realises it is the girl who stole her clasp.

"Ilyston," the nightingale says. "Welcome back."

Zanthi hesitates at the top step, holding her satchel tight against her side. She hadn't *meant* to come, but being here, she may as well return Madoc's writ. "Good afternoon. May I entrust you with something for Madoc Casca?"

The nightingale gives her an amused look. "We've your name, Ilyston. Go in." She cracks the door open in invitation. "Turn left and follow through for four rooms. Casca is minding the rehearsals."

She pauses, still clutching her satchel tight. "Thank you. What is your name?"

"Kit," she says. "I am sorry about the teasing. I see your clasp was returned safely."

"It was. There was no harm done. I'll see you around, Kit."

"I do hope so," Kit says, and sounds like she means it.

She goes where Kit had directed and regrets it as soon as she is faced with a squadron of dancers mid-spin, sweaty and stern-browed. There's a lot of bare skin. Beyond them, Thom and Madoc shift set pieces of a painted forest scene, all cut up into fragments like a puzzle. The room echoes under the *thump* of the dancer's feet, and she feels the beat of it right through her, right against her heartbeat.

Madoc's sleeves are pushed back, and he's faintly flush-cheeked, balancing an armful of wooden set pieces. He sees her the moment she sees him. A flicker of surprise disturbs his face, and then he tips his head in a beckoning way. She goes.

"Zanthi," he says. "What a delight to see you. Has something happened?"

"No, I only realised I still had your writ and thought I should return it. And maybe I ought to tell you that you should have returned Theron's robes to me, not him. The earful I got over it was entirely unpleasant."

Madoc winces. "I didn't mean to cause trouble."

"I imagine you never mean it," she says, and he laughs.

"Is that the only reason you came?"

She hesitates. He waits as if he has all the time in the day for her answer, like his armful of painted wood isn't a weighty one. "I didn't have any reason, I suppose. I didn't really mean to come, only I ended up here, anyway." It is maybe more of an answer than she'd intended, because his smile has a sharp hook of pleasure in it. "I see you're busy. It's no matter."

"I am," he says. He shifts his armful. "But if you don't mind waiting, perhaps we might have that tea?"

She hesitates. She doesn't want to go home, not yet, but neither does she want to sit here and watch the nightingales rehearse. "It's not that I'd be opposed, but I still have work I wish to do this afternoon—"

"Work in my rooms, then. You'll have them quite to yourself, and I promise you, you won't find a better place in all of Esk for quiet and comfort." He bends down, ducking his head. "Take my key."

If she hesitates, she'll look ridiculous, with him half-bowed to her. She slips her fingers under his collar, hooking the chain against his neck. The press of his skin is sun-warm and silk-soft, and she draws the chain and key out and over his hair. She's barely breathing, somehow, but when she does, it's all the scent of him, candle smoke and beeswax.

"Can you find your way up?" He straightens, and there's nothing of her own disquiet on his face.

"Yes," she says, trying to muster her thoughts back under control. She'd never thought herself weak to a pretty face before him. "Are you sure you don't mind?"

"Not in the least," he says. "Stay as long as you please. There is tea and a tin of biscuits in the kitchen and matches for the lanterns on the mantel."

"Thank you." She doesn't know what she's thanking him for. For the refuge, perhaps. For knowing she needs somewhere to hide away. For not hesitating in his offer, as if it didn't need a thought.

He hefts his armful up. Thom is calling for him. "It's an incentive for me to work harder."

His smile, just before he turns away, is a promising thing.

Chapter Ten

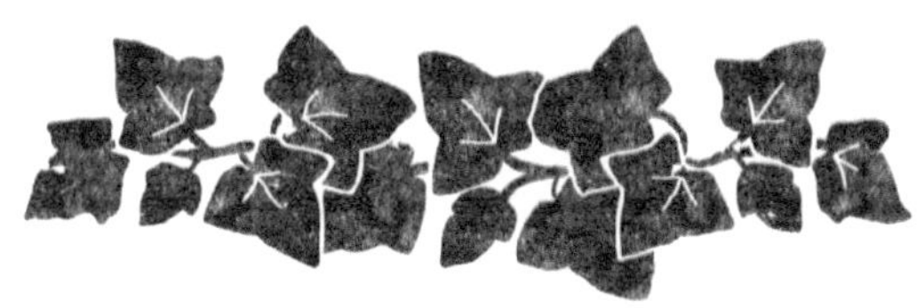

The gentle green of the garden swallows her entirely. She wanders, following the little quartz-gravel trails and mossy, paving-stone paths. Even the shift of the pebbles beneath her boots seems to whisper, as if everything is a secret. The whisper of wind-stirred leaves, the trickling streams linking the steaming bathing pools.

A nightingale, up on a ladder filling the lanterns, calls out a soft greeting to her. Another waves from within one of the smaller bathing pools. None seem even the slightest bit surprised to see her wandering when the Gardens are closed, and they greet her by name. She's not sure she's ever heard her name from so many lips in such a small space of time. Not even on the most packed days at the university.

As she turns through a latticed copse of birches, the path splits into frayed threads. The garden beds rise high and thick, spilling over with flowers and fragrant herbs. She turns in a slow circle. She doesn't remember this from her journey up with Chicory. She must have made a wrong turn.

"Ilyston?" A man pokes his head around a garden bed, and she recognises him. It's the doorman who had let her in that first time.

He's sandy-haired, wrapped in a bathing shift and linen robe. It's decent, but only barely so. "Are you lost?"

"I believe so, yes." She holds up the key. "I'm trying to get to the manor."

A breeze rustles the leaves above, and it sounds like laughter. He crooks a brow. At her and the key, both. "Here, let me show you. You aren't so far away."

"I hope I'm not disturbing your bathing."

"Not yet," he says pleasantly. "I'm called Rowan. I've heard a delightful lot about you, Ilyston."

"Zanthi," she says, falling in beside him. "Please."

He smiles at her. "Zanthi, then." He's as plain as she's ever seen a nightingale, ready for the waters. He has a strong body beneath his robes, as strong and lithe as Chicory's. "I'm dance-master at the Garden Hall during the Season," he adds.

The dance-master, as far as she is aware, is the one who calls the figures and leads the dances at a party, so that everyone else knows what to do. She supposes that to take such a role at the Hall is quite an honour.

"And what do you do the rest of the year?"

He laughs. "Oh, all sorts. I rake leaves and plant beds, work at the remedial baths. Learn new tricks. Help design new dances, both classical and more daring things. Have you ever seen nightingales perform? You're in for a treat this year."

"I shouldn't think so. I don't do the Season."

He looks entirely nonplussed. "Why ever not?"

"It's not my thing."

"You are standing in the Gardens, holding a Casca's key," he says. "I promise you, it's your thing."

With that, he laughs and waves her farewell, heading back to his bathing spot. He's left her at the gate to the private terrace, and Madoc's key unlocks it. She hangs it around her neck to return later and follows the main path to the manor.

On the second landing, the statue is haloed in the late afternoon light, turned golden. It still makes her blush. The outstretched hand, the tipped goblet. The face caught in a moment of reverent pleasure.

She's been thinking about this statue of late. It, and the pointing figure in the friezes of the archives. Their styles are vastly different, but both wear crowns of ivy. In all her reading, she hasn't come across a single mention of ivy crowns in any remnant religion or ritual. No river rushes, either. She's found mention of oak and laurel. Roses, holly, yarrow, and blossom. But never ivy.

She's still thinking about it when she sinks down on the sofa bench beneath the window. The sunlight coasts through the glass, kissing her knees and setting the carpet aglow. It drapes like a blanket, warm and heavy. She really *did* mean to continue with her reading while she waited, but the sofa is comfortable and the sun is a temptation.

The argument with Theron and her furious hiking about afterward has left her tired. Wrens chatter outside the window, and the distant trickle of the springs echoes like chimes. She lays her head on the arm of the sofa. A quick rest, she decides. No one needs to know. She'll hardly be out for a moment.

It's more than a moment.

She wakes to hearth flames and the clink of glass. She sits, and a velvet blanket crumples to her lap. Outside, lanterns gleam in the dark expanse of the Gardens. The room is aglow, sconces alight, and all the corners are softened in shadow. The wallpaper brambles coil deep and alive in the flickering light, like she might climb right into them. She is at the Gardens, she remembers. Madoc's rooms.

Glass clinks again.

Madoc.

He is at his drink cabinet, pouring a drink into a cut-glass tumbler. He's trying to be quiet about it and mostly succeeding. How long has she been asleep? An hour? No, certainly more.

"Madoc," she says, and he turns.

"Evening. I hope you don't mind that I didn't wake you. You looked so peaceful."

She should mind. It's a bit much, even for her, to be alone and asleep in his presence. But if she'd minded, she'd not have let herself sleep in his rooms, so she doesn't think he's the one who has overstepped. "I hope you don't mind that I fell asleep. I didn't mean to."

"Honestly, I envy you the opportunity. Would you like a drink?" He's changed from before, and his hair has the slightest curl of damp, so he's bathed, too. His pearl buttons are half-fastened at his neck, and he's wearing an evening shirt of fine, embroidered linen.

She's staring at his gaping collar. She looks away. "Have you somewhere to be?"

"I do, but not for a while yet."

"Then yes. But after that, I need to be getting home."

He sets a glass on the low table, then sits beside her. "I'll get you a carriage," he says. "Have you tried nectrine?"

She shakes her head, lifting the cup to her lips. It smells like the springs, earthy and heady, and there's a blossom-like perfume to it too. It melts into her mouth with a sharp bite of sweetness, and a hum that almost feels like aether, but isn't.

"Careful. It's strong if you haven't had it before."

"Worse than wine?"

"Depends on the wine." He takes a sip of his own. He holds his glass idly in a loose grip, entirely comfortable. "It's not so strong for me. We make it with spring water, and it fails to affect any with Casca blood. Don't try to match me."

"Noted," she says, tucking that away. "Do people often try?"

"More than is wise," he says, amused. "Though few know I'm hardly able to get drunk from it."

She smiles. She supposes he's drunk people into embarrassing situations more than once. "I'll keep your secret."

"Good. There'd be an uproar, otherwise. Speaking of, I am sorry about upsetting your brother."

"It wasn't just that. It was hardly that, really. He doesn't agree with some of my choices lately, is all." She sips. The sweetness lingers. "I hope I didn't get you into any strife with your mother the other day, either."

"No, not at all. Though I feel I should apologise for that too. She wasn't very welcoming."

"I'm used to it." She curtails his response, because she knows it will only be a platitude. "I can promise you, you don't know the half of it. I don't suppose you're ever refused anything."

His mouth turns up at the corners. "Not so. You've refused me a neat number of times."

She doesn't know what to say to that. "I didn't notice I was doing so."

"That only makes it worse," he says, but his smile is growing. He settles back into his seat. "Did you get your reading done, or did the wrens give you too much trouble? I find them awfully distracting when I try to read."

"Then why do you leave seed out for them?"

"Because they fret at me when I don't," he says, with no shame for being bullied by the tiny things.

She can't help it. She laughs. "The *Society Papers* have not painted an accurate portrait of you at all."

"It's accurate." He stretches out his legs to an embroidered footstool. He's wearing velvet parlour slippers. "But incomplete."

She dares another sip and takes a chance. "Might I ask you some questions about the journal?"

"I expected you might wish to do so," he says. "But not tonight. There's hardly time for it."

"Another time, then."

"If it will convince you to visit me again, then yes."

She smiles at the way he turns that, charming and enchanting, both. "Are you at such a loss for things to do? You seem very busy each time we cross paths."

His good mood falters. "I have many things to do, and hardly enough time. Still, I'd like the chance to enjoy the time I have for rest, now and then." Another sip. It's how he paces the conversation, she realises. Gives himself time to think, or makes someone wait, stewing. How fortunate for him that he can't make himself tipped with how often he's been doing it with her. "You've never done a Season, have you? It's a pity. Your company would have been entertaining."

"You, I think, are never short of entertaining company."

"Maybe not, but I insist you come by again. I've enjoyed our conversation, and I don't get many visitors." He rests his mouth against his glass, watching her.

She shifts, uncomfortable under such a gaze. "Truly? I feel you must have many friends."

"Not so." He looks thoughtful. "Other than the nightingales, there's not many."

"Only yesterday the papers were talking about a lunch party—"

"Oh? Following me in the papers?" There is laughter in his eyes now. "I'm flattered."

Flushed, she takes a deep sip. The nectrine melts through her words, keeping her silent.

"Truly, that is more work than friendship. As for friends, I have Nico and Eve. Mostly, though, there's Lettie. He's my dearest friend, but he hasn't been around for a long while."

"Is he...well?"

Madoc's smile is a little pained, though not at her. The sharpness, she thinks, is for someone else. "Well enough, considering. He's not in town anymore. I miss him, I suppose."

She can't help but study the way the lamplight falls across his face. It's almost infuriating how everything, every shadow and every drop of light, works to flatter him. "With all the stories about you, I didn't think your tally of friends would fail to exceed mine. Are you lonely, then?"

Gods, she's being nosy, now. As rude as he'd been in the archives, asking if she believed in the gods. But he only contemplates her over the edge of his glass. The nectrine shimmers golden, set aglow in the candlelight.

"Sometimes," he says. "Are you?"

"I didn't think so," she says, honestly. "But I've been told that these things creep up on you with you hardly knowing. I hope your friend comes home soon."

"As do I." He raises his glass. "To Lettie, coming home."

"To Lettie," she echoes. She likes the way it makes him smile.

"Well, I didn't mean to make things maudlin," he says suddenly. "I promise you I'm very skilled at conversation, usually."

"You needn't be skilled with me," she says, taking another mouthful. It really is pleasant, though it's very nearly gone. "It would be wasted. I think you're charming, regardless of what you're saying."

Madoc sets his glass aside. He tamps down his smile. She wishes he wouldn't. "I may have over-poured your cup."

"Because I complimented you?"

"That, and also this." He runs a thumb across her cheek. His skin is cool, and she realises how flushed she's become.

"Well, perhaps," she admits. She still finishes the last of her drink and savours the long, soft moments of it. Theron would probably call that a poor decision. When she sets her cup down, the *clink* is loud. "Will you walk me to a carriage? I don't like my chances in the Gardens in the dark."

"I think I am honour-bound to do so," he says, gathering the blanket from her so she can stand. "I'd not take any chances in a place like this."

"Is it not your domain?" She gathers her satchel and her papers, but she's sure she's forgotten something. Still, she can't see anything missing.

"It is, and that's why I know not to trust it," he says. "Come along, Ilyston. Let's get you home."

He rests a hand on her back as they wind their way down through the garden paths. She's not drunk so much as loose-tongued, and she hardly needs the support, but she still leans into it. It's an acceptable excuse, she thinks, for enjoying him so close. Then she cuts that thought short and throws it aside. She shouldn't be *enjoying* him anywhere.

His voice is low and close to her ear. "I'll call on you soon. I still owe you that tea."

"Surely not."

He laughs, and now it's a real one. Unaffected and handsome. "Getting you tipped on nectrine doesn't count."

He leads her back to the lower terrace. They don't go through the Hall, but instead through a neat series of more homely corridors that let out discreetly on a side street. He hands her into a lilac-painted town carriage like they've just come from a dinner party. The pony shifts, hooves stark against the cobblestones.

"Safe travels home." His smile still lingers, and even though he's laughing at her, she doesn't mind in the least.

"It's not so far. Enjoy your evening."

"It's already been delightful," he says, and closes the door for her.

She settles back, and that's when she notices the glint of gold resting on her chest. She sits up in alarm, pulling it free.

"Wait," she says, but the carriage is already lurching into motion. "I still have your key!"

She holds it up to the window, but Madoc only grins, waving as the carriage rolls away.

Chapter Eleven

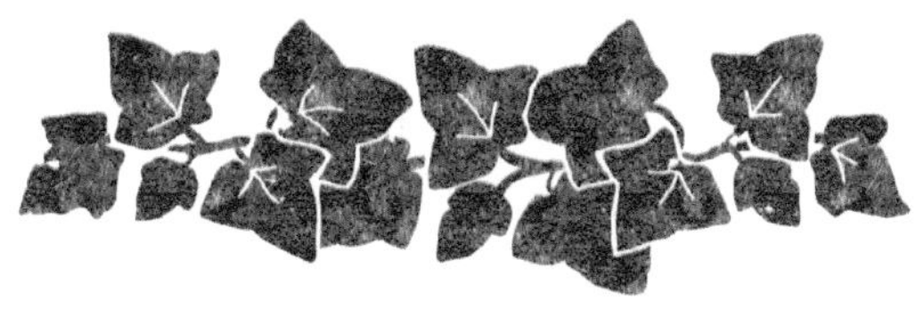

When she walks into Emlyn's studio, he's lying on the floor, staring at the ceiling.

She stands there until it is clear he hasn't noticed her arrival. "Painting not coming along?"

"Zanthi! I was just thinking of writing to you. I have news!" He scrambles to his feet, and his smile is startling in its ferocity.

"Good news?"

"Yes." He sits her on his painting stool, right in front of a half-done canvas. "No, don't look at that. Look at me."

She does. He's dressed properly, or as properly as an artist ever dresses, in a coat patterned with river wrens and a paint-free shirt.

"I've just had a studio visit," he says. "The Gallery came by to scout for the Annual."

That, she thinks, explains why he was on the floor. "And?"

"And I've a fair chance they'll accept one."

"As well they should," she says, smiling back. She tries to glance around the studio, but all the canvases are turned inwards, as Emlyn likes to keep them. "Which one?"

"I shan't spoil it. You'll come to the opening, of course."

She pulls a face. "Only for you." The Gallery's Annual Exhibition, falling on the cusp of the Season's start, is very much a society event. She'll need to find new clothes. But his smile is so very wide, and she can't be upset about it.

He draws up another seat, pushing the amassed pile of sketches upon it to the floor. A familiar shape tumbles out from between the pages. Braided rushwork, patterned like fish scales. Zanthi's breath chills in her throat.

"Where did you get that?"

Emlyn nudges it with his boot. "Oh, someone hung it on the door handle a while back. It's cute, isn't it?"

"I suppose it is," she says, her heart pounding in her chest. Who has been spreading these things through the town? "I've never seen them before this summer. They're turning up all over."

"I'm sure it's only some artisan trying to make a name for themselves. How is your work coming along? I've heard nothing from you in weeks, so I assume that means you're chasing something."

She's spent the last week researching all manner of odd and specific things. Mineral springs. Healing knowledge. The history and folklore of ivy. Her thoughts are all ivy, morning to night, and each day she thinks she's closer to becoming entirely unmoored. "Strangely, if I'm honest. I feel like I've lost track of my path. You were right about taking the researcher position, though. It's not been nearly as bad as I thought."

He nods, thoughtful. "And how did your research for the Gardens shake out?"

She freezes. It's a sliver of a moment, but he leaps on it like a pike on a minnow.

"Ilyston," he says, grinning. "There's a story there, isn't there?"

"There is not. I delivered some documents. That's all." She'd kept him very barely updated on her work for Madoc, because she knew he'd make a fuss over it. She never should have mentioned it in her letters to him at all.

Madoc's key is sitting in her dressing-table drawer, and she should have posted it back to him days ago. She can't bring herself to do it.

"You didn't stumble into any bathing pools? Steal away into an alcove with a nightingale?"

"Too far, Fairthorne," she says, kicking the leg of his stool and making it rattle. He laughs.

"And have you met the illustrious Madoc Casca?"

"Yes," she says. "Have you?"

"Mm. In passing. Quite the reputation." His face turns a shade of serious. "You will be careful, Zan? Don't get all trodden on."

"I'd never," she says. "We've been strictly professional."

"I believe Casca takes his profession very seriously. That is why I am warning you."

"He's charming. He's hardly a rake."

Emlyn makes a disagreeing sound. "Just because he doesn't mean to leave a trail of heartbreak, doesn't mean he doesn't. If he were anyone else, he'd be branded a trifler, but a Casca *does* get away with it."

"My heart is quite content where it is, never fear."

His gaze goes a little distant. "He'd be a wonder to paint, I think. I'd turn to portraits permanently, for those eyes. Lady Casca doesn't let any but the best painters get their hands on that face. Or any other part of him, for that matter." He laughs at whatever is on Zanthi's face. "Don't look so scandalised. There's hardly an artist in Esk who hasn't had at least one indecent thought about Madoc Casca. He rather invites it."

"I suppose he's pretty," she says, after a pause.

Emlyn's laugh is as rich as wine. "Oh, you must measure against celestial heights," he says.

"It's not that," she says, piqued. "It's only that—" She breaks off. Her cheeks burn. "I try not to think about it."

"Why? Why not think about it? You needn't spend your whole life paddling in the shallows, Zan."

"It's *Madoc Casca*."

"And? If he's given you any indication you'd be welcome..." He trails off leadingly.

Has he? He has sought her out, and held her hand, and let her sleep on his sofa while he changed his clothes with nothing between them but a curtain. He'd given her a key, in a roundabout sort of way. She really *must* return it. "No. No, he hasn't given me any indication."

She is far too retiring to mingle in his circles. Too boring to be his friend. She has a suspicion that no friend of Madoc's stays boring and retiring in his company for long. Or perhaps it's that they don't stay for long in his company.

A paintbrush jabs into her side. "You're having maudlin thoughts again. I can tell."

"Oh, sod off," she says, and he laughs. "Midsummer is coming. None of us will see any of them for weeks."

The Gardens close for midsummer. They do every year, though she's barely countenanced it in the past. The nightingales that live within the walls disappear, and Lady Casca and her son do, too. The rest of Esk celebrates with bonfires and thundering processions, and loud wooden clackers that fill the streets with gods-awful noise.

Zanthi has never liked the night of midsummer.

"I *do* wonder what happens at midsummer," Emlyn says. "I don't suppose you remember how you snuck into the Gardens that first time?"

The sound of a man clearing his throat has them both flinching. Zanthi turns to see Secretary Fairthorne in the doorway, a box in his hands. He is looking at his son with a world-weary look.

"Do not," he says, jabbing his cane in Emlyn's direction, "sneak into the Gardens."

Emlyn jumps to his feet. "Pa! What brings you here?"

"I had thought to surprise you with lunch and ask how the Gallery visit went. Though I see you have company already." He nods in Zanthi's direction, sheepish, as if he's embarrassed to be caught playing the part of doting father.

"It's only Zanthi." Emlyn takes the box and looks inside, and his eyes crease at the edges with his quiet smile. "And the visit was a success. I've got a good feeling about it."

The studio hasn't anywhere for them all to sit, so they troop out to the riverside and find a bench under the shade of a willow. The box contains spiced barley cakes, and Emlyn devours them like a child being allowed a treat. Zanthi nibbles while Emlyn regales his father with a far more detailed account of the visit than he delivered to her.

He still won't tell Joren which painting the Gallery was interested in, though.

Joren relaxes in the dappled light, looking for all the world like he's dozing. He's smiling, though. Just a hint in the corners of his mouth. "I look forward to seeing the exhibition," he says, when Emlyn finally winds down. "We'll celebrate tonight."

Emlyn stands, stretching his arms over his head. "Don't tell Mother. I want to surprise her myself."

Joren gives his solemn promise not to spoil the surprise, and Emlyn wishes them both a good day, jogging back to his studio with the rest of the barley cakes in hand.

She casts a sidelong glance at Joren. He's staring out at the river reeds and makes no move to leave. After a moment, she settles in to watch the river too, waiting for him to speak.

After a few minutes, he does. "Miss Ilyston."

"Zanthi. Please."

He makes a small sound. She doesn't know if it's an agreement or not. "Sneaking into the Gardens?"

"It was an archive passage," she says, after a pause. "If you must know."

The tip of his cane digs into the soil. "I see. The archives are closed now, of course."

"How did you know?"

"I know all sorts of things. It is the sum of my work." He sighs then, and it is as dry and rattling as the river rushes.

"Is everything well, Mr Fairthorne?"

"Nothing is ever well," he says, matter-of-fact. "And if you must, call me Joren."

"Joren, then. You are deliberating on something, aren't you?"

"I had truly not meant to draw you into any of this," he begins, "but you crossed my path, and that feels like uniquely fortuitous timing. May I show you something?"

"Something secret?"

"Entirely."

She gazes out at the river. The ducks weave amongst the rushes, there and gone. "Yes," she decides. "If I can help, I'd like to help."

She doesn't expect the small vial Joren pulls from his breast pocket. It's ornamental, capped with gold and cut from thick glass, like a perfume vial. It does not have perfume inside. She takes it from his hand, turning it in her palm.

Inside, thick, dark liquid rolls with the movement.

"Blood?"

"Yes. I'd like to know if you see anything else. With your talents."

"I can't summon it at will," she warns. But she tips her head, fixing the vial in the corner of her sight. For the longest time, there is nothing. The sun drifts above them, the rushes shiver, and then, ever so faintly, the blood ripples golden. Faint and *sickly*. There isn't a better word for it than that.

Pale, peach-gold aether ripples, that tremble and turn bruise-dark and bleeding. Gold again. Then bruised, as if it's fighting between whole and damaged. It's not like any aether she's seen before, but if she had to place it, it is most like the aether of the Well.

She passes it back, her skin crawling. *All* of her feels as if it is crawling, trying to get away from the vial. Her blood, her breath. All of it. Her throat is dry, and she clears it with a raspy noise. "Have you read *The Blooding of the Heirs*?"

Joren goes still all over. Then, "Yes. Ethram Hart. I have."

She tells him what she saw, and he listens, his fingers curled protectively over the vial. With his other hand, he grips his cane tightly, knuckles white. She doesn't ask if the vial contains an Heir's blood. She's sure he wouldn't tell her, if it were so. And she doesn't want to know how an Heir's blood ended up in a vial, or why Joren's facade cracks, just a sliver, when she describes the way the aether is fighting to cling to its gold.

"Thank you, Zanthi," he says, gravely. "You have confirmed, beyond doubt, what I needed to know."

"May I ask a favour in return?"

Joren tucks the vial away. He's not as old as Zanthi had thought when she first met him. Barely even fifty, maybe. It's only that he looks so weary. There are frown lines on his forehead and around his mouth, as if his life is entirely grim. Then she thinks of Emlyn, and the Admiral, and Madam Fairthorne with a garden full of flowers, and decides that it mustn't be entirely so. She hopes not.

"Of course."

"Could you provide me with Luminary Hart's address? You must know where to find it. I'd like to write him a letter, and I do not think he checks his university mail often."

Joren's mouth twitches. "No, I daresay he doesn't. Yes, I'll send it to you. It's hardly a favour at all." The tension bleeds from him. "And how have you been enjoying your work from the Crown?"

"Very well. It certainly leaves me with a lot of time for my own pursuits."

"At least someone has that privilege." He gathers himself. "Before I leave, I have one last thing to tell you. Your ability to see aether, and whatever else you see, makes you very valuable. To me, to the Crown, and to others who would not treat you so kindly. I tell you this because you are stepping into a world where you may need to know such things to protect yourself."

She frowns at him. His warning is too amorphous to chime any real alarm within her. "What world is that?"

"The world outside your brothers' protections. You have been well hidden."

"Then how did you find me? You sent me my offer of employment before you ever met me or saw my eyes."

"I saw a sketch of you in Emlyn's studio. I recognised the particulars of your gaze and asked for your name. And then I read some of your work and knew you'd be useful twice over."

So that first approach *had* been Emlyn's fault. "You said you had met someone with eyes like mine."

He hesitates, and then he sighs. “I was only partially truthful. I met a man who once *had* witch-eyes.”

“Had?”

“They had been cut out. The west is a cruel region for many reasons.”

“Then I am fortunate to live in Esk,” she says, blankly. Eyes *cut out*.

“The danger is less here, but not none.”

“I am careful. I stay out of people’s notice. I rarely leave the university. I have a small number of friends.”

He drops his voice, grim. “It is not entirely my place, mind. But you have been in Madoc Casca’s company, alone, more than once.”

She doesn’t know how he knows that. It is, she thinks, none of his business. “I have nothing to fear from Casca.”

“No, you do not. But everyone takes notice of who he takes notice of. You say you are careful. I am telling you, you are not.”

Chapter Twelve

She examines the papers more closely after that. She eats her toast slowly each morning, scanning between stories about artisans she doesn't know and socialites she knows even less. Madoc is there, of course. An appearance here, a sighting there. A rumour of a love affair, a scathing letter about his rakish behaviour. Now that Zanthi knows him, she can't imagine him being so heartless. He's been nothing but gentle. It scratches at her, all the gossip.

The storms are worse this year, or so the papers say. They all share grim looks when there is news of a large storm that made landfall and wreaked destruction on a northern town. The northern sky was usually Chester's charge, only she knows he's been sent east this year. He'll still feel responsible.

Her noble, dutiful brother.

She starts watching Esk's aether in a way she never has before, watching for any difference in the pattern. She hasn't forgotten the strange aether blood in the vial, and how it had made her feel like she was rotting inside her own skin. She's been called cursed, walked the archives with all its misfortune, but she's met nothing that felt as haunted as that blood.

It is a sweltering summer afternoon when she sees another of the woven rush charms. Her path home from the university weaves through a narrow street of townhouses, and it hangs in the front window, suspended on a green ribbon. It is a perfect match for the one she'd seen in Emlyn's studio. She continues on, but there's a growing suspicion in her. It only gets louder when she sees another woven knot in the window of a house a few doors down, too. And then another.

"Excuse me," she says to a woman pottering in the front garden. "Did you make that charm in your window?"

The woman smiles, cheeks creasing. "Oh, no. My son did." She points at a tumble of children playing down the street. "The children get cleverer and cleverer, don't you think? I've no idea where he learned it."

"Why did he hang it in the window?"

"That was me, Miss. I don't know why. It just seemed the place for it, didn't it?" She nods good day and continues snipping at her flowering yarrow.

Zanthi has delved into a great deal of Esk's little folklores and festive traditions lately. The festival of Rushtide is soon, but despite its name, she has never known woven river-reed charms to be a part of the celebrations. One of her favourite books, *The Legacy of Esk: Folklore, Rituals, and Traditions in a Historic City*, includes an almost complete documentation of festival favours. It does not have the woven river-rush charm, and she's searched through it a needless number of times to be sure.

And yet, they're appearing all over. Hanging on doorways and in windows. Sitting at the top of the archive stairs, marking the gateway to the darkness. A bell toll rolls through the street and she clutches her satchel, fear-struck, before her sensible thoughts catch up and she realises it is only the eventide bell.

She hurries on, a prickling at the back of her neck. As she passes the children, all tangled together in a clapping-jumping game, the edges of their song catch at her.

"*Through the ivy, through the deep—*"

The tune is itchingly familiar, settling in her mind like it's been there before, only she doesn't know it. The children clap in time to their paired steps as if they are dancing one of the rowdier dance hall favourites. The song comes in fragments. The children drop words and spaces into silence, different ones each time they sing through, though she can't pick up a pattern to it. Yet, there must be one, because they do it neatly, together. Without tripping.

It's a simple rhyme, when she hears it complete.

"*Through the ivy, through the deep, whisper low where waters sleep,*

Give to day and give to dark, by thorn and leaf and blood and bark."

It sends cold clawing up her back. Songs are a part of Esk and always have been. There are work songs and dances, operas and lullabies, river songs and children's games. Zanthi grew up on them. She is *sure* she's never heard that rhyme.

When she gets home, she borrows *The Legacy of Esk* from Theron's study and takes it upstairs to her room. She sits on the floor because there's no room to sit elsewhere. Neat stacks pile across her bed, the dressing table, the writing desk, and the floor in a chaotic spiral of theories. She's been rather obsessed as of late.

She has a lot of theories. One stack for everything that supports the existence of Esk's founding god. Another stack for the scant crumbs she's unearthed on the history of the Gardens and the existence of other springs in Esk. The largest stack is a gathering of archaeological records from all over Elveresk that detail and document motifs and myths that she feels are connected to Esk and the Well.

Now, a new stack, for all the odd happenings that are appearing across Esk. Charms in the archives. Charms in the houses. New songs. Before the words can fade from her mind, she writes the song out in her journal, and makes a note of the clapping, too. It's a rippling sort of pattern.

Fish scales, river songs, ripples.

She works her way through *The Legacy of Esk* once again. She runs down the index of festival songs, invocations, and folk rhymes, but finds nothing like it.

A knock at her door frame startles her.

"Zanthi," says Fletcher. He's got ink smudged on his cheek, and his hair is untidily clipped back from his face. He's managed to get a cardigan over his braces, but that's about the best thing that could be said for his state of dress, which is why it's alarming when the next thing he says is, "You've got a visitor."

Then he steps back, and Madoc leans around the door frame.

Zanthi stares, book forgotten. Gold specks glint in his ears and lamp-black darkens the curve of his eyes. He's wearing one of his draping velvet jackets, all elegance. In the frame of her door, he doesn't look entirely real.

"I'll leave you to it," Fletcher says, much too bright for how tired he appears. He turns to Madoc. "Word of advice. Don't interfere with the stacks."

"Noted." Madoc inches into the space. He looks around, cataloguing the safe areas as Fletcher's footsteps rattle back down the stairs. "I had come to ask you out for tea, but I see that this time, you are the one who is busy."

"You don't look dressed for tea," she says, because her mouth is a foolish thing. She hasn't quite caught up with Madoc in her house. *Here.*

"Do I not?" He glances in her dressing-table mirror. The velvet shifts. A subtle twist of thorns is burnt through the pile, and an embroidered golden moth sits at the back of the collar, wings spread across his shoulders.

If she wore her clasp while he wore that, they would match.

"Well, perhaps you do. I'm sure I wouldn't know." She returns to her page, finishing her search before she gets entirely distracted. When she next looks up, Madoc is sitting at her dressing table, watching her.

"I'm sorry," she says. "I'll finish this up."

"You needn't for my sake. I'll come back another day."

"Please don't. I could use a break from this."

"From the looks of it, it might need a break from you." He picks up the framed aethergraph on her dresser and smiles. "I've never known Captain Locksley to be anything other than bluntly charming and entirely unyielding."

"He's both those things," she agrees. The aethergraph is of her and her brothers when they had been much younger. It shows a gentler Chester, the way he had been before the airguard had whittled him into something sharper. Before the aether had reshaped him into the unstoppable force he is now.

Madoc moves on. He picks up the card with Hart's details. He clearly recognises something about it because he says, "Why has Joren written you an address?"

"Do you know him?"

"He's close to the family."

He must be close indeed, for Madoc to recognise him from his handwriting. "I work as a researcher for the Crown. Joren sent me that address so I can ask some questions."

Madoc peers at the address. "It's not too far if we take my carriage. Who lives there?"

"A scholar called Hart. I meant to write him a letter, though."

"Hart?" Madoc narrows his eyes, and then his face clears. "I've met him. Well, how about we go pay him a visit instead?"

"I don't think it's quite that vital—" she starts. A scraping noise interrupts her, and Madoc stiffens. Zanthi laughs. "Oh. That's Susan. She does that."

Susan is sitting in the doorway, shoulders hunched, staring at Madoc with her big eyes. In the gloom, she rather looks like she's appeared from nothing.

Madoc gives her an uneasy glance. "Your dog?"

Susan unfolds. There's a lot of her to unfold, sometimes. She picks her way over the paper stacks to give Zanthi a sniff and a bump of acknowledgement, then turns and trots back downstairs. Madoc is entirely ignored.

"Fletcher's," says Zanthi. "But we all love her dearly."

"She's very singular."

"Isn't she? Theron found her as a pup and carried her all the way home in a rainstorm."

"That seems entirely unlikely, and yet I can easily believe it," he says. "Your brother is an interesting creature."

"He doesn't like you much."

Madoc laughs. "For my part, I'm rather fond of him. No one ever dares treat me as sharply as he does, you know."

She supposes they cross paths in society, from time to time, because she can't countenance how they'd know each other otherwise. "Most people don't enjoy his temperament."

"I've always had obscure tastes," he says, and there is a weight in his words that makes her face feel flush. "How did you fare after the other night? I truly didn't mean to dose you so strongly."

"I was fine. Your key is in the drawer," she says. "If you'd like it back."

"I wouldn't," he says. There's the sound of the drawer opening, as if he's checking. "I have another. You should keep this one, in case you ever need to visit your garden door."

No custodian of the Gardens should be so free and easy with its secrets, and it makes her wary, the way he's both free and easy to her. She doesn't know what he's playing at. Or perhaps she does, and she wishes he wouldn't. "You should take it back."

He looks up. There's not much to read in his face.

"I suspect Lady Casca wouldn't like for me to have it, and I don't intend to cause strife."

"I can give my key to whoever I please."

"Madoc," she says, and he fixes her with that river-green gaze. "I don't wish to go places where I am not welcome. I've had quite enough of that, and I don't intend to invite any more of it."

"You are welcome with me."

"Perhaps. But I make people uneasy. Superstitious types think me cursed. And to be honest, I can't say for sure I am not."

"You are not cursed," he says, as if he is sure of it. As if he can *know*.

"I'm not normal, either." She stares at him, willing him to understand. "I'm not entirely Eskan-born. My father was from the west. I don't know who he was. *What* he was. But he gave me these eyes."

"I do like your eyes," he says, leaning on her dressing table. "I shan't like you any less just because you are a little from the west."

"They mark me as different."

His smile is slow and a bit sharp. "I'm a Casca. I know about being marked as different."

"Your mother does not like me."

"My mother is overcautious," he says.

"And you are not."

His smile stays. "I am, I promise you, but you are nothing to be wary of. Tell me, what is it that makes those eyes of yours so remarkable? Other than how pretty they are."

She takes a thin breath. She cannot fathom his teasing when she is trying to be honest. "I call it my side-sight. I see glimpses of aether, sometimes."

"Only aether?" There's no teasing in him now. "Because I think you saw something that day we found the buried spring. You came over faint. I've been wondering about it ever since."

The truth tugs at her tongue, but she weakens it before she lets it loose. "I saw water in the buried springs, as if they were full and brimming once more. And now I feel like I'm seeing ghosts of things everywhere, like I'm going half-mad and hearing things and finding things I should not be." She clutches her book and wonders why she's spilling this all to him. He is so loose with the Gardens' secrets. She should not trust him with hers. "In the west, they call what I have witch-eyes, and say I'm bad luck. For all I know, they may be right."

He comes to her, placing his socked feet carefully between her paper piles. He moves the last stack away from her, kneeling in its place, and meets her eyes, unflinching.

"Trust me," he says. "Who your father is, or where he is from, means nothing of who you are."

"It doesn't change my nature."

"There is nothing bad about your nature."

"You can hardly know that."

"I can," he says simply. "You might see strange things, Zanthi Ilyston, but you're not the strangest thing I've ever seen."

"No?"

"Not in the slightest," he says, smiling.

He meets her gaze so easily, and he hasn't even had to practice at it. She's thinking about that, and his lovely eyes, and then her thinking is quite thoroughly halted when he shifts forward and kisses her. It's a light kiss. A warm, easy press of his mouth. It still pins her in place.

Her breath hitches, loud in the quiet, and he draws back as if he's flinched.

She opens her lips, means to say something, but his gaze dips to her mouth and he's kissing her again. It's not the same this time. His hand threads through her hair, cradling the curve of her head and tilting her face back, and the kissing changes from something she knows to nothing like she's ever had before.

She curls her hand in the fabric of his shirt, not sure if she's trying to halt him or keep him there. She's not sure of much anymore, only that his mouth is hot, his hands are firm, and his scent is still all earth and moss and candle smoke, and everything else has ceased to matter.

When he draws back, he catches her lip in the lightest of grazes. It sends an uncurling of heat through her. She breathes raggedly, her heartbeat pounding in her veins. He looks entirely composed. Except maybe not entirely, because his hand tightens against her hair before he draws away.

He'd looked gentle before the kiss, but he doesn't any longer. His expression is wanton, dark-eyed and sweet-mouthed, and his voice is soft. "I shouldn't have done that."

She dampens her lip, chasing the feel of him. Her chest calms slowly. "I suppose you didn't mean to."

"Zanthi," he says, and his mouth curls. "I did mean to kiss you. Of course I did."

"You kiss a lot of people," she says, because she knows. Everyone knows.

"Yes," he says. "It doesn't mean I didn't very much want to kiss you just now, though."

There's a moment of silence. He still hasn't looked away.

"Then why shouldn't you have done it?"

"Because now is not the time for beginning such things." He pushes to his feet, a graceful curl of movement, and holds out a hand to help her up. It is as if everything has bled from him—the solemnity, the desire, the invitation. He touches his fingers to her hair, letting her know where it has come down. "I'll wait downstairs."

She looks around once he's gone. He's knocked a few stacks of paper over in his passage, but she finds it hard to be annoyed about it. She's finding it hard to do anything but remember his mouth over hers. She presses her hands to her cheeks, willing the warmth to simmer down.

She fixes her hair because it is needed. She wears the moth clasp, which is not needed, but she thinks Madoc will be pleased if she does. She doesn't wish to examine why she wants to please him. It has nothing to do with the kiss, and it has everything to do with it. It is complicated, and she needs more time to think on it.

Madoc Casca kisses a lot of people. Zanthi has known this from the moment she knew who he was, and she's not so surprised that he's kissed her, too. She's only surprised by how much she liked it.

Chapter Thirteen

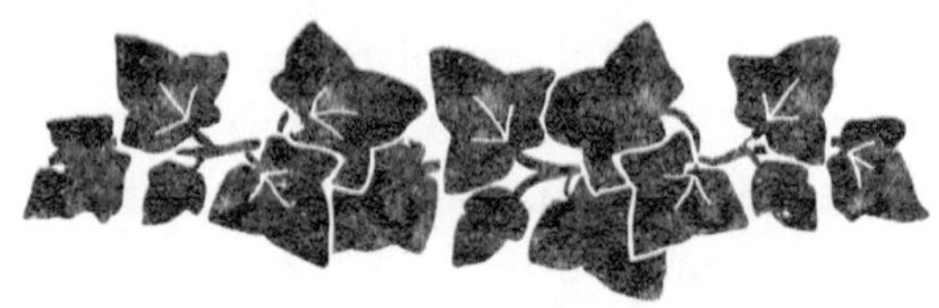

Madoc's carriage is all green velvet inside. She slides onto the plush cushions as Madoc talks to the driver, and then he's climbing in and settling across from her. His boot rests against hers. There's not much room, and they each must sit at side angles to the other, in order to fit without too much pressing together. For most people in a Gardens carriage, the pressing together is probably the fun of it.

She wets her lips, cursing herself for remembering the warmth of his mouth there. It's only that the carriage is scented like his smoke-sweet perfume, and every breath fills her with it, soaking through her thoughts.

Madoc has the curtain hooked back in his fingers, and he's studying the street outside as if it fascinates him. He fascinates *her*. The curves of his brow, his lashes, his cheek. His face is a handsome one. As soft as it is sharp. As kind as it is tempting.

He turns, and she is caught staring. She doesn't look away—if he thinks it fine to kiss her on her bedroom floor, she'll feel quite comfortable looking at him in a carriage.

"Zanthi," he says, then stops. His hand drops, and the curtain falls closed. He's wearing a thin gold bracelet on his wrist. A moth, matching his coat. Matching her hair. He glances away again.

"Would you tell me more of what you saw at the underground spring?"

The question startles her. She'd been thinking so much of his mouth, and he hadn't been thinking of hers at all. Perhaps she shouldn't have worn the moth, after all. "Water, as I said."

"It must have been more than water. You looked haunted."

Haunted is a good word. She feels haunted by it, entirely, and never so much as when she's close to him. He's so very *vibrant*, and that apparition had been dead-eyed and dead-mouthed. "I saw our reflections," she says, unwilling to tell him any more truth than that. "My eyes were black."

He smiles. "Your eyes are already black. And they're lovely."

"So you say."

"You are not easily flattered, are you?"

"Not by you." It comes out sharper than she means. His smile deepens.

"I rarely meet a skill I cannot master," he says, untroubled.

"If you truly regret kissing me, Madoc Casca, perhaps you should stop flirting."

"For now," he says, as if this is a truce. "And I don't regret it, not for a moment. One should never regret a kiss."

She supposes all the socialites in the Season who win a kiss from him never regret their kisses, either. Perhaps they collect them like Theron collects books or Fletcher collects stories. "The journal," she says, trying to wrest the topic back to firmer ground. "You know the language it is written in, then?"

"One of the few pieces of Casca heritage my mother was able to pass to me. I'm afraid we've lost most of it, and the history of our Gardens too. That's why the journal was such a gift to us." His words are warm, but a chill creeps into his features as he speaks. A shadow, stealing over him. "It told us a great deal we didn't know. A great deal we had forgotten."

"That there used to be more sacred springs in Esk," Zanthi guesses. She's pretty sure she's right, and he tips his head in agreement.

"Eight upwellings, according to our mysterious Casca. The Gardens were once the whole of Esk, spreading from the House to the river, though by the time the journal was written, most of it was already gone."

It is hard to imagine. All the honey-stone buildings and cobbled streets, gone. Instead, moss and old oaks and quartz sand and springs. The sound of water trickling down to the Lune. What happened to it all?

Across the river, above the town, the House sits. It is a palatial building, half-nestled in the sloping rise of the mountainside. Esk runs right up to its front steps, the streets unwinding from the House's doors and tangling into the maze of the town proper.

"Not a single history book mentions that," she says, after a long moment. "It must have been beautiful."

"It is humbling to realise my Gardens are nothing more than the remaining crumbs," Madoc adds. His voice is wry. "I can only suppose the Gardens did not survive the creation of the Well."

Her thoughts sharpen to a point. "The Well is not mentioned in the journals?"

"Oh, it is." He has a troubled sort of look, like she's focused on the one bit he didn't bother remembering. "But it wasn't here when the Gardens were at their height. It came after."

"You said they reached from the House to the river."

"Yes. The Gardens had the House before the House had the Well."

It goes against anything Zanthi has understood about Esk, about the entire isle of Elveresk. She had batted her theory around that the archives predated the Well, but for the *House* to predate the Well? Nonsensical. "Whatever was the House *for*, if not for the Well?"

He's silent. He watches the street pass by the window, and she thinks he will not say a word. And then he says, "Worship."

A prickle runs right over her. "And what did they worship?"

"The waters, of course. Did you know that in old songs, the Gardens are called the House of the Healing Waters?"

"A temple, then," she says. The carriage turns from the streets of Esk, down into the river meadows, and towards the dark blot of the Polling Woods. The House disappears from sight. "How curious. I didn't think Esk had any temples."

"We made a palace out of ours," Madoc says. "The Crown truly supplanted our god, whoever they were."

"You're sounding as heretical as I was accused of being."

He jostles her knee with his own, grinning. "Your face goes so serious when you're puzzling over your histories. Very like your brother when you look like that."

"Oh, so that's what you sound like when you aren't flirting."

His laugh distracts her from her thoughts, as sweetly as honey cake distracts her from her books.

It's raining by the time they climb out of the carriage, heavy drops pattering around them. The carriage has taken them into the Polling Woods, along a winding forest road. The village, when they reach it, is small. The houses sit far back from the street, sinking into the woodland, and everything is cool, drifting shade. A few early acorns lie across the path, green and small.

She hadn't realised that Luminary Hart did not live in the main town of Esk. He's entirely hidden away out here, far from any sort of society. She understands the impulse.

Silver moves at the edges of her sight. She looks, instinctively, and it disappears. No, it *darts away*. Whatever it is, it is moving, flowing like the wild aether of the storms. Esk's aether usually hovers or twists in place. She's never seen it move like that, like a living thing fleeing danger.

"Zanthi?"

"I thought I saw something," is all she says. She pushes the garden gate in.

Hart's cottage is built from hewn sandstone and neat shale tiles. It hunches under a low roof, with two small, square windows and a stone path to the door. The garden is awash with colour, yarrow and feverfew, rue and climbing roses. Two young crabapple trees stand on either side of the path, fruit bright and pink amongst the leaves.

It's quaint, in the best sense. It looks barely big enough for one person to live in, and she can't help but wonder how someone keeps their entire life inside. When she knocks, a swirl of movement slips under the door. Silver, again, but somehow not quite like aether.

She hasn't a moment to wonder at it, because the door opens.

Luminary Hart is not as old as she'd expected. She'd been thinking of someone grey and weathered, but instead she's faced with a severe man who looks solidly in his thirties. He has dark hair and grey eyes, and is dressed in a knitted jumper and corduroy trousers. He takes one look at them and sighs.

"Ilyston," he says, in the dourest of tones. "Come in, then. Best get out of the rain." He steps back and allows them entry to a small, recessed hall. "And Madoc Casca, too. An odd day, to be sure."

"It's been a while, Ethram," he says. "We're on a research trip."

Hart's mouth presses into an unhappy line. "Come into the kitchen. There's a fire, and I'll make you tea, but I can't promise you anything more."

She exchanges a glance with Madoc, and steps inside. Hart chivvies them on before they can remove their boots, as if he doesn't care about the mud they're tracking across his floorboards. "I suppose you want to ask some questions?"

"I do. How did you know?" Zanthi says.

"I remember you and your questions," Hart says, dire.

The kitchen is a small space, with a yawning, old-style hearth, a wooden table, and windows that look out onto a damp, lush garden. The garden is hedged in with thick woods, so that she might think they were out in the mountains and not at all a twenty-minute carriage ride from the city.

"I'm sorry, but I don't remember ever meeting you." Zanthi takes a seat at the table. Madoc doesn't. He stands behind her, hands in his pockets.

"No? That's gratitude for you, I suppose," Hart says. When he places the tea things on the table, his sleeve rides up to reveal stark silver scars around his arm.

Zanthi knows an aether burn when she sees one, but she can't fathom how a scholar ended up with aether wrapped around his arm in such a way. When he moves into the edges of her vision, that's odd, too. There *is* aether around him, the same colour as the strangeness outside. It's not true silver. It's almost like the inside of an ocean shell, shifting between gold and silver and grey and lilac.

She blinks herself back to the present. "I really don't think we've met before, Luminary Hart."

He takes down a set of cups from a high cupboard. There are already cups on the side of the sink, two of them, matching. The ones he takes down are nicer and less worn. How odd it is for someone as famously reclusive as Hart to have nice teaware for guests.

"Don't fret," he says. "You were a child. I don't imagine you would remember." He turns back to his task. "You wandered away from your mother and into the archives. I found you."

"Oh." She sits, stunned. "I didn't know."

"Never could understand her," he says. "You had gone into the archives for hours, and Therese didn't even notice until I brought you back. Scared half the life from me, running out of the darkness wailing like a ghost."

Madoc's laugh is soft, but a ripple of disquiet shivers through her. Running? From what? The archives were a grim, cold sort of place for a child to wander. Why had she ever gone into them?

"So," Hart says, when the silence has stretched out. "What did you come to bother me about?"

She reaches for her satchel and then realises she hasn't brought it. Her face heats. "I've been reading your work on festival traditions, and I had wanted to ask about a rush charm that has been appearing. No one can tell me where it came from."

Hart fumbles the teapot, catching it at the last moment. "River rushes?"

"Yes," she says, frowning.

"Do you have an example for me?"

"I...forgot it." She swallows. "It was a last-minute decision to come here."

Madoc shifts behind her, leaning closer. "I'm afraid that was my fault, Ethram."

"It usually is, isn't it?" He flicks them both a glance. "Alright, we'll sit and have tea, and you tell me all you can about these charms. But you shouldn't stay long if you're sensitive to aether, Ilyston."

"It is aether, then? It looks so—" she says, and then realises what she's said, and presses her lips tight. There really is a *lot* of the silver-not-silver aether pooling through the cottage. It's making her thoughts harder to arrange. She's never been much affected by aether before, other than the headaches her side-sight gives her from time to time. To feel it leeching her thoughts away from her is unpleasant, to say the least.

Hart catches her gaze and doesn't look the least bit surprised. He holds out for an admirable time before he looks away again. "You haven't changed, you know. You came out of those tunnels babbling about the things you'd seen, and I didn't believe you, at first."

"At first?"

He holds up his wrist, those aether burns stark against his skin. "I should have taken your warnings, little fish."

Little fish.

The name strikes a bell, and it rings through an empty space where her memories should be. On and on. Tightness claws up inside her chest, threatening to choke her.

"Tell me," he says, and so she does.

She tells him of the charms on the archive steps, in Emlyn's studio, and in the windows of the townhouses. She tells him of the song the children sang, and Madoc's hand tightens against her shoulder. She tells him of the friezes, and Madoc joins in there, describing them in a manner more graceful than she'd have ever managed.

Hart pours the tea as she speaks, but he is listening. As he lays out a plate of spiced honey-soaked biscuits usually reserved for festivals, his fingers twitch like he's curbing an instinct to reach for a pen.

"I have tried to link them," she admits. "The charms and the friezes seem alike with the fish scale pattern. And the children's song was the eeriest thing I've ever heard. And none of it seems to come from anywhere! I've looked through *The Legacy of Esk* more times than I could count."

"It won't be in there," he says. He glances out the window, towards the rain-wet tangle of garden. "It's only an old memory, coming back to the surface."

"Pardon?"

"Esk has forgotten much," Hart says. "And now it is remembering."

The words ring through her, much like the bell toll rang through her mind.

"What were the crowns woven of, on the friezes?" Hart says.

"Ivy," she says, the word coming slowly to her tongue. Then, her thoughts tumbling on, "Ivy and hawthorn, I think. Perhaps oak? And the statue by Madoc's door has an ivy crown, too."

Madoc looks down at her. Sitting as she is, he looks rather like the statue, amused and imperious. "It does," he says.

"Midsummer," Hart says. He's staring at Madoc. "Isn't that right?"

Zanthi leans back into Madoc's body, curious. "Since when has ivy been a motif of midsummer?"

"It's a Gardens thing. We've used it for midsummer for an age." He reaches past her for one of the biscuits, honey-dark and topped with almonds.

"That explains why I know nothing of it," she says, as she tucks that glimmer of information away. "No one knows anything of the Gardens at midsummer. Except, it seems, for you, Luminary Hart."

Hart smiles. "I spent some time as a habitant of the Gardens, Miss Ilyston."

"Alarming," she says before she can stop herself. She can't imagine Hart as a nightingale, not in a thousand years.

Hart laughs, almost as if he doesn't mean to. "What is your discipline? You can't be in languages, as your brother is."

"I was in history."

"Not anymore?"

Her tea is a fragrant, light brew with berry-sharp sweetness. She drinks and gathers herself. "I submitted a paper at the conclusion of my student year, speculating on the ancient history of Esk."

"That wouldn't have gone over well with that lot. Where did you end up?"

"I didn't," she says. The pressure of the aether is making her head spin. "It was considered too contentious, and I ended up nowhere."

He smiles, finally. "Now then," he says. "You are becoming interesting. What was your premise?"

She sets her cup down. Her fingers are aching like she's jammed them in a door. Her vision wavers at the edges. The aether is far too strong in this house. She's only been aethernipped once before, when Chester had come back from the docks saturated in it and she hadn't kept enough distance. It hadn't come as swiftly or strongly as this, though.

"I'm exploring the idea that Esk has a founding god. I wish to recover their name, at the very least, and restore it to our history books."

His silence is long and deep. "Is that so," he says finally. "I see why those fools balk at your research." He cuts his gaze to Madoc. "And do you have anything to do with this?"

"No, though our paths have overlapped."

"Inevitable," agrees Hart.

Madoc rests a hand on her shoulder. The touch is grounding, and for a moment, the aether is easier to think through. But when he speaks, his voice is weary. "It rather looks like the inevitable is coming for us at last. You should know, Mother and I intend to resurrect the midsummer ritual in full. We've nothing else left to try."

Ethram stills. "I thought that knowledge had been lost."

"It has been found."

"And will it be your mother?"

"It will not."

He looks at his teacup, as if the depths might tell him something. Finally, he says, "I understand, Casca. I wish you luck."

"I'd accept something a little more tangible, if you have it," Madoc says, as dry as she's ever heard him. He sucks the last of honey from his fingers.

"I can think of nothing to tell you that I haven't already told your mother once."

There's an odd taste on her tongue, like river water and rain. Alarm, too, beating in her, an echo of an old fear resurfaced. She stands and grabs Madoc's arm. She's not sure why, only that it feels very important that she doesn't let him go.

"Thank you for your answers, Professor. It really is time to be going."

Hart smiles. "Ah, your instincts are sharp."

With that, he ushers them back to the hall. The pounding of rain floods through the hall when he pulls open the front door. Even so, she hears the quiet creak of the kitchen door behind them.

"Go on," Hart says, shooing them out. Just before he closes the door entirely, he sticks his head out. "And Ilyston? Send me that paper of yours, and the research you've done since. I expect it by mid-week at the latest."

The door shuts with a final snap.

Chapter Fourteen

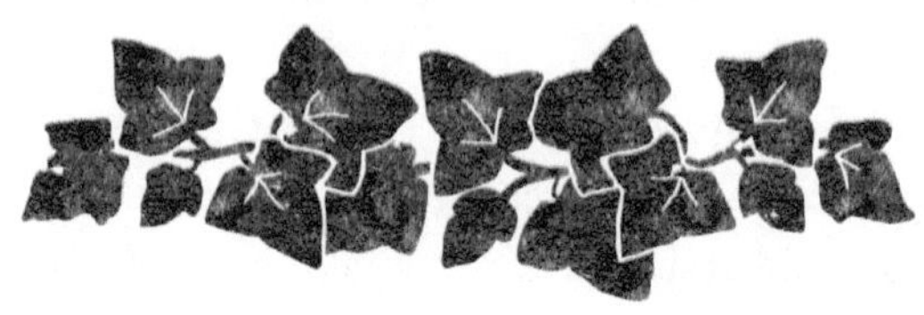

In the carriage, the sickness fades somewhat. A headache still clings to her temples, and her fingers are weak and unable to grasp much.

"How are you so unaffected?" she says, watching Madoc recline across his seat, entirely at ease.

"Aether doesn't really affect me."

"Lucky." She rubs her temple, trying to sort the conversation from the tangling effect of the aether. "Gods, what has he got hiding away in there to make it so aether-drenched?"

"Might be a natural spot. They occur in the woods around Esk. We've a few in the old forest. Not strong enough to be of any use for the airguard, but some aetherworkers visit them looking for wood and such."

There is a lot about aether that Zanthi has never learned. "What did you mean about the midsummer rituals? What are you intending to do?"

He winces. "I mentioned a few things that I should not have mentioned in your hearing."

"I won't tell a soul."

"I know." He presses his knee into hers. The headache abates, just a little. "Our springs are weakening. They flow less each year, and each year the healing effects are less."

Grim news. Without the springs, the casualties from the airguard would be much higher, and they're already too high. And all the aether the town flaunts, all the socialites in their aetherglass and aethercut gemstones. Without the springs, everyone would sicken, eventually. Gods, the *Well*. Could Esk even survive as a city without the springs?

No, she thinks. It could not. Not with the Well spilling over them, day and night.

When she looks up, the same dire thoughts are clear on his face.

"We're restoring the old rituals. It's foolish, perhaps." He leans his elbow against the carriage window ledge, resting his chin in his palm. "We're willing to try almost anything to keep the springs flowing, as unlikely as it sounds."

"It's not foolish," she says, barely thinking about it. He'd knelt at the dead springs like a priest in a temple shrine. He'd said *worship* as if it meant something. He's believed in the gods all along, she realises. No wonder he never laughed at her research. She reaches out, brushing his knee with her hand as if she means to place her palm there, only she withdraws at the last moment. She cannot bring herself to do it. "I won't talk of your secrets."

"I don't worry about my secrets with you."

In his face, she truly can't see anything but trust. She doesn't know what she's done to earn it. She doesn't know what she's done to earn his kiss or his kindness, either. She can't shake the feeling that he's just minding time, only she can't say what he is waiting for. Her head throbs.

"Zanthi? Are you well?" He says her name like a gentle thing. It sounds harsher in other mouths, but never his. He sits forward, rests a hand on her knee. He has no hesitation. His fingers press into the softness, and his golden rings catch the light. "Look at me."

She does. The nausea fades at his touch, as if whatever magic of the Gardens that keeps the aether away is wound through him, too. She wants to cling to that calm. She wants to cling to him. Hart told her she has sharp instincts, and her instincts are telling her that danger is coming. There is a dark spot in her mind where memories might have been, only when she tries to think through the darkness, all she gets is *sorrow*.

"Zanthi," he says, soft as moonlight. "Come to the Gardens. Bathe in the springs. It'll help."

The thought of bathing in the Gardens, with its wild pools and deep waters, makes her stomach tight. She does not want to sink into dark waters. Not even lovely, warm, healing ones.

But Madoc is looking at her, mouth curved in invitation. She has kissed that mouth. The thought is sweet. She has kissed Madoc Casca. She has delved under the river. She has defied the Luminaries and had tea with Ethram Hart. This cannot be any more terrifying.

She does not want to refuse. She wants to be brave enough.

"Very well," she says, and he smiles. "I'll come."

It is darkening when they enter the Gardens through a discreet door in the wall near the carriage house. Zanthi ducks under the thick grape vines, the gate bell chiming gently amongst the leaves, and the air changes against her lips. The evening is sweet with damp moss and sweet thyme.

As if summoned by the gate bell, a pair of nightingales flit from the trees. Madoc beckons one over.

"We're going to bathe," he tells them, and the nightingale, a solemn-looking creature with a long, ribbon-worked plait, nods and passes over their lantern. He rests a hand on the small of Zanthi's back, barely touching as he ushers her on. "Better? The effect is stronger in the water."

"It's already soothing my headache."

"I sometimes think half of Esk would be aethersick as a matter of course, if the springs weren't here, seeping through the stone."

It aligns too closely with her thoughts in the carriage. All of Esk washing away under an overspill of aether, until every last person wastes away, heart failing and breath rasping. She has seen the truly aethersick a few times in her life, the ones that pass a point that even the spring water cannot heal. It is a slow, inelegant death. Her mind catches on that horror, and then Madoc is there, taking her hand.

"None of that," he says. "You can write your thoughts down later. The pool is just ahead."

"I haven't any bathing dress. Maybe I could just put my feet in."

"You could," he says, all promise. "But it's best without any dress at all."

And like a heady draught of wine, her mind is entirely full of the night they first met. The way the steam had clung to his skin. The water pattering onto the moss. His invitation.

His smile crooks, as if he knows exactly what she's thinking.

The path dives into a deep hollow of trees and emerges again in a familiar glade. She breathes in her surprise. Steam hangs low across silk waters, and small whispers creep through the night, distant and indistinct. The stream, trickling. A cricket trilling in the hedge. All of it sheltered, secret. Vervain scents the air, and wind-struck leaves drift across the water's surface. The starlight drifts too, glinting like a dusting of gemstones.

She pauses, taking in the sight. "I must have gotten very turned around to have stumbled across this place."

"I thought a nightingale had snuck you in. It was my best guess how you got here." He slips his velvet coat from his shoulders, hanging it carelessly aside. The air is warm, dense, and she loosens her own vest.

All his movement is grace as he crouches by the pool and trails his fingers through the water like he's greeting it. The faintest shimmer dances in his wake. When he flicks his finger, the water vanishes into the air. She certainly doesn't catch any ripples of falling drops.

He doesn't notice any of it. "The water isn't too deep, but the natural pools do shift, so be careful when you're in. I won't be far away."

She takes off her boots and stockings to dip her toes in the water. The aether fades from her skin as easily as wet ink washes away. Despite her trepidation, she has a strong urge to jump into the delightful warmth. “Is this a poor time to tell you I can’t swim?”

“Truly? I should pick a shallower pool for you, then.”

The shallower pools, she thinks, are not so private, not so sheltered, and not at all secret. She doesn’t want another pool. She wants this one. Only she doesn’t want to be alone in the waters, either.

“Or you could join me,” she says, because darkness makes her bold. “Just for the bathing.”

“Or that,” he says easily. His gaze dips from her face, down the length of her, and then he’s turning away. He pulls at his shirt collar, barely a tug, and it falls apart under his fingers. The steam is pressing his hair into loose curls against his forehead, and it springs back tangled when he pulls his shirt over his head. “If you don’t mind sharing.”

His naked back is a revelation, and she stares until she realises she’s denying him the same courtesies he’s giving her.

“If I minded, I wouldn’t have said anything,” she says, turning away, and she catches his laugh.

She undresses, slipping her buttons free. A light-headed haze has hold of her, and she can’t help but smile as her skirt falls to the moss, and her blouse after it. She’s down to her slip, wondering whether to halt there or take it all off, when the water shifts with a gentle sound. She turns.

He’s entirely bare in the starlight, slipping into the pool. He dives under, and when he surfaces, water runs down the back of his neck.

She catches her startled breath. Well, then. All it is.

Her slip falls to the moss, too. The air is strange against her bare skin, damp and soft. She slips into the water behind him until she’s covered to her shoulders, and steam wraps around her neck. It’s achingly hot. It’s *bliss*.

Madoc turns at her satisfied sigh. Steam darkens his eyelashes, dampens his cheeks. He should look ridiculous, all sodden like that.

Instead, he looks as if he has grown from the moss and stone itself, as if he has been crafted to sit here with water clinging to his skin and nothing else.

"Good?"

She is keenly aware that she is naked, and so is he. She could reach out and touch him, feel his skin beneath her palm. Her heart thuds like a distant storm rumbles, threatening. "How do you not spend all your time here?"

"I very nearly do." He moves closer, and the water swirls around her.

Every bit of skin, every curve and point of her, is aware of where he is, and where he is not. As if she is dreaming, she reaches for his hand, finds his wrist, his lithe fingers, his hand turning palm-to-palm with hers. He catches her hand, draws her in deeper. Somehow, in all the heat of the water, his touch feels like a flame to her skin.

"Trust me?" he says, a damp whisper at the curve of her ear. "I want to show you something."

There is very little she would deny him in this moment, and so she nods, wordless. He guides her back, and she's falling, but the water balances her, lifting her up. It licks at her ears and her hair, until her hair fans out, floating, and is weightless. All of her is as light as air. She closes her eyes and breathes out the tight clench of fear in her throat.

Madoc's hands are still there, a light touch under her shoulders, and so she knows he is there too, somewhere behind her in the darkness. She is not alone.

Her toes crest free of the water, and her knees. Her thighs. The swell of her breasts and her stomach, too. She knows that if Madoc is looking, he might see all of her.

"Look up," he says, softly.

She does, and her world becomes nothing but the sky above.

It's a great painting of a sky, trimmed with the moth-bitten lace of the night-dark trees, and vast and generous with stars. She feels she could be falling upwards into that velvet dark, as if Madoc's touch is the only thing anchoring her.

"Oh." She forgets all about her knees and her toes. "I think I haven't spent nearly enough time looking at the stars."

"I'll never tire of the sight. I was very upset, once, when I was told I'd never be allowed to board an airship."

His palms press against her shoulders, though she barely needs him to hold her. She relaxes into the water, and it holds her all on its own. She stops thinking of the water entirely. The stars glitter through a thin veil of cloud, and a single falling streak of silver makes her breath catch. She doesn't know any of the names, can't pick a constellation from the sheer abundance of stars. Such strangeness doesn't matter. That they are without meaning to her does not make them any less beautiful.

And yet, Madoc would know their names if she asked him. She's sure of it. He would know so many things, if only she asked him.

"Come," he says, and she falls back into herself. "You'll get cold."

That seems an impossibility, with the water as warm as it is, but his hands gently turn her, bringing her back to him. Her feet find the sand at the bottom of the pool. The water laps nearly at her chin, though it doesn't reach his shoulders. He has very fine shoulders. He smiles, catching her gaze, and she finds herself following a droplet of water running down his cheek and around the handsome curve of his jaw.

She wonders if she kisses him, if he'll taste of the water.

The smile fades. "Stay along the shallower edge," he says. He steps back into deeper water. It's abrupt how quickly he moves apart from her.

Perhaps some of her thoughts had shown on her face. Perhaps they were not welcome.

At the edge of the pool, the natural stone makes an underwater bench, and she can sit with her head pillowed on the mossy bank. She closes her eyes and curls up, content to enjoy the warmth. The aether aches bleed from her until there's just the memory of them left.

She'd be content to stay for hours, but it hasn't been nearly that long before he gets out, water cascading onto the moss as he fetches a set of robes that hadn't been there earlier. Nightingales had delivered them, she assumes. She pulls herself out after him, her body weary and heavy in the air. It's not cold, exactly, but she wraps herself in the robe gratefully. Being bare in the pool wasn't uncomfortable, but she doesn't like it now. She gathers her clothes, slipping back into them as well as she can. Water drips down her back, and then Madoc is behind her, hands at her neck, gathering up her wet hair into a plait.

He doesn't speak, and she wonders if she should. But what could she say?

Heat brushes the nape of her neck. Madoc, pressing a kiss to her bare skin.

It all becomes too much. The kiss in her room. The carriage. The sight of his body, damp to the skin. His fingers, now, skating down her arms, over her clothes.

It does not take much to imagine them against her skin, like they had been in the pool.

She has never wanted someone the way she wants him. She has never wanted *anyone* before him.

"Madoc," she says, and she barely recognises her own voice.

"I know." His fingers brush against her cheek. She doesn't dare turn around. "Not yet."

Not yet, but *what* not yet? Another kiss?

He steps away. When she turns, he's bundling their damp robes over his arm. "It'll soon be midsummer. I'll be scarce for a time, after."

"After, then," she says, and now she doesn't know what she's asking for, either.

But his smile is small and honest as he agrees. "After, I will tell you all the things I haven't yet told you."

"You are as much a mystery to me as the stars," she says. "I cannot keep pace with your friendship."

"I do not think we are friends, exactly. Do you?"

"I cannot think what else we could be. You are well known for kissing your friends."

"That's not why I kissed you."

They are close again. They keep being close.

"Then why did you kiss me?" She reaches up, slowly, and tangles her fingers in his collar. He does not move. She tugs him down. Kisses him like she'd thought of kissing him when they had been bathing. He tastes of the springs, warm and earthy, and then he pulls away.

"Not here," he says, voice low. "Not here. Not now."

He takes her hand, pulls her fingers free from his collar, and runs his own across her palm before he places her hand back at her side. He's shadow-eyed and solemn in the steam drifts.

"Midsummer best, Zanthi," he says, though midsummer is still weeks away. He's looking at her like she's as distant and as unreachable as the stars above them. "Fortune's blessing."

"Fortune's blessing," she echoes.

He'd come to her house that afternoon to ask her to tea, and now he was telling her not to come back. He had cradled her in the waters, and now he was sending her away.

It is not quite a rejection, and yet it is.

It hits like one.

Chapter Fifteen

It is Theron's turn to make breakfast, and so the toast is burnt. She barely notices, because as soon as she sits down, Fletcher holds out a letter.

"You've been making friends." It's a tone that brooks trouble.

When she flips the envelope to see the name, she almost drops it. *Ethram Hart*. She had sent him a copy of her original paper last week, the morning after their visit. She hadn't expected a reply.

"He's a bit old for you, isn't he, sweetheart?"

Theron is listening. She can tell because he's still stirring his tea even though he never takes honey in it. He's not asking because he's still ignoring her, but he's listening like the nosy weasel he is. He'd been waiting up for her when she'd got back late after bathing at the Gardens. He'd pretended he hadn't, but she'd seen the light under his door, and the way it had turned out when she'd come upstairs.

"You're not as amusing as you think," she tells Fletcher. "I asked him some professional questions, is all."

"He's not known for being so obliging. Must have been quite some sweet talking."

"Besides, he's not really all that old," she carries on. "I thought he'd be older, but he looked barely into his thirties."

"You've visited him?" He narrows his eyes, trying to decide if she's teasing.

"He makes a nice pot of tea."

Theron's spoon clatters onto his saucer. "Who?"

"Oh, he speaks," says Fletcher. "Fancy that."

Zanthi peels the letter open. "Professor Hart," she says, and promptly ignores whatever her brother says next. Hart's letter just says, '*I have questions,*' and has the name of a tea shop, a time, and today's date. "Ah," she says.

"What does he want?"

"To get tea," she says, shoving the last of the toast in her mouth. "Must be fond of it, I suppose."

They both call after her like the insufferable gossips they are, but she's already leaving. There will be an interrogation later, no doubt. She hasn't time for it now. Hart has requested tea at ten o'clock, which doesn't give her much time.

It is a test. She will not fail it.

Hart is sitting at a terrace table in a second-floor tearoom in the old town quarter. It is very much a society spot, this place. He is dressed like a society man, too, all tailored trousers and a fine lawn shirt with an embroidered silk neck scarf. There's a summer coat hanging over the back of his chair, and when she nears, she sees his expensive boots that cling to his calves. It is a world away from the corduroy and jumper he had been wearing at his cottage.

"Who are you trying to impress?" She takes a seat. She's probably not dressed right for such an establishment.

Hart gives a cool smile. "You're not my only appointment today." He glances at the clock. "Aren't you prompt, though? Nicely done, Ilyston." He places a folio on the table. Her own folio, with her paper inside. "It's a good start. You'd do well to heed my notes."

Inside, his comments are scrawled in a looping, grey ink. "Thank you," she says, stunned.

"With significant edits to the proposal, and at least two major sources, you could submit this study for your first band."

"It would be wasted effort," she says. "I'm no longer a student."

"Then why did you send it to me?" He gestures to a server. "Be honest, Ilyston, at least with yourself. You haven't given up on the Luminary robes."

She is saved from answering by the server asking their tea preferences. By the time they have ordered, she's gotten herself settled once more. "You said you had questions."

"I have three," says Hart. "Answer them honestly." His burns are visible, peeking under his cuff, and she keeps coming back to them. They've scarred, so the wound must have been terrible when it first branded his skin. Aether burns usually fade with time. "Your paper is dated, I think. There is nothing in it of these friezes you found, and very little of your thoughts on Esk's founding god. Why have you not given me a copy of your current work?"

Zanthi presses her lips together. Hart looks at her evenly. He's not quite meeting her eyes, but he's looking so near enough that it's easy to pretend he is. "Half of my current work is speculation, and the rest has dubious sources at best."

"Ah, the Casca boy. What is the story there?"

"Is that one of your questions?"

"I won't insist on your honesty, no."

"There isn't a story, anyway. He asked me to search the archives for records about the Gardens."

"And then?"

"He—" She stops. There's a betraying heat in her cheeks. What had happened next? They kept finding each other, is what. A clasp, a key, a kiss, a dismissal. She doesn't know what to call it.

Ethram laughs. It's a strangely young sound, at odds with his dour words. "Some things are no mystery, after all," he says. "So, the current state of your work includes whatever you've turned up with Casca." He pauses, tapping the table. "Indeed, you can't publish any Gardens secrets. We'll have to think our way around that."

The server appears, loading their table with steaming teapots and a generous plate of small cakes. He offers them the option of lunch, roasted pike, and river greens, and Ethram dismisses him with a sharpness that even Zanthi finds startling.

"Not a fan of fish?" she hazards.

"Fervently against, in fact," he says. He pours his tea. The scent of it wafts across the table towards her. "Such river fish were sacred, once. I find myself reluctant to blaspheme."

"Were they? Sacred to whom?"

"That, Ilyston, is what you intend to find out, isn't it?"

"Have you come across anything on the subject?"

He tips his head back, gazing at the ceiling for a moment. He sighs. "I have," he says. "It is nothing I can talk about. You will find, as you delve deeper, that there is a strange manner of forgetting some things in Esk. I've never seen the like of it anywhere else in the archipelago, but here it is around every corner."

"Then how am I meant to discover anything?"

He smiles. "I am not Eskan-born," he says. It is a strange thing to say, the sort of information no one would freely offer, but he tips his head at her in a telling way, and she understands.

"You're western-born."

"I am. I recognised your eyes as soon as I saw you as a child. Witch-eyes, I would have called them, once."

"And what might you call them now?"

"Exceedingly useful. You as good as told me you can see aether, Ilyston."

She swallows. "Something like that."

"And you can walk into the archives at will. Do you know why most do not venture down there?"

"They are not allowed."

His laugh is dry. "There's no stricture against going deeper into those passages, no matter what the head archivist says—is it still Acanthus? Old grouch. No, Ilyston. There is old magic in that stone, and it keeps people out. None but the dead walk there. And don't give me that look. I know what I speak of. Most people could not stir their feet to get more than a yard down those tunnels, and of those that can, nearly all would be driven half out of their senses within an hour or two."

She wants to debate it, but she thinks of Orrey's face, pale and strung-out in the darkness. She's always known it has bothered others more than it's ever bothered her. Joren had told her it was unusual, the first time he had visited her.

"But you walked down there."

"Strung all over in warding charms and little superstitions from all over the isles," he admits. "It did me no good in the end."

"You think that my nature will allow me to see what others can't?"

"I certainly hope so." He gestures to the cakes, prompts her to take one. "Last question. I wish to know who you're working for. If you weren't picked up, you are no longer a scholar."

She swallows her mouthful. "I'm employed as a Crown clerk, under Secretary Fairthorne."

"Hm," he says, contemplative. "Surmountable. Certainly, better than the alternative."

"And that is?"

Hart takes a cake himself. "Do you know of the Landen Trading Company?"

The name is familiar, but in the end, she shakes her head, unable to place it. "I know of its existence. I have never met Landen."

"Don't, would be my suggestion. He'd have far too much interest in those eyes of yours."

She eats another cake, considering this. "Then he has an interest in the obscure?"

"That is a delightfully vague way of terming it. *The obscure*. But yes, he does, and I am thankful that you found me first."

"You didn't make it entirely easy."

A flash of amusement softens the angles of his face. "I think we will work well together. Now, I have some sources for you to investigate, if you please to do so."

Zanthi is caught on the *work well together*. She's not sure she's understanding it quite right.

"First, a volume on the mythological river systems of the underworld. I believe the translated title is most commonly *The Silent Springs*. It is rare, but I know your brother has it. How are you with ancient languages?"

"Poor," she admits.

"No matter. He'll likely help you if you need it. Second, a book of poetry by the poet Lydus. If you must read a translation, pick Ode. Tasen's work is rubbish, loses all the nuance."

She pulls her pen from her satchel and jots down the suggestions on the front page of her folio.

Hart makes an approving sound. "If you insist on delving into Esk's ancient history, I can tell you that of the small number of texts available to you, these are the two that will give you the truth. May you make better sense of it than I did."

"Pardon, Professor. I am not misunderstanding your intentions here, am I?"

"I should hope not." He slides over a small cream folder. It is the size of a letter. "I have another appointment to make, but don't hesitate to write if you have any further questions."

She opens it. Inside is a formal offer of mentorship. Hart has an unruly hand, the ink slash-dark and cutting across the page with no respect for margins or lines. But it has his university seal at the end. It has her *name*.

She can't manage a sound. Her words have flown from her mind.

"I expect good sense from you, Ilyston. Don't disappoint me." He rises, picking up his coat from the back of the chair. "I'll make it official this afternoon. I hope you didn't discard your robes too quickly."

Her heart is barely daring to beat. She can't look away from her name, twirled in Hart's hand. *Sopharion Zanthi Ilyston.*

In the moment before she glances up, her side-sight flares, sharp and blazing. Pearlescent apparitions twist against Hart, following him as he leaves. They eddy in the wake of his passage, as close to him as his shadow. Silver-not-silver. Almost like fish.

Chapter Sixteen

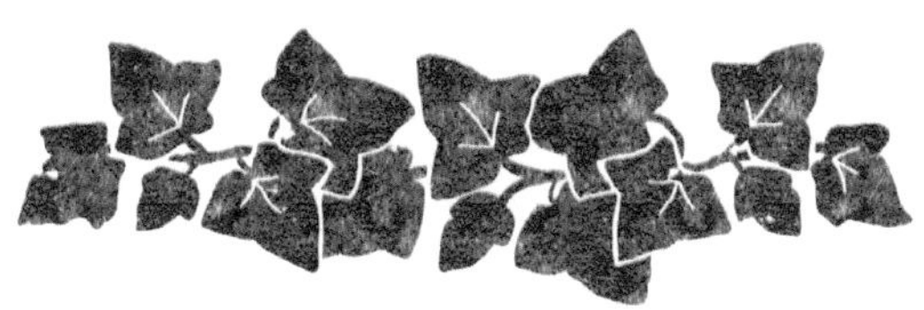

There is mail in the hall when she gets home. She clutches her offer to her chest and calls out, but there is only silence. Fletcher must be out. Theron, too.

She swallows back disappointment. "Here, Susan," she calls, and Susan lifts her head from her resting place at the bottom of the stairs. Susan sniffs the air when Zanthi holds up the offer, then slouches across the bottom of the stairs, unimpressed. "Ah, well. Someone is bound to be excited for me, eventually."

She's far more animated when Zanthi flicks through the stack of letters and finds the cream envelope of an airguard missive. "Chester has written," she says, and Susan's tail wags, once. "Come, help me raid Theron's study, and then I'll light the parlour hearth."

She does as she promises and curls up to read the first of Hart's suggestions, with Susan at her feet. She's struggling through the first chapter when the front door creaks. She keeps reading until the parlour door swings in, and the room is suddenly rather more crowded.

Theron peers over her shoulder. "Is that my copy of *The Silent Springs*?"

"Yes," she says. "I couldn't find Ode's translation of Lydus, though. Do you not have it?"

"I didn't think poetry was your style." He drops his gloves on the side table. "No, I know it's not."

"Well, maybe it is now."

"And haven't you read it before?"

She has, but it had been a few years back, and it hadn't had any relevance to her interests then. To be fair, other than the title, it doesn't seem entirely relevant now, either. It's not about springs, really. It's about the underworld.

She'd studied the folklore of the underworld until she'd moved on to researching antiquity. The underworld beliefs were notable in the folklore faction for being the most persistent and consistent mythology across the archipelago. From the witch-fearing West Isles to the rebellious northern islets, to the far-flung east and beyond, all agreed that beyond death, there was an upriver and a downriver. The name of the river changed, or there were many rivers, or a sea or a tide, but there was always water. There was always a way to be lost.

Even now, lovers in Esk would 'tie the ribbons' in marriage so their souls could find one another in the afterlife, and it was a ritual that none took lightly. It bound them entirely, life and death, and there was no undoing it.

No one tied the ribbons unless they were very sure of their lover's heart.

"Mm," she says, tucking those thoughts away. They make her own heart sore, in a way she didn't know it could be. "I've been tasked with reading it again." She holds out the letters. One to Theron, one to Fletcher.

"Oh, Chester has wri—" Fletcher starts, and is cut off by Theron's curse.

"Hart? You've been picked up by *Hart*?"

Fletcher looks at Zanthi in dawning delight. "You've been picked up?"

"By *Hart*," Theron adds, as if this qualifier is important.

"No one would be enough to please you. Just as her having no one hasn't pleased you either. This is excellent news. Well done!"

Theron drops the letter on the side table with the sort of obnoxious drama that makes her think he is, in fact, excited for her after all. "Well. It's *something*, I suppose. Has he opinions on your proposal?"

"He's given me comments."

"I'll read them. Make sure he's worth your time."

"You can keep your nose out of it," she says.

"Zanthi."

"*Theron*."

He raises his face to the ceiling, as if praying for patience. "Fine. May I please read the comments?"

She considers him. "Buy me the volume of Lydus, and I'll let you read them."

"I don't need to. I have it." He frowns, as if trying to remember where it might be. "I'll buy you something else instead."

She smiles, though she tries very hard to hide it. It seems their fight is over, if Theron is apologising. It's a very Theron apology, but she's used to those. "Very well. I accept."

"May I read Chester's letter now?" says Fletcher, entirely amused.

Fletcher has a flair for reading that neither Zanthi nor Theron can rival. He has them tense through Chester's account of a summer in the east, full of hacking at stormbeasts and weathering deluges of aether. But the usual harrowing tales are followed by welcome news. This year, Chester will be returning home early. Theron crouches by Susan, scratching behind her ears, and looks entirely cheered.

"It will be a busy Season," Fletcher says, when he's done. "Are you joining in this year, Zanthi?"

"No," she says, as she says every year. "Leave me out of your preparations."

Even if Fletcher and Theron don't quite do the circuit Chester does, there are still dinner parties and book readings and recitals and academic debates. Exhausting, all of it.

"Really?" Fletcher settles on the arm of her chair. "I thought your answer might have changed."

Had it changed? If Madoc had kissed her in the springs, if he'd done *more*, would it have changed? She doesn't think so. She tips her face up. "I wouldn't join a Society ball if the First Heir himself asked me," she says, quite sincerely, and Fletcher laughs.

"Careful," he says. "Chester could arrange that for you."

Zanthi shoves him off the arm. "Chester would never," she says. "Chester is the nice one."

Fletcher upends the entire chair in retaliation, tipping her to the carpet. He settles the chair back and sits down, looking smug. She gives him a rude gesture.

"Oh really? And Theron?"

"The clever one."

He grins, sharp. "And I?"

"The other one," she says, and dodges the glove he throws at her.

Theron wisely leaves the room before they can rope him into the ensuing squabble.

Theron delivers her his copy of Lydus, though he takes half a day to find. It is finally discovered shoved at the back of a shelf, behind the desk, and she finds out why in short order. The poetry is opaque in many ways, and stunningly explicit in others. Quite a lot about verdant crowns and blessed libations, with lurid verses on devotion that make her blush.

She takes days to wade through it. There is a secret hidden amongst the decadent words, but no matter how many times she reads it, she cannot find it. She's frowning over a painfully longing poem, dictionary in hand, when Theron lets himself into her room. He sits at her desk.

"Enjoying the poetry?"

"It's rather suggestive, isn't it?" she says, putting the book aside. "One could almost imagine it was written about the nightingales at the Gardens."

"Could one?" Theron says, flicking through the notes on her

desk. It's all raw research and quite unintelligible. "You've been expanding your theories. Hart will have his work cut out, keeping up with you."

"Do you mind so much?"

"Hart? No. Your work is well-suited to his expertise, and his manner is well-suited for your particular obstinacies." His mouth twitches, even as he reads. "I imagine your partnership will be a formidable force in the years to come."

"Something to look forward to when you've clawed your way to the top of the heap."

He sighs, like he always does when she claims he'll be chancellor one day. "Don't even joke." He closes her journal. "You're truly decided against participating in the Season?"

"Why would my answer have changed from any other year?"

"You didn't have tea dates with Madoc Casca on any other year."

She still hasn't been on an actual tea date with Madoc Casca, but she greatly suspects Theron is attempting to use the phrase as a euphemism. She's not about to explain how he's wrong. She's certainly not going to tell him about Madoc's curt and abrupt farewell in the Gardens.

"I don't see how that applies to anything."

"What is going on between the two of you?"

Nothing is a true answer, but it feels dishonest. That moment of bathing, the moment *after*, hadn't been nothing. "I'll tell you when I know."

"Just don't get in the papers," he mutters. "Hart stopped by my office today to pass this on."

He throws a small envelope at her. Inside are two keys on a university fob chain. She dangles them, giving him a questioning glance.

"The small one is for Hart's office. He says you may take it, as he never makes use of it. But be quiet about it."

"The other?"

"He did not elaborate on that one."

She checks the envelope. There's a thin line of writing under the flap.

Listen to your instincts.

There is only one door it could be for. She's not sure how he got her an archive key. She's not sure *why*.

"The university is in uproar about it already. Hart's never taken a sopharion student before," Theron says. "Does it affect your work for the Crown?"

"Joren is pleased. It works better for him, as I have a greater scope of access. Professor Hart doesn't care if I continue to take research and collect the university allowance at the same time." She pauses. "In fact, he suggested it."

"He would." He's amused.

"Theron—" she begins, but her brother shakes his head.

"No," he says. "Let's not. You've clearly shown me your research is valuable to more than one important patron. And you were right. I didn't help you as well as I might have. I should have put you onto Ethram myself, as he so sternly told me. So, consider me scolded."

She hides a smile at the thought of Theron suffering Ethram's sharpness. "I can pay my costs now."

"And if you are paying your costs, then what am I working for?" His mouth turns wry. "Put it aside, Zanthi. The river only knows what you'll need it for, if you keep going along so chaotically." He stands, and claps his palms together. "Now, come on. I believe I owe you a book or two, don't I? How about we go to the Reed Bed and see what is new on the shelves?"

It settles down after that. The *Society Papers* mark the annual closing of the Gardens with a note in the event pages. Theron glances at her, a question in his face, but she has no answer for him. Madoc has not written. She tries not to think too much about him. Not in the light of day, in any case.

Sometimes, in the dark of night, she thinks of stars in the sky and in the water, and tea-scented steam. Wrens by the window. Lips against her neck. Midsummer crawls closer, and the nights grow shorter and darker than ever.

Life trundles on. She has her scholar robes back, with the added gold band of a sopharion. The Luminary board isn't happy that Hart is encouraging her heretical research, but that is now Hart's battle to fight, not hers. She has nothing to do but chase myths and dig through the metaphorical mud of old stories and records.

Everything is almost perfect.

Chapter Seventeen

Midsummer dawns with a clinging heat, thick and unbearable. It builds through the morning until Zanthi almost wishes she could dive into the icy Lune with the rest of the festivalgoers. By the time afternoon comes around, she is desperate to escape the warmth and the noise of the growing festivities.

On midsummer, the town bells are silent, probably because nothing else could be heard over the cacophony of wooden clappers and drums. All the town is garlanded in oak and honeysweet, and all the people are garlanded in river-green or blue. Even Zanthi ties her hair with a green ribbon.

One of her recent purchases was an old edition of Hart's book on midsummer traditions throughout the archipelago, and she's read it cover to cover. He has a lot to say about Esk's midsummer festival, though if he knows any secrets about the Gardens' mysterious celebrations, he didn't put them down in ink.

Midsummer celebrates the Lune. The life-giver and soul-bearer, the marriage ribbon that binds Esk together. At sunset, a procession winds from the House to the river, ending with a plunge into the Lune's summer-gentled waters. It is strange, though, that Esk's oldest and richest festival doesn't celebrate the springs or the healing waters.

Just the river. A beloved and important river, but just a river.

When she heads for the university, the scatter of pleasure-rafts and river boats are visible all down the Lune. On the far bank, the river path is crowded with stalls of dried fruit and syrup-sweet jellies. She can hear the noise of it even from up on the hill. She can summon the memory of the scent and taste, and she smiles. When she'd been younger, her brothers would take her along the path, start to end, and let her eat her fill.

It's tempting, for a moment, to go explore, but she has other plans. Midsummer evening is one of the only times the university is sparsely occupied, and she intends to put her illicit archive key to use.

Hart has not acknowledged that he had given it to her, and so she had not asked. She suspects the key is Hart's own, that he has held onto for years. Certainly, no scholar should have such a thing, but Hart is not a scholar that cares much for what others think he should be doing.

She has chalk, charcoals, her rosemary cloak, and her journal. She intends to make a proper documentation of the pointing figure at the head of the procession, and some estimation as to the scale of it.

The university is crypt-silent and empty. Her footsteps echo in the vault, ringing off the rows and rows of empty desks. Perhaps everyone is off enjoying boat rides and violet apples. Perhaps Esk is still more devout than she thought.

The silence weighs heavier down in the archive. Stillness haunts everything, a breathless sort of absence. No one else is here. Her footsteps ring on the stone, her lantern sending out its familiar peach glow to dance alongside her. She cuts a swift path along the river tunnel, and the water echoes are muted and distant. She's turning down a familiar path, towards the friezes, when cold crawls up her back.

The feeling rises, clawing at her neck, her scalp. She glances behind her. It is as it always is, and yet, there is a strangeness too, as if things are not lining up as neatly as they once did. Even her heartbeats don't seem to line up as they should. The dark judders, as if it has been disturbed.

The darkness shifts.

She turns, but there is nothing. Cold stone paths, cold stone walls. Shadows stretch from her aether light, turning as she turns, circling her.

And a bell is ringing. There should be no bells. It is midsummer, and no bells are rung.

And yet, she can hear it, distant and unceasing, echoing behind her heartbeats, aching in that part of her mind that is darker than the deepest archives. She realises with sharp alarm that there are no bells ringing, except in that dark place in her mind where there aren't any memories at all.

She steps forward and knows immediately that she has stepped off her path. Her lantern flickers, and she holds it high. Forges on, one step at a time. Darkness seeps down the walls of the passage. Cold, dark water.

She stumbles forward, into a chamber she has never seen before.

The walls press in, close, and when she turns, her light skips shadows along the carvings that decorate the chamber, floor to ceiling. It is a tapestry of carvings. More figures, like the ones in the vaulted passage. At the heart of the gathering, a tall, elegant figure holds a hand aloft. The face is gone, lost to time, but she sees the arch of a stern brow, a noble nose. Their hair is long and drifting. Above their head is a stylised star. She's seen that star before. It is a god-star, used in ancient art to denote a celestial figure.

There is grace and strength in their body, and a frisson of a threat, too, in the way the head tilts, as if watching. Waiting. And she is sure the dark is listening to her. She steps forward. Her boots grate against the sand, and the echoes ripple around her. Her voice falls dead and dull in the air. The question is spoken before she thinks better of it.

"What is your name?"

The memory hits her, as sudden and startling as wash-water on a winter's morning.

Fish scales slipping from her hands. Darkness. Something lost in the water, taken from her. And strong arms swinging her up. Being held against a stranger's chest. The roughness of a university robe like her mother's, but it is not her mother.

Hart? It must be a memory from her childhood.

She wades through the dark spot in her mind, flicking through memories like catalogue cards. *Little fish.* Wet from head to toe. Aether burns shaped like fingermarks. Bells knelling. Always, always, the sound of a river.

Rivers and gateways to the underworld. Upriver and down. Ivy for endurance and devotion, and communion with the gods.

Ivy for midsummer.

The faint sounds of the festival drip through the streets and echo through the dark. And then a sound, closer and sharper. A stone-and-metal scrape that claws at her spine. Zanthi goes still all through. She is not alone in the archives, and her instincts are telling her to run, to hide, *hide, hide*.

And then she looks at that shining, crowned figure, and the fear fades away to nothing.

Forward, her thoughts say.

So, she goes forward. She creeps into the dark. It's hard, with the echoes, to hunt down the sound, but once she falls back into the vaulted passage, it rings louder than the midsummer racket. Loud, like the stone is screaming each time the metal gouges it.

Her heart is pounding. She twists her aether lantern to darkness and peers around the turn of the passage. There, in a flickering pool of aetherlight, a man is gouging at the passage wall, marking it with a chisel. His companion, standing beside him with a lantern, looks into the dark as if seeking something. Looks at her.

The lantern light swings around, and Zanthi turns and runs. She doesn't get far. Her braid snaps taut against her scalp, tearing her body backwards. She slips, boots skidding, and slams on her backside, hard.

Her captor forces his boot down on her chest. "Where the fuck did you come from?"

She tries to scramble away. His boot is wet, covered in mud, soaking through her blouse as he presses down. The fall has forced the breath from her, and the last of it gasps from her mouth.

"University?"

She nods. Her vision swims.

"Thought that was locked down," his companion says.

He pulls her up, throwing her back against the passage wall. He smells of salt, and he's dressed like a trader, wind-worn coat and leather belt. But it's his face that sends a chill through Zanthi. His eyes are wide and glazed, as if they're not seeing much at all, and he's twitching like a rabbit hearing the hunt near. His companion holds their one lantern, pulling in close. They fear something.

The chisel glints in his hand, but he doesn't seem overly concerned about threatening her with it. He keeps darting looks into the dark. "You tell me one thing, girl. You know the way out?"

"Yes," she says, and her voice is hoarse. She braces herself against the wall, looks at her feet.

"We keep going in circles. Been hours and hours. Days? I don't know." His voice blurs, going soft as an echo and fading back again. He pulls something from his pocket, slaps it into her hand. "You recognise this?"

It's a token. A coil of dread unwinds through her chest. Her whole body crawls with unease, like when she had held the vial of strange aether and blood. Everything in her wants to get away from him.

"We're with the Landen Trading Company. We pay our friends well," the man says. "And we're harsh to those who get in our way, understand?"

"I understand," she says. Her breath rattles. Her chest is aching. "I can show you back to the university."

His gaze is fervid in the lantern light, bright and feverish. "Not there. The way we came in. This is a cursed place full of cursed things. I'll not listen to any tricks."

She glances at the marks they've left in the wall and the aching dread inside her turns knife-sharp. She recognises those marks. She had seen them the first time she was in the archives, months ago. How many people had been down here, in those intervening months? How many lost explorers?

When she turns back, she looks him in the eyes. His dark-haunted face goes pale in shock, and she realises her mistake. Trader clothes, curses, salt. He's from the west.

He raises his chisel, the sharp edge glinting towards her. "*Witch*," he spits. "Another cursed thing from the dark, then? Won't trick me, river sprite."

He reaches for her, and her decision is barely a thought before she's acting on it. She dives for the lantern, grabbing it in her bare hand. Cold glass and burning aether flare across her palm, and she wrenches it down to smash over the stones. The sound shatters off the walls, glass on glass on glass.

She hurls herself into the darkness, runs for the hidden Gardens path she knows is ahead. There will be help at the other end. *Safety.* She scrambles up the rubble pile and squeezes through the gap. If the gods are kind, then it will be too small for them to follow.

Her knees tear on the stone, and then she's through, tumbling into the thick black of the other side.

Light shines through the gap. The rock groans, then a roar rattles the dark as stone slips free. They're breaking through. She has to get to the door. To the Gardens.

The thought has her on her feet again and running straight into the dark. And it is dark, darker than she thought possible. And the bell is ringing, ringing, ringing.

Not a single rock rises to trip her, no walls leap from the darkness. Her feet take her straight to the steps and through the door, into the spikes of the hawthorn hedge before she's able to stop. Her harsh breaths cave her chest and she slumps against the door, wedging it closed. From the dark behind it, there is only silence. Gently, the echoes of the bells fade from her mind.

Safe. But she must warn someone that there are people in the archives below the Gardens. That she may have led them here.

She fights her way out of the spiked hawthorns. Her blood

pounds and her heartbeat shakes, still out of time. Her breath, when she gets it under control, doesn't fill her chest.

She blames all of it for why she takes so long to hear what is all around her.

Music. Revelry.

The fading light thrums with voices, the air heavy with spiced smoke and burning sap. The cacophony resolves into drumming, singing. A high piping floats clear above it all. It's a strange and lovely tune, beckoning her on.

She is in the Gardens at midsummer.

Chapter Eighteen

The sun is setting, spilling its last velvet light.

Zanthi moves through the grove, chasing the sound of drums. Nightingales are everywhere. Wine soaks their lips, soaks the moss, drips like blood beside their footsteps. They're flocking down through the trees, towards something she can't see. She gathers her rosemary cloak tight around her and follows.

They are gathering near a trickling brook. A woman in a damp linen dress throws handfuls of flowers for the water to carry down to a dark, still pool that glints through the birches. Zanthi creeps among them, but her gaze keeps going to the pool, and the braziers that ring right around it. Eight of them.

Even from up the slope, the air is stained with a herb-rich, sweet smoke that coats her mouth with every breath. The drumming is a drowning beat, so thick she can barely hear. A woman slings her arm around Zanthi's shoulders, dragging her into the cloying warmth of her body. She's dark-haired and grey-eyed, and looks less wine-soaked than her peers. She is wearing a wreath of ivy around her hair, already half-loose and unfurling.

"Songbird?" She peers down. "You should not be here."

"I must talk with Madoc, or Lady Casca. I have something—"

She runs her hand down Zanthi's arm. "Not today. You had best wait at the manor."

"It is urgent. There are people who mean harm, breaking into the Gardens through a hidden passage—Madoc will know what I mean."

"Fret not, no one can enter the Gardens today except those allowed."

"I am here," Zanthi says.

"Oh, so you are." The nightingale bends down, brushes her mouth along Zanthi's jaw in a strange sort of kiss. "Then perhaps you should be here, after all. Enjoy the celebrations, little songbird."

And she is gone, weaving herself into the swaying dance of the crowd. Zanthi searches for a familiar face. Chicory, or Kit. Rowan. Thom, even.

The men will be through the cave-in by now. They might be coming through the door. Gritting her teeth, she forges into the heart of the procession. The nightingales draw her in, crowding around her like she is in an artisan-quarter dance hall. A hot mouth bites at her neck, and hands wind around her waist, but let her go easily when she twists away, cursing. There is laughter, layered and echoed, all around. Each face she sees is wet-mouthed and wine-hazed.

This is the Gardens' fabled midsummer celebrations? Wine and music? Drunkenness and dancing?

She wants to scoff, call it a disappointment, but she cannot help but be caught up in the sway of the dance and push onwards. Her heartbeat thunders with the drums, fills her head, louder and louder. Stumbling past a split-trunked oak, she finds the leader of the revelry.

Madoc. There is ivy in his hair. It twines up his wrists and over his shoulders like it is growing into him. Nightingales tug at his tunic, close around him, and his hands are in another's hair. He is kissing them. It is not a chaste kiss.

She stops in the shadow of the trees.

The drumming quickens, the sun sinks lower. A man grabs

Madoc, pulls him down to his mouth, and Madoc disappears in the growing tumult of dancing. Each nightingale is dressed in draping linen, thin as starlight. Like Madoc, they are crowned in ivy. She can hardly be blending in with her robes, but they are past noticing and past caring.

Tension thrums under all the dancing. It writhes in the music, in that frantic, fearful drumbeat. The nightingales cling to each other like fading souls in the River. They reach desperate hands for Madoc, tugging and pulling at him. He goes where they will him.

This is not a celebration. This is the worship of the Old Ways, and Madoc is leading it like a high priest from an ancient tale.

They kiss him, and kiss him, bestowing each like a blessing, like a devotion. The smoking pyres burn brighter as the night shadows move in, silken and half-speed. The procession winds down towards the fire-edged spring, strung out like the frieze on the archive wall, and she follows.

And then, with a cry, Madoc breaks from the crowd. He's laughing, sprinting the last of the distance, and the leading nightingales give chase like hounds after a stag. They howl like hounds, too, but they don't catch him. She glimpses Chicory, pale hair tangled and damp, and Rowan, face caught in some sort of desperation as he races, as if he can outrun whatever is coming for them. Madoc weaves them around the gardens, faster and faster, until he's flush-cheeked and panting. Until he disappears into the darkness and out of sight.

The crowd surges, carrying her forward. There is no standing against the tide. The nightingales keen—high and exultant, and spill into the glade at the fire-ringed pool.

Sabine Casca stands by the pool, her beautiful face as still as the dark waters. In her hands, she holds a bronze cup, and when Madoc comes to her, she passes it to him.

A shiver runs through the air, and everything stills.

Zanthi creeps closer as the revelry drops from the night. Around her, the nightingales stand with heaving chests, all smoke and wine-scented. It isn't so large a glade inside the birches, and it's brimming over. She can barely breathe. She cranes her neck, stands on her toes. She can't see more of him than shifting linen, and bare skin, and tousled hair all woven through with ivy.

He is speaking, though she has lost sight of him. She can hear his voice, though, clearer and deeper than she's heard it before. The drumming falls to nothing. Silence crashes in. In the sudden stillness, she forces closer, pushing past a tall nightingale, and she can see him again.

In the last fading moments of twilight, Madoc sets the bronze cup to his lips, and drinks. He sways, touches his fingers to his mouth. Glances at his mother once, before turning to the nearest brazier and pouring the last dregs into the coals. It drips like blood, hissing with viscous smoke.

The crowd is still. Breathlessly still, and a hand grasps Zanthi's, holding tight. They're all clutching at each other, all the nightingales. This time, when he speaks, she can hear every word. She knows the words, because everyone knows the words. He is speaking the blessings of the river. He is speaking the words bestowed on the dead.

Dread rises through her, cold and deep as the archives.

He lifts a clasp from his shoulder, and his tunic unravels. Standing there, a long line of bare skin, ivy-crowned and flame-kissed in the light of the brazier, he is beautiful.

And then he steps into the pool, and he falls.

There is nothing graceful about it. He collapses like he has been emptied and is crumpling. The water swallows him without a ripple. Without a sound. He is gone.

She staggers into the nearest body. An arm wraps around her, steadying her, but each face is turned to the waters. Feverish, avid. Unblinking. They all watch, and her heartbeats feel an age apart. Too many ages pass, and the water is still. Minutes pass, and still, no one moves. No one speaks. The arm around her holds her tight, and it is a warning.

She wants to push forward, drag him from the water. Why is no one else moving? And yet, arms hold her tight, and she can do nothing. She remains still, smoke bitter on her lips.

The darkness comes in, sweeps in, a river overflowing its banks. The braziers flicker. As the nearest flame cuts out, there is a moment of expression on Lady Casca's face. Despair, as sharp as any knife.

Only a moment, and then the fire flares back into ferocity.

The water ripples. Madoc breaks through the black mirror of the springs, mouth open and gasping, and the falling water sounds like drums. The nightingales surge ahead, crying out. She catches fragments, all mixed, but the words mean little. Blessings, devotions, affections.

Madoc is laughing, stretching out his arms, and the others go to him. Clothed, unclothed, somewhere between the two states, it does not seem to matter. They fill the springs, and all the night is the crystal sound of water and laughter.

The steam is thick. Someone is kissing his neck. Then the bodies shift, and she has lost him.

She stumbles back. The night empties as more and more nightingales dive into the pool, and she casts about. Sabine is gone. Not into the waters, but into the night. Lydus' poetry is coming to life around her, with all its fervent devotions and blessed libations, and she pushes through the dancing. There has to be someone unwined and un-drunk to listen to her.

When she breaks from the crowd, a pair of nightingales fall into pace beside her. They smile, jostle her in a friendly way.

"Sweet one," says one, running warm fingers along the edge of her ear. "Celebrate with us."

"I need to talk to Lady Casca," she says. She barely remembers why, though. The shock of the encounter in the archives has been faded by the shock of what came after.

The nightingale laughs, blinking bright eyes. Her hair is tangled, as if many hands have run through it already. "She'll have fled somewhere away," she says. "Take our midsummer blessings first?"

"A kiss for the Lord of the Waters," says her companion as they lean in to press a kiss to Zanthi's cheek.

"A kiss for his priest," murmurs the first, kissing her other cheek.

It is becoming increasingly clear that, whatever cursed ceremony she just witnessed, the rest of the evening will follow the sort of trajectory speculated about in the more scandalous gossip sheets. Wine and kisses and people bedding down under the stars. She can barely believe it, even as it is around her with damp, bare bodies and the scent of burning votives. She can think of nothing but that ritual, of Madoc falling beneath the water. It was, she hopes, only a play, acted out with remarkable verity. Wooden stage sets and rehearsals.

Only a performance.

The smoke stings her eyes, and she stumbles on the path. The nightingales catch her, bringing her back to her feet. Gods, she wants more light to see by. The air is too hot. The drumming is ceaseless.

"Thank you," she mutters.

There is no answer. The nightingales look over her shoulder and, like a pair of shadows, melt away. She has barely a moment to wonder why, and then Madoc is there. He's dripping in the spring waters, the heat steaming on his skin. His robe drapes, damp and clinging, and the ivy crown gleams dark in his hair.

"Oh," she whispers. Relief floods her. "Thank the gods. It's you."

He laughs. His pupils are so wide his eyes are almost as dark as hers, the green fled to the slightest ring around the edge. "And it's you," he says. His voice drops low, conspiratorial. "I thought you were a wine-ghost. I thought the river sent a dream to taunt me."

The last words are murmured as he bows to press his lips against her neck. He's certainly wine-tipped, and despite herself, she smiles.

"You smell like the dark places." He makes a dissatisfied noise, nuzzling into her hair. He's leaving her damp, but she hardly notices because he's burning up, fever-hot. "You don't belong to the river."

When one of her brothers comes home so drunk as to speak nonsense, she'll drag their boots off and let them sleep it off on the parlour couch. Madoc isn't wearing boots. He's not looking likely to sleep anytime soon.

All of him, she can feel, is quite awake.

"You're in a state," she says, but she can't help but laugh when his arms wrap around her and lift her, bringing her back into the shadows. He is warm and close against her, and *gods* she had missed him. "You had best go back to your revelry, Madoc."

"Come with me," he murmurs.

"I'll wait here, thank you," she says. He's running his hands up her back and down again, under her cloak. It's a lovely feeling. The thundering in her ears is finally calming. She tucks her face into his shoulder, all that bare skin against her cheek, against her brow, and her mouth. Her next breath is full of the scent of him.

He doesn't smell of any river. He smells of the springs, and pyre-smoke and sweat besides.

"Stay with me," he says, and he's laughing, coaxing. His fingers tug at her blouse, pull it from her trousers. "Promise me you'll stay."

"You told me to go, you know."

"I lied. I want you to stay," he says, and he hums against her temple. Satisfaction, maybe. The way he wraps those fingers along her waist, dips them beneath her trouser band, speaks of something rather more possessive. He backs her up against a birch. Water drips from his hair, runs down his cheek. "Zanthi," he says, and it is soft with longing. "I really did lie."

He bows his head towards hers, and then there is a hand between them, against his lips.

"No." Lady Casca pushes her son's head back. Madoc tips his face away from her. "*Madoc.* Not her. Not tonight."

It must get through to him, through the daze, because his fingers dig into Zanthi's skin, and then he's stepping back, snatching his hands away like they're burning.

"Zanthi Ilyston." Lady Casca says her name like a curse. "You are not supposed to be here."

"I came to warn you," she says, but she hasn't looked away from Madoc. He's reaching for her again, eyes wide and dark, as if he can't help but do so. She pulls her gaze away. "Lady Casca, I need to speak with you."

"I dare say, not in the least about whatever this is," says Lady Casca. She unhooks Zanthi's cloak clasp. It falls away, and Zanthi goes to catch it. Madoc stops her.

"Zanthi." There's no lightness left in him. "What happened?"

She looks down. The boot print is still recognisably a boot print across her front, mud smeared up her throat. There is a button missing, she realises. It hadn't felt so bad at the time. She lifts a hand, as if to cover it, but Madoc takes that too, turning her palm over. The aether burns are stark silver against her skin.

Strange, she didn't even feel them. Whatever power is in the Gardens tonight, it is potent.

"Madoc," Lady Casca says. Her voice is low. "Go back to the festivities. I'll look after this."

Madoc ignores her. He cradles his hand against Zanthi's neck, rubbing at the mud over her collarbones with a gentle touch. "Tell me who did this."

"Madoc," says his mother once more. "She's safe here. Go."

He pulls Zanthi in, presses her against him. His hand against her neck is coal-hot and restless. "I'll stay with her."

Lady Casca is not impressed. "Stay? You are half-drunk with poison and still have most of the night to go on it. It will only get worse, and you have proven you cannot be trusted with her."

Poison. She had known, she thinks, even if she hadn't wanted to know. The fear in the nightingales had been real. The despair on Sabine Casca's face had been real. It had all been real. He had said his own blessings and let the waters take him. And he had come back, somehow. *How*?

The look he gives his mother could draw blood. What Lady Casca says in response is in no language Zanthi knows. It's low and sharp. It's lovely. It's firm. It clearly means something, because Madoc releases Zanthi.

He cups her face instead and presses a kiss to her forehead, mouth hot. He murmurs in that same language, and the look he gives his mother is pure defiance.

Zanthi doesn't understand a word he says, but she can see in his face that he has made a declaration.

Lady Casca breathes out sharply. "You've made your point. Go, Madoc, before I change my mind."

"Zanthi." It's clear he's fighting the poison-induced haze to stay present, and it is not a fight he is winning. "Tell me you're well."

"I'm well," she says. "Go do what it is you do at midsummer."

"I'd rather you with me," he says, slipping his hands into her hair once more, and she doesn't need to have read Lydus to know what he means with that. "I'd rather have you."

She reaches for his other hand and brings it to her mouth. Her kiss is soft, and she lingers a little on the ridges of his knuckles. "A kiss for the Lord of the Waters," she says. "And for his priest." She lets his hand go. "There, take my blessing with you instead."

He dips his head, then catches himself. He laughs, already slipping back into that mania, and Zanthi can't help but think that despite the madness of it, it sits very well on him. He is entirely fey, sloe-eyed, and tangled. He is missing one earring, and the other glints gold as he tips his head down to whisper against her skin.

"I'd do a great many things for your blessing," he says, silken. "Things it would be a blessing to do."

"Enough," says Lady Casca, her patience ended. This time, when she commands him to go, he goes.

He gives Zanthi one last look before he is pulled into a writhing tangle of a dance. She thinks she'll be awake all night, thinking about that look.

Lady Casca sighs. "I'd like to blame the wine entirely," she says, once he's gone, "but that would be disingenuous."

"I truly didn't mean to trespass on your worship," she says, when she finally drags her gaze away from the dance. "I didn't mean to see."

"Come along, Ilyston," says Lady Casca. "You wished to talk, and so we shall talk."

Chapter Nineteen

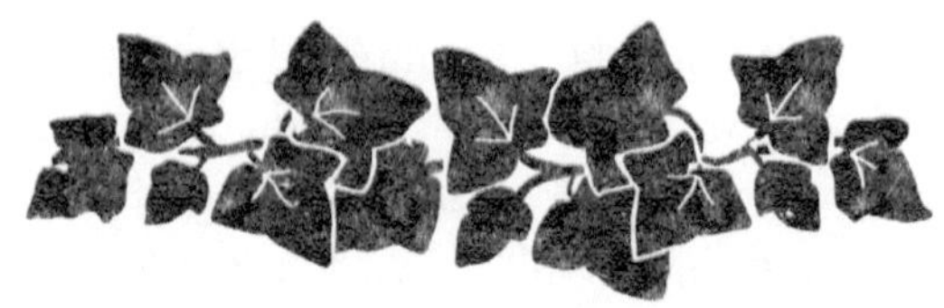

As Sabine walks, her black gown swirls around her. It's not until they pass under a flickering oil lantern that Zanthi sees the subtle pattern of fish twisting through river rushes, all beaded in fine, black gems.

Fish. It always loops back to fish.

Hart and his aether. Hart and his study of the old traditions and the Gardens, and his refusal to blaspheme. Did Madoc know, all this time, that the god she studied was here, in his Gardens? He must have. The fish scales on the archive wall, and the midsummer procession. The pointing figure crowned in ivy, and Madoc crowned just the same. *The Lord of the Waters and his priest.*

He didn't tell her, just as he did not tell her he kept the Old Ways. He did not tell her that midsummer meant a ritual staging of his death.

For it was only a staging, after all.

As they walk to the manor, Zanthi stumbles through an account of the men in the archives. It seems distant as a far-flung isle now, that encounter in the dark. Already soft and fading at the edges, as if she isn't meant to remember those men, and their chisel. She rubs at her chest, at the boot print.

"You were noble to come warn us," says Sabine, letting her into the manor. “But we have our own guardians, especially on a night like this. Nothing will come to pass.”

“Can you be sure of that?”

“They have not come, have they? I am well used to Landen. He has a long fascination with these Gardens, but that is not your trial to weather.” As they climb the stairs to Madoc’s apartments, she gives Zanthi an inscrutable look. “You should let yourself forget it ever happened.”

Madoc’s door is unlocked, and inside, a general untidiness has taken hold. Sabine sighs, picks up a shirt and a silk scarf, and drapes them over a chair.

“The ritual,” Zanthi says, and the words stick in her throat with thorns. “The poison was not a deadly one?”

“It was. I prepared it myself.”

She turns that each way, tries to make sense of the impossibility of it. “Then he did not take a full dose?”

“Ilyston.” She gestures for her to sit by the unlit hearth. “Do those cursed eyes of yours see nothing? It stopped his heart. It killed him.”

Zanthi takes the closest armchair, because her legs are leaden and she does not think they’ll hold her. “It did not. It was only a ritual.”

“And the ritual worked.” Her voice shakes. “Bless all our forgotten gods. It worked.” As she picks up a small stack of letters from Madoc’s desk, her hand trembles, and that is how Zanthi knows she speaks truly.

Real, all of it real.

Real, down to that neat stack of letters, waiting to be sent.

Was one for her? She does not wish to know. She does not want to find her name absent from Madoc’s farewells.

“Did they all know?” Her voice trembles, too. Did all those pleading, praying nightingales know what he was undertaking? Did they all know, and did he know, and did he not care to warn her?

“They knew. We are not just a pleasure garden, Ilyston. The nightingales are not just performers, though society likes to believe us so. We keep the Old Ways here, and they are acolytes. You should not have seen what you witnessed. It was not for uninitiated eyes. It was not for eyes like yours."

Zanthi looks at her hands, twists them in her lap.

Sabine's touch lifts her chin. "Are you unharmed?"

"Yes," she says honestly. "I was scared more than anything else, though it's worn away now." She can feel the forgetting. The darkness is lapping at her memories, wanting to swallow them, and she has the strangest, strongest sense that it may have swallowed those men, too. It doesn't manage to dislodge her memory entirely, though. Only softens it.

"I did not mean only from the Landen men."

"Nothing untoward happened in the Gardens," she says, and Sabine raises a perfectly arched eyebrow.

"We shall be glad I came along when I did," she murmurs. "Ah, my reckless son."

"If he kisses someone—"

"He will kiss nightingales aplenty, but they have all drunk deeply of the wine that will protect them from his poisoned tongue. You, my dear, have not." Sabine regards her for a long moment. "He spoke truthfully. He may choose to go with others, but he would have preferred to be with you."

Her chest aches at that—a deep wanting that sinks down, under her ribs and sits in her stomach. She wishes, for a dizzying moment, that she was someone who might have been brave enough to dance with him in the flamelight.

"Stay here tonight, and I will send a note to your household. You are, I think, familiar with these rooms? Latch the door. Come to my quarters in the morning, and I will have you seen home safely."

"I'm not as familiar as you think."

Sabine smiles. It is a slight, cold thing.

Madoc surely gets his smile from his father, because his mouth is the only feature that differs from his mother's. His smile is warm and generous and invites one into his secrets. Sabine's smile is a warning to keep away.

It is a warning that she should mind. She is a historian. What she studies is in the past, distant, and unreachable. It is not flame-light and poison, wine and ivy, and devotions given with kisses.

She gets very little sleep that night. The sounds of celebration last until the quiet, cold hours before dawn, and she lies in Madoc's bed, staring at the unfamiliar darkness. The pillows smell like him. It does not feel right to sleep here without his invitation, while he is elsewhere, sleeping or not sleeping.

She knows it is likely he'll have a lover in his arms tonight. Lovers, even. She feels some sort of way about that, and it's not how she thought she might feel. Her lines, it seems, are shifting faster than she can track them.

The thing is, she never really thought she might be his lover, too. A friend, yes. A kiss here and there, perhaps. But that kiss to her neck at the bathing pool had turned her thoughts entirely molten, and she had wanted him. And then tonight, he had wanted her more than any other.

She doesn't know what to do with that. She doesn't know what she *can* do with that.

In the morning, after far too little sleep, she steals a pleated chemise from Madoc's wardrobe to replace her ruined blouse. It is beautiful, because Madoc is a beautiful creature surrounded by beautiful things.

As she is lacing it, she tips her hand palm-side up and sees her lantern-scald is gone. The healing springs fade aether-burns, yes, but she had not touched the waters. And even if she had, it should not have healed within a night.

On the landing outside the room, Kit is waiting with Zanthi's cloak in her hands. She's tired-eyed but clear-faced. Evidently, not all the nightingales partook in the festivities. Between them, the statue of the ivy-crowned man looms large in the dawn light. His cup, held aloft, sends a chill across Zanthi's skin.

Kit smiles, amused. "It is rather a clue, isn't it?" she says.

Or a warning. One that Zanthi should have heeded.

Kit leads her up another set of stairs and along a hall that looks out over the gardens. At first glance, Zanthi thinks the moss lawns strewn with fabric and ribbons, and then her tired eyes pick out the shapes of limbs and tousled heads.

"They're lucky the weather is holding." Kit casts a fond look out the windows. "Though it'd take more than rain to wake them."

Madoc, she learns, is not strewn about on the moss lawns, because he is stretched out on a sofa in his mother's parlour, deep in sleep. Sabine is taking tea at a table by the window and greets her with no particular quietness.

"He won't wake anytime soon," she says. "You should return home."

"My brothers will be worrying," Zanthi says.

She stops by Madoc. His face is slack in sleep, his brow untroubled. Some sparse amount of ivy still clings in his hair, but it no longer looks like a crown. It only looks like he needs to brush his hair. She brushes her fingers across his cheek, but he doesn't stir. His breath is warm against her wrist.

Warm, but faint.

"His recovery will be slow," Sabine says, after a pause. "He will write when he is able. I expect your patience on the matter."

Zanthi takes that as Sabine means it. She is to stay away.

Madoc looks as he always has. She runs a light finger against the edge of his hairline, across his temple, frowning. She'd seen him blue-lipped and cold in the apparition in the dead springs, as if she had seen a glimpse of his midsummer ritual. But as he breathes, deep in sleep, it doesn't feel like the warning has passed.

Because even if he looks as he always has, she cannot shake the feeling that something about him has changed.

PART II
WHERE THE
RIVER
SLEEPS
autumn
-
winter

Chapter Twenty

The days after midsummer are gentle ones. The warmth lingers until even the ducks in the Lune seem fed up with it. There is only silence from the Gardens, even when she sends a brief letter to Madoc with well-wishes and an apology. The papers make no mention of him, not even when the Gardens reopen to society a fortnight after midsummer is past.

Folding the paper, she puts it aside and moves on. She has other things to do than sit and sigh over Madoc Casca. She makes sure to do them.

Midsummer has left her with more questions than she knows what to do with. There is a temptation to demand that Hart give her answers, but she suspects he is giving her all he can. He either knows nothing more or cannot tell her any more. She's not so eager to scoff at his claims of magic now.

Not after she witnessed that strange ritual. The morning after midsummer, when she'd walked past the dark pool, she'd found it nothing more than a sandy bathing spot. Shimmering in the morning light, strewn with the detritus of the celebrations: ribbons, sprigs of green, sodden ivy crowns. When Madoc had fallen, he had been swallowed whole and completely. But there, where he had disappeared, the water would barely reach his knees.

She does write to Hart, though, and tells him she witnessed midsummer at the Gardens. She asks him if she should continue her studies, if she should cease her searching. She doesn't mean to uncover what should remain hidden.

His reply is swift and firm.

Keep seeking. The course is set, and the ink is dry. Do not turn back.

At least, she thinks it is his reply. Because that line, and that line alone in the letter, is written in a hand that is not quite the same as the rest. It is as if another had reached over to pen it.

She spends her days in Hart's office, where the sunlight lights up all the drifting dust and leaves the air gold-stricken, and her nights in the parlour, buried deep in her research. Her roughly-constructed paper takes shape, only she isn't sure where to take it. She has very little in documentation. She cannot mention anything about the Gardens or the dead spring beneath the town. She can *maybe* mention the friezes, but she still has no proof of them, and no desire to delve back into those strange, dark passages alone. And even if she does, she doubts she'll easily find her way back to the chamber with the shining figure. That carven face drifts in her mind. That arched brow. The rest of the visage lost to time and faded away, just as their name, and nature, and purpose have faded.

Keep seeking.

Meticulously, she assembles a complete study of each of the archipelago's known aetherwells, no matter how small or insignificant. Most of this data is held by the airguard, but Joren agrees to send her what she needs. She finds sources on the history of each well, the towns that are built around them, and the gods they were once dedicated to. Because they nearly all have god-patrons, and the ones that do not are small and so long-faded that there is little known of them at all.

Esk's alone has never been dedicated to any god, and yet it is the most immense of them all. The only association it officially has is that of the Crown. And yet there are the fish and the river reeds laced through everything she uncovers, neither of which has ever been associated with the Crown.

It is Theron who gives her the next stepping stone. She is lying on the parlour rug, a stack of handwritten notes on her chest, and Susan being a tolerant pillow beneath her head. “Did you know fish used to be sacred in Esk?”

Theron looks up from his book. “Did they? I suppose I’m not surprised. They are everywhere.”

She rolls, so she’s able to frown at him. “How so?”

“There are fish etched into the threshold stones at the entrance to the remedial baths,” he says, bemused. “The old wing. Have you never noticed? Even our coins used to be called scales before they were crowns.”

That has her sitting up. “Really? Do you have a source for that?”

“Use the library, Zanthi,” he says, greatly exasperated. “I’m not your research assistant.”

She lies back down, her frown clinging. Susan shifts beneath her, somehow becoming even softer and more comfortable. “Do *you* remember my getting lost in the archives as a child?”

She expects him to laugh, maybe. The way he does when they share an absurd memory from their childhood, a sort of painful fondness of remembrance, tempered with loss. But she gets silence.

“Theron?”

He sighs. “Yes. Not Mother’s finest moment.”

She goes still. He so rarely mentions their mother. She doesn’t remember her passing. Instead, she remembers how Theron had picked her up from the town school one day, red-eyed and pale, with Chester beside him, more sombre than she had ever known him. They had taken her home, and mother had been gone.

She remembers Chester moving in to help them, and how he had never moved out again. They had become a family, the three of them. And then Fletcher had come along, and the family had grown.

She doesn’t miss her mother so much, to tell the truth. Even before her mother had died, it had been Theron who had comforted her, entertained her, and soothed her nightmares. But Theron misses their mother, she knows, because he never talks about her.

"It was Professor Hart who found me," she says, after a fraught moment.

A longer silence this time. "Was it? He has never mentioned that to me."

"It was right before he was injured," she says.

"I remember," Fletcher says, coming through with a tea tray. "There were all sorts of stories that year about a creature under the university waiting to drag students down and drown them."

"You had nightmares for months," Theron says. "Horrid ones. I thought it was just fear of the dark, from being so lost." He gives her a look. "I almost had a nerve attack when you told me you were going to study in the archives."

"He really did," adds Fletcher, all fondness.

"Mother used to wonder if you were some sort of seer of ill fortunes when you were young. You would say the most horrific things. But after a while, the nightmares stopped, and you never mentioned them again."

Unease ripples through her. *Seer of ill fortunes.* That is what she'd seen in the buried springs, wasn't it? An ill fortune. Madoc, dead, and she beside him. "I don't remember any of it. There's just a space in my mind where maybe memories were, and it's dark, and there's a bell knelling, and there's the sound of a river."

Porcelain clinks. Fletcher sets down the teapot. "Dark rivers and bells? You know what that sounds like."

She knows. "The dark river."

"The scholars already think you cursed," Theron says, amused. "Taking up with Hart and writing academic theories on the dark river? You'll frighten the codgers out of their wits."

"It could only be an improvement," she says, and he laughs. "It makes sense, though, does it not? Nearly all our festivals here celebrate the river. We all think it's the Lune, but what if they are born from a worship of another river?"

He hums in thought. "Then you'll suggest this founding god of Esk is of the underworld?"

"I even have an epithet. The Lord of the Waters." Then she quickly adds, "It's a theory. I don't know enough to be sure of anything."

There is silence. Theron has that slightly hazy look that means he's deep in the library he keeps in his mind. He's full of scholarly interest, not at all shaken by the concept. "There's no established literature for there ever being an underworld god. The dark river is the dark river. It has no figurative aspect. It has no worship."

"But don't you think that's strange when you dwell on it? Why does no one think that's strange?"

"The gods are more telluric in concept. Mountains, lakes, oceans, weather patterns," counters Theron. "The dark river isn't —" He breaks off. Even in such a conversation, saying the dark river isn't *real* is tempting ill fate.

"You'll have a hard time getting anyone to take your work seriously if you invent a god where there has never been one," Fletcher says.

"Uncover, not invent. And there *has* always been one. We just don't remember them." She holds up the volume of Lydus. All those suggestive lines about libations and devotions have since taken a different picture in her mind. A very specific picture of green eyes and crowned curls. "I think I am on a trail, something unbroken that I can follow back into the past."

"Through erotic poetry?" Fletcher says, with a shade of admiration. "You are going to cause a stir."

"I suppose you'll use the affinity debate?" Theron says.

Fletcher gives him a quizzing look, and Zanthi answers. "It's an old debate on whether the gods were different beings entirely, or whether they were people who had a particular affinity with aether. They could achieve tasks beyond their peers and so were revered because of it."

"There's an argument there that Chester could be exalted as a minor deity, and I think we all agree that it should never be made," says Fletcher, grinning.

She laughs. "Quite. And whoever the Lord of the Waters is, I do not think he was ever human."

Theron sighs. "I need to do some reading. I'll let you know if I find anything. And Zanthi, you realise you will upset quite a large swathe of scholars if you try to resurrect a forgotten deity of the underworld into our current literature. I'm glad this will be Hart's headache, and not mine."

That night, Susan follows her upstairs instead of trotting after Fletcher. Zanthi shuffles over in bed so Susan can curl up beside her. She smells as she always does, like almonds and parsley.

"I don't suppose you know anything of gods of the underworld?" Zanthi says, burying her face in Susan's fur.

Susan yawns and shows all her sharp, white teeth. She has a lot of teeth for a hound.

Chapter Twenty-One

It is amongst these dark thoughts that the festival of Sweet Night arrives, heralding the last weeks of summer. She rarely pays heed to it, and this year she ignores it with a furious intensity that Theron wisely does not comment on.

Sweet Night is for lovers. Shopkeepers string up rain-laurel and ferns, and cart-sellers roll out the gaily painted canvas awnings that will protect their wares from the weather. Those with lovers make plans together, and those without head to the dance halls to find a pretty face to smile at. Theron and Fletcher will buy each other favours—honeyed persimmon for Fletcher, spiced plums for Theron—and Zanthi will stay at the university as late as she dares and avoid the nonsense in its entirety.

The warmth of the last weeks is finally bleeding away. The evenings fall swifter, and the mornings have the crisp snap of distant cold. It's raining as Zanthi heads to the university, a light misting haze, and she tips her face to the skies and enjoys the kiss of water on her cheeks.

It's all the kissing she'll ever get on Sweet Night. She tries not to mind it. She'd resigned herself to a one-sided sort of life a long time ago. It's about time she remembered that.

When she makes her way into Hart's office, there is a faint echo of aether drifting through the air. Someone has been here, and recently. Hart, because the aether is pearly and water-thin. And so, she isn't startled when, a half-hour later, Hart strides in.

"Ah, Ilyston," he says. "We meet again at last."

She props her head on her hand, pausing in her writing. "So we do. Are you in need of your desk? I can move elsewhere."

"There is nowhere else." He pulls over the second chair and sets up crosswise from her. "We'll have to make do. If I'd been able to do so, I'd have avoided being here on a festival day. Especially Sweet Night. It's never been my favourite."

She can't help but be intrigued. "Do you have a favourite festival?"

"Midwinter," he says promptly. "Cosy, conducted at home, and none of the fuss."

"Isn't there usually some grand party at midwinter?"

"That's for Society people. The rest of us are much milder." He gives her a curious look. "You have no plans for Sweet Night?"

"Only to make myself as scarce as possible."

He nods and asks nothing more. Instead, he pulls one of the woven rush charms from his bag. She'd sent it to him weeks ago, when she'd first caught him up on her research. "I can tell you something about these things, but I can't give you a source. It's anecdotal at best."

It's not strange for folklorists to have half their best information entirely unverifiable. She readies her pen, expectant.

"Reed charms used to be far more common. We mostly use ferns and willow now. But in antiquity, rushes were more common. This one, I believe, is an old charm for lost souls. It is meant as a wayfinder, to help guide a lost person home."

"They're appearing all over Esk. No one knows where the knowledge of making them came from, only that they find themselves absently making them. I've been keeping a list of everywhere I've found them."

He looks over the page of her journal that she holds out. "No discernible pattern?"

"No, not in any way."

"I have told you Esk has had a forgetting over it for a very long time," he says. "I think this might be the start of a remembering."

She turns the rush charm over in her hands. "Is that a good thing?"

"I do not know," he says, troubled. She studies him from the corner of her gaze, but her side-sight is quiet. If his fish-shadows are about, they are hiding from her. Perhaps, they dislike being seen now they know she can spot them.

"If they are charms for guiding a lost soul home, then who is Esk trying to guide home?" She's thinking aloud because she has a creeping sense that she knows.

His smile is wry. "Don't relent from your studies. I think your answers are closer than either of us would like."

"I hope you are right," she says, because lately her studies are feeling rather like being caught in a river's eddy, swirling around and going nowhere.

A knock slices through their soft conversation. She looks up, but Hart is already going to answer it.

"Ah," he says, leaning in the doorway. "Casca."

Zanthi fumbles her pen, catching the cap just before she drops it.

"Ethram," Madoc says. He's speaking softly. "May I have a moment of Zanthi's time?"

"It's hardly mine to give," Hart says, dry. "But I'm near done with my work. I'll bid you an early evening, Zanthi."

"You needn't leave—" she begins, but Hart waves her off.

"I mean to pick up a festival favour before I go home," he says, packing his book into his bag. "Evening, Casca."

Madoc closes the door behind him, and then it's only them in a pocket of golden silence.

Zanthi caps her pen properly. She tries a smile. "Do you think he has a sweetheart?"

"It rather confounds the mind, doesn't it?" He's dressed down, for his own measure of it. It's still too stunning for a university office. Yet there's no smile on his face, not even the promise of one. "Good evening, Zanthi."

She presses her lips closed on the words that almost spill out. *Are you okay?* Or *I wrote to you*. Or *why didn't you tell me?* She thinks her face might say it all, anyway. His expression is hard to read, but she can see the shadows under his eyes clearly enough, and the way he's carrying himself like it's hard to do so. He's been very ill.

"I've been worrying over you," she says.

"I'm sorry. I never meant to worry you."

"No, you only meant to drink poison and drown yourself." She lays her pen aside. He's not even done his hair, just left it loose at the front and gathered the rest back into a messy clasp-up of curls. "Are you recovering well?"

"I am." He gives her a searching look, then places a parcel on the desk and sits in Hart's vacated chair. "It's all a blur that night. I'm told you came to us for aid, and I was no help to you."

He's doing everything carefully, and it's putting her on edge. She's used to his easy smiles and inviting warmth, and she's not sure what to do now that she has neither. The last she'd seen him, he'd been beautiful, like something of myth come to life. He'd been wild and wanton, and utterly, entirely, beyond her reach. He had not been hers, yet he had wanted her.

Now he's here, and he's Casca again. Still not hers and still beautiful. She doesn't know if he wants her like he'd wanted her at midsummer, but she still wants him. It hits her like a blow, how much she wants him.

"You were. I needed nothing but the sanctuary you gave. I intruded, as unintentional as it was."

A shade of something crosses his face. It's a curious expression. She's never seen anything like it. "Zanthi," he says. "I didn't mean for you to see what you did. I'm sorry."

"For what?" It comes out sharper than she intended, but not sharper than she means. "Tell me. What are you sorry for, exactly?"

He leans back. "You're upset," he says. "Did I do something unwelcome?"

"You tried to kiss me. *Twice*, you poison-tongued trial."

"Ah." His lips press down.

"It's not the kiss I'm objecting to," she adds, to be clear. "Only the poison."

"That is fair." He falls silent and doesn't quite meet her gaze.

She is, she realises, tired. She has been waiting on him for weeks, and now he is here, and alive, and *well*, he seems to be waiting on *her*.

"Why did you kiss me?" she asks finally. "In my bedroom. The first time."

She wants the truth. She wants to know if the desire she'd seen in his face had been the wine, or the poison, or the heated lust of the celebrations, or if it had been something truer. Something real.

"Because I wanted to," he says, and he says *wanted* like it is an easy thing to say. "Did you not want to, when you kissed me after we bathed?"

"More than I can say," she says, honestly. He doesn't meet her gaze, and her stomach tightens. "You promised you'd tell me everything you hadn't told me, once midsummer had passed."

"I did say that. But I never intended to tell you of the secret ways of the Gardens. I thought, after midsummer, if I survived, I could put it all behind me. I've always kept myself in separate halves. One part to face society, and be the host of the Season. The rest kept secret for worship and ritual in the way of the Casca family."

"And then I trespassed upon your worship and spoiled all your secrets."

"My intentions were to take you as a lover," he says. "I'd have given you half of me, and let you think you had all of me, until it was time to move on. It is what I've always done."

She grips her pen tight. "And now?"

He hesitates. "Since midsummer, things are changed. I feel the waters, all the time. I think I'd hear the water whisper, if I could only learn the right way to listen. I can't offer you what I had intended to offer you, not anymore. I'm not the same as I was."

"I thought maybe—" She cuts off. She'd thought he'd truly wanted her, as more than a passing lover. She thought he'd *seen* her. Carefully, she places her pen on her desk. She's been holding it too tightly. "It doesn't matter. I'm glad to see you well, Madoc."

His breath rushes out of him. "No," he says. "You thought right. I'm not making myself understood."

"I do understand," she says softly. "You're telling me that the Casca I saw at midsummer was you in truth. It wasn't a play, it wasn't a staging. It was who you are. And I understand you're not just yourself alone. Your nature can't be divided from your Gardens."

"I am sorry," he says, bleakly, "that I am not who I let you think I was."

The conversation has shifted again. She cannot follow its pattern, not as precisely as she wishes. She tries to parse more of an answer from his face, but can see only resignation. Regret. "You are exactly who you have always been," she says, her confusion bleeding into her voice. "If I were given the chance, knowing all of that, I would still choose you. Did you think I would not?"

"Zanthi," he says, and he has the gall to look shaken. "What do you mean, you'd choose me?"

A creak makes them both freeze, and the door opens. If it is her brother, Zanthi thinks, she will throw the inkwell at his head. But it is Professor Sol, Hart's neighbour, who frowns around the edge.

"I thought I heard voices. Ilyston, who is this?"

"My research assistant," she says, short.

"Assistant?" Sol gives Madoc a measuring look, eyeing his beaded collar.

"Is there a problem?" Madoc says, all pleasantry. He smiles, but it's not at all the friendly thing Zanthi expects. It's sharp-edged and full of warning.

Maybe she'd been wrong. He can smile just like his mother, after all.

"Right," says Sol, blanching. "Not at all." She closes the door.

Silence sits between them until Madoc shifts. "Did you mean it?"

"I meant it," she says. Her heart is rattling in its beating. "Just as I think you meant that you'd choose me, at midsummer. I ran to you when I wanted sanctuary, Madoc. I have kissed you, and disrobed with you, and watched you drink poison and stop your own heart. Would I be sitting here, listening to you, if I didn't want you?"

He's looking at her like he doesn't want to breathe. Like a breath might make everything crumble.

"I'm trying to figure out how you want me, though," she says. "We were friends, you said, and then we weren't that, quite. You ignored my letter, and now you are here. You say you intended for us to be lovers, but it sounds like you are bidding me farewell. What do you want of me, Madoc?"

"What I want, I can't have," he says. He pushes the parcel across the desk, and she takes it.

Inside is a glass jar of spiced plums. A Sweet Night favour. Her chest twists.

"I am a Casca. If it were just me, as myself, then perhaps it would be easier. But a Casca doesn't give their heart to anything but the Gardens. I have devoted myself to my path, and I don't mean to turn from it. You're not of the Gardens." He takes a steadying breath, short and sharp. "I want you, but you're right. I don't know how. I could have you as a lover for a while. We might see each other in society, this Season. But I could not keep you. And I find I wish that I could keep you."

She's seen the whole of him, right from the start. From the moment he'd kneeled at the dead springs, and she'd seen his reflection crowned in river rushes. He'd been all secrets, buried beneath the velvets and smiles and tempting invitations. Madoc, charm-sharp socialite, steadfast friend. Casca, devoted creature of worship, consecrated one.

And he is telling her she can only have one.

He is someone she could love, if she gave herself the chance, but she does not intend to love in halves. She wants the Madoc who sleeps on the sofa in the sunlight. She wants the Madoc who kisses with abandon under the midsummer sky.

"I would have you in full," she says, very softly.

"I cannot give you that. It is not mine to give."

She turns the jar of plums in her hands. "Then perhaps there is only friendship for us."

"And I am not content with that," he says, low. In his face, she sees a faint echo of that midsummer desire.

"Where does that leave us?"

"Nowhere good." He runs a hand down his face. "Gods, I came to apologise for midsummer, not to—"

"Break my heart?" She smiles to soften the jest. "Don't worry, it's only bruised."

"Zanthi—"

"I would rather have your friendship for as long as a friendship can last, than be a lover you will not let in. That is my answer."

His jaw tightens. "Don't decide yet. Would you wait for me a little longer?"

"I promise you, I'm patient." She sets the jar down on her stack of books. "And I have rather a lot of work to be getting on with."

She means it as a dismissal, and he takes it as one.

"Madoc," she says, as he reaches the door. "Tell me one thing. The letters your mother took from your writing desk. Had you written one for me?"

His mouth curls at the corner. "Yes," he said. "And I thank the gods that you never read it. You would have hated it."

When he leaves, the room seems smaller for the lack of him. She stares at her paper, the shape of her writing strange and unfamiliar until her thoughts pick back up and the world trickles back in.

The spiced plums crush down her pile of papers, and she wonders what he thought of as he had purchased them. If he were a simpler man, he might have given them to her, and kissed her, and perhaps invited her home with him.

He is not simple, not in any way. Madoc leads an enclave that worships a god that doesn't exist anymore. Not in any meaningful way, in any case.

Except in the way the healing waters flow, and cure injuries and ills. The Gardens are not a blessing from the Crown or from the Well, but instead a blessing from an entity so lost and sunk in time that even the acolytes of the Old Ways do not remember the name they worship. No wonder the springs had been failing. They have all forgotten far too much.

And none of it is a single thing she can put in her paper, because it's all secret. She pillows her head in her hands and curses, soft and heartfelt. What a *mess.*

She's never wanted a person like she wants Madoc. She's never known that there was a person who would look her in the eyes and might love her. And it doesn't seem fair that when she has found them, they cannot be hers.

Chapter Twenty-Two

The preserved plums don't go unnoticed, but a few quiet days pass before her brother gathers the courage to ask. Zanthi is at the kitchen table, eating the plums while she reads through Hart's latest letter, when Theron settles across from her.

Zanthi grabs for the jar, but he's faster. He spears the last plum just as Fletcher brings the tea.

"I've never known anyone to eat plums so miserably," he says, and bites into it. "Someone ought to enjoy them."

"I was enjoying them just fine."

"So, what is it, sweetheart?" Fletcher swipes the jar and clears out the last remnants with a spoon. "Are you seeing him, or are you not?"

Nosy rags, the both of them. "I'm not," she says. "And if I was, I would tell you so."

"But he gave you a Sweet Night favour." Theron takes the jar and considers the gold, handwritten label. "It was Casca, wasn't it? These are quality."

"I don't wish to talk about it." She finishes the last of Hart's letter, frowning at the list of reading suggestions. "Theron, you'll help me hunt these down, won't you? Some of them aren't even owned by the university."

He takes the page. "I have this one. I know someone I can borrow the others from. Hart is being troublesome, isn't he? *Song of Dark Waters?* I've never heard of it."

"He says I'll have to ask Sabine Casca for that last one, and to be prepared for her to say no. Either way, I'm not liking my chances." She puts her head in her hands. She feels, all of a sudden, exhausted. The tea steam dampens her cheek, makes her feel flushed.

Fletcher runs a hand over her hair. "He moved on, then? Casca, I mean."

She'd told him she was content to wait for him to figure out what he wants, and she is content to do so, mostly. Only, she's been thinking too, and even for her, the shape of what they could be escapes her. He has his society responsibilities, which she wants no part of, and he has his Gardens devotions, which she cannot be a part of. What part of his life does she fit in with, then? Madoc Casca is a shining jewel in Esk. He needs someone who can shine beside him.

"It might have been easier if he had."

"You never pick the easy way." Theron slides something across the table. "This was delivered before. It might cheer you up."

It's an Admiralty dispatch, and it does. Chester is coming home.

"He really is returning early this year," she says. But there it is, in official Admiralty ink. The *Lys* is to return in three weeks. "I'm glad. We've so much to fill him in on."

"You more than most," Theron mutters, and she kicks him under the table.

She's sure he's gossiped most of it to Chester already. The two of them exchange a steady stream of letters from spring right through until the ships come back, so Chester usually waltzes in already knowing every small detail of Zanthi's year. He and Theron have been like that since childhood. As long as Zanthi can remember, it has been Theron and Chester. They'd been fast friends, close as brothers. And then, when her and Theron's mother had died, Chester had moved in, and had taken care of them. And so he is her brother too, as truly as Theron is.

He'll have opinions on Zanthi's odd, careful dance around Madoc, surely. Chester is a society man, and he'll have been in circles with Madoc before. Perhaps he'll have some advice for her. He always gives good advice.

It's been half a year since Madoc appeared in the vault, dressed in dappled-shade hues and sorting her pottery fragments. He hasn't truly been a part of her days and her life, and yet her thoughts turn to him more than they should. Mostly, they're dark with midsummer smoke, and the drip of wine, and his eyes, so very green beneath his ivy crown.

What would it be like to be his lover? She might share him with others, and she isn't sure what to make of that. It's likely he'd never make a priority of her, and she'd be invisible compared to his more notable songbirds. There are so many reasons she should set him aside and not tangle herself with him any further. And that's before she thinks about the ritual, and the way his lips were made for blessings and devotions as much as they were made for kissing.

No. She cannot fall in love with him halfway. If she lets herself fall, she will fall entirely into the depths of him, and if she isn't careful, there will be no one to catch her.

Three weeks later, Zanthi wakes to the muffled clack of a pony's hooves and the rattle of carriage wheels.

Chester.

She slides from her warm sheets, pausing only to haul her dressing gown around her, and runs down the stairs. The front door creaks, and a familiar voice greets Susan. It's tired, a little gruff, and has been so *very* missed.

She is the first to fling her arms around him. He's cold with the morning air and hearth smoke, and rain clings silver on his captain's coat. He picks her up in his hug. It's the sort of hug that warms her top to toe.

"Aren't you a sight for sore eyes?" he says, holding her tight.

"Welcome home," she says, and the air is driven from her as Fletcher throws his arms around them both. "You could wait your turn," she mutters, peeling herself away.

Theron, the decorous one, waits for Fletcher to move along before he greets Chester. He gives Chester a restrained embrace, which Chester immediately disregards by picking him up and dragging him along to the breakfast room, all while squeezing tight enough to make Theron call him something very indecorous indeed.

Fletcher slips ahead of them to stoke the fire, poking the embers back into burning.

"Gods, it's good to be home." Chester finally releases Theron in favour of collapsing into the fourth dining chair, the one that sits empty most of the year. He's so clearly tired, heavy shadows under his eyes, and in her side-sight she can see the golden wash of the *Lys'* aether wrapped tight around him. The aether in his amber eyes, though, is something everyone can see. They've a gold ring, almost glowing. After he's eaten, he'll probably sleep the rest of the day and most of tomorrow, too.

Then he'll go to the remedial baths to wash the worst of the aether away. It will still be there, though. He's been captain of the *Lys* for three years, and after that first year, it never really went away.

He sighs, bone-deep, and then looks at each of them, long and in turn. "You all look well. That's good."

"We are well," Theron says. "You, on the other hand, look worn thin."

Chester grins. "I missed your henpecking. I'm meant to be worn thin. I'm the captain. Now, come on, Zan. I didn't miss that you have some gold on those robes hanging by the door. What's the story there?"

Susan, who is resting her head on Chester's knee in an adoring way, gives a slow wag of her tail. He scratches at her ears.

"You didn't tell him?" She frowns at Theron.

"You have hands," he says, heading off to put breakfast on. "And, last I knew, enough basic literacy to write a letter."

"Wait a moment," Fletcher says, hurrying after him. "I'll do the toast."

Chester laughs. The frightful shadows under his eyes do nothing to diminish him. His golden-brown hair is combed neatly, and he's got the beginnings of a beard that he'll let grow in over the Season. He always does. "Go on, then. Tell me your good news."

"I have a mentor. Professor Hart has taken me on."

"That's wonderful." He reaches over to ruffle her hair. "About damn time they noticed you."

Theron, having been pushed back to the breakfast room, makes a sour face. "Hart is acceptable," he allows. "He's taking good care of her, academically."

"As he should. I'd been thinking of finding you a job in the Admiralty somewhere, if the university kept being obtuse."

"I wouldn't last at the docks."

"No? I think you'd do fine. You'd wear an airguard coat very well." His eyes are creasing at the edges, bright with amusement. The *Lys'* aether flickers honey-gold, all the way through him. It curls around his cheeks, trickles down his arms, caresses him in light touches. It's not at all like the aetherghosts that drape over socialites and aetherworkers. It's reactive and shining, and entirely alive.

It doesn't give her a headache like looking at aetherghosts does, but it still isn't easy to focus with it there, flickering.

Fletcher brings out oats and poached fruit, as well as underdone toast and a honey-dripped currant cake. It's a rare feast, because they're celebrating. They've missed Chester, and none so much as Susan, who sinks down to lie over his feet.

"Tell me all about Hart," Chester says as they settle into eating. "I suppose I had better meet him soon."

"There's no need for that sort of formality," she says. "He's my mentor, not a lover."

Theron snorts. "Gods know, he might be preferable to your current debacle."

Fletcher smacks him with his literary periodical, and Chester chokes on his tea, and Zanthi rather wishes it had been Theron to choke, actually. *Honestly.*

"Pardon?" Chester says, all golden sternness. His honey-rich hair falls over his brow, and his mouth presses thin. "Are you saying Zanthi has a sweetheart?"

"I do not." It's been almost a month, and she hasn't heard from Madoc, hasn't had a visit or a letter, or a word. He asked her to wait, and so she is. She just isn't expecting anything to come of it.

"You brought home a Sweet Night gift," Fletcher says.

"You spent the night in his apartments," adds Theron.

Chester looks like he hears a storm bell ringing, like he's ready to do battle.

"I told you I'll tell you if there's anything to tell," she says. "Mind your own matters."

Theron opens his mouth, and Zanthi gives him such a sharp look that he closes it. Then she must quickly busy herself with her toast lest her surprise spoil her victory. She's *never* gotten Theron to shut his mouth about anything.

Chester tops up his tea. He likes it a good deal stronger than the rest of them, so they always leave some in the pot to keep steeping for his second cup. He takes a deep, even breath. "May I at least know a name?"

Zanthi cuts in on top of Theron. "No."

"You were never one to be coy, Zan," Chester says. Gods, but she forgets how *nosy* he is. He gives her a narrow look. "A name, please."

"I don't want to invite trouble," is all she says.

Theron peers over his teacup. "Fancy words, for a girl who spent midsummer night at the Gardens."

Chester jolts hard enough that his tea spills across the table. "Pardon?" He gives Theron an incredulous look, then turns it on Zanthi. "A nightingale? You?"

Fletcher puts his head in his hands, Theron is cat-satisfied at Chester's outrage, and Zanthi wonders which is worse: to prolong the humiliation or to admit, once and for all, that Casca has likely passed her over, just as they had all surely known he would.

And then there is a knock at the door.

Chapter Twenty-Three

As one, they fall silent. Theron glances at the clock. It is barely past eight. Fletcher stares at the hallway, an unhappy flush rising on his face. Chester pins her with a look. He stands, but she throws her chair back, heart pounding, odd and out of shape.

"I'll answer," she says, tripping over Susan in her rush to get to the hall first. "Don't move."

"That's hardly traditional," Theron snaps.

As she steps into the hall, she hears Fletcher reply, "Nothing about this is going to be traditional, and you know it. I'll get another chair."

Not traditional, but he's come at breakfast. That's about as traditional as one can get. She doesn't doubt it's Madoc, though, and when she opens the door, he's there.

The morning is gentle and sweet, the air bringing in the scent of the river. He smiles at her. "Good morning."

"You've come too early," she says, because she can't think of anything sensible to say instead. "We're still at breakfast."

"I'd hoped you would be," he says, like he isn't saying something absurd. Like he isn't making the exact statement of intent that he'd told her he could not give.

Zanthi grips the edge of the door. "It doesn't mean nothing, coming at breakfast."

"It didn't mean nothing when I let you keep my key," he replies. "Each time I have sought you out, it hasn't meant nothing. I kissed you, and it meant everything. I have my answer for you, Zanthi." He doesn't seem to care that she hasn't invited him in, nor that the woman across the road is peeking from her window. A set of university students crane over the stone wall, eyes wide.

There's not a soul in Esk that doesn't know what calling at breakfast means.

He's wearing his Gardens best, well-tailored trousers and high boots. His morning coat has a beaded moth across each shoulder. He's still a little sick-shadowed around the eyes, not entirely recovered, and she doesn't like that. He'd been so full of life, coming out of that midsummer pool, only to be ill for so long afterwards.

"It took you a while."

He takes that with a wry turn of his mouth. "I'm sorry I told you that you could not have the whole of me. You may. You may have the whole of me, and I would have the whole of you."

"Madoc—"

"You are my friend, Zanthi, and I'd have you always be the truest friend of my heart. I'd have you in my life and in my bed, too, when it comes to that. I'd have you hold all my secrets, as many as you wish to know. I think I'm well on my way to loving you, and I'd like to keep going, if you'd let me. I—"

He breaks off as Zanthi presses her fingers across his lips. She stares, eyes wide and cheeks burning as badly as any toast she's ever made. She feels the curve of his smile beneath her hand.

"Yes," she says. "Yes, only come inside now. You can't say things like that on the doorstep."

He's not in the least ruffled by everything he's just said. Not that he's unaffected. It's just that all she can see in his face is clear-eyed determination. The door shuts behind them, wrapping them in silence. She knows her brothers must be craning to hear every word.

"I know what it means to come to you like this. And we can talk it through, after, and I will answer every question you have. But for now, let me take breakfast with you?" He takes her hand, lifting it to his lips. His mouth is warm against the back of her fingers. "If you'll have me."

She takes a sharp little breath. "Then you'd better come through."

It's not until they're coming through into the breakfast room that she realises she should have warned him. There is a moment of blankness as he takes in Theron, dangerous-faced, and Fletcher, doing his best to look pleasant, and Chester, fury-pale in his gleaming uniform.

"Captain Locksley," says Madoc, and he rallies himself in a space of a breath. "Ilystons. Good morning."

Chester has a way of being entirely stone-faced and still having the danger of a storm in him. There are more questions in his gaze than the archive has shadows. "Madoc," he says, low. "You are very unexpected."

The familiar address startles her. Zanthi had supposed they knew each other, but it's strange to have it confirmed.

Madoc bows his head in a small apology. "Pardon my intrusion, then."

"You're very welcome," Fletcher manages.

Theron shakes out the *Society Papers* and chooses not to say anything at all. It's better than Zanthi could have hoped for, honestly.

Fletcher gestures at the extra chair he's pulled through from the kitchen. "I'm sure it's a simpler breakfast than you're used to, but please help yourself."

Madoc slides in beside Zanthi. The gold in his ears glints. "I'm afraid I'm not used to breakfast in any form. We usually start our day at morning tea."

"Quite understandable, considering. Then this is a diversion from your usual routine."

"Yes," says Madoc plainly. "But an important one."

Theron clicks his tongue. "So we're being upfront about it, are we?"

"Should we not be? I didn't think you'd accept anything less."

"You're brazen for thinking I'll accept anything," he mutters, but he backs down almost immediately, ducking back behind his paper.

Fletcher picks the conversation up smoothly. "I'm surprised to see you," is all he says. "I know you have your own speed of life at the Gardens, but breakfast visits are usually reserved for committed courtships."

"Yes, I do know that." Madoc catches Zanthi's gaze. "That's what I intend."

Theron bites his toast and still says nothing. Chester is staring Madoc down, unflinching. Zanthi takes a mouthful of poached fruit, because she's at risk of laughing if she doesn't.

It's a disaster. She's never felt quite as cloud-light as this. She wants to savour this morning forever. She looks at Madoc and he smiles at her, a flash of quiet amusement. Then she keeps looking at him, because she's suddenly struck at how very unordinary it is to see him there, in their breakfast room, with such a familiar, faded teacup in his hands. It is a picture she'd very much like to have become ordinary.

"Captain Locksley," he says, turning to Chester smoothly. "I apologise for interrupting your homecoming. I'm afraid I was distracted and missed the news that the *Lys* had come in."

"No doubt you were," Chester says. "But I'd rather have been here than not. What exactly are you playing at? Did the summer drag on too long for you? Did you get bored of your usual pastimes?"

Madoc's pleasant smile grows thorns. "I had heard the storms blew strong this year. I see the aether is biting badly."

"And I have heard rumour your year has been bountiful," grits Chester. "And quite generous."

"It has. We added a wing to the remedial baths. Perhaps you might consider visiting it?"

Fletcher sips his tea. Theron hides behind the paper. Chester looks like he considers saying a great number of things in quick succession, but he ends with waving a hand in their direction, as if he can make the picture of them seem any clearer.

"I hope to the gods that after a sleep, this whole thing will make more sense." He scrubs a hand down his face. "Ignore me, Madoc. I am merely tired, and yes, aetherbitten."

"Nothing minded in the least." He's not putting on any of his practised airs, but he still has a charm that never really fades. He leans his shoulder against Zanthi's in silent reassurance. "I see a fair few aetherbitten captains over the year. You won't scare me off."

"No, I daresay it takes a great deal more than that. Well, if you are truly determined, then let us have breakfast."

Zanthi lets out her breath. Fletcher takes the role of host, passing this and that to Madoc, and Madoc shows his talents just the same, turning the stilted welcome into a proper flow of conversation between him and Fletcher. He even has Chester chiming in from time to time. She watches all this as she works through her breakfast. It's remarkable, in the way Theron's debates are remarkable, and Fletcher's writing is remarkable.

Madoc must be magnificent in society. Almost as magnificent as he'd been wearing nothing but firelight, holding his bronze cup aloft. She winces and packs those thoughts away. Such things are not for the breakfast table.

Chester crooks a brow at her. She gives all her attention to her toast.

Madoc is reeling off a piece of town news that means very little to her, but clearly Theron and Fletcher know the people it concerns because they're leaning forward, intrigued. She's glad for it—her thoughts are entirely tangled up in Madoc, on the doorstep, saying, '*I'm well on my way to loving you.*'

A breakfast call needn't mean anything, in the end. It's not a proposal, but it's an intention. It's a statement. It's an old-fashioned and stately way of dedicating yourself to someone, to offer all you are and see if you fit with them. It means learning their household and their rhythms. The patterns of their life. Their days, and their nights, and their body. Gods, she's delving back into the sort of thoughts that aren't for the breakfast table again.

A touch on her arm startles her back to herself.

"Walk me to the door?" Madoc says.

Breakfast is winding up. They'll all be going about their day soon. She lets the rest of the toast sit uneaten on her plate and leads him out of the breakfast room without meeting any of her brothers' faces. Nosy weasels.

"I'm sorry," Madoc says, when they're as far from the others as they can get. "I didn't mean to make a show of it."

"I'm not convinced there's anything you don't make a show of."

He winces. "That may be true. Do you regret letting me in?"

"Not yet," she says, though in truth she is sure she never will. Letting him in might be the bravest and best thing she's ever done. "Breakfasts are...old-fashioned, aren't they? Scholars often skip such things. You needn't have, not for me."

"If I had asked you to my bed without it, what would you have understood?"

She flushes and can't quite meet his eyes. He brushes the back of her hand with his own.

"I thought so," he says. "So yes, I needed to."

She hooks one finger lightly around his and catches the surprised gleam of his smile. "I was gearing myself up to be passed over."

"Then you weren't listening to me properly," he says. "Nor watching me, either. This isn't a passing thing. I don't know how you fit into my life or how I fit into yours, and I don't know what we will become to each other, but I want us to find out together."

"And if you tire of my company when the Season begins? I don't take part, as a rule, and I don't intend to change that this year."

"You'll find out that I do not easily grow bored," he says, unbothered. "And once I decide on something, I am resolute. This is not the first breakfast I'll be at."

"Come any day. We've still not had that tea you've been promising."

He gets a stricken look. "Gods, we haven't, have we?"

She presses a palm into the soft wool of his morning coat. "Madoc," she says, with all the frustration she's had since midsummer. "I've been waiting for your kiss for weeks. Are you going to kiss me or not?"

That kiss in her bedroom has been haunting her waking thoughts, and her dreams, too. And so too that almost-kiss at midsummer, when his gaze had been so lust-dark and hazy. He's looking nothing like that now. It's something gentler than lust, but it strikes to her heart just the same.

"I'm sorry I kept you waiting," he murmurs, his breath against hers, and then he is kissing her.

He tastes of tea, of *her* tea that she drinks every morning. She'll never drink it without thinking of him now. His mouth is clever and hot against hers, and she melts for him, as much an instinct as breathing. He runs his fingers against her scalp, tangling her hair, holding her hard against him as he kisses her and kisses her some more. She's flushed-cheeked when he draws away. He smiles, and *now* there is hunger in his eyes.

"I won't leave you waiting again," he promises, low. "I know we've lots to say yet. We'll take it as it comes. But know that I want you like I've wanted no one before."

It's obvious, really, that it must be like that, but to hear it unhitches something that had been caught inside her. *Like I've wanted no one before*. In some ways, at least, this is as new to him as it is to her.

Well, she thinks. At least they can be matched in *some* things.

Her good mood holds throughout Theron's pointed teasing, through the afternoon, and right through her dreams that night, too. She sleeps late and then skips breakfast entirely to lie in bed and read until she cannot put off the day any longer. For once, she doesn't want to go to her studies.

She wants to stay in the strange, lovely wonder of a world where Madoc Casca visits her for breakfast. If the papers reported on it, no one would believe it. Even her brothers still don't quite believe it.

"Casca," Chester says when she makes it downstairs. He leans out of the parlour doorway and looks at her like she's a lost cause. Clearly, a night of good sleep has not made it make any more sense to him. "Lady Casca's son, delight of the Gardens, most desired man in Esk, *that* Casca. Must you?"

"Well, I'm sure he's not the *most* desired man," she says, a smile making her face feel entirely creased up. She's as light as air, and she's sure she's being insufferable. "You're quite popular these days, aren't you, Chester?"

Fletcher's bark of laughter is loud. He's curled up in the armchair by the fire, a stack of papers in his lap. "He's doing wonders for my book sales," he says, quite cheerily.

"Or maybe your book sales are doing wonders for my popularity," counters Chester, irritated. "You should pay for my winter wardrobe as compensation."

"Certainly. I'll put in an order for golden cloth at once."

"If you'll excuse me, Zan," says Chester, and pushes off the doorframe.

As she heads downstairs, she hears Fletcher's sound of outrage, followed by a solid thump, and she supposes he's been rather unceremoniously toppled to the floor.

Theron is waiting in the hall for her, tugging at the scholar's hat he insists on wearing. He insists on her wearing her own, too, so she pulls it on. It's being fussy over things like this that'll make him chancellor one day.

"It's going to be trouble," he says. "You and Casca."

"And?" she says, gearing up for another argument.

But he only shakes his head, giving her a hint of a smile. "And you had best be prepared for it." He holds up the stark ivory of a university memo, marked with the stamp of a post-runner. "And for this. It arrived a few moments ago."

She tears the seal open. It's a brief note telling her to report to a meeting room that morning. "I'm being pulled before the Luminary board," she realises, gritting her teeth.

"Relentless bastards," Theron mutters. "Come on. Won't do to have you late."

Chapter Twenty-Four

"You make a lot of alarming suppositions with no reputable sources," Acanthus says, looking down at her notes. "Or indeed *any* sources."

Zanthi keeps her face very pleasant. At least, she hopes she does. "I am studying an era of history made notable by its entire *lack* of sources, Luminary," she says evenly. "It is the absence of any reputable record that makes this era interesting."

"It is what makes it a poor subject of study. If you wish the university to uphold your mentorship, I would strongly suggest you find a new theory to chase."

The memo hadn't been for a meeting so much as it had summoned her to an animal trap, and she is the beast they are baiting. She suspected so, given the late notice. They hadn't wanted to give her any time to prepare.

They have very little chance of entirely disqualifying her study, not now Ethram has endorsed it, but they can certainly make it difficult enough that she's bullied into abandoning it. Theron didn't raise her to bow to bullies, though.

Theron hadn't accompanied her. They both know it wouldn't do to look like she's sheltering behind him, and so she'd come expecting to face the meeting alone.

Only when she'd walked through the doors, Hart had turned to her with a small smile and said, "Perfectly on time, as usual, Ilyston."

And everything had suddenly been a lot easier.

He is leaning against the back wall, society dress under his Luminary robes as if he's been interrupted from being somewhere more interesting. He hasn't said a word, but he doesn't need to. That he is there is message enough. No one could ever say he doesn't take his charge as a mentor seriously.

"You can't mean to truly use Lydus," adds another professor. He has a pale sort of face and a paler sort of voice. "A flight of fancy is not a historical record, Miss Ilyston. It is artistic expression, at best."

She pins him with her most open gaze. He quails. "You are Professor Quartz, yes? I read your Luminary work. It was an excellent account of early Southern seasonal culture."

He inclines his head, wary. The four of them are glowering at her like they intend to intimidate her, but she has stood before Lady Casca at midsummer. She watched Madoc drag himself from dark waters. Their scowls won't frighten her.

She continues, pleasantly. "It was a sheep-herding song, was it not, that formed the foundation of your research?"

"My research was based on local history," he says stiffly.

"Local history," she says. "Oral history. Tradition, you might say. Passed down for generations in a set of rhyming verses with no known author, and no documented origin. That sort of history."

"It's—" he starts, then stops. His jaw works.

"I would have thought you precisely the person to understand that cultural history and artistic expression are inextricably linked," she adds. Behind her, she hears a soft sound of amusement. Her mouth twitches as she tamps down on a smile. It wouldn't do to let the Luminaries see how much she is enjoying this. "Of course, the poetry in question in my paper *has* a known author, and a documented origin both in place and time. So it seems, Professor, that your line between historical record and artistic expression is a matter of your own convenience."

A fraught silence holds. Acanthus clears her throat.

"Step carefully, Ilyston," she says. "A mentorship is only as valuable as the mentor."

Zanthi glances up and catches Hart's gaze. His lips twitch, as close to a smile as he'll likely get in front of this lot. The meeting is over quickly, after that. Zanthi listens to their list of suggestions and knows she won't take any of them.

She sighs as she falls into step with Hart after. "I would have been lost without you there."

"You did just fine on your own."

"It's tiresome."

"Get used to it," he says with the tone of a man who has been very tired for a very long time. "The work you are presenting them is valid and sound, and they can't throw it out just because they don't like it. I've caught up on your latest sources, by-the-by. That last play fragment was an absolute pain to track down. I suppose your brother put you onto it?"

"He said you'd have a trial of a time verifying it."

Hart makes a sound deep in his throat. "I do pity the students he takes under his wing."

"Much less fortunate than I," she says. "You've been very good to me."

"I find you tolerable," he says. "It helps."

She tamps down on her smile. "I'll endeavour to continue being so."

"And are you truly intent on using Lydus?"

She tugs at her robe buttons, straightening the fall of the cloth. Beneath, she's dressed too lightly for the day. The cold weather is already crawling back, creeping down from the mountains. "You're the one who put me onto him."

He laughs. It's a breath of a sound. "I was trying to warn you."

"About midsummer? Yes, I figured that out after the fact."

He tuts, holding the door to the courtyard open for her. The wind tugs her out, biting at her bare wrists. Outside, Esk is tumbling straight into autumn. The first flush of russet is staining the poplars peeking over the university wall, and the scent of the mountains is in every breath.

"You'll need to be quicker than that, Ilyston. You've set yourself quite a task, delving into the forgotten annals of history."

"Apparently so. I suppose I will have to find some better sources or they'll keep picking at me about it."

"Have you not had a new avenue of research recently opened to you?" he says, all mildness. "I heard Casca came to breakfast."

It has been *one* day. Theron's gossiping is reaching new heights. "He did. I didn't think anyone knew."

"And you spent midsummer with the nightingales, as I heard. You're quite woven into the Gardens."

"Not like that," she says, staring at him, aghast. "There was no weaving."

"No? I must have heard wrong."

She takes it back. It's not Theron gossiping at all. Hart must take tea with the nightingales, though the idea of that seems so absurd as to be laughable.

"Zanthi." He stops, drawing her into the shadows of the university wall. In her side-sight, his strange, silver fish-shapes twist around him in lazy figures. "The Gardens are a different world. It is, I think, the right place for you to be, given your academic interests. Even so, be careful."

She stares at him. The laughter is gone from his face. "I will be," she says.

"As careful as you are in the archive tunnels," he adds, weighing his words. "As careful as you are in the dark."

"What must I be careful of?" she says, gripping her satchel tight.

He tips his head in a quiet shrug. "You are bound to walk strange paths, Ilyston. That's all." With that pronouncement, he bids her good day and strides off towards the tram. His dark shape cuts into the busy street and disappears, his aether-trails drifting behind him.

She rubs at her eyes until her side-sight settles and leans against the wall. *Did* she have a new source of research open to her with Madoc? She cannot write of the midsummer festivities, or Madoc's ritual, but perhaps there is something within the Gardens that could support her theories.

The rest of the day sits ahead of her, empty of any obligations. Is it too soon to visit Madoc? Breakfasts are usually a once-a-week or once-a-fortnight sort of occurrence. How often did he expect to see her otherwise?

If he's busy, she'll go elsewhere, she decides. She might at least try. She hops on a tram trundling in the opposite direction from where Hart went, and crowds in beside an academic with sickly aether wrapped around his wrist, the ghost-shapes fluttering hopelessly like a bird caught in a trap. On her other side is a woman with aether wrapped around her neck like a fur, dead and glossy. Like all aether-worked things, they're faded traces of power. Barely a smudge against the ever-present aether soaked through Esk's stones. It makes her shudder, regardless.

She rubs her eyes again and her side-sight fades. The man is wearing a watch with a glowing clock face. The woman has a necklace with a tiny aetherglass bead. Pretty mild things. Her head aches, dull and stony. Her side-sight has been playing up more than usual lately.

It's a relief to tumble into the Garden Hall. The nightingale stationed at the Hall door directs her towards the lower terrace, through a blissful haze of steam and into a thicket of birches. Dappled light falls in a gossamer veil, and all the air is sweet with drifting steam.

Madoc is lounging on the moss lawns amongst a scattering of his nightingales. They're steam-damp, draped in clinging shifts and chemises as if they're ready to slip into the springs. The quartz-gravel path crunches beneath her boots, and so they're all watching her as she approaches. She knows Chicory, and she recognises the dark-haired woman who she'd spoken with at midsummer. The other faces are unknown, but they all watch her like *she's* known to them.

Gossiping, she thinks. They all know who she is.

Madoc's smile widens like the day is dawning. He rolls to his feet and pads over to meet her. He's in fawn linen trousers, and they're damp in patches, clinging delightfully to his thighs and calves. Then she remembers she has an audience and looks away.

"What a lovely surprise," he says, catching her hand and drawing her in. "I didn't expect you to turn up so soon."

The laughter of the nightingales is as soft as the chatter of the streams tangled all around them. They pick themselves up, and even that is done gracefully. As they wander off, Madoc pulls her to the spot under the birches. He tugs her, coaxing, and she lets herself be drawn back to lie with him. The ground pillows beneath her, fragrant with thyme and the rich, heady scent of soil. She rolls on her side to better see him. They lie like that for a while, Madoc's gaze drifting up into the wind-dancing leaves. The light catches in his eyes, turns them glowing like aetherglass or sunlit waters. She cannot look away.

"I don't think I've ever caught you at rest before."

He tips his head, grinning. "You do always seem to catch me when I should be elsewhere."

"But not today?"

"Not today." He pauses then, lips apart, but whatever he was about to say is swallowed back, and he closes his eyes instead. The light drapes across his face. "How was your morning?"

"Oh, tiresome." She reaches out, hesitating just before her fingertips touch the damp linen of his shirt. "I have some questions."

His smile is slight, but true. He doesn't open his eyes. "Yes?"

"What marked the start and end of the midsummer ritual? I've been reading Hart's work, and he's always firm on the importance of a conclusion—" She breaks off, because he's rolled onto his side to stare at her, askance.

"The ritual?" he says, on the edge of laughter. "That's what you wanted to ask about?"

"Well, yes." She frowns. "What else?"

"I thought you might ask about us. About how we are courting."

And they are. She knew that. Obviously, she did. Only the word is different, coming from his lips. It feels like a kiss. "I didn't think there was much to ask. You made yourself very clear."

"Not so clear," he says. He's setting a strange sort of look at her. "I probably won't be an easy man to be courting."

"I shouldn't think I'll be much easier," she admits. "It's Vestmere soon, you know. You'll hardly see me."

"And then it will be the Season, and you'll hardly see me. We'll find each other, though."

"You, I think, are always very easy to spot." She's quite sure of that. Today, his earrings are small pearl drops that send rippling reflections across his cheek as he lies there. "About the ritual?"

"Zanthi," he says, and he is laughing now. "Tell me one thing. Am I to be your secret, or would you like to parade about a bit?"

Warmth spills up through her. "I think I'd hate a parade of any sort. Let's be a little secret, for now. After the Season is done, we can do some promenading." She brushes her fingers against his shirt. It's so much finer than anything she has, and she had never thought her clothes were poor quality. "Do you mind?"

He is watching her, unflinching. He doesn't look away from her eyes once. "Then we'll be secret. I don't mind. I'm quite used to all the important things being secrets, you know." He catches her fingers, brings them to his lips. "As secret and slow as you wish."

Zanthi doesn't recall saying anything about *slow*, but perhaps that is Madoc's way of asking for her consideration. "The ritual?"

He hums, eyes fluttering closed again. "I don't know. I suppose it started when I drank the poison?"

"How can you not know?"

"Should I?" He waves a lazy hand through the air. "We do many rituals. I visit the springheart in the mornings, I cleanse it on the first day of each month. Some days, we sing or say blessings. We celebrate all of Esk's festival days, and a good number of others, besides. There is midsummer and there is midwinter, sitting in counterpart—"

She sits up, tense. "What happens at midwinter?"

"Nothing like midsummer," he promises. "And that won't happen again. I need only undertake that ritual once."

"You were alarming enough when I thought you nothing more than a socialite. What are you now that the ritual is done?" She wishes she had a notebook to jot down what he is telling her. "What can you tell me of this ritual for which you do not know a beginning or an end?"

He laughs. "Surely it ended when I came back from the dark river, didn't it?"

"I don't know. I haven't much made a study of rituals. I should ask Hart—that is his area of expertise."

"He won't know much about this one. I think the journal you uncovered is the last remaining record of it. I must be the only Casca to have completed it in two centuries or more. Longer, perhaps."

"Would you translate the journal for me?"

Laid out on the moss as he is, his neck is a golden line leading down to where his chemise gaps against his collarbones. The linen clings to his steam-damp skin, thin as mist. He hums.

"Of course. I don't think you'll find much use in it, though." There is silence, and when she looks up, Madoc's gaze is on her. His throat shifts. "As for what it makes me, I suppose I am a full initiated attendant of the waters now. A high priest, to be exact. An archon, I think, is the term that is sometimes used."

It is the term Lydus uses in his poetry, though she hadn't associated it with the Gardens at first. It must be what he was writing of, though. A high priest of the sacred springs, bound in worship to the lost god of the dark river. A creature of the underworld. The sort of thing that should only exist in stories and songs, and ancient poetry. If only she could trot Madoc out in front of the

Luminaries. She'd like to see them claim his existence as an disreputable source.

"You've had more time to think on it. On me," he says, when she's been silent too long. "Do you find it bothers you?"

"What bothers me is how little we know about it," she says, wry. It has been stuck in her mind like a thorn. It had been a strange ritual, and she didn't see it end. And all she has learned tells her an unfinished ritual is a dangerous thing. "It bothers me that I cannot remember there being a ritual end to the ceremony."

"Well," he says, drawing out the word. "There was a lot of—"

"No," she says, feeling her cheeks darkening. "I don't think that counts."

"A lot of our ceremonies end with a kiss," he says, and raises himself, propped on one elbow. The sunlight dapples him in gold and lights the green in his gaze. "And I didn't get one from you, then."

"I try not to kiss poisoned tongues."

"I promise there's no poison now," he says, his gaze dipping to her mouth.

She leans in and lays her lips to his. He's smiling, watching her under half-lowered lashes. She kisses him once, soft and chaste, and she expects to taste the sun and the springs on his lips.

He's cold. His mouth is as earth-cold as the archives, without a speck of warmth to be found. And then he wraps his arm around her and pulls her over him. His lips *are* sweet with steam, and warm as a cup of tea, and the strange moment flees her mind entirely.

Chapter Twenty-Five

The month of Vestmere passes in its usual raging flood of academic clamour. Vestmere is as close to a Season as the scholars have, only instead of evening parties and soirees, it is full of debates, presentations, assessments, and awards.

Madoc takes it all in stride admirably and never misses a weekly breakfast. No scholar is at their best in Vestmere. It is the time of year that merits are measured and weighted, and Theron, who is aiming for another band on his robes and is eyeing the Head of Languages role when the current head retires, becomes as vicious as a small stormbeast. Chester, usually still in the north at this time of year, avoids both her and Theron with increasing alarm. Fletcher only laughs and puts them in separate rooms when they start to squabble at one another.

Her studies progress slowly, though. Her time is taken up with endless university happenings, and when she gets home one day to find Madoc has delivered his promised journal translation, she grits her teeth against the frustration of missing him. He had been right about the contents, though. There isn't much there to use. He has not given her the section involving the ritual and the poison, which are the parts she suspects might be the most useful.

She still doesn't know when the ritual ended. Hart, when she had asked him about it, had given her an intense look and simply told her that such things end when all the steps are danced.

There had certainly been a lot of dancing, but that is not quite what he means, she thinks.

Esk comes alive as autumn tumbles them towards the Wintering Season. Vestmere finally ends, and the fashion showcases start. The docks fill up with returning airships. The *Tisk*, the *Foxpoint*, the *Sepha*.

The town fills up, too, all the winter accommodation starting to fill. The streets are choked with carriages, and the air takes on the hazy golden shimmer in Zanthi's side-sight that makes her feel like the world is always twisting away from her. It won't stop *moving*.

This is why she mostly becomes a recluse during the Season. She keeps her head down, pulls her cloak's hood up when the weather allows the indulgence. It gets dire as airguards fill the streets, too. When they're fresh from the sky, they're wound full of twisting sparks of bright ship-aether, and it leaves her eyes aching. She isn't aether-sensitive in the way most people are, isn't susceptible to the sickening and wasting that some suffer, but her side-sight does reliably give her atrocious headaches when everything is glimmering from every corner. Perhaps she's under the weather, but it feels worse than ever this year.

The artisan markets grow, and the artisan quarter ceases to sleep. Merchant ferries arrive in the town most days, hauling in fabrics and wood, and the airships bring back skulking, glowing heaps of raw aethermaterial—bones, scales, teeth.

Zanthi hates those most of all.

But she still must venture across the river and through the town some days, and today is one of those days.

It is the opening of the Gallery Annual, and she promised Emlyn she'd be there to admire his painting. She dresses with more care than usual. She kisses Susan's head and wishes Fletcher a good day, and hurries out.

All of Esk is pretty and sparkling in a heavy rain, and she rushes up her street to catch a tram. She doesn't see the Admiralty goods carriage until it's too late. She presses herself to a garden fence as it trundles by, close enough to touch. Her side-sight flares, but she barely needs the warning. She can feel the dead aether dripping from it, and it twists the air right out of her chest. In her side-sight, it drips from the carriage, pools beneath the stones of the street, sinking down.

The carriage must be loaded with aethermaterial from the stormbeasts. Bone, scale, teeth, all heading to the artisan quarter. She's rarely seen so much raw, dead aether all in one hit, and as she braces herself, she realises why it looks familiar. The bruised, sticky aspect of it reminds her of the damaged aether in the blood vial.

That aether hadn't been dead, but it had, perhaps, been dying. Did Joren know?

"Are you alright?"

She looks up, startled. There is a man leaning out of his front door, watching her clutch at his garden wall. She knows his face, but not his name. She's seen him often enough over the years, handsome in his airguard uniform. Even without the uniform, the aetherburn scars curling up his neck would clue anyone in to his occupation.

"Fine," she says, gathering her thoughts back. She straightens from her slump. She'd half-collapsed and hadn't realised. No wonder he looks so concerned. "Thank you."

He gives her a once-over, as if unconvinced, and steps out of his doorway. He's in his slippers. "I keep telling them they shouldn't haul those carriages through the streets like that," he says. He pulls a tin from his pocket and offers it to her. "Aniseed drops? They help somewhat."

She hasn't the heart to tell him she isn't aether-sensitive, so she thanks him again and takes the tin.

She's *not* aether-sensitive, but the aniseed helps.

She gets to the gallery late. She slips into the back of the crowd as the speeches finish, adding her polite applause to whatever has been said. Giant, domed skylights send watery light scattering across the gathering, illuminating the paintings hung floor to ceiling in a riotous patchwork, though there is barely a glimpse of them through the shining crowds.

There's a lot of aetherwork being worn. She sneaks another aniseed drop and finds it helps. *Fancy that.* All this time, she should have just been eating aniseed sweets.

There's a lovely, towering fern in a glazed pot, and she shuffles into its shadow, hoping the room will thin out once people move through to the galleries. From where she stands, she can see a portrait of a grouping of youths in a riverboat, and a whole wall of airguard captains—she squints and makes out a very idealised representation of Chester's profile—and another of a woman in a beautiful, beaded gown. Not one, she thinks, has a chance of being Emlyn's. He would never paint anything so tame.

"You smell like aniseed," says a voice in her ear. "Not been kissing any airguards, have you?" Emlyn spins her around and clasps her forearms. "You're certainly dressed bonny enough for it."

Emlyn is looking rather bonny himself. She forgets, sometimes, that he's actually rather well-off and well-born, because she's so used to seeing him half in paint rags and stinking of linseed oil. He still smells a little of linseed oil, to be perfectly honest.

"I feel like I haven't seen you in an age," she says, and despite everything, she can't help but smile. "I might not have recognised your face."

"I certainly recognise yours. I've been staring at it enough lately."

She blinks, trying to make any sense of that, and then she does. "No."

"It's much better in the flesh," he adds. "I see I didn't do you justice."

All her flattering thoughts are buried under the sudden, stomach-dropping dread. "Tell me you didn't."

He turns the lovely smile on her, the one he uses to charm collectors and clients. It has never worked on her, and it never will, and he knows it. "Sorry, Zan. Can't."

"*Fairthorne.*"

"If I'd told you, you wouldn't have come," he says, which is fair, because it is true. "Come on, I want you to see it. I painted it for you, you know."

He finds a way through the crowd, mostly by judicious use of his shoulder, and pulls her into the main gallery. His painting is halfway up a wall, in prime position. It's a magnificent painting. He's made a mistake in spending his talent on it, because there's no one in society that would want that painting. There's no way he's going to sell it.

It's clearly her, though she's never reclined on any window seat with that elegance. One leg is peeking out beneath the fold of her skirts, a line of pale stocking that his brush has made beautiful. All the light is indistinct, a riot of colours that aren't really colours, just softness and greys. He hasn't changed her eyes, and even though they're nothing more than brush marks of darkest umber, it shows her why her gaze makes people uncomfortable in a way the mirror never has.

It's a gentle painting, but damning too, because the girl in that painting looks like she's weathering a storm and knows the viewer will not help her.

"Emlyn," she says. She grabs at his arm, holds him. "I do not look like that."

"You do, a bit," he says, and he leans into her. "You were so sad that day. I only want to show you that you should go where you want, and you should reach for what you want. I didn't want you hiding yourself away."

She clutches at his sleeve, linseed smell and all. "I did," she says. "I have. Em, I have so much to tell you—"

"I know you do," he says, grinning. "Do you like it?"

Gods, she adores his smug face. "Of course I do, you wretch. But you shouldn't have. You'll never sell it."

His grin grows to a new shade of insufferable. "It's already sold."

She stares at him.

"You have *so* much to tell me, darling mouse." He grabs her hands for a quick squeeze, which is about as affectionate as he ever gets and probably a touch too affectionate for such a setting. "This is wonderful for me, you know."

"Whatever do you mean?"

He doesn't get his reply out before there is a solid presence at Zanthi's side, and a hand settling at her back. And a familiar scent, that candle-smoke perfume that makes her whole body sigh right through.

"Zanthi," Madoc says, right against her ear. "What a lovely surprise."

And everything is entirely different in a moment. Her throat goes dry. She hasn't seen Madoc since breakfast last week, and she's grown so used to him as a pleasing, amiable addition to her morning that she is entirely unprepared for the creature that has appeared beside her. He's drenched in a muted evening blue, and it turns his green eyes river-deep. He's never looked so much like Lady Casca, all aloof, unconcerned, and charming distance.

She can't help but stiffen. "Good morning, Madoc."

"Morning, dearest," he says, and the endearment does exactly what he surely meant it to do. Her ears burn. He tucks her into his side while she's still processing the sweetness of that word said for her. Madoc tips his gaze to Emlyn, and the charm winks out of him. "Is he a friend of yours, then?"

"Casca," Emlyn says, unruffled. "It's been a long while."

"And yet, not long enough."

Emlyn laughs. "Not still sore about that river painting, are you?"

"Depends. Are you ready to make it up to me?"

"I still can't give it to you," Emlyn says, palms up. "I told you, it's been sold."

"Remarkable, seeing as when the Gardens claimed it, it was available."

"I never took any payment from you." Emlyn winks at Zanthi so fast she thinks Madoc wasn't meant to catch it, but she knows he did. "No harm."

Madoc makes an unhappy noise in his chest. He looks at the painting on the wall. His jaw unclenches. "It's well done, Fairthorne," he says, after a moment. "You're reaching new strides with your work."

Emlyn preens. "I am honoured, of course."

"Don't take it too much to heart," Madoc mutters.

"I look forward to seeing my work hanging at the Gardens," Emlyn adds. "My darling model deserves no lesser throne."

Zanthi could kick him. She also wants to pinch his dear, *dear* face, with his combed hair and ridiculous dimples and endearing brashness. Only Emlyn Fairthorne would paint a larger-than-life portrait of a friend to cheer them up. Only he would get it into the Gallery's Annual. Only he would sell it to—

"*Madoc*," she says, realisation dawning. "You didn't."

Madoc gives an elegant one-shouldered shrug. "Was it ever a question? Of course I did."

"Come by for tea soon, Zan," Emlyn says, still smiling wide and handsome. "I want to hear *everything*. And thank you, Casca, for the patronage. Truly an unexpected honour."

"Oh, go charm someone else," she says, a bit airless.

He grins and goes off buoyed up by the sort of manic delight that must result from trotting an artist out to have his work admired for hours on end. Madoc mutters something very unflattering under his breath.

She steps away from him, because they are still in a crowded room and she has no plan to make the papers. "I didn't know you knew Emlyn."

"I'm rather more surprised that you know him."

She tips her face to the painting. It's so strange to see her face looking back at her, so noble and unknown. It's good Madoc bought it, though she'd hate to know the cost. It would be odd to think of it hanging in some stranger's collection. "He's very sweet, in his own way."

"I suppose you think Theron is sweet, too."

"No, he's a moss-asp waiting to strike, and that's on a good day."

His eyes are bright. "I don't suppose you'd wait a little longer for me? We can go for that tea we keep missing."

She hesitates. She's only been in the scratchy-bright room for a half-hour, and already she's about reached her limit. The aether glimmers in her side-sight are making her head scratchy and sore.

Madoc scoops her around and points. "There are some quieter galleries over there. Very unfashionable stuff. You could browse in peace."

"Well, if it's *unfashionable*," she says, and he laughs.

"I have a few more conversations to get through. I'll come get you soon." He brushes his fingers across the back of her hand, and then he's gone too, slipping back into the crowd.

Madoc is right, though. The far gallery *is* quiet. The light sits soft and muted over the empty viewing benches. Everything, she notes, is landscapes. She wanders a while, admiring the artisanship. There is nothing lesser in the work as far as she can see, nothing to mark them as unlovable compared to the portraits in the main gallery. She drifts towards a vignette of a misty country scene. The artist has dragged their brush along the canvas sparsely, as if they'd not had enough paint to make the journey, and the result is strangely lovely but also sort of miserable. She's trying to decide if she likes it when another viewer joins her.

"Casemer Lake," says a man. He's got a fine voice, smooth as milk. "Fed by the Lune. There's some interesting local folklore that it was made by the desperate grief of a young wife clawing herself out of the dark river itself."

Zanthi looks up, thoroughly startled.

He turns more fully to her. "You are the model for Fairthorne's remarkable portrait, are you not? It's had quite the illustrious buyer, too." He smiles. He's got a pleasant face, his brown hair styled in a fashionable tumble over his forehead, and his aetherglass necklace shines knife-like at the edges of her vision. At his collar is the star-and-quill pin of the Writer's Guild.

She goes prey-still all over. "Pardon, but you are?"

His smile widens. "I'm a writer for the *Society Papers*. And you are?"

"Uninterested," she says, turning back to the painting.

His laugh is loud, grating in her aching head. "I'd like to have some words with the most talked of model of the show."

"I'd rather not."

"I'm sure I can convince you," he says, and she's sure he usually can convince his targets. He's charming, but it's nothing that will ever hook Zanthi. Compared to Madoc, this man's charm is like poorly applied gilt on a low-quality book. "I've heard rumours that Madoc Casca has been entertaining a regular visitor to the Gardens this year. There are rumours of morning visits in the outer town, too."

She stares furiously at the painting, at the too-thin scrapes of paint. "I have nothing to say to you."

"Come, miss. It won't be hard to find your name, not now that I know of you. I'll have it in the papers by morning, whether you have a word to say to me or not." He shifts, and in her side-sight, the aetherglass is painfully bright. "If you agree to give me a few words, I promise that my work will be kind."

"And if I don't?"

"Then I have no promises to give you." His eyes glint, as if that prospect is more pleasing to him, after all.

The sound of footsteps has them turning. Madoc stands in the archway, and she's never seen him look so cold. She's never seen him look so much like his mother.

"Archer Colt," he says, and his words are dripping with warning. "I didn't think landscapes were to your tastes."

"They're not. But a good story is," Colt says, all brightness. "And do *you* have any words to share with me? I think I might make it to the top of the gossip section, with a catch like this."

Madoc comes to her side, and he makes no secret of the way he rests his palm to the small of her back. "Not with this story."

Colt's smile falters. "Pardon?"

"Not this story," Madoc says. "Not her."

Colt's gaze flits between them, and if he'd been curious earlier, he's ravenous now. "Gods. Don't tell me the morning visits are true?"

Madoc's jaw tenses, mouth pressed tight, and Colt watches him in fascination. This is not a face Madoc lets show outside, she realises. This man has never seen Madoc when he is obstinate, when he is set on something. When he is more of the Gardens than he is of Society.

Somehow, without meaning to, she knows more of him than the people who have moved in his circles for years.

"I'll talk to you about the Gardens' latest acquisitions," Madoc says, and he has that dangerously pleasant timbre to his voice. "Do you have an aethergrapher with you? You may take an aethergraph. But if I see a single word published about her, Colt, you will never publish in the papers again. I will have you thrown from your guild. I will have the Gardens closed to you. I will make sure no one worth anything ever speaks to you again."

The humour drains from Colt's face. She can see there is no doubt in his face that Madoc means it, that he could follow through on each and every one of his promises.

"I see." He shoves his hands in his pockets, and he doesn't so much as look at Zanthi again. It is as if she has ceased to exist. He drags a thready breath through his teeth. "I have Sanderton with me. He'll be delighted to be given the allowance of an aethergraph."

Madoc is unflinching. "Then go get him set up, and I will find you. Leave."

"I should thank you for such a generous offer." His face is set mulishly, clearly rattled. He runs a hand through his hair and leaves, hurrying off through the arch. The gallery falls back to silence.

"I've never seen an aethergraph of you in the papers," she says after a moment.

Madoc presses his lips to the crown of her hair. It's the briefest of kisses, so gentle she almost misses it happening. "I try to avoid it," he admits. "Mother has strictly forbidden me from getting my face in the papers if I can help it."

"Then you shouldn't have rewarded him like that."

"Zanthi," he says, moving his hand to brush against her fingers. "I didn't do it because I intend to keep you a secret. There'll be gossip, eventually. There will be articles and aethergraphs and more speculation than either of us will like. But let it happen on our terms, when we wish it."

"And perhaps for a writer you like better," she adds, a little wry.

"When they print your name, it won't be because they've intimidated it from either of us. That weasel had better enjoy his interview, because it is the last time I will ever speak to him."

Now it's quiet and her sight is less aetherstruck, she notices what she hadn't before. There are shadows beneath his eyes. He's tried to cover them up, but they're there, if one looks for them. She touches a light finger to his cheek, right under the hint of darkness, and traces across the arch of his cheek.

"Are you well?"

"I'm fine," he says. He gently tips his face away, but with clear reluctance. "I'm sorry. We'll have to postpone our tea again."

She doesn't mind. Honestly, she's had enough of society for one day. And when she tells him so, he smiles with a look that makes her think that, for once, so has he.

Chapter Twenty-Six

Madoc's purchases at the Annual do make the papers. Alongside her portrait, the article says he also acquired a set-piece of lounging festivalgoers in a garden, a suggestive piece of bathers in the river, and a pair of gentle, rolling landscapes. The portrait of her is the only one that appears in aethergraph form.

She stares at the ink-brown aethergraph, the grainy print not doing justice to Emlyn's work. Her face is still recognisable, though. Her face. On every breakfast table in Esk. She thinks she might be ill.

"Did we know you had a portrait painted?" Fletcher says, running a hand through his uncombed hair.

"*I* didn't know, not until yesterday," she says and folds the paper back up. The first page has the rare aethergraph of Madoc, perfectly framed amongst the well-dressed crowd. "I think I'll keep my head down for a few days. Be unremarkable and boring."

"It is what you do best," Theron murmurs, and she throws a crust of bread at him.

She doesn't see Madoc for the rest of the week. That isn't unusual. It's her mood that is unusual, because she hesitates at the thought of going to see him and then backs away from it. Her own indecision rubs her raw. She catches her reflection in shop windows and puddles, and thinks of the Gallery Annual and *Society Papers*, and the way Colt had looked delighted at the thought of spreading her secrets around. She has the creeping thought that she's invited in a whole host of trouble, accepting Madoc in for breakfast.

Seeing him at the Annual had set her all adrift. She'd gotten used to him being amiable and well-dressed and talking of lovely things like rituals and ancient worship. She'd forgotten, somehow, that temple boy or not, he is still a socialite at heart.

She's still in a bit of a mood when she climbs the stairs to Emlyn's studio on a rainy evening at the end of the week. The door is ajar, but she hasn't even cracked it an inch more before his voice rings out, curt.

"Go away. I don't have time for you."

Zanthi pauses. She recognises the stress in his voice, and she recognises it on a rather personal level. "Very well," she calls. "Can I fetch you supper before I go?"

The door is wrenched from her hands. "Zanthi," he says, tugging her in. "Of course I have time for you. Well, I don't, really, but I'll make it."

He's a mess. There is paint on his cheek and through his hair, and his shirt is undone past his collarbones. Behind him is a disaster of creation, which can only mean the painting is going very, very well.

"No, I daren't interrupt genius at work," she says, grinning. "I take it that your career has taken off?"

"More commissions than I can hope to do." He leans in, pickled with the scent of linseed oil and turps. "To tell the truth, all I want to paint are the river willows, but these society types *do* insist on having their faces done."

A dour-faced woman looms on the canvas behind Emlyn. It's a finished portrait, likely painted from life, and he's touching a few final bits after the fact. "I'm glad it went well for you."

"I'm an artist with a work hanging at the Gardens, now," he says. "I'm made." He taps her on the nose and turns back to his canvas. “You are my luckiest charm, Ilyston. To think, one day soon I’ll paint Casca himself.”

“How do you make that?”

He glances over his shoulder. “*Please.* Tell me the breakfasts you hinted at having are not with Casca.”

“I can’t. They are.”

The paintbrush flips through his fingers and lands precisely in his grip. “Thought so,” he says. “I suddenly find myself very well-connected indeed.”

“You’re the admiral’s son. You couldn’t be less connected if you tried.”

“That connection only bears fruit with the airguard, and I’d cut my own hands off before I stepped foot into a uniform.” He darkens a discreet corner of the painting. It makes no discernible difference. “So, what have you wandered into my domain to tell me?”

“I only wanted to see how you were. I left the Annual rather abruptly.”

He shrugs. “I didn’t notice. I *am* glad you came, though. Why didn’t you go with Casca, if you’re breakfasting and everything? I’ve never seen a man so floored as he was when he saw your painting. Whatever spell you’ve woven, it’s a good one.”

“If that was a witch joke, Fairthorne—”

He laughs. “No, truly. Why aren’t you planning your Season debut?”

“We’re being quiet. I’m not doing the Season.”

That gets her a look. “You’re taking breakfasts with Casca, and you’re not doing the Season? Zanthi, Casca *is* the Season.”

“I’d hate it.”

“You hate crowds, but you came to the Annual for me. Why?”

“Because you asked.” She sits on the painter’s stool when Emlyn pushes her down, and looks up at him. “Because you’ve been working so hard for it for so long, and I wanted to see what you’d made. Because you’re my friend.”

His mouth curls a little. It’s a fond look. “Love you too, Zan.”

He kicks the stool, and it spins, and she curses his name very thoroughly. Then the stool stops, so her back is to him. "I hate being sincere, so I'll only say this once. Casca is a trial, but he takes his work seriously. You've never seen a Season Opening, so you wouldn't know, but it's as much a work of art as any painting I've ever done. Casca is a director on a stage. A conductor of an orchestra. A dance-master of a hundred moving parts. And I know you aren't a society type, so maybe the Opening is beyond you. That's fine, too. If you hadn't wanted to come to the Annual, I would have done a private showing for you, when all the crowds were gone. But if you'd refused to see my painting hanging in the exhibition at all? That would have felt vile. I'd have been hurt."

She kicks herself back around so she can face him. Her throat is all twisted. "Em—"

"Don't," he says, looking very put upon. "Pretend I never said it."

She looks at her feet, at the paint-smudged floorboards below. "I don't want to go to the Opening."

"Then you won't, and I daresay Casca is too smitten with you to mind it. But you should find a way to see all of him and all he does, regardless."

She's seen far more of him than anyone might suspect. She's seen him and his Gardens at their darkest and most secret. Still, she groans, putting her head in her hands. "I'm going to have to do it, aren't I?"

"'Fraid so, darling. You can't just ignore the bits you don't like."

"I don't dislike it," she admits, peeking over her fingers. "I don't dislike any of him."

He clicks his tongue. "Well then," he says, "there isn't any problem, is there?"

It is Chester's turn to make breakfast, and so the toast is perfect.

Zanthi glares at it, all golden, even pieces, but Chester is frowning at Madoc, who had arrived while he was preparing the meal.

Madoc is looking rather lovely, with gold in his ears and gold up his wrists, and a twist of gold pinning his hair back from his face. It makes his cheekbones look lethal, but that's surely not what has Chester staring.

"Madoc," Chester says. "Are you well?"

Madoc smiles as he pours the tea. "Quite well. Busy."

Zanthi shares a sharp look with her brother. She knows he has noticed the shadows under Madoc's eyes, too. It's a bit much, even for a nightingale, even for a Casca, to wear any sort of cosmetics to breakfast. He's done his best to make it look like he isn't, but there's the tell of it, of creams to smooth out the shadows and hide them away. When she brushes her finger along his hand under the table, his skin is cool.

Chester gives him a measured look, then moves on with serving. "I suppose you would be. How are the Season preparations coming along?"

"Are you sure you want to ask that? It's a heated topic at this table lately," Madoc says.

"It's hardly heated," returns Theron. "Your opinions are just flawed."

"*You're* the one turning down an invitation to the Opening on principle," mutters Fletcher. "So don't talk about flawed opinions."

Zanthi sips her tea. Chester's mouth tugs up on one side.

"You'll be there, Locksley?" says Madoc. "Please say yes. I'd like to think all my hard work will be witnessed by at least *one* soul at this table."

"Of course I will be," he says. "You never fail to make a spectacle."

There's certainly a slight buried in the compliment, because Madoc laughs. "I do try."

She glances up, but Theron is the only one who is looking at her. He gives her a very neutral look, the one she calls his *nothing* look, then turns back to the papers. She nibbles at her toast. His nothing look is sharper than a book-knife slicing paper. He's judging her for something.

Zanthi wants to argue his silent insult. It's not that she thinks the ballrooms beneath her. It's not even the pageantry. She wouldn't mind wearing beautiful things and following ribbon-wisps of gossip through the night. It might even be enjoyable, in the same way hunting through a history book for crumbs of a story is enjoyable.

But she's avoided such things for so long that she wouldn't know how to wade into it now. And she's spent enough of her life feeling awkward, out-of-place, and unwanted in the halls of the university to ever willingly bring herself into such an environment ever again.

Then Theron shakes out the morning's issue of the *Society Papers* and says, "Oh? The Second Heir is back in town."

Madoc's toast clatters back onto his plate. He looks, for a sharp moment, outraged. "Pardon?" he says, voice low. "Arlet Harbourne is back in Esk?"

Chester frowns, cup halfway to his mouth. "You know Heir Auguste?"

"Wait," says Zanthi. An old conversation is slotting into place in her memories. "Is Arlet Harbourne your *Lettie*?"

"Yes, and a first-rate weasel, what's more. I can't believe he didn't write to me." Madoc reaches over the table and takes the paper right from Theron's hands. Theron stares in shock.

"Perhaps he had more important business to attend to, being an important sort of person," Theron says, piqued.

"The only business he manages is poetry and being pecked at by people who should know better. Gods, he only got in yesterday. How did they get the news?"

Zanthi leans over his arm to see the paper. There's no aethergraph, only a slim article at the top of the gossip pages. It claims the Second Heir was seen slinking back into the town on the dawn ferry. That's the word they use. *Slinking*. Like a fox, or a stoat, or a thief.

"It's not nicely worded, is it?" she says.

"It's only the beginning," Madoc says. He gives her a quick glance from the corner of his eye. She isn't sure what to make of his expression. It's somewhere between resignation and concern, and she doesn't know if it's for her or his friend. "The papers were horrid to him last time. No wonder he tried to sneak in."

Chester makes a so-so noise. "He's an Heir. He really shouldn't be sneaking anywhere."

"Have you met him?" Madoc says, sharply.

Chester is silent for a beat. "No. But I know the First Heir well. And I can't imagine Eve sneaking in anywhere. Whether it's a tearoom or an aetherstorm, he strides in like he's got a personal invitation."

"Yes, well. Going against Eve is like inviting a moss-asp in for a kiss," Madoc says, grim. "Going against Lettie is like refusing honey from an open hand. And yet, people do. Repeatedly."

"Perhaps you'd best go see him," Zanthi suggests, tugging the paper from his hands. He's creasing it with how tightly he's holding it.

He glances at the clock. Breakfast hours are well past. "I think I must. Walk with me to the river, then?"

Zanthi passes the paper back to Theron as they leave, and her brothers fall on the gossip, all intrigued faces and speculation. Madoc's face holds only trouble.

The walk to the river twists through rough-stepped lanes and stone walls and leafy gardens. They pass under an overspilling of grapevines, and it sends a shower of morning raindrops down on them.

Madoc ducks his head, the light-dapples kissing his face. "You'd be very welcome to come with me."

"I think you had better visit your Lettie on your own," she says. Dropping in on an Heir, even the second one, is going a touch too far for her sensibilities. "That article was terrible. He'll probably need a friend, if that's the homecoming he's being given."

He brushes the back of her hand with his own. She knows they're both thinking of Colt at the Annual.

"The papers wouldn't be any kinder to you, if you were to appear on my arm this Season," he says.

"I'll have to figure it out someday, but not this year." And she would, in time. Perhaps, if she made herself very boring, they wouldn't find anything worth remarking over. "Will you have someone else on your arm instead?"

He's frozen for a moment. She sees it from the corner of her eye. "Probably," he says, at last. "I hadn't thought of that. But I can't go around alone for all of winter, or I'll have the town in uproar."

She laughs, because there is something sweet about the mulishness of his face as he confronts this thought. "I thought so. Perhaps Lettie will accompany you, now he's back."

"Maybe," he says, without much hope. "If you read things in the paper this Season, Zanthi, know it's most likely rubbish."

"You're the one who told me the papers described you truly."

"Forget I ever said that. I was wrong."

She stops them below a plum tree, right beside the river. "I'm a scholar. I'm well-versed in reading rubbish."

He laughs, that lovely, rough one that means she's startled him. The river reed beds below them whisper like gossips at a ball, but there is no one else to pass comment on the kiss he brushes against her mouth in the shadow of the plum tree.

Chapter Twenty-Seven

The truth, when she admits it to herself, is that it is easier for her to accept Madoc as a temple priest than it is to accept him as a jewel of the Season. As a follower of forgotten gods and the ancient ways, he still feels like he belongs with her. He belongs in the dark and secret places, in the quiet spaces between words on faded pages.

Madoc Casca, heir to the Gardens and society darling, does not belong to her at all. She's not sure he ever can. She is not a socialite, and she never will be one. It is not her style, just as debates and academic intrigue are not Madoc's. She worries there is no way for them to fit together entirely. There is no way for them ever to make any sort of sense.

She is the one that asked for all of him. She is the one who asked for everything. The Season Opening may be beyond her, but Emlyn is right. She can't ignore half of who he is and call it fair.

Not when he arrives on her doorstep every week, even when he's tired, even when he's surely barely slept the night before.

Not when he'd held her hand in the archives and kept her close in the dark.

The next time she is left alone with the *Society Papers*, she trawls through the town schedule for the next event at the Gardens. It's a small music recital. It won't be too large, because the Season isn't truly open yet. And besides, she doesn't intend to *attend*, exactly. She's going to research.

That evening, the carriages are lined up across the cobblestones. Floating visions of silk and ribbon tumble out, laughing and chattering, and drift up the stairs to the grand oak doors. Nightingales stand sentry at the door, checking invitations and guiding guests to the entertainments.

She skirts the square entirely, and knocks on one of the discreet, hidden doors set into the far side of the Hall. A breath of relief escapes her when she knows the face that peers out.

"Kit," she says. "What luck!"

"Evening, Zanthi." Kit draws her in. "Madoc is hosting tonight."

"I know. That's why I came. I don't suppose there's any way to —" She breaks off, wondering how best to phrase it. "Peek?"

"Spy?" Kit says, delighted. "Oh, yes. We'll make you a nightingale, yet."

Which is an entirely alarming phrase, but she lets Kit tug her away through a warren of hidden corridors. Spying, it turns out, is a popular nightingale pastime.

Kit leads her to a tapestried corridor that opens onto a shadowy balcony. The railing is heavy wood, carved with a thicket of woodland plants, and a gathering of off-duty nightingales crouch behind it and peer through the gaps in the carving to watch the stage below.

Zanthi kneels beside Kit. The great chandelier above them is lit aflame, glittering in candlelight, and all the guests below are glittering, too. The crowd turns and mingles like the paints on Emlyn's palette, distinct but running together, blending into odd shapes and motions. It's a music performance, so there isn't dancing so much as conversational groupings, all the guests vying to be included in the *right* circles. And there is a lot of conversation. It drifts up in a ringing swell of noise, louder than the music, and she can barely snatch a word or two of meaning out of it.

"There," says Kit, nodding, and Zanthi sees him.

He's dressed in a wine-dark velvet that sweeps to his wrists like wings, all richly embroidered around the collar and hems. She understands where the moth motif comes from, seeing that. He's walking, a woman on his arm and her companion leaning into him, and his smile is a beautiful thing. It's not *his* smile, though, not the one she knows. She'd met something like it the first time he'd visited the archives, but that smile had been polite and sweet. This one is polite in that it is mannered, but there is nothing sweet about it.

Madoc speaks; his companions laugh. Then he's handing them off to a set of people. Introducing them, perhaps? As soon as they are connected, he's off again. He has a way of walking that seems aimless and easy, but from up here, the pattern is clear. He has a target each time.

"What is he doing?"

"Making sure the right people have the right conversations. Making sure the wrong conversations are interrupted. Ensuring everyone feels like he has given them his personal attention tonight, but without actually doing so. It can shape how the Season opens, this sort of thing. Having the favour of the Gardens can elevate someone's entire Season."

"That sounds exhausting."

"I suppose so. At least *we* get a night off, now and then. He doesn't get to rest, not until spring."

"Not that we use it to rest," mutters the nightingale on Zanthi's other side. "Oh, look. There's Frederic Masey. What *is* he wearing?"

The nightingales fall silent as a man struts across the scene in bold blue, much stronger than the twilight-haze shade that is clearly in style.

"The Maseys are always competitive weasels. He's trying to outshine Casca, I'd bet."

There's another silence as they all contemplate the futility of that, and then someone snorts. "Good luck to him."

Madoc charms his way through a group of artisans in pretty spring-blossom colours. Once, he draws a man into a private conversation, and when the conversation is done, he slides his hand against the back of the man's neck and kisses him.

She's heard much about Madoc bestowing kisses like blessings at his parties, but he doesn't kiss his chosen one like he kisses her. It is a brief brush of lips, barely remarkable. Barely even a *kiss*. It still changes the course of the crowd. From the balcony, it is easy to see how the currents shift, as people angle to be the next to engage with the chosen one.

"Ryley Rose. An artisan," says Kit, low in her ear, as Madoc murmurs something and the artisan laughs. "I suppose he'll be a notable for the Season, now. Madoc is very discerning when it comes to picking his favourites."

"I shall have to look up Mr Rose's work," Zanthi says, mildly, and Kit gives her a stunning smile. She feels she has passed a test, but it wasn't such a hard test, after all.

This is the Madoc that Emlyn first warned her of, that Fletcher cautioned her against. She might laugh, seeing it, because while it is him, truthfully, it's barely a scratch to the surface of all the things that require caution about Madoc. Better to warn her of a poisoned mouth and inviting darkness, of rituals and river-green eyes. Of steam-damp linen and the many unspoken promises that she has been waiting for him to speak.

It's like midsummer, when she'd watched him disappear into that dance and felt only molten warmth. She curls her fingers against the wooden railing and watches the crowd envy the sparse kiss he had given. Madoc is never shy about kissing her. He is always generous and never demanding.

Her gaze catches on a woman in blue heading straight for Ryley Rose, and continues on, following the flit of conversation from face to face. She can see the story spread, from a gasp here, to a laugh there, to a moue of shock just beyond. And then her gaze falls on Madoc again, and he is looking up at her.

He is so dark-eyed in the candlelight. His mouth curves in a small smile, meant only for her. She wishes, for a fleeting instant, that he *would* be demanding.

Madoc must gesture for a nightingale, because one appears at his shoulder. He whispers something, and the nightingale disappears with a smile, weaving into the crowd. Madoc glances up at her once more, inscrutable, and then he turns back to his work. Perhaps she's imagining that his smile is softer at the corners now, that his face looks more handsome than ever.

She isn't so surprised when the nightingale from below crouches down beside her. She carries the mingled perfume of the crowd, thick when she leans in.

"Pardon, Miss Ilyston," she says. "Casca says that if it pleases you, he'd have you stay a little longer and wait for him." The nightingale doesn't wait for an answer, just delivers her message and leaves.

A gentle invitation. Not demanding at all.

Zanthi is expected home. Her brothers will notice her absence, and the evening is still young. It might be hours before he's free from his obligations. She rests her forehead against the railing and watches the crowd tangle around him.

Kit leans her head against Zanthi's. "I'll walk you to the manor, if you'd like. The Gardens can be strange in the dark."

Zanthi shakes her head. She doesn't mind the dark. She slips away in the middle of a violinist's performance, as the crowd is watching the soloist, enrapt. The walk to the manor takes an age, but only because she is drifting along without haste. Music curls amongst the trees, and the autumn leaves lay in thick blankets to either side of the quartz trails.

It *is* different in the dark. Behind her, the Hall is glittering, and all the stars are dipping down to kiss the trees of the old forest. The rush and tumble of the creeks and streams echo through the dark, and if she were to close her eyes, she might as easily be back in her archive tunnels, with the echo of the river all around.

With that thought, she realises the air is not nearly so warm and steam-damp as she has grown used to. She crouches by a stream, and the water laps at her fingers, tepid and faint.

Strange, but perhaps it's winter's chill, creeping in early.

She's never been in the Gardens in the cold weather. Not even the magical warmth of the healing springs could be expected to banish winter entirely.

Madoc's rooms, when she reaches them, are cold, too. She stirs the hearth and adds wood to the fire until the warmth creeps back to the room. She settles down in the armchair by the fire, the faint strains of music drifting up from the Hall, and lets her eyes fall closed.

She had been a fool for worrying herself over this. She had glimpsed Madoc's society face at last, and it had been very easy to see him beneath the mask. No matter the strangeness of the scenery, he hadn't been a stranger at all.

The music fades, eventually, and she must doze, because she wakes to a drift of perfume against her cheek, and a kiss to her mouth. Madoc is there, draped in wine-velvet and dark-eyed. "You stayed," he says, soft. "I'd hoped so."

She uncurls. "Is it late? I didn't mean to doze."

"I'm sorry to disturb you, only it didn't look entirely comfortable."

A crick in her neck proves him right. She stretches, rubbing at her neck, as he leaves her to go sit at the dressing table across the room. Velvet pools, water-like, around him, and he reaches for his hair, removing pearl hairpins with deft, clever hands. He hadn't looked like he was wearing so many, but once his hair is free to shift and fall around his face, she realises just how carefully he'd been done up. So much of him is artifice, but it isn't at all apparent until it is undone.

"It was a very pretty sight," she says, "to see the Hall all lit up."

He glances at her in the mirror's reflection. "It is one of my favourite things in this world. I am glad you came to see it." He works at a tangled pin, then, his focus shifting. It leaves him open to her gaze, and she follows the line of his velvet moth coat where it dips at the nape of his neck, revealing the barest hint of his smooth back. Even the way he sits is studied elegance, a long line like a careless artist's mark. Emlyn had said there wasn't an artist in Esk who hadn't had an indecent thought about him, and she thinks he must be right. That dip of skin, his hair falling dark and tangled. The glint of gold at his wrists. She isn't an artist, and she doesn't wish to paint him. What she wants is to lie herself alongside him, her body against his.

Madoc in repose on the mossy lawns. In firelight and darkness. Dancing under candlelight with music.

All Madoc. All hers.

There is no reason why she shouldn't.

He is talking again. "It's late, but not so late as all that. Perhaps we could have a drink before I walk you to a carriage?"

She goes to him, slides herself beside him on the bench. She watches him in the mirror; the smile at his mouth, and the way his gaze goes half-lidded and thoughtful.

"We could," she says, and it takes more courage than she thought to voice her desire. "Or I might stay."

He doesn't react, really, except for the way he goes still entirely.

She watches his reflection, but he is turned, watching her, so she faces him. He's been wanting her, she's sure of it. *He* was so very sure of it, by the dark pool, when nothing stayed his tongue. But he is still, and he doesn't move.

"Or not," she says, with a wry smile. "It was only a thought."

He melts into movement, a flame catching, and takes her cheek in his palm. "It needn't be only a thought. You caught me off guard." His kiss is slow and petal-soft. "I would very much like for you to stay." He leans in again, resting his mouth against her temple. "It need not be that, though. Stay, and I'll keep to myself, if you'd like that better. But please, stay."

Each word ripples against her skin, his breath stirring her hair, skating her ear. She can feel it echo all the way through her.

"I'd like you to take me to bed," she says. "If you'd like that better."

"I'd like that the best of all."

She raises her hand to his, rests her fingers on the gold at his wrist. Traces the thrum of his pulse. "I should say, I drink the tea. Do you?"

"I do." He smiles, gentle. "So, we have nothing to worry about in that quarter." He draws her to her feet.

The making of the offer was a moment of courage, but this requires courage again. The shadows stretch along the carpet as he leads her into the dark of the bedroom. The soft hearth light falls in through the arch, low and golden and lapping at their heels. His room is as she remembers it. The bed is unmade, spilled around the shape of him when he'd risen that morning, and the rumpled covers are more inviting, more calming, than something unspoiled would be.

He presses a kiss against the crook of her neck and holds there for a long moment. She can feel his steady breathing through her back. "What do you like?" he asks, softly. "What do you want?"

When she turns, there's a shadow of that midsummer desire in his face. It's not so far to stretch to kiss him, to catch his lip the way he does to her sometimes. He laughs, like he recognises what she is doing.

"I don't know," she says, all honesty. "Not yet."

"Not at all?"

She's not sure of his tone. "Is that a problem?"

"Not for me." He kisses her again, a little deeper. Teasing. "And you only need to tell me if you dislike anything. There is nothing you can do wrong."

That, she thinks, cannot be true. She's read books, of course. There are absolutely ways she could do things wrong. But back when she had read those books, she had also thought that such things might be quick.

It isn't quick. It takes exactly the time it takes and not a moment less. He slips her buttons free, slips her blouse free, slides her camisole up the lines of her sides, and pulls it away with a whisper of silk against her lips. She's not so practised at disrobing another, but she slides her hands against him, tracing down his ribs, and his body shifts against her touch like he's working to hold himself still. He steps out of his trousers, lets his shirt fall somewhere to the floor beneath them. She stops noticing, too distracted by the shape of his body beneath her palms.

"Come here," he murmurs, settling back against the pillows, pulling her over him. His kisses steal the words from her until she almost forgets she's wearing nothing but the night against her. She breaks away to breathe, head spinning with it, and he keeps going, down her jaw, down her neck. His hands press in the small of her back, and when she arches into it, his mouth is against her breast. The touch of it makes her jump, and she can feel his soft laugh against her skin.

That is what soothes her, and the heat of his mouth is what pulls her thoughts off course again. He is gentle with her. He is still and steady beneath her, letting her go where she pleases, as her hands dip down his sides, to his hips, where he's still wearing his undergarments. She knows why he's kept them on, out of some attempt at modesty—as if she hadn't seen all of him the moment she had first seen him. As if she hasn't already felt him against her, in the springs, and in the summer night.

His hands settle at the crook of her hips, thumbs against her thighs, dipping desperately near where she wants him and is also wary of him going. Yet, he's being so careful. He does not go there. Her breath catches in frustration. It makes her brave, brave enough to wrap her fingers in his hair and drag his head back from where he is working across her neck and sending all her mind to threads.

"Madoc," she says, though she doesn't know how she has the breath spare. She barely has the thoughts to spare. In all she'd read of this, she'd never once considered she'd lose the ability to string her thoughts together. "*Enough.*"

He's gentle-faced and pulling away before she realises what he's understood, and then she laughs, because it wasn't at all what she meant.

"Enough holding back," she says, pressing close again. Her teeth graze his lip. "I'm inexperienced, not—" She's distracted by the softness of his mouth and has to chase down the tail end of her thought. “Not unsure. You can have what you want of me.”

He smiles against her lips. His hand slips down her thigh. “Do you think I’m not?”

“I think you’re not being honest,” she says, leaning in. Her weight shifts against him, and she likes the way his lips fall open, a dark gap. It’s making her mind go all sideways again. “Be honest with me.”

“You’ll always have my honesty,” he promises.

The next kiss is the sort of kiss he might have given her on midsummer, if he’d had the chance. There is the honesty she’s been longing for, and there are his hands, firm against her thighs, and the press of his body right against hers, all the way along. Things turn, and pillows cradle her head, and he’s over her, and warmth, she thinks, is all of it. The heady, heart-aching warmth of it. Nothing compares, not even the spring water around her and the stars above her.

Instead, there is the salt-kiss of his shoulder against her lips, his whispered blessing-curse against the curve of her ear. The way his hair sticks, damp, to her cheek.

He makes it very easy, loving him.

He makes it make perfect sense.

Chapter Twenty-Eight

Morning comes in with a loud and incessant knocking. Zanthi pushes herself up and blinks at her own pale arms against the green sheets. The daylight is strong, brighter than she usually wakes to, and there isn't a carriage or tram-rattle to be heard.

Then Madoc swears, low and heartfelt, right beside her. All the bed shifts as he rolls to his feet.

Her memories rush up like a cup overflowing, and she drops back into the sheets, pulling them high around her. Madoc reaches for his robe, and she glimpses the smooth skin of his back before he shrugs the robe up over his shoulders and heads through the archway.

A murmur of voices goes back and forth, then the door closes again, and he's back. His curls are a briar-tangle around his face, his cheek creased from the pillow. She's never seen him so unmade.

"For you," he says, bemused, and places a holdall on the end of the bed.

It is her own holdall, the one that usually sits at the top of her closet, and she takes a moment to realise what it means.

"Gods, what is the time?" She flings the sheets aside. If one of her brothers has dropped a bag around to the Gardens for her, then that means it's well past breakfast. It means that her absence has been noticed, remarked upon, and extrapolated against. It means they knew she'd need fresh clothes. Sometimes, she thinks there is such a thing as being *too* well cared after.

"A little past ten," says Madoc. He sits beside the bag, taking her hands away from the fastening.

She blinks down at him and remembers she's wearing nothing at all. He tugs her down into his lap and gives her a kiss that makes her forget why that was a problem.

"Good morning," he says, smiling at her. Then his words catch up to her again.

"Past ten?" She stares at him. "I'm supposed to be at the university."

He presses another kiss to the corner of her mouth. "There are indoor baths downstairs. Bathe, get dressed. I've something to attend to, but I'll fetch morning tea when I'm done. I'd like to sit with you a bit before you go."

It's the way he says it that catches at her. "Something to attend to? Is there trouble?"

His hand traces against her waist. They're close. She could lean in again, taste his mouth, but she does not.

"Some," he admits. "In truth, the springs are still in strife."

Cold drips through her, despite the warmth of Madoc's body beneath her. "But the ritual worked. Didn't it?"

"Surely it did, or I would not be here," he says, wry. "It was meant to strengthen the waters of the springs, and it did. The healing waters are working remarkably well, of late. But there are other things coming to the surface in the pools...tangles of dead rushes, and dark sand, and sometimes dead fish. There should be no fish in our springs. It's very puzzling."

Puzzling is not the word she would use. Puzzling is a word for parlour games and riddles. And the river rushes...it's been river rushes from the beginning, from the first woven rush charm on the archive stairs. Madoc runs light fingers down to the dimple at the small of her back, but she barely feels it. "Are they river fish?"

"Pardon?" He looks up, distracted. The morning light catches the green of his eyes.

"The fish. Are they river fish?"

He smiles, sharp and wide. "Yes, love. They're river fish." He catches her face between his palms, brings her in to kiss her once, chaste, and soft. "I see I've lost you to your thoughts. Take one of my robes and go bathe. I promise the waters are safe, and the baths downstairs are not so deep that I will fear losing you to them."

The manor's indoor baths are fed by the sacred springs, the water trickling in from a large urn held aloft by a gathering of stone nymphs. The upper pool curves beneath a large window, deep and shaped for lounging, and the water trickles over a lip and into the lower pool, clearly for more practical bathing.

She hangs Madoc's robes on one of the wooden partitions and slips into the lower pool. She is glad to have the baths to herself, for these are proper baths, and there are no bathing shifts to wear.

After some exploration, she settles on a simple, honey-scented body oil. It's far finer than anything she's ever used at home. She stays in the lower pool, even after she's washed. Even as safe as it surely is, the deeper water of the upper pool unnerves her.

Water cascades around the room, lively and echoing, and she relaxes into the warmth. Her thoughts are foolish, giddy things this morning. Madoc's face, and the sound of his voice, raw and low, against her ear. She sinks further into the water. It had been so frightfully easy, following his lead. She hadn't been worried, exactly, about the thought of bedding him, but she'd be a liar to say she hadn't been apprehensive. But he'd made her feel as if she were as much a revelation to him as he was to her. And that morning, he had said her name like he always had, gentle and low. It had been different, too, like it was his to say now, his to have between his lips.

He'd called her *love*. Not, she thinks, an endearment he uses easily. Something just for her.

The door creaks, and alarm drops through her. She sits up and sees Sabine Casca, bare and unconcerned, taking down her hair. It's long and dark, curling gently as it tumbles all the way down her back.

Zanthi does not know what to do.

Sabine steps into the water with a little sound of pleasure. Her hair drifts out around her in a sweep of curls. Zanthi tries to hold still, as if she might just fade into the tiles and disappear. Sabine settles herself across the bath, gathers her hair up, and looks over at her.

"Good morning," she says. "Are you enjoying the waters?"

"Very much so," she manages, shifting away. "I didn't mean to intrude upon your time. I'll leave you to bathe in peace."

Sabine reaches into an alcove beside the bath, picking out an ornate wooden comb. "Stay. I'd like to talk with you."

Zanthi casts a desperate look at the door. No one appears to save her. She is left to slide along the recess until she is beside Sabine, who takes her gently by the shoulders and angles her away. She gathers up Zanthi's wet hair, pulling it over her shoulders, and begins to comb. It's startlingly gentle.

"So, you finally stayed the night," she says, perfectly opaque. She has a quiet, rolling sort of voice that is as lovely as it is uncompromising. "Might I understand this as you accepting my son's suit?"

Comb. Tug. "I accepted it weeks ago, when he came to breakfast."

"Did you?" Sabine works for a while in silence, then sets aside the comb. A jar lid scrapes, and a perfumed hit of thyme and blossom cuts through the air. She takes Zanthi's hair between her palms, working the hair oil through it. "You gazed so clearly upon him at midsummer. All you thought, and all you desired, was clear to see. And yet, it took you so long to come to him." She reaches Zanthi's scalp, drags her fingers back through the length of hair, and then picks up the comb once more. "I wondered if you were hesitant to claim him, as he has claimed you."

Zanthi does not know what to say to such a thing. She doesn't need to, because Sabine carries on over her silence.

"The Gardens were quiet, when they were under my hand. I

held power, but I did not draw the crowds like Madoc does. Under him, the Gardens are a force to be reckoned with. Our ranks of nightingales finally grow instead of shrink. The Season turns and spins on his smiles, and half of his charm is that his favourites change with the months. But you, I believe, are not something he is willing to ever let change."

Zanthi turns, and the comb snarls in her hair. "Have I misstepped somewhere?"

"Misstepped? No, not lately." She twists gently at Zanthi's damp hair. "He needs all the tethers we can give him until we reach the end of this tangled path."

She can do nothing but sit there, pinned, until Sabine finishes. "What path is that?"

"If I knew that, I would worry less," she says. "Our healer can find nothing wrong with him but weariness. Madoc has never suffered from weariness before. The waters have always sustained him."

"He said the waters are stronger than ever."

"The power in them waxes and wanes, and so too does my son."

Ripples lap against her skin. Water clings to her eyelashes, and she can almost imagine it shimmers. When Madoc had drawn his hand through the springs that night before midsummer, the water had shimmered where he had touched it. Not aether, but she'd seen it all the same. "Then he is sick."

"He is fading," Sabine corrects.

"Lady Casca," she says, "you know I am a scholar. I'm studying the history of Esk's god."

"Esk hasn't a god." She says this very carefully.

"But your Gardens do, and your Gardens were once Esk. Who is the Lord of the Waters? Why does the Casca family serve them?"

"Serve is an interesting word. I would not choose it, I do not think."

"What word, then?"

"Dedicate. Celebrate. Carry forth into the world. Remember,

when all have forgotten. Venerate." Her voice trails off. "As for who? The Lord of the Waters is he who brought our healing waters to the surface. It is he that was the balance, who kept the worlds together, yet apart. He who was the guardian, and the echo, and the first carekeeper."

Remember when all have forgotten. She turns, now hardly caring that they are sitting in a bath without a stitch of linen between them. "Remember? Remember what? His name?"

Sabine's lovely face creases in a slight frown. "Name? No. I do not know the names of the gods."

"Then what good is your duty of remembering?" she says, before she thinks better of it.

Sabine, though, only smiles with a quiet, slight pull of her mouth. "We haven't fulfilled our duties, no. We forget more and more with each generation. Perhaps that is why the waters fade. Perhaps that is why my son does, too. But you are a historian, are you not? You make a study of remembering."

"I am trying," she says, earnestly. "Gods know, I am trying. But it is hard when everything is forgotten and faded."

"Nothing is ever entirely forgotten. Even stone holds the shape of water that has long since vanished. The very earth holds the shape of rivers that have not flowed since the world dawned."

She tips her head when Sabine's hands prompt her to do so. Her knees are red with the heat of the water. "May I ask you a favour?"

"You may ask."

"My mentor is Luminary Hart. Ethram Hart."

An amused sound. "I know him well," she says, all warmth. "What a fitting partnership."

"He told me of a book in your possession. *The Song of Dark Waters.*"

"It is in my keeping, yes. And yes, you may read it, though you may not take it away from this manor. Come to me on a day I am free, and I will show you the Casca collection of antiquities. It is small, but important."

"You have a collection?"

"We do. You shall have to be patient. I haven't time to show you today." She runs her palms over Zanthi's hair and draws away. "There. We do not do breakfast courtships at the Gardens, Zanthi. I expect to see you at all the ritual festivities going forward. You are one of ours now."

Zanthi touches a hand to her head. Sabine has braided her hair around her head in a wreath. She's seen the style on some nightingales. It is a way of dressing hair that is unique to the Gardens, and to those who belong to it.

It's a strange weight on her head, her neck bare and open to the air as she heads back upstairs. Entirely strange, and yet, she doesn't dislike the glimpse of it she sees in the landing mirror.

Madoc is in his rooms, and he's not alone. Chicory sits on the sofa, worrying at something in her lap as Madoc paces the room across from her. She blinks at Zanthi, and her face loses some of its strain.

"Good morning," she says. "The Gardens crown looks very good on you."

Madoc turns, startled, and the frown fades from his brow. "It does," he says, coming to greet her. He traces the shape of her plaited hair along her temples. "Who?"

"Sabine," she says. She tightens her robe around her. "Do you mind it?"

"I like it very much," he says, but his smile is a pale thing compared to what she is used to.

She leans past him. On the table by the bench seat, where she had once stacked stolen journals, is a small box. It looks like the sort of woven rush punnet one might get when purchasing berries from the markets, but when she peers inside, it's holding an assortment of muddy objects. The earthy, tea-rich scent of the springs is strong.

"What are these?"

Madoc's hand settles at the small of Zanthi's back. "They washed up in the lower pool this morning. We've had all sorts of odd things since midsummer, but this is the first time there has been gold."

Dark sand, river rushes, fish. And there is indeed a dead fish there, small and silver, amongst tangled reeds. She reaches for it in a daze. Her bath had been too hot and too long, maybe, because her mind is drifting, unmoored. Her fingers brush cold, wet scales, and a bell chimes somewhere in the distance.

She jerks her head up. Esk is silent. It was no hour-chime. Only the dark tolling in her own mind.

"Zanthi?"

She gathers herself. "I thought you said they were river fish."

"Are they not?" Madoc picks up the poor thing, holding it in his palm in a gentle way. It's as long as his finger, elegant and silvered even in death.

"I'm no naturalist, but no, I don't think so."

It's not a minnow, nor is it one of the tiny river fish with the ribboned fins that are called dancers. It has rippled fins that might fan, a little *like* a dancer, but the shape is different. She tries to imagine what it would look like in movement and realises why it looks familiar.

It is exactly like the silver aether-fish that follow Hart.

"What did you mean by gold?" she asks, looking back at the punnet. It holds only sand, mud, and broken rushes.

Chicory stirs, holding up the handkerchief in her lap. "These," she says, and passes the handkerchief to Zanthi.

It's heavier than she expected, and when she pulls back the cloth, she finds a pair of golden bracelets. Chicory had been cleaning them of mud, and they shine, brilliant, in the morning light. They are plain, and despite the heft, fairly thin, and very, very old. She tilts them to the corner of her vision, but there is nothing to be seen clinging to it. She slips one on. It fits well.

"Does it not remind you of the offerings in the dead springs?" she says, angling her wrist in Madoc's direction. "The ones you told me not to touch."

"I thought them offerings too, only now I wonder. What if they were things the springs washed up as they died?" He runs his thumb down her wrist to sit against the bracelet. Her pulse flutters against the press of his hand. "Are my springs still dying?"

Chicory stands. She looks as pale and silvered as the fish. "I should go," she says. "I want to finish searching the pools."

"Be careful," Madoc says, and Chicory brushes a kiss to his cheek, squeezing his other hand tight. Madoc sighs when she leaves. "I shouldn't have said that in front of her. She'll worry."

Zanthi makes a noise of commiseration, but she is distracted by the bracelet on her wrist. The gold is cool against her skin and does not warm despite the heat of the baths still clinging to her. And now she thinks on it, shouldn't the gold be warm from the springs already?

"What are the marks?" Madoc asks.

She slips it off, peering closer. He rests his nail against the faintest scratch. She hadn't noticed it before, and she squints, tilting the bracelet into the light. "Oh," she says. The marks are familiar. She's read about them in *The Silent Springs* a dozen times these past months. "Ancient funerary bracelets."

Madoc's face goes grim.

"I haven't seen any in person before. We don't send our loved ones off with jewellery any longer, not now they go to the ashgrounds, but the ancients buried their dead, or sank them in bogs and fens. They'd send them off with gold, so that they might be seen in the river of the underworld and souls could find each other." She traces the bracelet. "We tie the ribbons now, and say the ribbons will lead us to each other. But once they used gold."

"You have so many disturbing facts under that lovely face of yours." He tangles his fingers in hers and takes the bracelets, setting them aside. "Please don't wear it again."

"It might have been a name," she adds. "The markings, I mean."

"I'm more concerned with how they ended up here. Surely no one was ever sinking their dead in our sacred springs, or we'd have found more by now."

"No, I shouldn't think they were." She glances at the fish, placed back in the box. "But I need to ask Hart some questions. Can we take these to show him?"

He hesitates. "I don't see why not," he says. "Now?"

"Have you anything on?"

He circles her wrist where the bracelet had sat, as if the hot press of his fingers can erase the trace of it. She thinks of the wrist that gold had once adorned—someone loved enough for another to hope to find them in the after. Once, she'd believed she would live alone and go into the dark river alone, too. Now? Perhaps not. She hopes not. She doesn't know if tying the marriage ribbons is something Madoc can offer her, but if it is, she thinks she would be willing. She would find him in the river.

She winds her hands through Madoc's hair and tugs him down to press his mouth against hers. He makes a startled noise, then melts into her, and his kiss is cold.

She pulls back, shocked. He smiles at her.

"Nothing on at all," he says, and kisses her again.

This time, his mouth is warm and sweet like always. She makes a soft sound of relief, and he smiles against her lips, runs the tip of his tongue there in a question. She lets him in, and the kiss turns hot and wanting, like he hasn't even begun to have enough of her. She could persuade him back to the bedroom, she thinks. So easily. She could have him unveil more mysteries for her in the soft light of the day. She almost does.

But his kiss had been cold, and the bracelets were cold, and the strange, silver fish looks up with dark, dead eyes, and she remembers how dark Madoc's eyes had been at midsummer. How dark and dead they had been in the vision in the underground springs.

She shivers and pulls away.

She needs to talk to Hart. She has to ask the right questions, so he will tell her the answers she needs.

Chapter Twenty-Nine

The carriage trundles through the town, making slow progress through crowded streets. It's no hardship to be sitting beside Madoc. He smiles at her, runs his hand across her hair once more. "It really does suit you."

"I'll have to learn how it's done," she says. She has the punnet cradled on her lap, and she's trying not to look at the dead fish. She doesn't like its vacant stare. "All I know is a sensible, academic plait."

"I know how to do it. If you wish to wear it more, you need only ask."

"Perhaps in time I'll get used to wearing your Gardens crown," she says. "Best not make a habit of it yet."

He settles back, a satisfied curl to his mouth. "My crown. I like that."

"I never asked. Were you able to see your Lettie?" she says, then, because she thinks if she lets his thoughts wind on, she'll learn what a couple can do in a carriage, and she'd rather not do it with a dead fish staring her down.

She regrets her impulse when his smile goes strained and grim. "I did."

"Did it not go well?"

"It is a delight to have him back. Only, he's been alone for a long time." The air runs out of him. "I would like you to meet him, but perhaps not yet. He is changed, from what I remember. He's quiet. I don't think he's well."

"Quiet is not so bad, as it goes."

He presses his nose to her temple. "No," he says, and she feels his smile. "It isn't."

"Besides," she adds. "It must be hard to adjust to Esk after all that time away. Even I struggle to adjust each time the Season comes around. Maybe it'll just take time."

He hums, peeking around the curtain as the carriage finally makes it across Holloway Bridge and heads towards the velvet tumble of the old Polling Woods. "Ah, won't be long now. Tell me, why are you bringing a dead fish to your mentor?"

"I see aether around him sometimes. It takes the form of fish just like this one. I know he has some connection with the Gardens, doesn't he?"

"He's been digging into our history for a decade or more. He's never been too concerned with the god-aspect, though, like you. He's always been more interested in our remnant rituals. He's documented a great many of them, though my mother has never let him publish any."

She leans back to see him better. "Not midsummer, surely? Not *Hart*."

"He has, actually. But it was before I partook, when mother still led the dance." He smiles, then, at her expression. "Don't look so scandalised. Taking part in the more carnal aspects isn't a necessity, you know. Plenty of nightingales do nothing more than dance."

"Even him dancing is a stretch of the imagination," she mutters, and Madoc laughs.

The carriage rumbles to a stop on the same tree-lined street as last time. The canopy of oaks has long since turned gold and grown sparse, and the rattle of wind-blown leaves chases them to the cottage door. The garden has turned rambling in the rain, gone to seed and tangling thick.

She knocks. There is no answer for a long time. She's exchanging a glance with Madoc, wondering if they should retreat, when the sound of the lock unlatching breaks through the quiet and the door swings open.

A man leans on the other side, and it is not Professor Hart. He's neck-creakingly tall. Zanthi has to tip her head up to see his face. His pale hair is gathered in a knot at the base of his neck.

"Yes?" he says. He has to bend to look out the small cottage door. "Can I help you?"

She meets his gaze. She hardly means to do so, but then she's looking right into his eyes, and they're pale grey. As light as hers are dark, really. Something shifts in her memories.

"Is Professor Hart in?" she says. Madoc places a hand on the small of her back. Guiding. Guarding, perhaps.

"No," says the man. He's got a hint of an accent, but a very pleasant voice. "Perhaps I can be a poor substitute? You must be his student. Zanthi Ilyston?"

She nods.

"Come inside. I'll take your message and let Ethram know you've been by."

He exits the doorway, and there is quite suddenly a lot more space. She takes a breath, clearing her head.

"If this is the sweetheart," says Madoc, close to her ear and rich through with amusement, "he is exactly as confounding as I thought he might be."

Confounding is a gentle way of putting it. Zanthi is entirely rattled.

The man leads them to the front parlour, overrun with books. Stacked shelves line every free wall, and a fire crackles away in a blue-tiled hearth. Their host gestures them to a worn sofa in ticked linen. A set of woollen blankets are slung over the back, as if Hart and this gentleman spend evenings here, curled up. Because this is Hart's lover, she's sure of it. The way he'd said *Ethram* sounded like the way Madoc says her name.

"So, Ilyston," says the man. He looks to Madoc, sitting close to

Zanthi's side. There is a flicker to his expression, almost a blur, and Madoc goes tense as a linen cord pulled tight. "And Madoc Casca, I believe." He picks up what he had abandoned to answer the door—a half-complete knitted vest. The needles flash between his fingers. "What brings you here?"

"I had some questions to put to Hart," says Zanthi, watching his hands on the needles. There is a strange pressure in the room, like the aether that made her so sick last time. She cannot stay long. "On the matter of funerary bracelets."

"I'm afraid I know little of those," he says, but there is something unnatural about it. It's not a lie, but it's not the truth, either. "Antiquities are more Ethram's style."

"And what is your work?"

"Growing things," he says. "Chopping wood, baking bread. Fact-checking Ethram's flights of fancy."

"Hart never strikes me as fanciful."

"No? Well, you haven't known him as long as I have." He glances at the punnet in Zanthi's lap. "And what have you there?"

She sees no reason not to let him indulge his curiosity, so she passes it over. "They were found in the healing springs this morning. They should not have been there."

He sets his knitting aside again. "What an interesting fish," he says, after a very long moment. "Your springs are turning up startling things, Casca."

"Only since midsummer," Madoc says, and the words sound smudged, as if he's talking from very far away.

"And it is dead. One would expect anything emerging from those waters to be alive," adds the man. He looks up, pinning Madoc with his gaze. "Or maybe not." He picks the fish up, gentle as a caress. It is nothing more than a splinter of silver in his large hand. His fingers are long, too, and his nails are pearly white and pointed in snub droplets. When he curls his fingers around the dead fish, the whole room shivers.

She flinches away, turning her head, and her side-sight leaps into focus. In it, he's not really a man. He's some of a man, surely, for he has flesh and blood and form. But in the edges of her vision, he is taller still and indistinct, a space where the world is being pushed aside, pulled apart, being remade anew in each mere moment of his existing in it.

It is monstrous and shifting, this thing in the shadow of him, eddying like a reflection broken up on the surface of ripples. A stormbeast? Something worse, even.

She pulls herself back together, blinking the side-sight away. He's a man again, knitted sweater and grey trousers cuffed up, knitted socks poking out beneath. He's watching her with a curl of a smile.

"Apologies, little fish," he says. "Did I startle you?"

In her mind, the bell rings in the dark place. It's echoing, and in the echoes, she hears his voice.

Madoc grips her hand tight, but when she looks at him, his eyes are glazed as if he is wine-drunk. A chill creeps through her.

"Who are you?" she says, as silvery aether slips between the man's fingers and dashes away into the shadows. The same as the fish that follow Hart.

"Hm? Oh. You may call me Ky." When he opens his fingers, one after the other, the fish is gone. "Rather like Ethram, I am an enthusiast of things both ancient and forgotten."

"What are you?" she asks, then. When she tips her head to the side, there is nothing around him but a haze. The monstrous shape is gone.

"Something peculiar," he admits. "But so are you. My heart tells me so." He smiles. She fancies his teeth are sharp, but when she looks at him properly, it's only a normal, rather lovely, smile. "You should be on your way."

The aether is building around her, the pressure crumbling at her mind, and Ky's infuriating, vague answers twist away from her like minnows from a net. She swallows. "Yes. We should."

"I'll keep these for Ethram, when he returns."

She nods, not trusting her tongue to move. There is an

undertow to his words that brooks no argument, and Madoc quietly tugs her hand, urging her to stand.

Ky remains seated as they leave, but before they exit the parlour, he speaks once more.

"Casca?"

Madoc freezes in the doorway, locked up.

"There are no words in the old tongue carelessly spoken, or they would not be spoken. Do remember that when the time comes. Because it will come. It is not finished yet."

And then he turns back to his knitting.

When Chester had taken her to the seaside as a child, they had played a game, chasing the waves into the ocean and then turning and running back up before the next wave could catch them. That is how it feels, leaving the cottage. Running out before a wave catches them and drags them under.

She's trembling as they climb into the carriage. "Madoc," she says. Her voice is thin at the edges.

"Yes," he says, the air rushing out of him. He yawns, and rubs at his face. "What a strange man."

She stares. "A man," she says. She's sure he was half stormbeast. More, even. Whatever he was, he wasn't human.

He looks at her. His eyes are wide, winter-green. "Odd, wasn't he? It shouldn't surprise me. Ethram always was a curious sort." He pauses and his face flickers, as if he's held a frown back. "I think I must be more tired than I thought. I can barely remember the conversation."

The bell rings in the back of Zanthi's mind. She twists to watch the street dwindle behind them. The last autumn leaves are pushed aside by a sweep of wind and coming rain.

"It wasn't much of a conversation," she says, turning back to him. The trouble is bleeding from his face, and she knows he's already moving past the strange encounter. Whatever aether-induced forgetting had been laced through the cottage has worked on him. It hasn't worked on her. She can remember every strange moment.

You remember when others forget.

Hart had told her that. Her true-sight, the same sight that had revealed the monster lurking in Ky's shadow.

Did Hart know what he had living beside him in his cottage? Whatever Ky is, he is no ordinary man. There are strange bloodlines in Esk, Zanthi knows, but that had always meant something like the Casca family and their beauty, or the Heirs and their aether resistance. Remnants stemming from the first inklings of Esk, little quirks unique to Elveresk blood.

But Ky was something else again. That shifting beast in his aethershadow was monstrous. Did Hart know?

"Gods, is it that late already?" Madoc searches his pockets until he finds a small gold timepiece. Shadows play across his face as they move through the woods, pooling deep beneath his eyes.

She leans into him, pressing the frown from his face with her thumb. "You'll wear yourself out."

"I've got a fair amount in me until that happens. Trust me."

"The Season hasn't even begun yet."

"Don't remind me," he says, catching her hand and kissing her thumb. "First, I have my birthday to get through."

Madoc's birthday party is the sort of thing the papers report on every year, and so she'd decided to stay well away. The encounter at the Annual had made her more cautious than she'd been before. She runs her thumb along his lip. "Should I reconsider refusing your invite?"

"Perhaps next year." She feels his smile against her hand. "I don't wish to disrupt the lovely plans I'm sure you have. Tell me what you'll be doing while I am celebrating, so I can imagine it as I go."

"I'll be in the parlour reading," she says, sure of it. "And my brothers will be there too, so really, you're probably better being where you'll be."

He makes a noise of disagreement. "Let me give you something to think on while you sit reading, and you can imagine me as I imagine you." He takes her wrists and gently tugs her up and over to sit in his lap. Her head is worryingly close to the roof of the carriage, but he cups his hand over the back of it. If the carriage were to bump suddenly, his hand would protect her.

"You've clearly kissed in a carriage before," she says, smiling.

"Once or twice," he says. "But I think they're about to fade from my memory."

He's kissing her neck as he speaks, so he doesn't see the way his words make her flinch.

Chapter Thirty

In an admirable show of restraint, her brothers make no mention of her night at the Gardens. She makes it through a week of very careful sibling indifference and considers herself safe. On the night of Madoc's birthday, she is curled up in the parlour, the flames in the hearth leaping high as Chester pokes at the coals. Soon, he has it crackling along comfortably, and he settles in his chair with Susan curled up at his feet like a skein of wool. He's got a thick tome of some past captain's journal in his hands, and Zanthi is stretched out on the small sofa with her favourite Aster Starling novel. Theron settles in his armchair, and Fletcher sits at his feet, draping himself back against him.

It's the sort of night she spends so much of the year craving. All of them together, nothing to disturb them but the rustle of pages and Theron's vicious pen-scratch as he annotates whatever paper he is reading.

They're all jolted by the loud knocking at the door. It's nearing midnight, and as they stare at the clock and each other, the knocking comes again.

"Susan isn't bothered."

Susan, indeed, is just lying there, watching the flames in the hearth. It can't be anything serious, then. Susan glances at her, dark eyes bright with firelight.

Theron levers himself to his feet. "I'll get it," he says, with a sour note that promises ill for whoever is disturbing them.

They hear the door open, and a few moments later, Theron's laugh. It's his proper, genuine laugh, and she and Fletcher exchange curious looks. It's rare to hear that sound, and of the people who have ever sparked it, all three are in the parlour. Two sets of footsteps come back up the stairs, and then Theron is showing Madoc into the parlour.

He is startlingly out of place. They are all in dressing gowns, and he is there in a linen so fine it might be gossamer, and velvet that looks like it would be bliss to run her hands down. She's sure his lariat has genuine northern spring pearls.

"Good evening," he says. "Please pardon my intrusion."

Fletcher seems lost for words. Chester raises his brows at Zanthi, then goes back to reading, as if he wants nothing to do with whatever is occurring. Theron pauses by the bookshelf and, after a space of consideration, plucks a volume. He hands it to Madoc.

"I assume you're not so tipped that you can't read," says Theron, and goes back to his armchair.

She pulls up her legs, making room for Madoc on the sofa. Once he's seated, she stretches her legs back out, piling them into his lap. That seems to alarm him, though she has not a clue why. There's been rather more of her in his lap than that, after all.

"Birthday party over?" Fletcher says, peering over his book.

Madoc smiles, though it mostly seems directed at himself. "Not so much. I slipped away."

"To come here? And read?"

"It's my birthday. I'll spend it as I please."

There is a restrained touch of lash-black at the line of his eyes, and she suspects something on his lips to make them look wine-kissed. He is a little wine-kissed in the other sense, too, though not so badly as she might have expected. He wraps a hand around her ankle, thumb running up and down, and turns the book over in his other hand. The cover is very familiar.

"That is my favourite series," she says, laughing. It has been since she'd been seventeen and wildly enchanted by all the scandalous pieces of ancient myth she could get her hands on. "It's set in the ancient times, and it's very thrilling."

Madoc takes this endorsement with a raised brow. "*The Mystery of the Thorns.* I have heard of it."

"I'm sure you have. The hero is an alluring devotee of the moon god who never fails to find trouble. Or a willing lover."

He gives her a vaguely pained look. She bites down on a smile. Theron *would* think it amusing to hand it over to Madoc. Fletcher only looks resigned.

Though his hand is restless against her ankle, the rest of him relaxes into the calm of the evening. She stops reading, after a time. She watches him, but he must be quite enraptured by the mysteries of the thorns, because he doesn't notice in the slightest.

Emlyn *should* paint him, she thinks. He's very beautiful. The flicker of firelight dresses his skin in licks of gold and burnished copper, but a painting could never capture what she sees when she looks at him. It's nothing so tangible as pigment and colour. Nothing could ever portray the warmth she feels when he is close.

She'd never thought she'd enjoy being touched like this. Easy, and unconscious. Like Fletcher kissing Theron's cheek at the breakfast table. As thoughtless and as vital as breathing.

The clap of a book closing brings her back to herself. Her brothers are on their feet, and Fletcher is yawning.

"We're off," he says. He drops a kiss to Zanthi's head, ruffling her hair.

Madoc makes a note of his page and closes his book, too. Theron gives him a quelling look.

"We'll see you for breakfast, Casca," he says as he follows his husband from the room.

Chester nods at them both and follows, looking amused all through.

Madoc laughs, settling back against the sofa. "I honestly wasn't sure if I'd even be let in the house this late," he says, tipping his head to her. "But I was certain I needed to try."

"Did you really slip your celebrations? I was hoping you were enjoying yourself."

He smiles. "It was a lovely night. A dear friend helped me climb out a window to escape it."

"I must thank them sometime." She puts her book down entirely, because even Starling has nothing on Madoc lounging on the sofa beside her. "Tell me everything."

"Everyone was very celebratory, and I found myself with no shortage of conversation or dance partners. And some hellion has devised a new variation of the Autumn Marches, which is sure to take off once everyone has untangled their limbs from the collisions. Honestly, even the best among us were getting turned around." He taps his fingers against her ankle. "I suspect I know who is at fault for that creation, because Mey Roslin was more competent than most at it, and her sister is known for her talents as a dance-weaver. There are also some new figures floating around for the Dance of Nettles, though those are much more friendly."

"Isn't the nettle dance rather common for the Season?"

"Mm, it's a fancier version of it," he says. "But the basic steps are rather the same. Quite a lot of the popular society dances start out in the dance halls, as it goes." He circles her ankle with his hand. It goes around quite easily. "You told me once that you don't know how to dance."

"I don't, not properly. I've never learned."

"Would you like to?"

She's quite distracted by that implacable grip around her leg. "Maybe. If there is no one to witness it, at first."

"I suspect you'll be good at it once you set your nerves aside."

"How do you figure that?"

His smile is telling. "It's quite like other things you're rather good at."

"You must have had more wine than I thought," she mutters, and he laughs and releases her ankle.

"I had barely any, or I'd never have made it through the dancing. As it was, I was thinking of you curled up somewhere with a book and blessed silence, and there was nothing I wanted more than to be there with you, too. So I came."

She leans over to steal a kiss and almost jumps out of her skin when there's a sharp scratch of claws on wood. Susan stretches, and in the dying firelight, she seems to stretch impossibly long, all teeth when she yawns.

"Perhaps we might go upstairs," whispers Madoc.

"Yes," she says, remembering what is sitting on her dressing table. She'd bought it weeks ago, waiting for his celebrations. "I have something for you."

Susan follows them to the top of the stairs, then turns around and heads down to her usual nighttime haunt at the foot of Chester's bed. Madoc makes a small noise of relief as he closes the door.

"It's much less papery than last time," he says, sitting on the edge of her bed. "How are the studies coming along?"

"Rubbish," she admits.

He makes a commiserating noise as he twists his rings off, pooling them in the palm of his hand. They're each very beautiful, finely wrought and shaped like golden sprigs of flowers, sparkling with chips of emerald and sapphire. The last is a dark, clear gem like a night sky, and when he places the handful on her bedside with casual irreverence, she can only stare. She's been entirely foolish to think she's picked anything to rival what he already has.

"You looked very fine, coming into the parlour like that," she says, sitting beside him. She strokes a thumb against the gold at the corner of his eye. It lifts against her skin. "I'm sorry, I'm dull with these things. I don't want to dampen what you enjoy because I haven't figured out how to like them yet."

"You don't *have* to figure out how to like anything. You do, or you don't, and both are fine. I know my life is far out of step with yours." He smiles, his lashes soft against his cheek as his gaze dips down. "I keep waiting for you to run."

"Is there something from which I should run?"

She means it as a jest, but he looks up and his face bleeds into a serious sort of look.

"Perhaps. Zanthi. I should have spoken more frankly before I took you to bed. I promised you all of me, and you shall have me, but I cannot promise that every small thing will be yours only."

He is watching her, tense as a heron waiting to strike. She wonders how much he's ever had to find the words for his nature. Explain it. Measure it against another's expectations. For all he is the leader of the Season, he has never been tasked to keep himself polite. She's hardly going to ask him to start. Not when he's so beautiful, bestowing his kisses.

"Is this about you being so generous?" she suggests. "Madoc, I'm not fussed if you kiss and flirt, now and then. I saw you at the recital. I think I understand the difference between that, and between this."

"Do you?" he says, intent. He has such an easy charm of a face that it surprises her to see it so focused. She forgets how sharp those eyes can be. "Because there is a difference. It is different with you. And I should have made it clearer before now."

"Remarkable as it is for a scholar, I am able to grasp both context and nuance," she says. "Did you think I minded?"

"I expected you to," he says, and his mouth turns down. "I didn't think to explain, because I am so used to being what I am, and being known as such. And you didn't run from me after midsummer, and so I didn't think, either, that you might expect that I never do anything like midsummer again. I can moderate such things, but I cannot remove myself from them entirely. But anything more than Season kisses and festival blessings, that is yours, and it is ours."

"See? Hardly a thing to be fretting over at all." She slips to her feet. "No, stay there. I said I have something for you. Perhaps then you'll understand."

She takes the box from her dresser. She is probably just as nervous about this as she was asking him to bed. Or maybe more, because she'd been sure that he'd wanted that, and she isn't sure he'll want this. But she needs to give it to him, because she needs him to understand.

It's like the breakfasts, when he'd come to her door to show her she would not be a songbird or a passing fancy. That he intended her to be woven into his life. She wants to show him the same.

The box is velvet, embroidered with a maker's mark. He brushes a thumb across it, recognising it. "You're gifting me fine things indeed." She can't see his face as he opens it. She watches his hands instead, his neat nails and graceful fingers. He lifts the hair clasp, tilts it through the light of her lamp. "Ivy?"

It's an elegant thing, worked in gold and glass. Simple enough to be practical, lovely enough to be worthy of him. His gaze is clear and unguarded when he looks at her.

"You looked very fine with ivy in your hair," she says. She wants him to understand that she hadn't disliked *any* of it.

"I regretted you seeing me at midsummer, so very bitterly. I thought it would scare you off."

"I'm glad I saw it, even though I was never supposed to." She settles back down beside him, traces his fingers with her own. "You were fearless."

"I was a lot of other things, too."

"Yes. I saw you in truth at midsummer," she says. "Midsummer was when I knew I would love you if I let myself have the chance."

He goes still. Her cheeks burn with the words she's saying.

"I saw it all, every moment, and I liked every moment of what I saw." Her voice trembles, and she hopes he understands what she is so desperately trying to tell him. "You are as you are, Madoc. I told you on Sweet Night that I would have you in full. I meant that, with all my heart." She takes his hand and brings it to her lips. "Kiss who you please. We'll be ourselves between us, as we are."

He twists his hand, catching the back of her head in his palm and drawing her in for a kiss. It is a long, lingering caress. "And you?" he says, soft against her mouth. "Who will you kiss?"

"Whoever I please." She drops her voice, as if with a secret. "To be truthful, it's only you. No one else is nearly interesting enough."

"How fortunate I am, then, that no one else is worth your time." He kisses her again, as if showing her why it should stay that way.

She smiles. "You *are* welcome to stay. My bed is a fair sight smaller than yours, but I'm sure we'll figure it out."

He slips her back until the pillows sink beneath her. "I would love to stay," he murmurs, leaning in to kiss her.

She chases the trace of wine on his tongue. He must have looked as striking in motion, dancing in a sea of velvets and silks, as he had looked in pensive stillness with firelight on his skin.

He is strange and complicated and so very different from anyone else she has ever known. And he is hers.

Chapter Thirty-One

Madoc is entirely unimpressed with the tiny washroom they all share, with its barely more-than-cold water and frost-paned window looking over a scrap of a courtyard.

"That was gods-fucking miserable," he says, when he emerges into the kitchen. His face is washed, and his hands are damp, but she thinks he hasn't attempted anything more than that. "Harrowing."

She flips the bread on the toasting griddle. She's left it too long, again, and it's edging towards umber. "Have you never used an ordinary washroom before?"

"I've never stayed a night outside the Gardens," he admits. Then considers and says, "Well, maybe a few times at Eve's townhouse, back when. But his bathrooms rival my own." He ushers her away from the stove. "Here, let me."

She fixes up the tea and cuts up a plate of apples, and by the time her brothers have made their way down, Madoc is bringing out a tray of toast that is burnt on one side, and temptingly golden on the other.

"A joint effort, I see," says Theron, taking a serving. "Interesting."

The first round of post arrives after that, and the table falls to silence as they read. Zanthi has a note from Joren, warning that he will have no work for her for some weeks and wishing her well on her studies in the meantime, and another from Hart, saying that he was sorry he missed her, and that he promises to look over the items she had brought.

There is no mention of Ky, or who, or *what*, he is.

Madoc has stolen the *Society Papers* before Theron could get them and is flicking through the first pages with a distinctly displeased air. "Someone last night spilled too much to the papers," he says, and she peers over his arm to see that the entire first pages are devoted to the events of Madoc's birthday.

No aethergraphs, of course. The lenses wouldn't work in the Gardens. She glimpses names she doesn't know, and names she does —Masey, Heir Evelyn, and then another. Heir Auguste.

"Lettie didn't attend?" she says, halting him when he tries to turn the page.

"No. He wasn't well," Madoc says. There's a bit of tightness in his voice. He turns the page, but it's no help. The next story is all speculation about the Second Heir's refusal to take part in society despite returning to town. There *is* an aethergraph here, though it must be an older one. It shows a sweet-faced person, only just of age, handsome in a gentle way. He's all adoring eyes and full mouth, and Zanthi sees in an instant why Madoc is so fond of him. He seems lit up from within. Incandescent.

"Oh," she says. "He's handsome."

Madoc's smile is bright. "Is he, now?"

She likes that look on him. "He has a lovely smile."

And the look fades. "Yes," he says, softly. "He did, didn't he?"

Chester is watching them. No, he's staring at the pages in Madoc's hand.

"He'll have to make some appearances, illness or not," Theron says, reaching over to steal the papers. "It's rather his whole point as heir, isn't it?"

She sees the way Madoc bristles all over, like a hound gearing up to growl, but it's not Madoc who speaks.

"He's doing just fine as heir," Chester says, blunt as worn-down pencil. He rarely uses that voice at home. "Leave him be."

Theron gives Zanthi a brief flicker of raised brows, and she ducks her smile. Chester's friendship with the First Heir means his Crown loyalty is unflinching, apparently.

"The papers certainly don't think he's doing fine. The way they write it, he's wasting half to death." He flicks through the papers, as if he's searching for something he expects to find in the gossip columns. "Here. They're speculating all sorts of things. Wasting illness, melancholia, sinking fever. Mostly, they say he's aethersick."

"He can't be. He's an heir," Zanthi says.

Madoc is silent. It's a very telling sort of silence.

"He *can't* be," she repeats, turning on him. "Hart's paper is clear on it. The heirs *are* aether. It's in them. Taking the aether away would be like cutting their soul away from them."

Madoc cuts his toast with a jarring motion. His face is resigned, and cut through with a deep, restless tide of anger. The papers aren't just gossiping, she realises. Heir Auguste is truly sick.

"They have nothing more than rumours, for now," he says, finally. "I will do my best to make sure everyone keeps thinking it rumours. But the fact of the matter is that Arlet can't be around aether for long. It sickens him greatly, and the waters do not help."

She tips her tea in her cup, watches the liquid shift with the motion. The springs waxing and waning, but ultimately fading. The Crown failing. The Second Heir sick. Madoc sick, too. The Well and the Gardens. She feels like she's walked a long, ambling loop and she's come back around to face her beginning again, but from the other side of a river she cannot pass through. The answer is somewhere ahead.

Through the ivy, through the deep, whisper low where waters sleep.

"Zanthi?"

She startles back to the present. "Sorry?"

Fletcher looks between them all. "I only asked if you were going to the university presentations with Theron tonight."

"Oh. I suppose so, yes."

Theron huffs, spreading his preserves thickly on his toast. "I remember you being more enthusiastic about them last year. Will Hart be there?"

"I don't think so. He's retreated for the Season."

"Are you expected to get another accolade?" Madoc asks, his ill mood slipping away.

"No," Theron says.

"Yes," Zanthi says loyally. "Don't be modest, Theron. It doesn't suit you."

"We certainly didn't spend so much on your robes for you to be modest about them." Chester folds his paper open. It is not the *Society Papers*, or even the *Esk Gazette*. It's the *Ledger*, a weekly paper distributed by the admiralty to its members. He's got it open to a page of tiny, even numbers, all marching down the page in columns of little ink marks. He's scanning them like they mean something.

When he puts the paper down, frowning, Madoc glances it over. "Those readings seem higher than they should be."

Chester's frown fades. "You know how to read them? That's a unique skill for a socialite."

"I'm taught all things, as the future head of the Gardens," he says, like it's not so remarkable.

"What are they?" Zanthi tugs the paper over. The numbers make no more sense up close than they did from across the table.

"Aetheric readings from the Elveresk waypoints. And Madoc is right. They are much higher than they should be, this time of year." Chester scrubs a hand down his face. "I don't know if you have noticed, but there's more airguard in town than usual."

"I've been distracted," she admits.

Madoc makes a small noise of amusement. She presses her knee to his in warning.

"It's not meant to be widely known, but the storms are showing no signs of stopping for winter."

Fletcher looks up sharply. "Not at all?"

"A village went under in northern Pickett yesterday. Fifteen dead. It brewed too fast for the Crown to intervene, and by the time a ship got there, it was over."

"What does that mean?" The storms have always stopped in winter. That is why the Wintering Season is what it is—a time for excess and festivity, when there is no danger brewing in the skies. "All the ships are in, are they not?"

Chester tucks the paper away and gives her a scratchy sort of smile. "It means that we're all very lucky to live so far inland, where the storms can't blow."

The clock chimes, and the room breaks into the scuffled sounds of various people getting ready to go about their day. Madoc is dressed in his extravagant jacket and a creased chemise, his pockets full of last night's jewellery. He looks exactly like he spent the night somewhere unplanned and ill-advised.

"I don't suppose you want to borrow something?" she says, smiling a little as he brushes toast crumbs from his silk velvet. "You can't catch a tram looking like that. The papers would certainly have gossip to print."

Chester laughs. "If you don't mind a short walk to the carriage house, I'll take you home. It's on my way."

"There," says Madoc. "Easily solved."

She kisses him goodbye in the entry hall, and thinks that if any of her brothers are around to see, then that is their own problem, and they can mind their business.

"Good luck with the Opening," she says, drawing away. "I can hardly avoid talking about it, no matter where I go. I suppose you won't be by for breakfast for a while."

"You're welcome at the Gardens any time of day or night," he says. "Come, please. It'll make it easier, to know that you are somewhere at the end of the dancing and drinking."

And he truly means it. She kisses him again, tries to sink the taste of him into her memories where she can always find it. "I'll come by," she promises. "Make a good show for everyone."

His smile is like candlelight. "I always do."

On the night of the Opening, she cracks her attic window to the cold snap of winter wind sleeting down the valley. Through the mist, she can see the over-river glow of the Gardens, lit like a bonfire against the night sky. She can hear the faintest strains of music, too, carried by the wind right to her window. She sleeps with the window ajar, and lies with Susan curled around her like a fearsome and overlarge festival wreath.

The music sinks into her dreams, and in her dreams, she is dancing too.

Chapter Thirty-Two

It's not that she had forgotten Sabine's offer to share her collection, exactly. But catching the Lady of the Gardens proves a more arduous task than she had expected. Even Madoc confesses to not knowing where his mother is half the time.

It is a week after the Opening, when she finally strays from Madoc's rooms to find Sabine in her upstairs parlour, sitting at a writing desk with her hair undressed.

"Pardon my intrusion," Zanthi says, but Sabine only waves her to sit on the sofa. It's the same one that Madoc had been sprawled on, poison-hazed and asleep.

"I didn't realise you had come by." Sabine finishes her note and caps her pen. She rings a little bell, and a nightingale comes to take the letter. "Do you have need of me?"

"Do you have some time for me this evening?" It is almost evening, the Gardens outside slowly lighting up with lantern-gold. "I wondered if I might look at the book I asked after last time."

"I don't see why not. I'm not needed at the Hall tonight." Sabine fetches a small, tasselled key from her desk and gestures her back into the hall.

The antiquities collection is housed in a small room that appears unimportant until the door is open. Sabine lights an oil lantern, casting light around the space, and Zanthi takes a moment to gather her thoughts. There is a complete frieze of marble, set on the wall. She has no idea where it might have once sat, only that it depicts a procession she finds startlingly familiar.

"Midsummer," she says, voice soft. The figures, stylised and simple, are dancing and chasing, and ahead of them all is an ivy-crowned man holding a cup aloft. They are, all of them, wading through a river. It is a match for the faded, crumbled stone frieze in the archive passageway.

Sabine brings a case to the small table by the door. It holds clay tablets, each pressed with inscriptions. Zanthi recognises some indecipherable ancient script, a lot of the middle dialect, and even some old northern and an archaic form of eastern valley script. She picks one up. She knows enough to recognise a prayer for health. "They certainly all appear to be linked to worship. Has anyone ever studied them?"

"I allowed Ethram to look over them, because I am fond of him. No one else."

"And these are all from the Gardens?"

"For the most part. Knowing what we know now, I assume some came from the springs that are since lost to us."

"And they have never been documented? Catalogued?"

Sabine's mouth has a touch of deep amusement. "Never. What provenance can we give them? No, I shouldn't think there is much point."

Zanthi wants to argue that. It might be difficult to place them historically, but that didn't mean they had no value. And they certainly had value to the Casca family, limping along with no knowledge of their own history, when perhaps they already have so much of it here, hiding in dust and shadows.

Sabine gestures her closer, close enough that her plum-blossom scent grows strong. "Do you know what this is?"

It is a stone, sitting in what might be a boot box from decades ago. The stone is far, far older. She recognises it by the markings, the remnants of the carvings.

"From a temple?" She reaches out, then tucks her hand back away again. It is the match for the kneeling stone by the dead springs in the archives. "I saw something similar in an aethergraph of an old temple ruin. It was an altar, I think."

Sabine gives her a thoughtful look. "It is called a veilstone, or a limenstone. Traditionally, only a consecrated Casca may kneel upon the one at our springs, but I do not know the function of them elsewhere. This one isn't from Esk. It came from far west."

Zanthi looks up, startled, and Sabine meets her gaze steadily.

"I have let two others into my collection before your mentor ever stepped foot in here. Friends. One was your mother. She found this stone as fascinating as I did. The conversations we had over it! Speculating over other springs, in other parts of the archipelago. Wondering if there were other bloodlines like mine. I had been alone in this world since I was thirteen, and while Madoc is my great blessing, there were no others after him. I was desperate at the thought of family."

"I didn't realise you were so close."

"Once, we were. She went west for me, because I could not. She found no springs nor answers, but when she came back, she was growing with you." She covers the stone once more. "Behind the tapestry is a door. Inside are the oldest things we own, including the book. You may look, but you may remove nothing beyond this room. Take the lantern."

Zanthi does, though her head is still spinning with Sabine's revelation. The lantern light sends the shadows stretching, long and hungry, across the shelves. The tapestry is faded, and in the pale colours, Zanthi sees the faint shape of the Gardens. Even at a glance, she can tell it depicts far more pools and streams than exist in the Gardens now.

The alcove behind the tapestry is as dark as the archives. A breath of dust and stone sighs out.

"What is in here?" she asks, barely above a whisper.

"All we have left of the Lord of the Waters."

Inside the alcove, there is barely room enough for her to take a full square-step in. Four hollows line the walls, but only one holds a wooden chest. She takes it and sits on the floor of the space, the oil lantern flickering beside her.

The book lies on top. She knows as soon as she opens it that reading it will be the work of weeks, perhaps months. The translation will be slow, doubly so if she must work on it here without Theron to help. The ink is faded in places, but she can read the inscription on the frontispiece, in part.

The tale, or perhaps, *account...of the...death* or perhaps *murder*, she can't quite remember, only that it means a violent act, *of*...a word here that she doesn't know. Perhaps something like lord or king? And then after it, where she might expect a name, a great mark of dark ink.

She hisses, pure academic frustration, and turns the page. It is not a long book. From the way the pages are jagged and the writing cut off in places, it might not have even been a book when it was first written. A scroll, perhaps, that had been damaged, and the remnants stitched into a book for safe-keeping.

And again and again, there is that dark mark. Each time the god of Esk is named, the word has been smudged out with a thick fingermark of the same ink, as if it has been written and erased in the same moment.

"Has the book been translated?" she asks, her voice carrying back to the main room.

"Ethram has read it through," Sabine says, after a moment. "But he wrote nothing down and claimed he remembered nothing after."

The forgetting, then. He had warned her, as well as he could, and he had set her on this path, hoping that she would remember where he had not.

She turns the pages carefully, gleaning a sparse word here and there. *Flood. Guardian. Sheltering. Sacrifice.*

Sacrifice. Death.

A brazier flame going dark.

She has tried not to think about it, mostly. Tries, instead, to let her memories linger on his beauty in the firelight, and the way he had desired her, and his laughter as he'd entangled himself in the nightingale's dance. But the fact that Madoc had been sent back to them did not change the horrifying, unshakeable truth that, first, he had died.

The book ends abruptly, a word broken right through the middle. Zanthi lays it aside, exhausted, as if the few words she had understood take all her strength to hold in her mind. One day she will sit and translate it, but the answer she needs now is not there. It has already been erased from those pages.

She sifts through the rest of the chest. There is very little inside. There are grains and dust in the bottom. Some sort of plant material, long since ground away. A set of gold earrings, the fine wire bent in the shape of twisting fish. Silver hairpins. Pearls strung on a gold chain. A shell comb. A thin tablet of river clay, impressed with one of the ancient scripts that she has never been strong at reading.

The last item is a pressed gold box, thin and delicate in her hands. She unlatches the hinge and lifts it. A pale shimmer gleams, and as she blinks, it takes shape in the lantern light. A lock of hair sits in a thin, intricate braid, curled end on end in a twisting figure.

A death-lock. Even now, mourners cut a death-lock before they send their loved ones downriver. She has one from her mother, and it sits in a silver box in Theron's study. Her mother's lock is the same shade of russet brown as Zanthi's hair, but the lock in her hands is pale moonlight, almost glowing in the dark. It doesn't look ancient. It looks as if it was cut a moment ago. She closes the box once more, a strange, foreign grief twisting in her chest. It tilts her, shakes all her thoughts into new shapes. For all her many, many hours of thinking about Esk's lost god, she'd never once thought of them as a person. A real, tangible creature who wore a favourite pair of earrings. Who had to comb their hair in the morning. Who might have sat at an ancient dressing table like Madoc sat at his, picking pearl hairpins from their curls.

More than ever, she is sure she must find their true name. If only so they can be remembered as they were, and not remain a shifting, shapeless void in history.

She packs it all away except for the tablet, which she takes to Sabine. Unlike the book, it does not have the heavy blanket of forgetting on it. "Do you know what it says?"

"Your mother told me once." She taps her fingers to her dark lips, thinking. "*If the moonlight fades, send me after the river's child.*"

There seems to be a great more writing on the tablet than that single line. "Is that all?"

"There may have been more. That is the line I remember. It was pretty, is what I thought of it."

Zanthi knows the word for moon and finds it there, and the word for light, and the possessive form of *river* is recognisable, though she couldn't parse much more than that without a dictionary or three, or perhaps Theron.

"May I take a copy of it?"

Sabine gives her a very long look. In the dull light, her green eyes seem black as coal. "Very well," she says, eventually. "But only that. Nothing else." She places the key on the shelf beside her. "Spend as long as you wish here. You may keep the key in Madoc's rooms."

Once Sabine is gone, Zanthi pulls her notebook from her pocket. She finds with it a stub of charcoal that has been left abandoned since last winter and makes a passable rubbing of the inscription. Then, overleaf, she also makes a copy as accurately as she can, drawing out the strange, angular forms.

After, as she locks the door behind her, she realises the collection has wearied her as much as a day in the archives used to weary her. It has the same heavy impact.

Night has fallen while she has been cloistered away, and outside, the Gardens are aglow. From the hallway windows, the trailing ribbons of lanterns and garlands and light-bright streams unfurl down to the glittering Hall. The Season is well and truly underway. The Hall is open, the crowds are gathered, and the pools will be open for society bathing.

She hesitates as she comes to the second landing. A small bundle of nightingales, decked in evening finery, mill about the feet of the ivy-crowned statue. Rowan stands on the stairs just below her, and he looks up. There's gold powder brushed against his cheeks and touching his lips, and he's almost a stranger as he smiles at her.

"Good evening," he says, holding out a hand to help her down on the landing. "How lovely to see you again, Ilyston."

She lands amongst a cloud of silk and velvet, the air scented like the sweetest of Esk's flower shops. There are six of them, all looking like visions from a dream. She tucks her hands tightly into herself, so as not to get charcoal on their silks, and mutters an *excuse me*. The nightingales part, and she wriggles through them and slips through Madoc's door.

He's there, no less fine than any of his creatures.

"Zanthi," he says, and her name is a chime on his lips. He's fixing green glass earrings in his ears, each bordered with a fine twist of gold. There's a matching gold twist in his hair, circling his curls. He's so very fey, with his wine-dark lips and a touch of gold high on his cheekbones. "I thought you'd left."

"I was just on my way out. I see you are, too."

He checks himself over in his mirror, then holds out his arms in display. "I am. Do you approve?"

"You needn't my approval," she says, tugging him around so she can admire the fine work in his top. It's more structured than the velvet drapery he so likes, with a high collar and pleated work at the shoulders that sweeps down to his wrists. Each thing he wears must cost more than a month of her university stipend. A lot more, perhaps. "But yes. You are very handsome."

"And you look haunted again. Did something happen?"

"I saw your room of antiquities," she says. "Madoc, your Lord of the Waters. Do you think him dead?"

Madoc, fastening a bracelet to his wrist, goes still. "Dead? I suppose not. He is gone and forgotten. But I never thought him dead. Why?"

"There is a book in your mother's collection. I couldn't read it very well, to be honest, but I know enough to know it is an account of a murder."

His face is grave. "A death is one thing. A murder is another entirely." He snaps the bracelet clasp together. "No, Zanthi. I do not think my god is dead, or I'd be long dead too, floating in the lower pool."

A nightingale whistles, sharp, from the landing.

"That's my call," he says, and his face clears of its troubled air. "I've been dallying. Here, walk with us to the gate so I know you've safely reached the carriages."

He takes her hand—he's not wearing his gloves yet and his hands are delightfully warm against hers—and leads her out onto the landing and down the stairs. The nightingales follow in a cloud of delight, chattering brightly.

He pauses at the overgrown gate of the first terrace, before they delve down into the open terraces.

"Safe journey home," he says, cupping her face. What was handsome in the brighter light of the manor is devastating in the glowing night-dark of the Gardens. He leans in close, his mouth brushing against her ear. He smells of some wickedly crafted scent, the sort of perfume one wants to press their face against, sink into, eat up. "I'll be thinking of you all night, my love. Draped over my sheets where I laid you, ready for worship."

Heat scorches her face. The nightingales laugh, bright and merry, and without shame or hesitation, he is kissing her. She melts into it, into the hot bite of his mouth, and then all her mouth is flooded with the ice touch of winter. Of the archives.

Of cold. Stone. River mud.

Madoc is already moving away, kissing the corner of her lips, then her fingers. "Goodnight," he says, soft as moonlight, and then he strides away down the lanterned pathway. His nightingales flock after him, glittering apparitions in the golden light. He leads them like he'd led them at midsummer, and they fade into the dark.

Zanthi presses her fingers to her mouth. The river-taste is fading, but it sinks heavily in her memory. And as she turns, her side-sight leaps into sharp, startling focus. It has never flared like this in the Gardens before. But now it is there, and she is not seeing aether. Dark water rises in the mossy hollows of the nightingales' boot prints, welling over. It is darker than water should be, darker even than ink.

It floods, covering the moss, and flows off into the night after Madoc, as if it is chasing him.

Chapter Thirty-Three

The skies hang low, the morning of midwinter. The week has been one of the busiest she can remember. Madoc is in the papers, and nowhere else. Society gossip and scandal wind on, pulling in Madoc and the Heirs and Chester, too, though Zanthi can barely keep track of it day to day. Chester had caused some fuss at the Opening, and it's still haunting him through the pages.

She comes down to breakfast and finds her midwinter gift from her brothers sitting on the table by her teacup. She has nothing for them, as it is customary to only give gifts downwards. Parents to children, older siblings to younger, teachers to students.

Her gift is a pretty pair of gold and emerald earrings, and she knows they've picked them so she will have something to wear to the Gardens. Madoc had invited her to the inner Gardens' midwinter celebrations, and with Sabine's request echoing in her mind, she had agreed.

"Hart hasn't forgotten you entirely," says Theron when he brings in the morning post. He drops a small box on the table before her, and then drops a brief kiss to the top of her head, an affection so rare that it almost distracts her from her mail. "Go on, I'm deeply curious to know what sort of thing the famous recluse gifts a sopharion."

Inside the box is a twist of dark linen, and atop it, a small, woven charm of river rushes. Her heart beats dully.

"Oh?" Fletcher reaches to take it. "I've been seeing these everywhere lately. Are they good luck?"

Zanthi barely hears him. She unwraps the linen, and a set of golden bracelets fall onto the table with a dull jingle. Delicate, thin bracelets. Polished to a gleam, with not a speck of mud or river sand on them.

"Is it appropriate for a mentor to gift jewellery?" Chester asks, looking up from a slim volume of poetry that they're all politely pretending he is not reading.

It's not jewellery, though. Not the sort one adorns a lover with, or at least, not while they're alive. She picks one up, runs her thumb over worn patterns, and knows it is the same pair Madoc had found in the Gardens. Why had Hart returned them to her in such a manner?

Funerary bracelets, and a charm for guiding a lost soul home.

"You're frowning up a storm," says Theron.

She slips the bracelets onto her arms. "Did you look at the inscription I gave you?"

"That charcoal rubbing? Yes, I did. The translation is on my desk, if you'd like to fetch it."

She does. It is passed around the table.

"What an odd story," says Fletcher, keenly. It's exactly the sort of thing he delights in. "What do you suppose it means?"

Here are the words of [...], heard as the dark water rises.

"The way will close. The water will cease. I cannot stay. If the moonlight fades, send after me one who comes from the river. Find me in the rushes. Find me in the current. I cannot stay and I will not go."

She reads it over twice. "Send after me one who comes from the river? Sabine said the line was '*send me after the river's child.*'"

Theron tips his teacup in disagreement. "Mm. Both are possible. Truly, it means '*the river's one,*' but there is a sense of inheritance that suggests ancestry. It is not talking about a literal child, though. And it *is* 'send after me,' not 'send me after.' She must have misremembered."

Fletcher makes a musing sound. "Is it talking about the Casca lineage, perhaps?"

"I don't think so," says Chester, over his book. "That's what the moonlight represents."

The silence at the table is profound.

"Pardon?" says Fletcher, aghast. "Since when did you have opinions on *metaphor*?"

He frowns. "Since it is obvious? The moon seems to always mean protection or guidance, or guardianship, in old poetry. The Cascas are guardians and protectors, are they not?"

Theron's cup is an inch from his lips, with no sign of movement.

Zanthi stares, too. "I'd no inkling you had such an interest in poetry."

"Well, the reason for *that* is hardly a mystery," says Theron, recovering. "My compliments on your continued mental improvement."

"I will carry you all the way to Conning Street and dunk you in a water trough," says Chester, very pleasantly. "You see if I don't, you wretch."

"You can't carry me to Conning Street. You can't even carry a midwinter invitation to the post box."

"Theron," says Fletcher, breaking into their squabble. He's holding the paper aloft. "What is this bit at the back?"

Theron sips his tea. He takes a moment to respond, as if he has to remember what he'd written. "Oh, that's something else. The whole 'river's descendant' subject put me in mind of one of mother's old books. She was always on about ancient genealogy. There are a few families that have connections to rivers, both real and myth, Casca being one."

"You didn't finish whatever you were writing out," says Fletcher, puzzled.

"I suppose I got distracted."

Zanthi plucks the paper back. Theron's neat handwriting is stark on the page. There's a list of old names. Casca, Vye, and Holloway, all from Esk. And others she doesn't know, Wenwood, Asatos, and Selanna. She flips the paper frontwards again.

If the moonlight fades.

The Casca light has been fading, for generation upon generation. Dying young. Dying without children. Sabine being the last Casca before she even came of age. Madoc being the only child she'd been blessed with. Madoc's health fading more and more with each passing week.

"I should take this to Madoc," she says. "He should know."

Chester casts an unhappy look at the window. It's a grey, writhing mass of rainwater. There is little to be heard of the outside world but the drum of rain and the distant rumble of thunder.

"I feel fretful for saying, but it feels like aether," he says, voice dark. "I don't like the look of the sky."

Perhaps she is anxious, too, because she watches the sky while she gets dressed for the day. Clouds skulk across the rooftops of Esk, so thick she cannot see the river, or what lies across it. The old town, the Gardens, the House, and all the high street—gone. There's a faint glow and rattle as a tram passes along a distant street, and then that, too, is swallowed by rain and mist.

She slips her new earrings into her ears, and then, after a pause, puts the golden bracelets in her pocket. She isn't bold enough to wear them after Madoc asked her not to, but she feels a strong instinct to keep them on her. They're important, only she doesn't know *how*.

Susan paces the entranceway, restless, as Zanthi waits for the promised Gardens carriage to arrive. She sniffs at the bracelets in Zanthi's pocket, and her teeth show beneath a silent snarl, white and thorn-sharp.

"Sorry, Susan," she says, kissing Susan's snowy head. "But I'm afraid I rather like them."

The hour winds on, and no carriage comes. She stands at the doorway, barely able to see the street through the curtain of water that is pummelling from the edge of the portico. What is left of the winter garden is bowed under the strength of it.

"Take Chester's carriage," says Fletcher, coming up behind her. "It'll be back with plenty of time for him."

She shakes her head. Chester's carriage is boarded a few streets away, and walking there would get her as sodden as walking up to Conning Street. "I'll walk to a tram. It'll amount to the same, anyway."

"I don't suppose you'd consider not going? It's raining rather a lot."

"And there are hot springs at the other end of the walk. Don't fret about me," she says. There's a worry gnawing at her, but it's nothing to do with the rain. "I have my cloak."

Chester comes in, then. He's holding one of his old airguard cloaks, from before he was a captain. It's pale grey with silver buttons, and far too large for her. Still, it has a hood and a thick collar, and the dense wool will keep the rain at bay.

She dutifully stands still as he settles it around her shoulders, layering it over her rosemary cloak.

"Keep the hood up," he says, tugging it over her head. "It'll keep you dry."

"I'll bet good money you didn't fret half as much when Theron left," she mutters, and Fletcher laughs.

"You'd bet wrong. He tried to make Theron wear the cloak too."

Chester smooths the hood down, and his palms rest briefly, cradling her head. "Keep sharp. Keep your eyes open. If you see silver in the sky, get indoors and away from the windows."

Chester's uniform is by the door. Fleet boots, sword, coat. She doesn't like the tense worry in his voice. "We're safe in Esk."

"I know," he says with a touch of a smile. "But indulge me."

She kisses his cheek in farewell, and Fletcher's too. "Happy Midwinter," she tells them, and they echo the blessing as the door shuts behind her.

The cloak does an admirable job of keeping her dry on the way to the tram, though it causes the nightingales to double-take when she comes into the Garden Hall. There's a crowd of them lounging around, as if there isn't a care in the world to fret over. The air feels better here, too. The oppressive weight of the storm fades entirely away.

"Did you disrobe an airguard?" Rowan is draped on a window seat, watching the grey haze of the gardens beyond the glass. "In this weather, I hardly blame you. I'd be next in line."

"I rather think you'd shove me out of the way to be first," she says before she can think better of her tartness, and Rowan gives a bark of laughter. It's such an undignified thing that she laughs too.

"You're not wrong. If I'm not mistaken, that must have once been Captain Locksley's." He tips his head at the mess of weather outside. It lashes against the windows and washes his face into an unhealthy sort of grey. "Madoc has been gone all day. He's at the springheart."

"I don't know where that is," she admits. "Should I?"

"It is where the springs rise from the stone. Or so I am told. No one but the Casca family is allowed in there."

"I'll take you," says a voice behind her. Thom. She has not spoken with him since that first visit, when he had sat back and let the nightingales taunt her. Now though, he seems to find her barely remarkable, just gestures her along with him.

Outside, the rain shatters everything. It is worse than bells in a festival procession. Or perhaps it is more like the drums had been at midsummer, loud and faster than her heart, and never letting up.

"If you can convince him to rest before the celebrations, you'd be doing good work." Thom leads her up to the private terrace and then past the manor. He's wet to the skin with rain, his shirt sticking to his shoulders and neck, but he doesn't seem to mind it.

The steam is cool, almost cold, and she realises it is not steam, but mist. The clouds are sinking lower and lower. None of the pools and streams look peaceful now, all cut and torn by the rain. He leads her down pencil-scratch paths, almost gone in the rain-swollen moss, until they are in the dark tangle of the old forest.

Ahead is a wooden door built into an outcropping of stone, mostly draped in moss and ferns, and myrtle trees.

Thom stops. "Call him from the threshold," he says. "No one but a Casca is allowed beyond the gate."

She watches him disappear back into the rain and mist, and only then does she approach. The air is thick with the scent of earth and rich, rotting wood.

She knocks, then pushes the door in a sliver. "Madoc?"

Nothing.

"It's Zanthi."

Silence.

She looks around. Thom has gone, and there is nothing but the drumbeat of the rain, all around. She slips over the threshold, and into the dark.

Chapter Thirty-Four

Inside, the quiet is sudden and complete. The rain vanishes, becomes a muted whisper, and then nothing at all, as she follows the twisting path through the stone. It loops once, twice, and then all the dark lights with a gentle, shifting grey.

She is in an underground chamber, all enclosed in natural cave walls. A steep rise of steps leads to the lip of a natural pool, and the trickle of water echoes all around. The light—stealing in through cleverly hidden channels cut into the stone above—sends reflections shifting across the walls, shimmering in the steam. Dripping water matches her heartbeat, steady and ceaseless, and the air is hot and damp against her tongue.

Madoc is sitting at the top of the stone stairs, on a veilstone that matches the one in Sabine's collection. He isn't kneeling. He's sitting on the edge like a child at the river, one leg pulled up to his chest and the other dangling over into the water.

His shoes are sitting at the base of the steps, and so she removes hers, too. The stone burns beneath her stockinged feet, as if there is a gentle furnace beneath them. He doesn't stir as she climbs up to him. It isn't until she is beside him that he blinks, as if coming awake.

"Is it that late?" he says. His voice is rough, and he looks her over. "I meant to send a carriage for you."

"It's barely mid-morning. And the rain wasn't so bad."

He smiles, tugs at the edge of her cloak. "Worse than I thought, if you had to enlist in order to get through it."

She has the strange urge to pull him from the edge, as if, were he to slip, he'd fall right through the endless depths to the bottom. It's a strange notion, she knows, because the pool is brimming with steaming water and Madoc swims as well as a fish. These are his waters. He has nothing to fear from them.

"Have you been here all morning?"

"Since last night," he admits. "I can't sleep. Or if I do, it doesn't feel like sleep. I wake more tired than before and have nothing but a strange tolling in the back of my thoughts. In my dreams."

The cold seeps in through her, despite the cloying warmth of the cave. She licks the gathered springs-steam from her lips. It tastes of earth and stone. "Like a bell?"

"Yes, exactly like. It tolls on and on."

Her bell, the bell she has been hearing since that first visit to Hart's cottage. She'd been thinking it a manifestation of her own fears and anxieties, but how can it be if he hears it too?

He blinks, and some of the worry fades from his face. "But if you are here, the day must be late," he says, and his smile is as it always is for her. An invitation. He holds out a hand. "Come. Careful, it's damp."

"Your mother said only a consecrated—"

"I am the only truly consecrated Casca there is," he says. Steam pearls at the edge of his eyebrow, runs down his temple. "I say who can be here."

The pool is deep. That is the first thing Zanthi thinks. The water is clear and jewel-toned, and it goes on and on, until the clearness fades into darkness. There's nothing comforting about it. It is endless, and it could swallow her, and she could be sinking forever.

"May I give you a midwinter blessing?" he asks, softly.

She nods, wetting her lips. He murmurs something in his old language and traces over the water's surface. The water shimmers under his touch. Each time he changes direction, the ripple reflections change too, leaping at his movement, and all light around them turns.

She's quite dizzy by the time he raises his fingers to his lips, presses the water there. Then he dips his hand again and brings his fingers to her lips. He holds them there a moment longer, warm and damp against her mouth.

"Blessings, Zanthi," he whispers. The echoes seem to whisper her name back to her.

He's never looked closer to that strange version of himself that had led the procession at midsummer. She doesn't know if she's allowed to kiss him here, but the question must show in her face, because he's leaning in on the next breath. He tastes of the springs, of earth and rain. When he slides his hand around the curve of her neck and into her hair, he leaves water against her skin.

"I didn't get to bless you at midsummer," he says, and smiles at the heat that floods her face.

She thinks she knows exactly what a midsummer blessing entails. His face tells her that she is right.

"I forgot so much of that night," he continues, running his fingers down the curve of her jaw. "I wish I could see through the blur of my memories."

"There are parts of that night that I am sure are better for you to forget."

"Perhaps. But I'd have them all back, to remember every moment of you."

Her breath catches. He says it so easily.

"I do remember some," he says. "You, in the firelight, like a piece of my desires summoned into breath. I saw you in the waters, and then you were there, waiting. I thought you must have been a dream."

"It wasn't a dream. It was only me wandering in where I wasn't welcome."

"You weren't permitted," he corrects. "You were always welcome."

Midsummer Madoc had been nothing but welcome, and invitation, and promises. She remembers his kiss, pressed to her forehead like an offering. "You said something to me, too, in your strange language. What was that, if not a blessing?"

His face changes. He looks away, and his cheeks are a shade darker than usual. "It was something else."

"Will you tell me?"

He trails his fingers through the water. "Not yet," he says, after a moment. "But I promise I will."

She resigns herself to another answer left just out of her reach. He looks so weary, though, and she has no appetite for prying secrets from someone who so clearly needs a nap. "Come, I've been tasked with making sure you rest a while before the evening begins."

He sighs and gets to his feet. "With you beside me, perhaps I can."

As they leave, she turns back to the pool. The water is, for a ripple of a moment, dark like night. The bell tolls, faint, under the echoing drips of the chamber.

It would be so easy to fall in.

She shivers back a sudden chill and follows Madoc, reaching for his hand. By the time they are ducking back out into the weather, the thought has faded from her mind entirely.

Madoc does sleep, sprawled on the sofa with his head on Zanthi's lap. Zanthi reads until he stirs in the late afternoon, blinking awake. He looks up at her for a long, sleep-soft moment.

"I think I was dreaming of you," he says. He reaches up to touch her lips. "Or maybe it was a memory."

"Or maybe it is something yet to come," she says, warm-hearted, and ducks to kiss him properly awake. "How are you feeling?"

"Better," he says, though he barely looks at it.

Outside the windows, the storm rages on. She's been watching it thicken all day.

"I don't think the midwinter procession happened," she says. "No one would have survived a dip in the Lune in this weather."

"They can just stand in the street and count themselves drenched," says Madoc, amused at the thought. "Come, let's bathe, dress. There's lots to do before evening."

Chicory is in the baths when they get there. Zanthi hesitates, even as Madoc disrobes without pausing. Other than her alarming encounter with Sabine, she has yet to encounter any of the nightingales in the indoor baths. Chicory is kind about it, though. She turns away as they disrobe and doesn't turn back until they're both done in the lower bath and settled in the upper. The water is a milky green colour today, added by some salt or soak, and Zanthi is glad that it covers her so completely.

"You look better," Chicory says, eyeing Madoc.

"I got some rest. Has anyone been out in the town?" He runs his hands through his hair, working a scented oil through the ends.

"Rowan's been at Willow Isle. He says the flood flags are raised."

"Understandable, in this weather."

Zanthi sinks into the water, letting their conversation flow over her. She curls up on one of the submerged benches, and it's deep enough that she's covered over her shoulders. Chicory is leaning back on the edge of the baths with the curve of her breasts above the water, and she wonders if she'll ever be that brazen. She can't imagine it.

When Chicory steps from the water, glistening, her wet hair trails across her pale shoulders, and Zanthi looks away, right into Madoc's laughing face.

"I'll dress your hair," he says, pulling her to sit against him. His skin is warm against hers, warmer even than the water. He kisses the side of her neck. "And then you can watch me prepare for midwinter. I promise you, it's a sight."

It is exactly as he promises.

She drinks tea, still easy and loose from the bathing, as he dresses himself in midwinter finery. The evening is only for the inner circle of nightingales—those who celebrated midsummer, those who keep the Old Ways. For everyone else, the Gardens are closed and silent.

Tonight, the storm is another layer of secrecy, closing Esk in mist. The rain has lessened, fading off to a silver dampness that clings to the windows, and through the silence, she can hear music drifting over the Gardens' walls, coming from the old town. Society's midwinter ball is well underway, the Winter Pavilion full of society's richest and most elegant.

She thinks she has the superior view, though, as she watches Madoc make himself up. His hair is glittering with clips and clasps shaped like oak leaves and buttercups and primroses, and he's set a golden wreath of miniature hellebores amongst it all like a crown. Over his loose chemise, one with beautiful embroidery along the hem, he has a velvet short jacket that he is liberally ornamenting with an assortment of beribboned pins and brooches. He slips a set of necklaces around his neck, and strings bracelets on his wrists. Rings, too, on his fingers.

"You should look ridiculous," she says, in awe. "You don't."

"I've got a better eye for it," he admits. "I used to look thoroughly ridiculous when I first took over this task."

He finishes with a light touch of adornment to his face. Lips rain-touched, eyes dark at the corners, until he seems like a creature of the woods, wandered out.

"You are making a very promising face," he says, catching her gaze in the mirror's reflection. "Would you like to be made up to match me?"

She smiles wider than she means to. The thought isn't as unappealing as it might have been, once. "Not tonight. Let me enjoy the spectacle as the wallpaper does."

"Perhaps," he says, coming to draw her to her feet. "Or perhaps not."

She thinks he might put one of his many rings or bracelets on her, as he is wont to do, but he only bundles her to the door.

"Go ahead of me," he says. "They'll all be downstairs in the hearth room."

Midwinter is one tradition that takes place entirely indoors, and Zanthi is glad of it. The night has a cruel edge, the cold seeping at the windows as she passes them on her way down. She slips into the hearth room—a low-lit room papered in a pale pattern of twisting willow, and dominated by a giant, roaring hearth—and tries to skirt along the edges and into the shadows.

It is a very full room. Every nightingale that had filled the Gardens at midsummer is here, dressed in layers of finery. She had not realised that she was expected to be in evening dress. Thank the gods for her brothers and their gift of golden earrings. At least she has *some* finery on her. Before she can lose herself to a dark corner, Sabine catches the crook of her arm and draws her in beside her.

"I am glad to see you came," she says, implacable, as she traps Zanthi there.

The nightingales cheer when Madoc enters. Some bow, or flourish, or blow kisses. He bows back gracefully, jingling as he does, and the nightingales arrange themselves in a loose circle around him, and the gifting begins. There is a hierarchy to it. The newest to the ranks go first, and the more senior nightingales wait for later. Each asks Madoc for something, and he gives it. Most take something from him—a brooch, or a bracelet, or a pin. Some ask for a kiss, or a sweet. If it's the former, he'll kiss them, or if the latter, he'll pull something small and brightly wrapped from his pocket. She recognises the sweets—they are from the finest confectionery store in Esk. Madoc, it seems, uses this opportunity to spoil his nightingales in every way.

There is a lot of laughter. There's endless chatter, cheering, and smiling faces. Zanthi can't help but laugh when a nightingale tries to take one of the oak-leaf clasps and gets it snarled in Madoc's hair instead, and the struggle that follows involves three nightingales to free him.

It takes a long while to move around the circle. Madoc never rushes things, lets his nightingales deliberate for as long as they wish. But finally, the turn reaches Thom, the last nightingale in rank, and he asks for Madoc's shirt. By then, there is very little left pinned to his coat or on his wrists. Madoc pulls the shirt over his head, laughing, and throws it at Thom's face.

Zanthi supposes Sabine will finish the ritual then, but Sabine presses on her back, urging her forward. Madoc stands there bare-chested, holding the coat with a few last pins left, and his smile is low and lovely when he sees her step up.

She hadn't expected to take part. He might have warned her, and she might have made some plan for what to take from him. She wonders if she's brave enough to ask for a kiss, but the room is watching, the chatter softening down, and their gazes are too heavy upon her.

"What would you have from me?" he asks.

She's reaching before she thinks her decision through. She should have reached for his hand, perhaps, and taken one of his rings. Or the coat. Instead, she reaches up, and when he understands, he bows his head down to her.

She takes the golden wreath half-hidden in his curls, lifting it free. Then, as he straightens, she places it on her own head. She's chosen right, she thinks, because Madoc is looking at her with that dark-eyed look she's come to love so well.

The nightingales cheer for her, and then Zanthi has Chicory's arm around her waist and someone else's around her shoulders, and well-wishers are pulling her into a celebration.

Madoc turns to his mother, but his eyes track her as Chicory leans to whisper in her ear.

"A lovely choice," she says gleefully. "It suits you very well."

"Is there ever any wrong choice?"

"Not so much. We try to leave the finest thing for Madam, though sometimes she flips it on all of us and just asks for a chocolate."

Not this year. Sabine smiles at her son and lifts the last necklace from around his neck. It is a very fine thing indeed, so richly made that Zanthi hadn't even thought about claiming it. It makes sense, if it had been meant for Sabine all along.

"And Thom would get sour if someone claimed the shirt before it got to him," Chicory adds.

"Does he often lose his shirt?"

"Sometimes his trousers too," chirps a nightingale beside her. "If someone is daring enough."

They're each sporting their gifts proudly, glints of gold and gemstones under the lantern light. Not a single favour has been lightly chosen. Zanthi's usual gift-giving tradition is much more sedate than this one, but she thinks she could love this, too. Everyone is so merry, even with the nectrine yet to be poured, and there had been something lovely, too, about the quiet pleasure on Madoc's face each time a nightingale had found a gift that delighted them.

Warm arms wrap around her, and Madoc is against her back. He props his head against hers, and the nightingales fall back.

"You've all quite exhausted me of generosity," says Madoc, though she can hear the smile in his voice. "I'll not share a whit more tonight."

Thom calls them all to the table, then, and Zanthi finds the table seating another mystery again. She cannot parse a pattern to it, or even if there *is* one, but she is beside Madoc and is glad enough for that. The food is feast-like, venison and tart sauces and vegetables with goat cheese, and lentil soup with spiced flatbreads, and rabbit cooked down into a rich, creamy stew. There is not, she notices, any river fish anywhere.

She drops her hand to find Madoc's under the table, and they tangle their fingers together. He gives her a smile over the curve of his wine cup. She leans in, and she could not even say what is balancing on her lips, only that it is happy and bright. Before she can voice it, a clamour crashes over them, shattering the night.

The room falls silent. Madoc gets to his feet, eyes wide.

The sound comes again, and this time it doesn't stop. A discordant alarm of bells, ringing and ringing, in a way she has never heard in her life. But she knows what it must be. Every soul in Esk does.

The storm bells.

Chapter Thirty-Five

The room swells with movement, all the nightingales lurching to their feet. Madoc commands them with quiet, quick directions, sending them off to prepare for the storm. She clutches the back of the chair as he calls up nightingales to go with the head healer, Rue, to wait out the storm in the healing rooms of the remedial baths.

She understands why. If an aetherstorm is going to land on Esk, then the healing waters will be needed for townsfolk and airguard both. Chester will be running to the docks, even now, along with the neighbour who had given her aniseed drops, and the First Heir, and every other brave soul who has chosen to run into the storms rather than hide from them.

"Zanthi," says Madoc, coming to her. He's pulled on a shirt, tied his hair back. "I'll be needed all over, I think. Would you stay here and help shutter the manor?"

"Of course," she says, and spots Thom in the doorway. He gives her an apologetic look.

"Admiralty runners at the Hall. They want Lord Casca."

"I'm coming." He slips off the last of his bracelets and places them in her hands. "If I don't come back before the storm hits, it's because I've gone to the springheart." He squeezes her hands, but there's an absent worry in his face, as if his mind is already elsewhere, planning. "Stay safe."

She watches from the window until he and Thom disappear into the storm. The bells have stopped, but she hears the echoes of them, ringing and ringing and never quite fading. Rain slices through the mist, the clouds writhing above in bruise-dark greys and purples. She closes the shutters in Madoc's room, locking the storm out. On the landing, she finds Kit struggling with the giant shutters behind the statue.

"I don't think these have been closed in decades," Kit groans, arms straining.

In the moments before they drag them closed, she sees the first aether in the sky. It twists silver-sharp and wild, and Kit makes a low noise of wonder. The storm light spills through the last hall window, striping the tiles in silver shadows. Chester's warning echoes in her head. She runs to slam the last shutters closed.

With all the windows shuttered, the manor is dark. She takes an oil lantern from the wall and goes back downstairs. The hearth room is empty, and so she sits at the base of the stairs and waits. Madoc does not return. Chicory staggers in as the hour turns late, pale as milk, and Zanthi catches her before she can fall entirely. She is wet through, the colour bled from her.

"Baths," she grits out, and Zanthi takes her there.

She helps her sink into the water, still wearing her slip and chemise, and the heat of the water brings a flush of pink to her cheeks.

"Gods," Chicory says, pressing her palms to her face. "Aether. I can't stand the stuff."

She is the first, but there are many others. Both the lower and upper baths are full within the hour with wan-faced nightingales. There is very little she can do to help, but on a faint thread of memory, she runs upstairs to find her satchel. In the inner pocket is a tin of aniseed sweets.

She is passing the sweets around the baths when the healer, Rue, comes through the door, shaking rain from his hair.

"Aniseed," he says, all approval. "You know an airguard or two."

"I'm afraid I do," she says, feeling pale.

"It is a pleasure to finally meet you, though I wish it had been under better conditions."

She's seen him before, she realises. At midsummer, in the knot of revellers around Madoc. "I have seen your face," she says, and he gives her a flicker of a smile, as if he knows exactly what she is thinking of.

"Are you faring well?"

"I'm fine. I have a moderate tolerance."

Rue has a lovely way of smiling, with barely a flicker of movement in his face. It's in the eyes, she thinks. He's got eyes of such incredible warmth. Perhaps it's a healer thing. "Come to the healing rooms when the storms are over, if you are able. I can always use hands that can suffer the snap of an aetherbitten guard or two."

"Do you think there will be many?"

There are no shutters in the baths, and so they all see when the sky flashes. Not silver this time. The gold of ship aether. Somewhere in the mountains around Esk, a ship has fired its guns. Rue's face turns grave.

"I hope there will be many," he says, turning back to her. "It's the thought of an empty healing hall that I fear."

It's not until he's bustled off, kneeling to check on a slumping nightingale, that she understands what he meant.

She slips from the bathing room and stands by the manor door, cracking it open. The rain writhes through the air, torn apart by the wind before it can fall in any pattern.

The cold seeps through her, and she wants to be huddled by the hearth with Theron and Fletcher and Susan, watching the rain together.

She wants to be with Madoc, pressed in the warmth of his arms. She wants to be anywhere but here, alone.

She knows the way to the springheart, she thinks, even with the world torn up like this. And so, silent, she goes.

Madoc is kneeling at the lip of the pool, where the waters are brimming up, spilling over. The steps are steep and smooth beneath her toes, and the water runs down, tumbling over her feet and away. It does not feel as warm as it had that morning.

"Madoc?"

He startles slowly, as if he's been asleep. "Is the storm worsening?"

"I think so. The baths at the manor are full of nightingales. Rue is with them."

"You should not have risked coming through that, not even in the Gardens."

He draws her down to kneel beside him, as they had kneeled at the dry and dead springs underground. The Gardens' spring is not dead. It is writhing like a living thing, the surface cut and rippled like a storm is tearing it apart, though there is not a stir of breath in the entire chamber.

Madoc holds her close against him, as if he is seeking her warmth. "The longer I sit here, the more I think the waters are fading. They are cooler, are they not?"

She skims her hand across the surface of the pool. The strange ripples jump against her skin, and there is no warmth at all. "It is cold," she says. "It will do nothing to help the nightingales, like this. Or anyone injured on the ships," she realises. "Is there nothing we can do?"

He shakes his head. He slips down, until he is sitting on the wide, recessed step that marks the top of the springs. The spilling water rises higher, pouring over the veilstone to cascade around him. He does not react to it.

She falls to her knees beside him, and as she presses a palm to the veilstone to steady herself, she feels the faint impression of letters. They are worn deep into the stone and faded almost entirely away. Another remnant of the past, lost to time.

"Why are the waters overflowing like this?"

There is no answer.

"Madoc?"

His eyes are closed. She presses a hand to his cheek, and when he opens his eyes, they are black as the dark river itself. Then he blinks, and his gaze is green and clear once more.

"It is the echo," he says, as if he is speaking from far away. "The storm will not end. The springs will not return."

"All storms end," she says. "The storm will pass."

"The waters are cold."

"Then bless them." She weaves her fingers through his, presses her palm to his cold one.

"I don't think any blessing I make will fall right, not now," he says, faint. He draws her in, kisses her, and she expects the river taste, expects the icy bite of stone and mud, and so she does not flinch.

The river is in him. It is flowing through him and taking him with it.

"Hold on to me," he says, so softly. "I feel as if I am washing away."

"You are only tired," she says, even as her heart pounds in her chest.

She kisses him again, because she will kiss him even through the silt of the dark river, even if the cold burns. His skin is chilled when she slides her hands through his hair, and the spring water is cold when she slips herself over his lap, and cradles herself against him.

"I'm sorry," he says, against her mouth. "I thought I could fix it. But it's so cold, and there is nothing I can do."

She hushes him. "Calm, now," she murmurs, kissing the edge of his eyebrow, his hairline. "I am warm, am I not?"

"You are like a burning ember in my grasp."

"Then take my warmth." She takes his hands and slides them up under her chemise. He digs his thumbs into the softness of her stomach, and then up, to rest under her breastband.

He sighs, and there is warmth in his breath. Heat, when he mouths at her neck. She feels the curve of his smile. His voice, when it comes, is stronger. "And if I wanted to take more?"

"Here?" She pulls back. Behind Madoc, the springs ripple and shake, the waters dark, but his face is clear, and all his focus is on her.

"Here," he says. He slips her buttons free. "Now."

She does not wait for him to undress her. She pulls her chemise over her head, and he loosens her breastband, and then that, too, is gone. The midwinter crown catches in her hair, and he steadies it, sets it closer into her curls.

"Wear my crown," he says, kissing over her breast. Kissing over her heart. "You are mine, Zanthi Ilyston."

"And you are mine," she says, tugging his head back so she might kiss him again, fiercely, through the river taste. She wants him like she did at midsummer, and this time, she will not lose him to the waters.

"Always," he promises.

She presses her face to the crook of his neck, and longing aches through her. For his candle smoke scent. For the perfume he wears. For the warmth of him, all over her, instead of this coldness. She tugs at his trouser buttons, slips her hands inside and tastes his gasp as she wraps her hand around him.

Here, at last, is warmth.

Water spills around them as she presses their bodies together, kisses the damp curve of his shoulder. His hands grip her waist, urging her on. He holds her tight enough to hurt, and she holds him just the same. The echoes layer, on and on, until all the chamber is her wanting breaths and the hitch in his throat as he says her name, and it is nothing any river will ever take from her.

She presses her face to the crook of his neck, mouths her desperation against his skin. He burns beneath her, his hand spread against her skin and holding her down, holding her against him.

She kisses his neck, and his cheek, and his mouth, until the river has fled from him. Until he is salt and candle smoke again.

Not here. Not now. He is *hers*.

And all around them, the waters run warm.

Chapter Thirty-Six

In the dim light of the springheart, Zanthi lies against Madoc's chest, his knees caging her in, and watches the water ripples fade back to a gentle, calm sway. Madoc might well be dozing, his lashes dark against his cheeks, but for the way he is tracing patterns against her damp skin.

"Fading moonlight," says Madoc, when she tells him of the translation. "That is exactly our situation. We are fading away. Blood and waters, both."

She listens to the steady beat of his pulse in his neck, strong and firm. She wants to ask him about so many things, but again and again, her tongue stops silent in her mouth. It's not the forgetting or any curse, keeping her silent. It's only her own reluctance.

"I've been thinking about the Lord of the Waters," she said. "You say he isn't dead, but I think he was killed. Maybe the Well is what was left of him when he was killed. The gods are aether, as far as we know. Surely the killing of one would cause an overspill."

Like the springheart had overflowed, as Madoc had been lying faded and cold on the stone. She presses her face into the crook of his neck.

"What a grim thought that is. Like a bleeding wound that never ceases."

"Usually, a wound ceases to bleed when the body dies. I think we are cursed with whatever it is for eternity."

Outside, the storm wails on, the sound sharp and violent even in the deep rock of the chamber. There are fourteen airships in the airfleet, and any single one of them can cut down a storm on its own. Surely, with almost the full fleet out, the storm should have been over hours ago.

And yet it goes on.

"The inscription gives me hope there is a way to stop the fading, though," he muses. "If we can figure out what it is asking of us."

Zanthi is barely listening. She is thinking of Madoc being washed away by the river. And the forgettings that have haunted her all year, one after another, all rippling out from one moment in distant history.

The moment Esk lost its god. The moment the god lost their name. The ruin of the archives. The overspilling Well of aether. The fading of the Gardens. It is as if a balance was upset, and ever since, all of Esk has been barely clinging on, unaware of its own danger.

Without the Casca family, the healing springs would not be there to heal and protect Esk. Without the Heirs, there would be nothing to hold the Well back from scouring Esk from the soil and stone of Elveresk. And without the Crown, there would be nothing to guide the airships, and nothing to help the people of the archipelago outrun and outlast the aetherstorms.

It is a vast and spiralling problem, but she can do one small thing. She can find the missing name and restore it. A small thing, to begin to balance the forgetting. As soon as the storm is over, and she knows her family is safe, she will go to Hart. He will help her dig free the answers. Him and that strange fey, Ky, for Ky is certainly linked to the old magic of Esk as much as the Casca lineage is.

Madoc stirs beneath her and disrupts her thoughts. "Listen. Is the storm getting quiet?"

It is. Slowly, but it is. They fall silent, listening to the distant wailing of wind and sky. She hopes it is only wind and sky. It seems a long time before the sound finally falls to silence.

"I think it's over," he says, with a breath of relief.

The springs are still as a mirror once more. Steam drifts in the air as it should, and the both of them are soaked through. Water clings to Madoc's hair, to his lashes. There are still shadows under his eyes. His lips are still pale. And when she tilts her head just so, his eyes seem darker than they should. But that fading, falling mood has gone away with the storm.

He helps her to her feet and passes over her abandoned chemise he'd thrown aside earlier. "Let's go see what damage has been done."

In a handful of hours, the storm has left Esk in shambles. They emerge, wet clothes donned again, to a world torn like paper scraps and scattered wide. Broken boughs lie across the path and in the pools, and uprooted bushes, and one old, twisted tree lies sidelong, all the roots bare and dark in the morning light.

"The manor," Madoc says, taking her hand and going forwards at a run.

The rain has left an ankle-deep lake of water over the landscape, so it seems the entire world has been drowned. There is no storm, no wind at all, but the water still ripples as they pass, as if stirred in all directions. No, not all directions. Only in one. Towards Madoc.

She falls back, watching him forge forward, watching all the water shiver towards him. Neither of them had stopped to put their shoes on, and so they are barefoot and sinking in moss and mud as the manor comes into view. The door opens, and Sabine runs to meet them.

"Gods be kind," she says, sweeping her son into her arms. "I feared the worst when the waters cooled."

"I am fine," he tells her. "How have you fared?"

"All is well," Sabine says. "Rue is opening the lower terraces to the street. Already, the aethersick are flowing in."

"It will be a long day," says Madoc, grim.

He insists she change into dry clothes, and so she trudges to his rooms where someone has laid out a shift-like dress for her to borrow. She takes her satchel, too, because she doesn't know where she'll be going after this. By the time she has changed, Madoc is gone.

Downstairs, Rowan and Chicory are waiting to take her to the healing rooms. She has never seen them so plain and so wan. They wade through the terraces, silent. The path is piled with broken branches and cut up moss, and when Zanthi enters the healing rooms, she gets her first glimpse of the streets outside the Gardens. The buildings are still standing. Most of the windows are intact. But gods, only barely.

Zanthi finds the rhythm of helping. Some need only be directed to the pools or the baths to bathe. Some fare fine with sitting and taking a quick shot of Rue's tonic, made with spring water. Others are bleeding or bruised, and need stitching or compresses, or salves. The ones with open wounds need to be taken to a particular part of the baths. Others need somebody to carry them there. With her side-sight, she can quickly ascertain how much aether is wound around a person, and what they might best need to help.

"How are you doing that?" Rue asks, coming to her side. "I've not seen you send a person wrong."

"A personal quirk," she says, accepting the glass of thyme-water he passes her.

"An entirely practical one, which is refreshing to see," he says, with a shadow of a smile. "I'll tell you now, none of the other nightingales have any talents that are of use to me here."

"But of such use elsewhere," Chicory says, coming to join them. There is blood smeared down her chemise. "The first ship has come back."

Rue gets his wish. The healing rooms are full. Zanthi watches each group of airguards keenly, looking for a familiar face, or for the crest of the *Lys* on a collar or a coat. When she hears mutterings of a ship crashed on the docks, she must stop a moment, breathe out the panic in her chest. The only way an airship can crash is if the captain is dead.

"Zanthi?" Rowan is there, touching her shoulder. "There is someone who wishes to speak with you."

Zanthi goes pale, dread turning her to ice. "My brother?"

Understanding floods his face. "No, it's not—" He breaks off. "I heard that Captain Locksley has been injured. We sent some healers to his home. I'm sorry, that's all I know."

She lets that settle in her chest. *Injured.* But back. Safe. Not dead.

But if it is not an Admiralty clerk coming to tell her grim news, then who could be waiting for her? Rowan leads her out of the healing rooms and into the Hall. It is eerie in its emptiness, each sound echoing mournfully from wall to wall.

"Here," Rowan says, and points her down a narrow side-hall.

When Zanthi ventures through, she finds Ethram Hart sitting at a small conversation table by a shuttered window. He is as colourless as hearth ash. Zanthi sinks down in the chair across from him.

"You haven't replied to my letters in weeks."

Hart looks her in the face, and she realises how full of shadows he is. "Forgive me. I have been unwell."

She swallows, because he does look unwell. He looks aethersick. "I need your help, Hart. I think you know what is sickening the Gardens."

"They have forgotten too much," he says. "I have tried to restore as much as I could, but not even Ky has escaped the forgetting. He does not remember enough to help."

"Ky," she says, weakly, because she suspects, even if her mind cannot comprehend it. Silver fish, moonlight hair, claws, and monstrous shrouds. "What is he?"

"You have read the *Song of Dark Waters*, have you not?"

Zanthi runs a tired hand down her face. "I couldn't read it at all."

Hart makes a thin, tired noise. "Of course."

"Hart," she says, staring at the pale, old aetherburns on his arm. The ones that look like fingers wrapped around his arm. Fingers tipped in sharp divots of claws. "The thing you found in the archives. Was it who I think?"

"In a manner, yes. In a manner, no," he says. "I'm afraid you won't get any straightforward answers, Zanthi. It's all tangled."

It echoes through her, a drop of water falling into a still lake and sending ripples spinning. The strange feeling takes her again, from her toes to her ears. It's like she is back in the archives, walking through the damp dark, hearing a river echo all around her. "Ky."

"You met him," says Hart. "What did you see in your side-sight?"

She swallows. "Something monstrous. Something in his shadow, only it wasn't his shadow, it was him."

"Yes, that's him," says Hart, and through the worry there's a softness that makes her chest ache just to hear. "Monstrous."

"I'm sorry," she mumbles. "I didn't mean—"

"You did, and you needn't apologise. He is what he is."

She stares at her mentor, but he is a stranger to her in this moment. "He is a god."

"Only an echo of one."

"What does that mean?"

Hart's eyes slide closed. "For a long time, Ky has been nothing but a strange remnant. I knew where he came from, and what he had been, but he was only a ghost. A wraith who escaped the river, while the rest of him remained, locked fast. We need to rescue the whole of him, and for all my years of searching, I have never found how."

"Why did you not tell me earlier?"

"I could not. Such things I cannot easily speak. Or, I could not. Now the magic enshrouding him is gone, and I find I can."

"Oh," she says, realising what is different about him. "The fish."

"Pardon?"

"You've always had these strange, ghostly fish in your shadow. They go everywhere with you."

His expression turns pained. "They're not here anymore, are they?"

"No. Has something happened to him?"

"His ghost has slipped back into the river. He is gone."

She stares at her hands, gripped tight around the edge of the table. Hart settles his hand gently over her own. The aetherscars she has grown so used to are fading. Even as she watches, they seem to be fading.

"Zanthi. I do not know how long I will last without him. I came to say farewell."

He is cold, like Madoc had been cold when the dark river had been rushing through him. She lifts her head, and she thinks she can see it, dark and silent, all through him. "But he's not gone forever, is he? We can get him back."

Hart squeezes her hand before he lets her go. "I do not see how."

"He is a god. He cannot be *dead*. Not in the sense you and I can be dead."

Hart's mouth crooks, as if she has said something that amuses him. "In a way, I suppose so. Ky is and was, and isn't and will always be the Lord of the Waters, whether he is dead or not. He doesn't exist quite so simply as you and I. He will be dead, and also not, because it is not that simple. Like ripples, like echoes, except he is also the stone that cut the water or the cry that started the call. Perhaps you can ask him yourself, if you can pull the tangles free. And I pray to all the stars that you can, because we are lost unless you do."

She looks away, because the raw grief in his face is too sharp for her.

"Tell me what happened that day in the archives, when I was lost as a child. Tell me what Ky has made me forget."

Hart looks weary again. "Ah, that day. You unleashed a great deal of change upon my life. And then again, this year. It was you who brought Madoc the secrets that sent him to the dark river. And it is you who has spent so long trying to discover a name that Esk has forgotten, and has forgotten it ever knew. So why you, Zanthi Ilyston?"

It's a good question. She'd rather like to know herself. She puts her head in her hands. "I can't believe you knew all this time. Gods,

I feel ridiculous. All my speculations, all my theories. And you knew his name, his nature, his *fate*, from the very start."

"Don't feel so. I've enjoyed watching you work immensely," he says. Then, getting to his feet. "Come. Walk in the Gardens with me. The rest of this conversation must be had amongst the old groves."

He takes them into the cradle of an old, gnarled oak grove. The storm-snapped branches sweep down to encase them in a wicker of bare twigs, the silence is thick, nothing about but the drip of rain from the branches and the distant trickle of water. The walk is long, because Hart shuffles along like a man twice his age. A sharpness sits in his weary gaze, in the slopes of his tired face.

There is a bell ringing somewhere. In her mind. In the air. In the faint breeze that ripples the waters.

"You know his name," says Hart, tipping his head to the wind, as if he can hear the bell, too. "It's the first word you ever spoke to me."

She clutches the strap of her satchel, her heart barely more than a pale thud in her chest. "I cannot remember it."

"Then I will tell you, but only once. I haven't the strength for more. His name cannot last in a world where he is not."

His mouth moves, but it is a long moment before her thoughts hear the word he speaks. A shiver runs through the Gardens. In her side-sight, the echoes of all the rain, the steam, all the glass-gems of dripping water, lean towards Hart. The Lord of the Waters, reaching for him.

Not gone. Still here. Still in the waters of his sacred springs.

Hope flares through her, bright as moonlight. The name rings in her mind, fitting perfectly into that dark space where something had been missing. *Kyrillos*. He is still here to find.

"Take care of his name. While we have it, we have some chance of finding him again. A true forgetting is what will kill him entirely." He looks through the rain-dark branches. "It will kill him, and all he sustains."

Madoc. She swallows back her sudden, sick fear. "But there *is* a way to find him," she says. "Did you never read the clay tablet in Sabine's collection?"

He stares at her. "What tablet?"

She tugs her satchel open, digging for a piece of paper, and finds it tucked inside an inner pocket. "It holds the last words of the Lord of the Waters. Ky's words. Theron translated it."

Hart reads it, then flips it over and reads the rest of Theron's notes. "Old bloodlines?"

"Mother was a fanatic about them. I suppose he was trying to see if he could figure out the origin of those 'born of the river.'"

"This one. Asatos." Hart gives her a look. "Theron certainly must have realised. Did you not?"

"Languages are not my strongest skill."

"No, I do know that." He passes the paper back. "Asatos is a long-dead family line from the west. The family name means seeing-unseen, roughly."

"Oh," says Zanthi. The realisation drifts through her. "Long dead?"

He is watching her carefully. "So they say. Cursed into oblivion centuries ago."

They can't have been. Not entirely. Because her mother had returned from the west with *her*. Her witch-eyes and her side-sight, and her ability to see what others don't. *Asatos.*

She opens her mouth, her thought barely formed, when a cry shakes through the air. They turn to see Kit running downhill towards them.

"Ilyston," she calls. Then, "Zanthi!" She stops a wide pace away from them. Her cheeks are flushed. "You need to come to the manor. Madoc is there."

It's the way she says it. *Madoc is there.* And the flush to her cheeks. Not exertion, not from her run down the hill. Flushed because she is upset. Because her eyes are red.

"Go," says Hart, low and urgent.

Zanthi doesn't need to be told. She's already running.

Chapter Thirty-Seven

Rue is sitting in the armchair by the smouldering hearth, head in his hands. He doesn't stir as Zanthi passes him. Through the arch, Madoc is in his bed, sunk into a nest of cushions. She can easily imagine his nightingales fussing, piling them about him, kissing his brow, settling him in. It makes her smile, even through her worry.

She runs a hand down his cheek, traces the curve of his nose. He does not stir in all the long moments she sits there, tangling her hand through his curls. A strange grief curls in her chest like a creature stirring from a long, quiet slumber. It is her midsummer grief. It is older than that, too. Her chest aches, as if she has no air, and her throat burns. All of her feels like an open wound.

Rue looks up when she sits in the armchair across from him.

"It is not a sickness of the body," Zanthi says, fixing her gaze on him. It has been a long while since she's looked at someone so directly.

Rue barely flinches. "No," he says. "The illness is not a physical one."

"It is not getting better."

"It is getting worse," he corrects her gently. "It does no good to talk around things, Miss Ilyston. Ever since midsummer, he has been fading. I do not understand it. The ritual worked. I know what went into that poison, and no mortal body could have survived it. And yet, he did."

"Then the fault lies not with the poison, nor with Madoc, nor with the ritual." She stares at the flames in the hearth. "The tangle is deeper than that."

The very first time she'd gone into the archives as a student, she had been fascinated with it. The endless dark, the promise of what might be found. The strange feeling, always present, that she was searching for something. That she had lost something.

Trust your instincts, she'd been told.

Her instincts are telling her to seek. They always have been.

"I must talk with the Lord of the Waters," she says. "Where would I go to do that?"

Rue looks at her in alarm. "Talk?"

"Pray, I suppose. You are a devotee, aren't you?"

He takes a thin breath. "I am. I was born in these Gardens."

"Where do you go, when you wish to be close to your god?"

"There is a shrine out in the old forest. That's where the nightingales go."

She stands, and he holds out a hand, staying her.

"Lady Casca and Madoc, though, they go to the springheart. If you truly want to be heard, then I would go there."

"Am I allowed to go there without a Casca beside me?"

His laugh is dry, like autumn leaves. "Gods, no. But if you think you might help Madoc? I'm not going to tell you that you can't."

She leaves her satchel by the desk and glances down to see the two golden bracelets sitting on a pile of books. Someone must have removed them from her skirt pocket when she had left it crumpled on the floor. She picks up one, and then the other, and slips them onto her wrists. They are as cold as the storm had been.

They were made for the wrists of some unfortunate soul she'll never know, but in that moment, they feel as if they were made for her, and her alone.

"Wish me luck," she says.

"Luck and fortune." Rue stands. He's a tall man, and he has to bend to place a kiss to Zanthi's cheek. "And blessings. I hope your prayers turn up more than mine."

"I've never done one before," she says, summoning up a smile. "But I am excellent at dissertations."

If the Lord of the Waters is at all like Ky, she might have a fair chance at swaying him. Ky must appreciate a good dissertation. He fell in love with Ethram Hart, after all.

❧

The quartz gravel shimmers in the pale winter light. A few wrens pick over storm-torn moss, and the remnants of the morning rain clings to the bare branches above. It's a perfectly still moment.

And a bell rings. It's in her thoughts, and through her body, shaking the blood in her veins. Her side-sight shifts into movement. The water, ghost-water, not real water, flows past her, sweeping in from all directions and urging her forward. It is as she had seen in the archives, those months ago, and she knows where it is flowing.

It isn't leading her to the moss-scratch pathways to the door of the springheart. It's taking her to the hawthorn hedge.

The last time she had struggled through these hedges, it had been a sweet midsummer evening, with drums rippling the air and everything smelling of smoke. Now, the branches are thorned and bare, broken by the storm and dripping with rain.

She finds the old door hidden in the crumble of ancient stone and overgrown ivy. It opens silently for her, and the darkness wells up from inside. In her side-sight, the dark waters flow around her legs and into the passage.

She hasn't got her aether lantern, but she barely needs it. Her feet find their way in the darkness, as if remembering the steps to a dance. The old stairs, the stretch of silence, and the crumbled cave-in she must scramble over.

Her feet kick up dust when she slides down the other side. It settles across her tongue, as bitter as grave dirt.

The darkness turns murky, stops being sheltering, and starts threatening. She can feel it, like Madoc must have felt it when they had last walked here. The difference between the Gardens, where the springs still flowed, and the rest of the darkness.

The old archives, where only the dead walk.

The dark brushes gentle touches to her neck, her wrists. She can't see a whit, except at the edges of her vision. The water flows on, and she follows, and within a step or two, her side-sight has bled across all her vision. Through the dark, she can see the dark arch of the vaulted passage above her. She can see the twisted, fractured figures of the dancing frieze, and as she passes beneath the waymarker, the crowned figure with the outstretched arm, she pauses.

The figure is wearing bracelets, just like the ones Zanthi is wearing.

How had she never noticed? It is a midsummer procession, after all. It is a funerary procession. She knows where the figure is pointing now. Where the procession is headed. They are going to the springs.

She runs. The echo of the midsummer drums beats in her memory, alongside her heartbeats, and in the darkness, a bell rings, on and on.

The hidden passage swallows her, drawing her down into the ancient dirt and wild stone. The chill settles over her, and there is no one beside her this time to hold her hand and anchor her. She follows the current and it leads her where she knew it would. The dead springs.

She *knew* the ritual wasn't finished. Something has been left undone, and it is sinking Madoc. She will not let him sink. She will find out what must be done and bring him back to the surface, to the stars.

The dark current flows into the mirror-like pool at the heart of the little chamber. There is no sign of that dry, dead spring, full of sand. There is only water.

A silver shape darts around her, urging her on. She glimpses fins, scales. A memory stirs in the depths of her mind and sinks again before she can seize it. It tastes of river mud and rain.

The stone is slick as she climbs the steps, and inside the spring, water is brimming as full and deep as the spring in the Gardens. The stone is black with an ancient damp, and the water wells down and down, into endless night. It is as clear as air, clear as nothing at all.

She sinks to her knees at the veilstone. Surely, if she pleads, Ky will hear her here. He will answer her. She opens her mouth to say something, anything, and her voice sticks in her throat, shrivelling.

In the darkness, the bell rings.

This isn't right. The Lord of the Waters is not here. This is not where she will find him. She *knows* where to find him.

Find me in the rushes. Find me in the current.

When she leans over, there's not a single reflection in the pool. She holds her hand over it, and the water shows her nothing back. Only the glint of her bracelet, shining with some fey light in all the gloom.

She thinks she knows, now, what Ethram and Ky had been telling her when they had gifted the bracelets to her. *A place only the dead go.* The dark river.

The bell rings.

"Send after me one born of the river," she mutters. "Oh, you *wretch*."

She dampens her lips, tastes the springs there.

She *can't.*

She goes back down the steps. Steps up and turns back again.

The bell rings.

It's only water.

She just needs to step. It's dark, and it's deep, but Madoc has taught her how to stay afloat, how to let her body be borne. His hands, warm against her skin. His mouth, hot against her neck. That is what she is thinking of as she undresses. When she is in only her slip and her bracelets, she climbs back up.

It's only water, and Madoc needs her. And if she doesn't go, she'll have to return to the Gardens damp and empty-handed and sit by Madoc's bedside to watch him fade.

She is one born of the river. She has the forgotten name. She will find Ky, and she will bring him back so he can heal Madoc.

She will not accept anything less.

The last of the ghost-water flickers around her and disappears into the spring. Her side-sight fades away. She must go now. It has to be now, or the water will vanish.

Her toes hang over the edge of the final step. The veilstone, like the one in the Gardens springheart, like the one in Sabine's collection. All the same. Thresholds. A stopping point between two places. Two worlds. A thing to cross over.

The bell rings. She steps. The water swallows her down.

Chapter Thirty-Eight

When Madoc had taken her bathing, the water had cradled her, borne her up towards the stars. She remembers, in a strange, hazy moment, the way his fingers had pressed against her shoulders. The way water had run down his neck and into the hollow of his collarbones. The way she had watched the stars. The way he had watched her.

This is no star-pierced pool. When she steps into the water, she falls.

It's a rush of water and shadow, and she plummets down into the endless dark. Yet it's only a moment of falling, only long enough for her to fear she'll fall forever, and then her feet land in sand.

A river drags at her. It's warm, the same warmth as her skin so that she barely feels it there, only that it tugs at her, tugs her downstream. There is no wind, no air at all, really, for all that she still breathes. The light is the grey of night, and all the sky is stars.

Through the dim light, the world swims back into focus. Old trees bow gracefully, and mossy islands rise from dark waters. She knows this flooded place. The water is ankle-deep, and the silt is soft under her toes.

The Gardens are silent, dark. Ragged lanterns hang unlit, strung between trees thick with dark, silent leaves. The springs spill over, the pools flooding, and all the space between them is hollowed with water. Here and there are stands of dark rushes, and they rattle with the echo of faded whispers. Like the last pen nib, rolling in the box. Like pottery shards, shifting under searching hands.

She follows the paths, hidden beneath spilling waters, through rush beds almost taller than she is. She is pushing through a thicket of reeds growing tangled across her path when gold glints from within the dark leaves.

Like a bell ringing in the darkness, it is familiar. She stoops to fish the gleam from the water and finds a golden droplet of an earring. She's seen its pair once before, amber in firelight, set against dark curls.

A stillness seizes her.

Beyond the rushes, a flame bursts to life, bright in the velvet dark. She turns towards it. The water ripples around her ankles, and all the rushes whisper.

Through the trees, Ky is standing in the rushes. She is not surprised to see him, but there's still a strange sort of alarm that runs through her. He's dressed in moonlight-silk, his hair long and garlanded with river daisies. His teeth, when his lips part, are dark and sharp.

"You came," he says. "I wondered when you would."

Zanthi stares at him. She knows him, and yet she feels she is staring at a stranger, too. "I came to speak to the Lord of the Waters."

"I am he," he says, with that dark, sharp smile.

A chill crawls through. It startles her, because it is the first sensation she has felt since landing in the greyness. "But I met you. You were Ky, then."

"I am he," he says, again.

"Why did you not tell me? Why did you not tell Madoc?"

"I was not your Lord of the Waters, not then."

"And you are now?"

"As I always have been."

Zanthi, quite suddenly, wishes she had a book in hand, so she might throw it at him. Hart's excess of books makes sense, if he must be in constant conversation with this creature.

Ky's sharp smile grows, as if he can hear the echo of her thoughts. Perhaps he can.

"I was waiting for you. I could not go until you came."

The rushes are wound up around him, twisting around his calves and up to his knees, growing through the restless linens of his tunic. There is no breeze, but all of him is in movement, as if he is underwater. It is clear he cannot move. It looks as if he has been here for an eon.

"I came to ask what is ailing Madoc." She wades forwards and the rushes rattle around her. "How do we cure him?"

"Cure?" Ky looks thoughtful. "No, that is not the tangle we are here to pull free."

She steps into the dark water of the pool that traps him. It is the midsummer pool, she realises. The braziers stand around the banks, all eight of them.

One is alight.

She stares at that light, and a yawning ache opens through her. It is an old, old grief. Older than weeks, or months. A grief of a lifetime. It makes no sense that it is hers, and yet she knows it is.

She scrubs her hands down her face. "Hart is waiting for you."

"Yes." It's a sigh of a sound. "I hear him, sometimes. Has he been waiting long?"

"No," she says, but it feels like a lie. "Not yet. Why are you here?"

"I am the river, but the river is not me, little fish. I cannot command it." Ky tips his head. His eyes shine flat, reflecting moonlight from nowhere. "Even a god can die, after all."

"But you are not dead."

"Not yet," he says. "But almost."

It makes a sharp sort of sense. The springs have been dying, because Ky has been dying. He was not dead in an instant, centuries ago, but stuck here, dying slowly, for an eon. It makes her mind faint to think of.

He makes a sound like the rattling rushes, a harsh intake of breath. "I had tethers in the mortal world. The Well, and the sacrifices that it fed me. And my worshippers and their worship."

"But then the worship stopped."

"It faded," he corrects. "My true death was inevitable, then. My tethers broke, one by one, until only the Well remained. And then you came."

The memory is there, faint at the edges. She can't quite make out the detail of it. "I found you in the archives."

"Not the archives, little fish. They are but a way. You found me here."

"In the river?"

He inclines his head. "I have been here for an age, and for no time at all. You dragged me from the rushes a moment ago, and years ago. I have lived a mortal life between then and now, have brewed tea and made jam and planted thyme, and neither have I moved from this place. But you know this, too, don't you? You've grown to age, and all with part of yourself left behind."

She knows it is true. "Then I have been here before."

"Haven't we all?" He considers. "Or perhaps it is that we all will be. When you first freed me from my suffering, I followed you out of the river, breaking myself in the doing of it. And you, too, got caught in the echoes."

The bell is still ringing, somewhere in the distance. Madoc's earring is cold in her palm.

"Everything is tangled. *I* am tangled." His expression shifts, and she sees some of the man he had been in the cottage, wry and warm. "We are here to pull the tangle, little fish, to get us both free."

"How?" She tries to tug at the rushes that hold him, but they are vicious things and cut at her hands. "I am sick of hints and half-truths. If you know, then tell me."

"I need a river child to free me, and I need a consecrated Casca in the Gardens to tether me. Only then will I have the strength to walk free of my death."

"You have that," she says. "He did the ritual. You *have* that."

"Do I? I won't be free until he comes into his full power. He cannot come into his power until I complete the ritual and send him back. I cannot send him back unless I am free to catch him in the river."

And he is not free. He is caught tight in the silent, vicious reeds.

"But you sent him back. You have done it already."

"I have not. I cannot. He was always fated to fail his consecration."

She makes a thin noise of frustration.

"My last faint flame of a priest turned out to be a very brave one. Or, perhaps, an entirely foolish one." His gaze darkens. "Do you not see the shape of what he has done?"

She sees nothing but the ripples in the water, bearing a dark shadow into view.

She is running into the water before she can think. Sand slips beneath her toes, and she claws herself deeper. The river drags at her, but she only sees Madoc, face tipped to the stars, drifting, still. The water runs over his face, stirring his hair against his ashen cheeks. There is ivy in his curls, dark and glistening.

As soon as she takes him in her arms, the water rises against her. She drags him with her, pushes for the safety of the rushes. Sinks. Pushes again. The water swallows her, then raises her. Madoc slumps against her shoulders, and she holds him with a death grip, pulling him towards shallower waters, towards Ky.

The water is to her chest now. It is deepening. Her breath is loud, harsh, and wet.

She knows this.

A memory shakes loose from a dark place in her mind. Madoc, and a funeral bell ringing, so loud and so long. Her arms shake. It is an old memory, older than it has any right to be. Somehow, she's been here before.

"This didn't happen," she says, pressing her words into the chill of his cheek. His lips are bloodless and pale. "He lived."

Ky watches her. "Because you were here."

"I was *there*," she says. "I am there watching for him to return."

"You are here," he says, and the water becomes alive with silver shadows, darting around them. "Here, to catch him when I could not. Here, where it all gets tangled."

Zanthi drags Madoc to Ky, and the silver fish in the water help bear him up, keep him floating.

"Why are you not doing anything? He is your priest. He is yours," she says, and it comes out as a snarl. "*Heal him.*"

"Yes. He is mine." Ky moves his arms, limited though he is, and takes Madoc. And that is all it takes.

The rushes sigh and shiver and fall back, and Ky smiles. His mouth is cruel. A mouth that could swallow a city, batter down walls, bring the night in swift and unstoppable.

"Why are you grieving, river's daughter?"

She is, she realises. Her eyes sting, and against her lips is the taste of not river water, but salt. She feels the river is in her. A roaring, scouring tide of it. She knows that the Madoc of midsummer is well. He is going to step from the water and lift her up. He will bear her into the shadow of a birch tree and say strange and solemn words over her.

And yet that is a memory and hasn't happened yet. All through, she is cold with the fear that it might never happen. That it never happened. That he has been dead in the river this whole time.

That even now, he is dead in his rooms in the manor.

But. *No.*

"Do you understand?" says Ky. "My priest, but not only mine."

No, not only his.

Madoc is hers. She has chased the river away once already, has claimed him in the spilling waters.

"The ritual must be finished," she says. "How?"

"That is your choice, river's daughter."

She brushes the ivy crown, remembers him in the midsummer firelight, reaching for her. She rests a hand against his cheek. Madoc has taught her, again and again, how such things are ended. He's pale-lipped with poison as she leans in to kiss him. His mouth tastes of river water and wine, and things more potent than either. It's just a touch, but that's all she needs in a place like this.

His eyes open. Dark, green, still hazy with wine, just as she remembers. He looks at her, and there is wonder there, wonder and a longing so raw she thinks her chest might split. He reaches for her.

"That is certainly one way to go about it," murmurs Ky.

Madoc looks up, face slack in shock, and Ky releases him back to the river. He is gone in a swirl of dark water.

"And so it is done," says Ky, as the ripples die back to stillness. "It is finished."

She reaches through the water, but there is nothing there. Madoc is beyond her reach.

On a distant wind, she hears music, exultant cheers, the splash of water, and people laughing. Her heart aches.

"Things are as they are," Ky says. "The ritual is finally complete. Ah, little fish. The river is coming for you."

Her head is growing heavy, the bitter taste in her mouth growing strong even as she grows numb. She doesn't know how she'll escape the river again. She can't remember how she did it last time.

She can feel echoes of her all the way back, like a bell ringing into the night. Muddy hands, small and sore. Cold hands, holding a lantern aloft. Damp hands, dragging Madoc from dark waters. Fractured grief, jagged fear, ossified loneliness.

"There is something more you must say," Ky says. "Do you remember?"

He stands just as the carven frieze had, a shining figure with flowing hair. He was made for this place, to drift amongst the souls and usher them on into the world that comes after. And yet, on the wind, she hears the patter of rain on a windowpane, the crackle of a hearth. The sound of a door closing, and boots being removed.

He is not where he belongs, not anymore.

"Hart is waiting for you," she says, and the words feel right, even as they fall like stone from her lips. "Go home, Kyrillos."

All the rushes sigh, as if a great breath has bowed them, and in that breath, all the rustling sounds like his name, over and over. *Kyrillos. Kyrillos. Kyrillos.*

"That is all I needed you to say, river's daughter." His hands settle on her shoulders, curve around her. Cruel hands with pearly claws, and she's barely noticed that before he is pushing her back, pushing her down. The water rises around her, as if she's falling smaller and he is growing impossibly large. "My blessings go with you."

The water closes over her head. Her heart stutters, and the sound is loud in her ears.

She is alone, and the loss is a great, clawing thing.

Then there is only silence.

The water drags at her feet, and the rushes tower around her. They're very tall. She pushes them aside and realises that it's only that she's very small. Her hands are soft and round, with short fingers that struggle to balance a pen.

A memory, she thinks. She's in a memory. An echo.

In the memory, she has gotten lost, and has found a river. She likes the river. It sounds like home.

She is looking for ducks, with the dark waters murmuring around her. Instead, she finds a thread of pale golden moonlight caught in the reeds.

Her child hands are pulling the reeds aside, following the thread. A flash catches her eye, and she finds a heap of crumpled silver at the base of the rushes, caught in a thick-grown net of stalks. Something shining and shifting like moonlight.

"Fish," says her mouth, even though her watching mind knows it is no fish.

She watches her hands free Ky from his shroud of rushes. He's a strange creature of scales and spines, beautiful and sleek, curled in a twist of silvered form. He shivers under her touch. She watches, caught in horror and shame, as her child body hauls Ky from the rushes like she'd drag an over-large book from the shelf.

"Go home, fishy," she says, and hefts him into the water. He wakes when he hits the open river, a frozen frisson of shock, and then a twist of sleek muscle transforms him into something else entirely. The silver-shine of his body writhes, circles her once, and is gone, down into the depths.

Her laugh is bright in the darkness.

A bell rings, and she stops to listen.

Beyond the rushes, a flame bursts to life, bright in the velvet dark. She turns towards it. The water ripples around her ankles, and all the rushes whisper.

She is running through the archives, wailing, her footprints wet. Strong arms swing her up, cradle her against a warm chest. There is a grief in her, too large and jagged for her to understand. She cries for what she has lost, only she can't remember what she has lost. Her mind is an echoing place, and a single word is all she can say.

In the darkness, a bell rings.

. . .

She walks in the archives, following a bell. There is a darkness in her mind, an aching space where something isn't. She is looking for it, only she cannot remember what she seeks. She only knows that it slipped from her hands.

She only knows that it was hers.

She is in the archives, and she is alone. Her lantern flickers out, but the darkness draws her on. There is something on the edges of her thoughts, almost taking shape, and she's close to finding it. With a whispered creak, the door opens to a night sky. Stars glint through a hawthorn hedge.

Then, air. Cold and sharp on her skin.

Chapter Thirty-Nine

There are hands tilting her head up, and solid, cold ground beneath her. Her chest seizes in a violent ache, more painful than anything she's ever felt, and she arches in a great, chest-splitting gasp.

The person falls back. They're talking, low, fast.

"You're okay, Zanthi," they say. "I've got you."

It sounds jarringly loud. Harsh.

She is rolled to her side as she retches up water. It's thick and dark and leaves a stained patch of moss beneath her. She's wet and cold. There are people leaning over her, all damp too, bathing shifts clinging to skin.

The night shatters, torn apart by the sound of the manor door slamming wide. Her vision is swimming, as if there's water overlaid over everything, but she sees the ripples of a scene. Lantern light spinning. Manor light. Dark trees like stage sets.

Madoc is running. His feet are bare, and his hair is dry and plaited at his temples, and he's calling for her. When he drops to his knees beside her, the force of it tears dark scars in the moss. He pulls her into his arms, and the sound he makes when he presses his face to her wet hair is only her name, over and over.

"I'm well," she says, and her voice feels strange in her mouth. "It is done, now."

It is done. The ritual Madoc undertook at midsummer is finally complete, and he will be well. Safe.

The nightingales are around her, trying to make sense of it. They were bathing, they say. She came up from the water, still as the dead. No, they didn't see her fall in the water. No, they can't explain it. Yes, the water turned cold as ice, and they all felt it.

She opens her fingers, and Madoc's earring shines in her palm. He sees it and his face is struck open, bare shock and then fear. His hand comes over hers, hiding it from view. Then he's lifting her, as easily as Ky had lifted him in that dark pool.

The memory stutters, then slides into place. Stays. For the first time in a long while, the bells are silent.

She curves into him, head on his shoulder, as he bears her back to the manor.

"Where did you go?" His voice is low. He shoulders the door shut behind him.

"I didn't go," she says. "I'd already been. I hadn't left." As she says it, she knows it is true. She's been in that river half her life and hadn't known it. She had wandered into death as a child and had seen a glimpse of what her future held, and it had been too much, too grief-stricken, for her memory to hold. "I'm here now. All of me is here now."

He sets her down on the sofa, the cushions cradling her. There are no shadows under his eyes. There is no fading to him any longer.

"You are awake," she says, suddenly wondering at the marvel of it. He is awake, and as bright and lovely as he had been when he'd first wandered into her little alcove in the vault. More so, even, because in her side-sight, his shadow is rippling with dark waters. Not chasing him, not any longer. Waiting beside him like a patient hound.

"Yes. I am. I woke, and you were gone. Rue and I were standing here when we saw them drag you from the water."

From the window, there is a perfect view down to the pool.

"I must have frightened you."

"You must have frightened me? Zanthi, my love, nothing has stopped my heart so soundly."

"That's not true," she says, reaching out to drop the earring in his palm. "One thing has."

He rolls it over, the gold glinting between his fingers, then gone entirely, tucked away somewhere. "I lost this at midsummer."

She shivers, running her hands down her thighs. There is nothing in her side-sight now. Only the quiet stillness that the Gardens bring. "I spoke with the Lord of the Waters. Or perhaps I spoke with Ky. Both, I think. They are the same once more. He is healed, too." Her head aches, and she wants to feel his warmth against her. "I'm cold, Madoc. Come here, help me be warm."

He does. He eases the damp shift over her head, wraps a blanket over her, and then he's slipping in behind her, bundling her into the warmth of his body. He presses his lips to the curve of her cheek, the end of her brow. "I'm teaching you to swim," he says, against her skin. He's hollow-voiced. "I never want to see that again."

"You may teach me whatever you please," she agrees. She traces her fingers down his arm, over his fingers, chasing the lines of his rings. His skin is warm, and she will never cease being grateful for that. She loops her fingers around his wrist as far as they'll go, feels the muscles flex as his hand twitches. "Only tell me first what you spoke to me at midsummer. You did promise."

His breath is almost a laugh. It's mostly a release of tension, a hot brush against her. "I spoke the first devotion to you," he says at last. Then, "The one that binds me to the Gardens and to the Lord of the Waters. The one that makes me his."

The tug that pulled the tangle free, she thinks. Kyrillos was right. Madoc was brave and foolish both. But then she remembers the way he'd cupped her cheek. The defiance he'd given his mother.

"All the way back then?" is what she manages.

He tucks his head into the crook of her neck. Kisses the skin there. He is, she thinks, hiding his face. "All the way back then," he says. "From the very start."

"What..." She dampens her lips. "What are the devotions?"

He lifts his head. She's always thought his eyes were wonderful. Such a rich colour, so full of life. But now they're peerless. Midsummer-dark. They're full of secrets and they hide nothing. His lips move, and the words that come from them mean nothing to her, except they do. She can feel them tug inside her chest.

"I don't know what they mean," she says, softly. "Tell me."

He hesitates. "*I give my heart to the river's course, and my life as the rushes that grow in the current. To bend and be broken and grow anew, but stay, always, in your waters.*" He ducks his head again. Presses his lips to the curve of her ear. "It sounds better in the old tongue."

She twists, pressing up against him. His breath is against her mouth, and she kisses him. She doesn't wait for him to catch up. She kisses him how she'd wished to kiss him at midsummer, when he'd been drunk with life and beautiful in his ivy garlands, and the sound he makes is dragged from deep within him.

"I will stay in your waters, too," she says. "There is very little, now, that can ever keep me from you."

"Where did you go?" He barely moves his lips against hers. "Zanthi, tell me."

"You know where," she says. "Don't you remember me?"

His eyes flutter shut. "I thought I'd dreamed you. Even now, I could be dreaming you."

If anyone has ever been summoned from a dream, made up from dark desires and longing hearts, then it is Madoc Casca. "Not dreaming," she says. She rests her head against his chest, listens to the steady beat of his heart. "Somehow, we're not dreaming."

She hammers on Hart's door until he answers her. It is early. She is beyond caring.

He blinks, taking her in. "Is everything well, Zanthi?"

"I need to talk to Ky," she says, and pushes in. Hart seems too startled to say anything at all.

She has given him three days, and that's only for the sake of Hart. She thinks three days is plenty of time. She wants answers.

Ky is in the kitchen. He's washing dishes. When she comes in, he puts down the last bowl and turns to her, damp rag in his hands. Water drips on the floor. It is soapy.

"*Why are you grieving?*" Zanthi says, rage making her voice pinch. "You had me drag his *dead body* from the cursed dark river, and you ask me *why I'm grieving*?"

To his credit, Ky does look a tad sheepish. Or as possible as it is for a man wreathed in the grace of an ancient god to look sheepish. "He wasn't truly dead," he offers. He sets the rag aside. "Not while we were there."

Hart's hand settles on her shoulder. "What in the isles is she talking about, Ky?" He sounds very tired, as if he isn't near recovered from his illness. The aether cannot be helping. Even now, the cottage is thick with it. She hopes, for Hart's sake, that Ky is in better control of it now.

"It's nothing that needs dredging up. Just a tangle of happenings that we managed to pull free." He crosses to the table, and sits. He's easier to look at like that. She doesn't feel so small.

"Explain," she says.

"When you were a child, I was able to follow you free of the waters and into Esk because you carry the blood of those who see the unseen, who can pass all boundaries and find all ways. No one else would have been able to find me. And the second time, you were able to stand in my place and catch Madoc in the river because Madoc said words to you that should never have been said to another but me. And so, the river accepted your claim and allowed you to drag Madoc from its clutches when he was beyond my reach."

"That cannot be. Madoc did not say those things to me until after he had returned."

"The echoes layer and roll over one another. At some point, a beginning ceases to exist."

"I despise talking with you," she decides. Hart gives a sound rather like muffled laughter.

Though Ky doesn't laugh, she gets the distinct impression of amusement. "You have done me a great service, twice. You have favours to collect from me, when you are in need of them."

She looks over his shoulder at the pot of thyme on the windowsill. The jar of jam by the stove. "If I freed you as a child, why didn't it work the first time?"

"It did, for a while, but you were a child, and your words did not have strength enough to stand against the river. You told me to go home, and I did not have a home." He smiles, then, at Hart, who is fussing with the tea things. "Ah, but I do now."

Hart sighs. "Thank you for what you did. Returning him to me."

"I don't know why you wanted it," she mutters. She catches Hart's smile before he turns away. For all she doesn't quite trust Ky and his face that looks far too gentle, far too mortal, for what she saw in the dark river, she is so fond of Hart.

"We still have work to do," Hart says. "Esk won't be truly safe until Ky is restored to the histories and stories of Esk."

"It had better be enough to earn me my Luminary robes," she says, eying Ky.

He catches her looking and tips a brow at her. It's something he must have stolen from Hart, and it suits his strange, beautiful face very well.

"Madoc told me the meaning of the devotions he said to me at midsummer," she says.

Now he laughs. It's a sound as gentle as the water trickling through the Gardens. "Tangle after tangle," he says. "Without those devotions, he would have perished in that ritual, and I would have faded away, and all Esk would have been lost under the Well. With those words, he gave us a chance. It shouldn't have worked. He shouldn't have been able to mean what he said. What a startling creature he is. What a startling creature you are, too."

Startling, he says. Zanthi watches Hart choose between a stack of well-used tea tins, and in her side-sight, Ky's aether-shroud shifts between all his monstrous forms. Though they are none of them monstrous, not truly. They are all nothing more than a man sitting at his kitchen table, watching his beloved make tea.

He turns back to her, and there's a flat moonshine in his eyes, once and gone. "In the dark river, we are nothing more than echoes. You, I, Madoc, every Casca, and every Heir to ever have been Blooded. We stay there, layering over one another. You will always be there, pulling me from the rushes. You will always be there, waking Madoc with a kiss."

"Then you will always be there, dying in the rushes. And Madoc will always be there, cold in the water."

"He wasn't dead," says Ky, with great exasperation. "And besides, that's what makes him my priest, does it not? He's always there, in the river, even as he brings life and laughter to my Gardens."

"But you're back now," says Hart, a dangerous edge to his words. "You're both of you back now."

"Yes, my heart," says Ky. His smile is not at all wreckful and dark. It's fond, and as gentle as ripples on a morning lake. "You scholars take everything so literally. I am back. I will stay."

Chapter Forty

The storm left Esk in pieces, and it takes a long two weeks for the fragments to be gathered, sorted, and mended. Chester had not come through the battle unscathed, and it is days before he sits her down and tells her how close he had come to falling into the dark river himself. The aether of the *Lys*, always so brightly wound through him, is burnt into him, now. With her side-sight, she can see how it wraps around him like creeping vines, holding him together, keeping him tethered.

Not all the captains were so fortunate. Not all the ships returned. When the last missing ships are found and their crews home, some alive and some in shrouds, and the funeral bells have rung for a day and a night, and the barges have borne the dead downriver, then, all of Esk takes a shuddering breath and continues on. By the dawn of the last month of the year, the town is shining with aetherlamps again, the shops are open, and the *Society Papers* announce the Season is resuming.

There is still a pall to Chester's face, and a black ribbon on his wrist for those he lost. His eyes burn with aether-gold, and she thinks they'll never see the warm brown of his eyes without the aether ever again. The First Heir has made the papers by choosing to don a grieving veil when outside his residence. Rue's healing halls are still overrun with the injured. But Esk, as a whole, is not a town inclined to melancholy.

Zanthi watches it stir back to life and wonders what it was about ballrooms and candlelight that she ever found so off-putting. She cannot summon that bone-chilling aversion back through her. Nothing seems so bad if Madoc is there, too. How could it be?

She is sitting by the hearth, Susan sprawled across her lap, when Theron shakes out the evening paper and reads out a list of upcoming events and parties. She looks up, still holding Susan's silky paws. There will be an evening party at the Gardens next week, by invitation only. She runs a thumb over Susan's snub, pearly claws and decides.

"Theron? Might you help me with something?"

"You've a good chance of it," he says, and follows her upstairs when she asks him. He settles at her desk, all curiosity.

When she pulls Madoc's chemise out of her wardrobe and lays it on her bed, his face takes a calculating air.

"This is a very fine thing. What do you wish to do with it?"

"Can you help me have it tailored?"

He pins her with a sharp look. "You changed your mind?"

"Only for something small. A starting point to dip my toes in." She passes the chemise over when he gestures for it. "I thought you and I might go to the evening party at the end of the week."

"I haven't an invitation."

"That's no matter," she says. "I'll sort it." Privately, she thinks she won't even need to. She's entirely sure Madoc has had all her brothers on his list since he first came for breakfast.

A handful of nights later, Zanthi contemplates the wisdom of her decision. In her side-sight, Susan yawns with her white-thorn teeth and lies across the doorway, a grey puddle of sleek shadow. Zanthi blinks back at Theron's dressing-table mirror. She frowns. Behind her, her brothers do the same.

"You could just leave it out," suggests Fletcher. "The Gardens allow for *some* informality."

"Do your usual braid," says Theron. "That will look perfectly acceptable."

Chester sighs. "Here, pass me your clasp, Zan."

She does, resigning herself to whatever Chester has in mind. Theron's mirror is more flattering than hers, perhaps, which is why she thinks that the lot of them look like a lovely aethergraph waiting to be taken.

Madoc's chemise is hers now, quite permanently. It's been altered to sit properly against her neck, slipping gracefully over her shoulders, the sleeves falling like water to her wrists. They'd found some silk, nicer than any she'd owned before, and Theron's tailor had summoned up a skirt to match. Then Theron and Fletcher had conspired to gift her a hairpiece finer than anything she's ever owned.

It is, she thinks, their idea of an amusing reference. And, perhaps, an acceptance of everything this is, and everything it will become, in time.

"There," Chester says.

He's pinned her hair in a gathering at the base of her neck, and the hairpiece, a garland of golden ivy, is draped across the crown of her head and woven right through her hair. She gives him a grateful smile.

"I think you've saved the night before it even began," she says.

"Don't say that. There's still plenty to go," he says, rather more cheerily than such a statement deserves, and takes her downstairs to hand her into his carriage. He hands Theron in just the same and waves them off.

"Nervous?" Theron asks, as the Garden Hall rises beyond the carriage window, lit with candlelight and glittering glass.

"Horribly," she says.

He smiles. "Not a whit to fear," he promises her. "You've faced down hostile Luminaries for half a year. Socialites will have nothing to concern you."

She hopes it is so. When they reach the top of the Garden Hall steps, the nightingale at the door opens his mouth. Closes it again. Lights up like a lantern.

"Ilystons!" It is Rowan, and he is gleaming. "Fancy that!"

"May we come in?"

"You may, and curse you for coming by on a day I'm stuck on the door." He grazes a kiss to her cheek as she passes inside. "He's over by the windows, looking pretty."

He *is* looking lovely, is all Zanthi can think when they step inside the receiving hall. And then she sees the clasp he is wearing, gold and glass. Her ivy leaf, glinting in his hair as if it is the crowning jewel of his entire look.

They cross the hall, and she's watching only Madoc, so she sees the moment he sees them. To her immense amusement, he notices Theron first. Then his wide-eyed gaze skates down to her, and *that* is the smile that she loves best. It is soft, and open, and not at all the sort of face he should show in this sort of place. The people surrounding him look askance, but he's already moving.

"Sabine Casca will exile us all over again if her son spends the night looking like that," Theron mutters. Then, as Madoc reaches them, "Evening, Casca."

"Theron," says Madoc, all rich delight.

Theron's face twitches. "Madoc," he corrects, though a tad reluctantly.

Madoc is trying to tamp down on his smile, she knows. He isn't managing it.

"Zanthi," he says. His rings glint as he cups her cheek, and it's all the warning she has before he kisses her. It's a gentle, chaste thing, and he holds her face in one hand, barely touching, as he draws back. He's smiling, still. "You're here."

She had forgotten, somehow, about Madoc and the Gardens' liberties and the kissing.

Theron, also, seems to have forgotten because he looks alarmed for a split moment, then wisely says, "Enjoy your evening," before abandoning them.

"He's concerned you'll give him the same treatment," she says.

Madoc laughs. "Pity he ran. I might have, for bringing you here."

He's still resting his hand against her cheek. They're just looking at each other. It's not at all Madoc's usual style. They should certainly move somewhere else.

"You're very nicely made-up," she says, instead. "I chose a good night to come."

"Zanthi," he says again. His soft look is going a little dark-eyed, and she understands what Theron had meant. "Is that my chemise?"

"It was. It's mine now."

"As it should be. It looks far better on you." He runs a hand along the collar edge, against her skin. "I thought I'd misplaced that months ago."

"Yes," she says, smiling. "Since midsummer."

"All the way back then?" His eyes are bright. The candlelight of the salon seems to be working to flatter him above all others. She can hardly blame it.

She truly loves him. There's not a ballroom she'd hesitate to enter if he was beside her. Not a passage, not a storm, not a river.

"From the very start." She puts her arm through his, and he tugs her in tight against him. "Show me your waters, Madoc Casca. I must learn to swim in them."

Epilogue

The ink gleams on the page, wet and dark. The weather is wet and dark too, the rain drumming against the window in a ceaseless dance. A carriage rattles outside, draws to a stop, and she lifts her head.

Susan pads from the room. A visitor for Fletcher, perhaps. It is too early in the day for Madoc to be by, and Theron is teaching a lecture until mid-afternoon.

Already moving on with her thoughts, she finishes her sentence and sets the paper to dry. It is a letter for Hart, and it outlines her latest thoughts for her paper. A paper that will restore the name *Kyrillos* to the ink and stone of Esk and, if she's planned it all right, in a way that won't reveal the ancient secrets of the Gardens.

It will likely take her years to see it all through. Theron will translate the *Song of Dark Waters*, now the forgetting is fading, and she'll catalogue the Gardens' treasures. It will be painstaking. Careful discoveries, pulled from the archives. Old stories, uncovered. Archaeological finds, recategorised. Her fingers are aching to get started.

A knock at the door frame disturbs her. She is in Theron's study, but it isn't Theron in the doorway. It is Joren, Susan close on his heels.

"Good afternoon, Miss Ilyston," he says.

She carefully draws a clean sheet of paper over her letter. "Joren. I thought you were done with me."

"I'm afraid you'll find that once the Crown has you, it is never done with you." He sits in Chester's armchair, crossing his ankles. "I read about your evening appearance in the papers. How are you finding society?"

"Exceedingly nosy," she admits. "But I suppose I'm used to that. Scholars, after all."

His smile is faint. "Indeed."

"But not as tiresome as I feared," she adds. "Madoc makes it very easy."

He leans back in the chair, and for a moment, looks at rest. His gaze falls upon the painting behind the sofa. A lush, verdant river scene. It's a small painting, but Joren, of course, recognises it in a heartbeat.

"Ah," he says. "The painting that caused my darling son so much strife with the Gardens. I've always wondered where it ended up."

Zanthi hides a smile. "*Is* it that one, then? I suspected, but Madoc didn't seem to notice it at all when he was here."

"I imagine he was quite distracted by his company," Joren says, amused. A flicker of trouble creases his brow, then. "I have come here to ask for your help, I'm afraid. You are free to refuse, of course."

"You know I'm unlikely to refuse."

"I do," he admits. It has been barely a year since they had first met, and yet he seems to have grown wearier than a handful of months and a storm could account for. "May I introduce you to someone? I believe he would benefit from your help."

Zanthi lays her pen down. "How so?"

"He has developed an aversion to aether, and for all our efforts, we cannot fix him. And it is quite imperative that we do."

She frowns. It seems to her that such a problem should be

brought to Rue at the Gardens, or to Madoc, with his blessings and custodianship over the healing waters.

And then she remembers Madoc's grieving, solemn face when he spoke of the one person his Gardens could not help, and a suspicion grows in her. "Who?"

Joren sighs. "Your secrecy will be required."

"Yes, Joren. I know about secrets."

He nods. It takes a moment more before he speaks, but by then she already knows. In some way, she has known since Joren had shown her that blood-filled vial with its dying, tortured aether.

"Heir Auguste. Arlet," he says at last, but all she hears is *Lettie.* Madoc's dearest friend. "Unless we can figure out his illness, he will not survive."

"And you think I might be able to help?"

"At this point, Miss Ilyston? You are the last one left who can."

The story continues with Arlet in

ALL THE RUINOUS GODS

A little more?

Wondering if Madoc and Zanthi ever get their tea date? Join my newsletter and receive the bonus scene right to your inbox.

www.theahawthorne.com/ivy

Acknowledgements

Thank you to my darling Elsie for believing in me and indulging all my thoughts and whimsies, all the characters and *what-ifs* and moodboards and playlists. Without you, Esk and all the stories within it would not be what they are. This one is for you, as all my stories are for you.

And thank you to Christina, whose conversation last year brought me back to writing after so many quiet years.

To my wonderful team of beta readers and cheerleaders: Alyx, who bolstered me with honesty and enthusiasm. Fatiha, who delivered such a generous and gentle read-through that I was able to see it through new eyes. Zaylee, who shared such honest, emotional reactions and made me excited for my own story again. Emma, who picked up almost every crumb and clue I tucked away in the text, and who genuinely uplifted my soul with her comments. Elsa, who gallantly saved me from more than one plot hole, and who made me grin all through my morning tea with her feedback. Fiona, who was sincere and generous with her time, responses and encouragement. Claire, who likened my worldbuilding descriptions to a snuggly blanket, a phrase which continues to delight me. Vivien, who gave me such a unique view of my work and some truly valuable feedback.

To all the Esk Readers: that you believed in my work enough to give me your time and thoughts means the world. I hope all of you are never short of books to delight you and tea to bolster you.

And thank you to every writing and art friend I've had over the years, some of whom might recognise a character name or idea from a story I've shared in the past.

This story was built on a foundation made of pieces of my older stories, and the journey of creating it has been cathartic and full of joy. In that way, this book is also a love letter to all the stories that weave through our life alongside us, changing and diverting, but never straying far.

And with a final cheer, thank you to everyone who purchases and reads my work. Without you, these stories would never live in ink and paper.

About the Author

Thea Hawthorne writes queer, cosy fantasy from her home in Tasmania, Australia, always with a cup of tea close to hand. She enjoys rainy days, both in books and in real life, and will always talk about the weather. In her books, you'll find a delightful blend of found family, folklore, quiet pursuits, a lot of warmth and a little dash of steaminess.

www.theahawthorne.com

Also by Thea Hawthorne

THE MUSES OF ESK SERIES

The Muse of Missing Pieces

A Reverie of Roses

THE RIVERSENT SERIES

All Woven With Ivy